Hard Landing

STEPHEN LEATHER

Hard Landing

Hodder & Stoughton

Copyright © 2004 by Stephen Leather

First published in Great Britain in 2004 by Hodder and Stoughton
A division of Hodder Headline

A CIP catalogue record for this title is available from the British Library

Trade Paperback ISBN 0 340 83176 6
Hardback ISBN 0 340 73410 8

Typeset in Plantin Light by Palimpsest Book Production Limited,
Polmont, Stirlingshire
Printed and bound by
Mackays of Chatham Ltd, Chatham, Kent

Hodder and Stoughton
A division of Hodder Headline
338 Euston Road
London NW1 3BH

For Barbara

Acknowledgements

I am indebted to Ian West and John Newman who helped me to understand what it's like to work in the prison system and I am grateful for their help and advice. Any errors of fact are mine, not theirs.

Alistair Cumming was invaluable for guidance on police matters and Sam Jenner gave me his expert advice on matters military.

I was lucky enough to have Denis O'Donoghue on hand to cast his professional eye over the manuscript and to have Hazel Orme's editing skills on the case.

It was a pleasure to work with Carolyn Mays at Hodder and Stoughton again and *Hard Landing* is a better book for her creative input and unwavering support.

Trish Elliott ran her hand across her stomach for the hundredth time since she'd left the doctor's surgery. It didn't feel as if there was a new life growing inside her – it was far too early for any movement or kicks, for the baby to make its presence felt. But Trish had known straight away this time, after years of trying, she was pregnant. The third pregnancy test had confirmed what her body had been telling her.

She hadn't said anything to her husband and she'd left it another month before seeing her doctor, but now there was no doubt. 'Pregnant'. She whispered the word to herself as she parked the car at the side of the road, relishing the sound of it. 'I'm pregnant,' she said softly. 'I am having a baby.' She wanted to run down the street and tell everybody, shout it to the sky, phone every friend and relative she had. But she also enjoyed having such a delicious secret. She knew. The doctor knew. And that was all. For a while, at least, the baby belonged solely to her.

She switched off the engine and shuffled across to sit in the passenger seat. Her husband loved to drive. It wasn't a macho thing, or that he didn't trust her at the wheel, it was just that he enjoyed it so much that she was happy to let him do it. Trish thought that she was probably the better driver. She took more care, followed the *Highway Code* religiously, checked her mirrors constantly, and was always happy to let other motorists get ahead of her. Jonathon – well, Jonathon drove like a man, there was no getting away from it. She sat in the passenger seat and waited for him to leave the office.

That was something else that would change, she thought, with a smile. Jonathon had promised that when they had a family he'd get a desk job. No more late nights, no more weeks away from home, no more putting his life on the line. He'd take a regular job, with regular hours, and he'd be there for her when she needed him. Someone else could take the risks and have the glory. He'd be a husband and father. A family man. He'd promised, and she would keep him to it.

She saw her husband walking along the pavement towards the car and waved. Jonathon got in and kissed her cheek. Trish slipped her hand round his neck and pressed her lips to his, kissing him deeply. He kissed her back, with passion, and slid his hand down to cup her breast. 'That was nice,' he said, as she released him.

'You deserve it,' she said.

'For what?' He started the engine and revved the accelerator, as he always did, boy-racer style.

'For being such a good husband.' She stroked his thigh. She wasn't going to tell him yet, not until the time was absolutely right. The food was in the boot, all the ingredients for his favourite meal, and a bottle of wine. She'd only have a sip to celebrate and that would be the last alcohol she'd touch until the baby was born. She wasn't going to do anything that might remotely jeopardise the health of her child. Their child. The child they'd been waiting for for almost three years. Their doctor had insisted there was no medical reason for her inability to conceive. She was fine. Jonathon was fine. There was no need yet for intervention, they just had to keep trying. They were young, fit and healthy. Jonathon's job meant he was under a lot of stress, but other than that all they needed was lots of sex and a bit of luck. They'd had lots of sex, all right, thought Trish, with a smile. It had always been great, from the very beginning.

'What are you smiling at?' asked Jonathon, putting the car in gear and driving away from the herb. He pushed his way into the traffic without indicating, and waved a careless thanks to a BMW that had had to brake sharply to let him in.

'Nothing,' she said. She wanted to tell him there and then, but she wanted it to be perfect. She wanted it to be a moment they'd both remember for ever.

'Come on, come on,' muttered Jonathon. There was a set of traffic lights ahead. Jonathon groaned as they turned red. 'See that?' he said. 'Now we're stuck here.'

'There's no rush,' she said. She looked across at him. He was so good-looking. Tall, broad-shouldered, with a mop of black hair that kept falling across his face. Perfect teeth – a toothpaste-advert smile.

He grinned at her, the grin of a mischievous schoolboy who had never grown up. 'What is it?' he asked.

'What?'

'You. You're smiling like the cat that got the cream.'

She wanted to tell him. She wanted to grab him and kiss him and hug him and tell him he was going to be a father. But she shook her head. 'Nothing,' she said.

A large black motorcycle pulled up next to them. The pillion passenger leaned down so that he could look into the car. For a moment Trish thought he wanted to ask directions. Then she saw the gun, and frowned. It was so unexpected that for a few seconds it didn't register. Then time seemed to stop and she saw everything clearly. The gun was a dull grey automatic in a brown-gloved hand. The pillion passenger wore a bright red full-face helmet with a black visor. The driver had a black helmet, his visor also impenetrable. Men without faces. The driver revved the engine. The passenger held the gun with both hands.

Jonathon turned to follow her gaze. As he moved, the gun kicked, the window exploded and cubes of glass splattered across Trish's face.

The explosion was so loud that it deafened her and she felt rather than heard the next two shots. Her face was wet and she thought she'd been cut, but then she realised it wasn't her blood: her face and chest were soaked with her husband's and she screamed as he toppled forward on to the steering wheel.

There were eight of them in the minibus, all wearing blue overalls, training shoes and baseball caps with the logo of the pest-control company above the peak. As the minibus stopped at the gate a bored security guard with a clipboard waited until the driver wound down the window, then peered at the plastic ID card clipped to his overall pocket. He did a head count and made a note.

'No one off sick tonight, then?' On a bad night there'd only be four in the squad. Eight was a full complement and, with the company barely paying above minimum wage, they were usually at least one man short. No women. The work was unpleasant and physically demanding, and while sex-discrimination laws meant that women couldn't be refused a job, few made it beyond the first night.

'New blood,' said the driver. 'Still keen.'

The security guard shrugged. 'Yeah, I remember keen,' he said wearily. He was in his late twenties but looked older, with hair greying at the temples and a spreading waistline. 'Okay, gentlemen, hold your ID cards where I can see them, please.'

The men did as they were asked and the security guard shone his torch at the cards one by one. He was too far away to check that the faces of the men matched those on the cards, but even if he had studied them he would have seen nothing wrong. Time had been taken to ensure that the ID cards were faultless. The van was genuine, as were the overalls and baseball caps, but its original occupants were in their underwear in a disused factory in east London, gagged, bound and guarded by another member of the gang. He would stay with them until he was told that the job was done.

The faces that looked back at the security guard showed the bored resignation of men about to start eight hours of tedious night work. Three were West Indian, including the driver. The rest were white, all aged under forty. One of the youngest yawned, showing a mouthful of bad teeth.

The security guard stepped back from the minibus. He waved across at his colleague and the white pole barrier with its STOP sign rose. Two uniformed policemen, wearing bullet-proof vests and cradling black Heckler and Koch automatics, were standing at the gatehouse. They watched the minibus drive by, their fingers inside the trigger-guards of their weapons. The driver gave them

4

a friendly wave and drove towards the warehouses. Overhead, a British Airways 747 swooped low, its landing gear down, wheels ready to bite into the runway, engines roaring in the night sky.

The man with bad teeth ducked involuntarily and one of the West Indians laughed and slapped him on the back.

'Don't fuck around,' said the man sitting next to the driver. He was wide-shouldered, in his late thirties, with sandy brown hair cropped close to his skull. He scanned the darkness between the warehouses. He wasn't expecting trouble: virtually all the security was at the perimeter of the airport.

In the rear of the minibus, the men were pulling sports bags from under their seats.

'Right, final name check,' said the front-seat passenger. His name was Ted Verity and he'd been planning the robbery for the best part of three months. 'Archie,' he said. He opened the glove compartment, took out a portable scanner, switched it on and clipped it to his belt.

'Bert,' said the man directly behind him. His real name was Jeff Owen and he'd worked with Verity on more than a dozen robberies. Owen pulled a Fairy Liquid bottle out of his sports bag. He sniffed the top and wrinkled his twice-broken nose.

Verity took a second scanner from the glove compartment, switched it on and placed it on the dashboard.

'Charlie,' said the man next to Owen. He was Bob Macdonald, a former squaddie who'd been kicked out of the army for bullying. Verity didn't know Macdonald well, but Owen had vouched for him and Verity trusted Owen with his life. Macdonald pulled a sawn-off shotgun from his holdall and slotted a red cartridge into the breech.

'Doug,' said the man next to Macdonald. He shoved a clip into the butt of a handgun and pulled back the slider. He was the youngest of the West Indians, a career criminal who'd graduated from car theft and protection rackets to armed robbery after a six-month stretch in Brixton prison. That was where Verity had met him and spotted his potential.

The alphabetical roll-call continued. A to H. The young guy with the bad teeth was Eddie. He had a revolver in his right gloved hand and a stun gun in the left. He pressed the trigger of the stun gun and blue sparks crackled between two metal prongs. The high voltage charge was enough to disable a man without causing permanent injury. The tall, lanky West Indian next to Eddie was Fred. He had a twin-barrelled sawn-off shotgun. A thirty-something Glaswegian, with a shaved head and football tattoos hidden under his overall sleeves, was sitting on his own in the back cradling a pump-action shotgun. He was George and he had an annoying habit of cracking his knuckles.

The West Indian driver was Harry. Verity didn't know Harry's real name. Over five years he'd worked with him on a dozen jobs but had only ever known him by his initials, PJ. He was one of the best drivers in London and claimed to have been Elton John's personal chauffeur. Verity nodded at PJ, who brought the minibus to a halt.

'Anyone uses any name other than the ones you've been given and I'll personally blow their head off,' said Verity, turning in his seat.

'Right, Ted,' called George, then slapped his forehead theatrically. 'Shit, I forgot already.'

'Very funny,' said Verity. He pulled a sawn-off shotgun out of his bag and flicked off the safety. 'Remember, we go in hard – hearts and minds. Don't give them time to think. They sound the alarm and we've got less than six minutes before the blues and twos arrive and we're up to our arses in Hecklers. Everybody set?'

The six men in the back nodded.

'Masks on,' said Verity.

They took off their baseball caps and pulled on black ski masks with holes for eyes and mouths. Verity nodded at PJ and the West Indian drove forward. Verity's heart raced. No matter how many jobs he did, no matter how many times he'd piled in with a gun, the fear and excitement always coursed through him like electricity. Nothing compared with the high of an armed robbery. Not even sex. All his senses were intensified as if his whole body had gone into overdrive. Verity pulled on his mask. He connected

6

an earphone to the scanner, then slipped it on under his mask. Just static.

PJ turned sharply to the right and pulled up in front of the warehouse. Verity swung open the door and jumped down, keeping the sawn-off close to his body. His earpiece buzzed. A suspicious passenger in the arrivals terminal. An IC6 male. An Arab. Good, thought Verity. Anything that drew attention away from the commercial area of the airport was a Godsend.

Owen pulled back the side door and jumped out. He had stuck a revolver into the belt of his overalls. The rest of the team piled out and rushed over to the warehouse entrance. There was a large loading area with space for three trucks but the metal shutters were down. To the right of the loading bay there was a metal door. The men stood at either side of it, weapons at the ready.

Verity walked up to the door and put his gloved hand on the handle. It was never locked, even at night: there were men working in the warehouse twenty-four hours a day, but only a skeleton staff at night. Four men at most. Two fork-lift truck drivers, a security guard and a warehouseman. Four unarmed men in charge of a warehouse containing the best part of twenty million pounds' worth of goods. Verity smiled to himself. Like taking candy from a baby.

Verity pulled open the door and rushed in, holding his shotgun high. To the right of the door he saw a small office containing three desks and wall-to-wall shelving filled with cardboard files. A uniformed security officer was sitting at one of the desks, reading a newspaper. Verity levelled his shotgun and motioned with it for him to stand up. Eddie rushed past and pressed the prongs of the stun gun to the guard's neck and squeezed the trigger. The man went into spasm and slumped to the floor. Eddie dragged him behind the office door. He took a roll of duct tape from his overall pocket and used it to bind the man's hands and feet as the rest of the gang fanned out, moving through the warehouse. It was about half the size of a football pitch with cartons of cardboard boxes piled high on wooden pallets. Most were marked 'Fragile' and came from the Far East. Japan. Korea. Hong Kong.

7

An orange fork-lift truck reversed round a stack of boxes. Doug ran up to it and jammed his pistol against the neck of the operator, a middle-aged man in white overalls. He grabbed his collar and pulled him off the vehicle, then clubbed him across the head with the gun.

Verity could hear the second fork-lift whining in the distance and pointed in the direction of the sound. Fred and the Glaswegian ran off, their trainers making dull thuds on the concrete floor.

Doug rolled the fork-lift driver on to his front and wound duct tape round his mouth, then bound his arms.

Verity motioned at Macdonald and Owen to start moving through the stacked pallets. They were looking for the warehouseman, weapons at the ready. Macdonald looked at his watch. 'Plenty of time,' whispered Verity. 'Radio's quiet.'

The second fork-lift truck stopped, and there was a bump as if something soft had hit the ground hard. Then silence.

The three men stopped and listened. Off to their right they heard a soft whistle. Verity pointed and they headed towards it.

The warehouseman was in his early thirties with receding hair and wire-framed glasses. He was holding a palm computer and making notes with a small stylus as he whistled. He was so engrossed in it that he didn't see the three masked men until they were almost upon him. His jaw dropped and he took half a step backwards, but Verity jammed his gun into the man's stomach. 'Don't say a word,' hissed Verity. 'Do as you're told and we'll be out of here in a few minutes.'

He grabbed the man's collar with his left hand, swung him round so that he was facing in the direction of the office, then frogmarched him towards it with the gun pressed into the base of his spine. 'There's no m-m-money here,' the man stammered.

'I said, don't talk,' said Verity. He rammed the barrel into the man's back for emphasis.

When they reached the office the two fork-lift drivers were lying on the ground outside the door, gagged and bound. Owen was standing over them, his gun in one hand, the Fairy Liquid bottle in the other.

Verity pushed the warehouseman to the floor next to them. He rolled on to his back and his glasses fell off, clattering on the concrete. Verity pointed his gun at him. 'The Intel chips,' he said, through gritted teeth. 'The ones that came in from the States this morning.' Voices buzzed in his earpiece. A Police National Computer check on the Arab, name, date of birth, nationality. Iraqi. 'Bastard ragheads,' muttered Verity.

'What?' said the warehouseman, confused. He groped for his spectacles with his right hand.

Verity nodded at Owen, who sprayed the contents of the Fairy Liquid bottle over the three men. Macdonald frowned as he recognised the smell. Petrol. The fork-lift drivers bucked and kicked, but the warehouseman lay still in shock, clutching his spectacles.

Owen emptied the plastic bottle, then tossed it to the side. He took a gunmetal Zippo from the pocket of his overalls and flicked it open. 'You heard what the man said, now where are the chips?' He spun the wheel of the lighter with his thumb and waved a two-inch smoky flame over the three men.

'Archie, what the hell's going on?' shouted Macdonald. He took a step towards Verity. 'No one said we were going to set fire to anyone.'

'You've got a shotgun in your hands, this is no different.'

'Have you seen what third-degree burns look like?'

Verity levelled his weapon at Macdonald's legs. 'Have you seen what a kneecapping looks like?'

Macdonald raised the barrel of his shotgun skywards. 'Just wished I'd been fully briefed, that's all.' He shrugged. 'You're right. In for a penny . . .'

The warehouseman scrabbled on his back, away from Owen. Owen followed him, bending down to wave the flaming Zippo closer to his legs. The warehouseman backed against the wall of the office, his hands in front of his face. 'I'm not sure how close I can get before you go up in flames,' said Owen. 'The Intel chips,' he hissed. 'Where are they?'

'I'll have to check the computer,' stammered the warehouseman. A dark stain spread down his left trouser leg.

Owen clicked the Zippo shut, grabbed the man by the scruff of the neck and dragged him to the office door. Verity followed. The earpiece buzzed and crackled. There'd been a car crash outside the departures terminal. Two minicabs had collided and the drivers were fighting. Verity grinned under his mask. The more distractions, the better.

Owen threw the warehouseman into the office. 'You've got ten seconds, then it's barbecue time,' he snarled. He pushed him down on to a swivel chair.

The man's hands trembled over the keyboard. 'I have to think,' he said. 'I'm only the n-n-night man.'

'Remember this,' said Owen, lighting the Zippo again and waving the flame close to the man's face.

The warehouseman shrieked. 'Okay, okay, wait!' He stabbed at the keyboard. 'I've got it.' He wiped his sweating forehead with the arm of his coat. 'Row G. Section Six. Twelve b-b-boxes.'

Verity turned to the office door. 'Fred, Doug!' he called. 'Row G. Section Six.' The earpiece buzzed. Despite the clean PNC check, the Arab was being taken into custody.

Owen closed the Zippo and used duct tape to tie the warehouseman to the chair. 'I d-d-did what you wanted, d-d-didn't I?' asked the man fearfully. Owen slapped a piece of tape across his mouth.

Verity pointed at Owen. 'Tell Harry to get the minibus ready,' he said, then jogged towards Row G.

'I'll do it,' said Macdonald.

Verity stopped in his tracks. He pointed a gloved finger at Macdonald. 'I said him. If I'd wanted you to do it I'd have told you.' He pointed at Owen. 'Do it!' he shouted. Then to Macdonald: 'You stay with me where I can keep my eye on you.' He jogged down the centre aisle, Macdonald and the Glaswegian following him while Owen ran towards the main door.

Doug was already sitting at the controls of a fork-lift truck. 'Here they are.' Fred gestured at a pallet loaded with cardboard boxes.

'Come on, get them loaded and let's get out of here!' yelled Verity. The boxes contained the latest Pentium chips from the

States. According to Verity's man on the west coast, there were twenty-four boxes in the shipment worth almost a million pounds, wholesale.

In the distance, the metal door slammed. They all turned at the sound of running feet. Verity and Macdonald raced into the main aisle and saw Owen hurtling towards them. 'Cops!' yelled Owen. 'There's cops everywhere!'

Verity whirled round. 'What?'

'They've got PJ. There's armed cops all over the place.'

Verity's hand dropped towards his scanner. He checked the frequency and the volume. Everything was as it should be. 'They can't be,' he said.

'They must have hit a silent alarm!' shouted Owen.

Verity ran towards the office, where Eddie was standing with both hands on his pistol. 'What do we do?' asked Eddie.

Verity gestured at the metal door. There were bolts top and bottom. 'Lock it,' he said. Eddie ran over, slid the bolts, then ducked away. There were no windows in the warehouse, no way of seeing what was going on outside. Owen was panting hard. Verity put a hand on his shoulder. 'How many?' he asked.

'Shit, I don't know. They were all over the minibus. Three unmarked cars. A dozen, maybe. I didn't hang around to count.'

Verity rushed into the office, slapped the warehouseman across the face, then ripped the tape off his mouth. 'Did you trip an alarm?'

The man was shaking. 'How c-c-could I?' he stammered. 'You were w-w-watching me all the time. You know you were.'

'What are we going to do?' asked Eddie.

'Shut the fuck up and let me think,' said Verity.

'There's nothing we can do,' said Macdonald. 'If the cops are outside, it's all over.'

Verity ignored him and turned to Owen. 'You said they had PJ?'

'He was bent over the bonnet of one of the cars and a cop was handcuffing him.'

'Did they see you?'

Owen nodded.

'The minibus was still there?'

Owen nodded again.

'Okay,' said Verity. If the cops knew they'd been seen then he and his men had only seconds. He gestured with his shotgun at the two on the floor. 'Free their legs,' he said. 'And untie the twat in the chair. They're our ticket out of here.'

Eddie rushed into the office. Fred and the Glaswegian bent down and ripped the tape off the fork-lift drivers' legs.

Verity cradled his shotgun as he stared at the bolted metal door. If the cops knew they were armed, they wouldn't come storming in. And if they went out with hostages, the police wouldn't be able to shoot. Verity tried to visualise the geography around the warehouse. As far as he could recall, there were no vantage-points for snipers. It would all be up close and personal, and that meant the cops wouldn't be able to fire without risking the hostages. But they had to move quickly. 'Come on, come on!' he shouted.

Eddie pushed the warehouseman out of the office. 'The security guard's still out cold,' he said.

'Three's enough,' said Verity.

'Enough for what?' asked Macdonald.

'To get us out of here.' Verity went over to the warehouseman. 'Give me the duct tape.' He held out his hand to Owen, who tossed him the roll. The warehouseman tried to speak but Verity pushed the barrel of the shotgun under his nose and told him to shut up. 'George, come over here.' The Glaswegian walked over to him. 'Put your shotgun against the back of his neck.' The Glaswegian did as he was told, and Verity wound duct tape round the weapon and the warehouseman's neck.

'You use him like that and it's kidnapping,' said Macdonald. 'Shoot him and it's cold-blooded murder.'

'If the cops let us go, no one'll get hurt,' said Verity. He nodded at Fred. 'Do the same with him.' He gestured at one of the fork lift drivers. The West Indian hauled the man to his feet and did as he was told.

'They won't let us walk out of here,' said Macdonald. 'Even with hostages.'

'Armed robbery will get us twelve years, maybe fifteen,' said Verity. 'If a gun goes off and one of these sad fucks gets it, it'll be manslaughter. Ten to twelve. We've got nothing to lose.'

'Ted Verity, I know you can hear me,' said a voice. Verity spun round, then realised that the voice had come through the scanner earpiece. It was being broadcast on the police frequency. 'This is the police. It's over, Ted, come out now before this gets out of hand.'

Verity roared and ran over to the fork-lift driver Fred was tying up. He slammed his shotgun against the man's chin, then kicked him between the legs, hard. He fell back, and Verity hit him again as he went down.

Macdonald grabbed Verity's arm. 'What the hell's got into you?'

Verity shook him off. The earpiece buzzed again. 'There's armed police out here, Ted. There's nowhere for you to go. Leave your weapons where they are and come out with your hands in the air. If we have to come in and get you, people are going to get hurt.'

A telephone began to ring in the office.

'Answer the phone, Ted,' said the voice in Verity's ear.

'It's the cops,' said the Glaswegian. 'They'll be wanting to talk to us.'

Eddie hurried over to Verity.

'They've already talked to us,' said Verity. He slapped the scanner on his belt. 'On the radio.'

'How did they know we had a scanner?' asked Eddie, his face just inches away from Verity's.

Verity could smell garlic on his breath. 'They knew everything,' he said. 'We've been set up.' He swore, then pushed Eddie in the chest. 'Get the fuck away from me!' he said.

'It's over,' said Macdonald. He turned to the Glaswegian, looking for his support. The Glaswegian shrugged, but said nothing. 'If we go out with hostages, they'll throw away the key,' said Macdonald. The Glaswegian's finger was on the trigger of the

13

shotgun. Most of the barrel was covered with duct tape, binding it to the warehouseman's neck. The man was trembling and the tape across his mouth pulsed in and out as he breathed.

'They'll throw away the key for me, anyway,' said the Glaswegian. 'One look at my record.' He jabbed the shotgun against the warehouseman's neck. 'Let's just do what we've got to do.'

Macdonald groaned. 'Jeff,' he said to Owen, 'help me out. This mad bastard's gonna get us all killed.'

'No names!' screamed Verity, brandishing his shotgun. 'No fucking names!'

'Ted,' said Macdonald calmly, 'them knowing who we are is the least of our problems.'

'He's right,' said Doug. 'If the cops are outside it's thank you and good night.' He gestured at the door with his handgun. 'This pea-shooter's gonna do me no good against pigs with heavy artillery.'

'We're not gonna shoot at them,' shouted Verity. 'All we're gonna do is tell them if they try to stop us the hostages get it. Look, the minibus is out there. PJ's there. If we move now, we can still get out of here. If we keep yapping they'll be firing tear gas and God knows what else in here.'

The phone stopped ringing. Fred went to stand by Doug. The Glaswegian pulled the warehouseman back so that he was closer to Verity. Battle lines were being drawn. Owen cursed and moved over to Verity, his sawn-off shotgun at the ready. He gestured with his chin for Macdonald to join him but Macdonald shook his head.

'Eddie,' said Verity, 'get the hell over here.'

Eddie looked across at the two West Indians, then at Verity. 'I didn't sign up for a shoot-out,' he said. 'In and out, you said.'

'Eddie, get over here or I'll shoot you myself.' Eddie gritted his teeth. Verity levelled his shotgun at Eddie's groin. 'I swear to God,' said Verity. 'Get your fucking arse over here.'

Tears welled in Eddie's eyes but he did as he was told.

'Answer the phone, Ted,' said the voice in Verity's ear. 'What we've got to say is better said over a secure line, right? Don't you agree?'

Verity ripped off the earpiece and pointed at the fork-lift truck driver on the floor. 'Get a shotgun taped to his neck, now,' he shouted to Owen, keeping his own weapon aimed at the West Indians.

Owen grabbed the duct tape and pulled the injured man to his feet. 'Give me a hand,' he said to Eddie.

'If you're going to go through with this, I'm out of here,' said Doug.

'You're not going anywhere,' said Verity.

'This ain't no Three Musketeers thing,' said Doug. 'You do what you've got to do, but I'm walking out now.'

'I'm with him,' said Fred, shifting his weight from foot to foot.

The telephone rang again.

'We're going out together,' said Verity.

Eddie was winding tape round the fork-lift truck driver's neck.

'They're not going to let you drive away,' said Macdonald.

'They won't have a choice,' said Verity. 'What are they going to do? Shoot at us while we've got these guys by the short and curlies?'

'And what are you going to do when they say there's no deal?' said Macdonald. 'Blow the heads off civilians?'

'They'll deal,' said Verity.

'If that's what you think you don't know the cops.'

'Do you?' yelled Verity. 'Is that how they knew we were here? Did you grass us up?'

'Screw you, Verity,' said Macdonald. 'I don't need this shit.'

Verity pointed his shotgun at Macdonald's midriff, his finger on the trigger. Macdonald swung his own shotgun up so that it was levelled at Verity.

'Guys, for fuck's sake!' shouted Owen. 'We're on the same side here!'

'We're in this together,' said Verity. 'If we split up now, it's over.'

'It's over anyway!' roared Macdonald. 'You just don't see it.'

'Bob, we're damned if we do and damned if we don't,' said Owen.

Macdonald snarled at Owen, though he kept his weapon on Verity. 'You told me this was a straight robbery,' he said. 'In and out before anyone was the wiser, you said. Now we're taking hostages.'

'The cops are going to say we took hostages anyway,' said Owen calmly. 'Soon as we tied them up we were holding them against their will. Look, I brought you in on this because you were a cool head. Don't let me down now.'

The phone stopped ringing. Outside the warehouse they heard rapid footsteps. Then silence.

Macdonald lowered his weapon. 'Okay,' he said.

Verity stared at him, then nodded curtly, acknowledging Macdonald's change of heart. 'Check the door,' Verity said. 'Don't open it, just listen.'

Macdonald walked towards it. As he passed Verity, he turned suddenly and slammed the cut-down stock of his shotgun into the man's stomach. The breath exploded from Verity's lungs and he doubled over. Macdonald brought the stock crashing down on the back of Verity's head and Verity dropped like a dead weight.

Owen stared at Macdonald in amazement. Doug and Fred cheered. The Glaswegian tried to rip his shotgun away from the warehouseman's neck but the duct tape held firm and he cursed. Macdonald swung his gun towards him. 'Don't even think about it, Jock,' he said.

'You're dead,' said Owen. 'When he gets hold of you, you'll be wearing your balls around your neck.'

'If we go out there tooled up, we're dead anyway,' said Macdonald. He backed away from Owen. The Glaswegian ripped his shotgun free with a roar. He aimed it at Macdonald as the warehouseman slumped to his knees.

Macdonald kept backing away. 'I've no problem with you, Jock,' he said, 'or you, Jeff. I just want out of here.'

There was a loud bang at the entrance and they all jumped. As the Glaswegian turned to look at the metal door, Macdonald sprinted down the warehouse. He ducked between two towering stacks of pallets, then zigzagged right, left and right again. He dropped the shotgun and kicked it under a pallet, then sprinted towards the rear of the warehouse. Behind him he heard the metal door crash open, then the staccato shouts of men who were used to their orders being obeyed. 'Armed police! Down on the floor, now! Down, down, down!'

Macdonald zigzagged again, and reached the warehouse wall. The emergency exit was at the mid-point and he ran towards it. From the front of the warehouse he heard a single shotgun blast, a burst of automatic fire, then more shouts. He wondered who had fired. Owen was too much of a pro to shoot at armed police. It was probably the Glaswegian. Macdonald hoped he hadn't hit anybody and that the police had been firing warning shots. A pump-action shotgun against half a dozen Hecklers was no contest.

Macdonald kicked the metal bar in the middle of the door, which sprang open. An alarm sounded in the distance. The door bounced back and he shouldered his way through.

'Armed police!' shouted a Cockney accent. 'Drop your weapon!'

Macdonald stopped dead and raised his hands in the air. 'I'm not carrying a weapon, dipshit!' he shouted, then stood where he was, breathing heavily.

'Down on the ground, keep your hands where we can see them!' shouted the officer. He was in his mid-twenties, dressed all in black with a Kevlar vest and a black baseball cap with POLICE written across it in white capital letters. His Heckler was aimed at Macdonald's chest. Two more armed officers stood behind him, their guns aimed at Macdonald.

'Can we all just relax here?' said Macdonald. He took off his ski mask and stared sullenly at the three policemen. 'Okay now?' he said. They looked at him grimly.

'Down on the floor!' said the oldest of the three, gesturing with his Heckler.

'Yeah, right,' said Macdonald. 'Look, I don't have time for this.' He moved to walk by them. The Cockney swore at him, raised his weapon and slammed the butt against the side of the Macdonald's head. Macdonald went down without a sound.

★   ★   ★

Macdonald came to lying on his back, staring up at a man in a white mask wearing a dark green anorak, shining a small flashlight into his left eye. Macdonald groaned. He heard the wail of a siren and realised he was in an ambulance. He tried to sit up but the paramedic put a hand in the middle of his chest and pushed him down. 'Lie still, you've had a nasty bang on the head.'

'He hit me,' said Macdonald. 'Why the hell did he hit me?'

'Because you were resisting arrest, you twat,' said a Cockney voice.

Macdonald tried to sit up again.

'Really, sir, I wouldn't,' said the paramedic. 'There's a good chance of concussion. We're going to have to give you a scan.'

Macdonald tried to push away the paramedic but his arm wouldn't move more than a few inches. He looked down. His wrist was handcuffed to the metal bar of the stretcher he was lying on. He tried to raise the other. That was cuffed, too. The cop who'd hit him was sitting next to him, the Heckler cradled in his lap. He had a long face with deep-set eyes and he'd turned the baseball cap round so that the peak was at the back. 'I should have hit you harder,' he said.

'What the hell's going on?' asked Macdonald, groggily.

'Your mate shot one of ours,' said the cop. 'You're all going down for attempted murder on top of armed robbery.'

'He's okay?'

'Your mate? Took one in the arm. He'll live.'

'Screw him, he almost got us killed. The cop who was shot, is he okay?'

'Now you're worried, aren't you?' The cop slapped his Kevlar vest. 'Vest took most of the shot, bit of damage to his lower jaw. But the intent was there and you're all in it together.'

Macdonald lay back and stared up at the roof of the ambulance. They were moving at speed, the siren still wailing, but he could tell he wasn't badly hurt. He'd been hit before, by experts, and the butt of the Heckler hadn't done any serious damage. What worried Macdonald was why the job had gone so wrong.

*　　*　　*

Macdonald was wheeled into cubicle where an Indian doctor examined the head wound, shone another light in his eyes, tested his hearing and tapped the soles of his feet before pronouncing him in no need of a brain scan. 'Frankly,' he said to Macdonald, 'the queue for the MRI is so long that if there was a problem you'd be dead long before we got you checked out.'

Macdonald wasn't sure if he was joking or not. The doctor put antiseptic on the wound and told Macdonald he didn't think it required stitching. 'Any chance of me being kept in for a day or two?' Macdonald asked. The longer he stayed out of a police station the better.

'Even if you were at death's door we'd have trouble finding you a bed,' said the doctor, scribbling on a clipboard. He glanced at the paramedic. 'You did the right thing bringing him in, but he's fine.'

'Told you I should have hit you harder,' said the armed policeman, who was standing at the end of the trolley cradling his Heckler.

The paramedic looked across at the cop. 'What do we do with him?'

'I've been told to keep him here until the forensic boys give him the once-over.'

The doctor pointed at a curtained-off area on the opposite side of the emergency room. 'You can put him in there unless we get busy,' he said, and walked over to where an old man with shoulder-length grey hair and a stained raincoat was haranguing a young nurse.

The paramedic wheeled Macdonald across the room and pulled the pale green curtain round him. The armed cop dragged a chair over to the side of the bed and sat down, facing him.

'Haven't you got anything better to do?' asked Macdonald.

'I'm not to let you out of my sight,' said the cop. 'Not until CID get here.'

'How about a coffee, then?'

'Fuck you,' said the cop.

'Hey, I didn't shoot anyone,' said Macdonald.

'You were carrying, and the intent was there. The fact that you didn't pull the trigger doesn't mean shit.'

Macdonald stared up at the ceiling.

'I should have shot you when I had the chance,' said the cop. Macdonald ignored him. The cop kicked the trolley. 'You hear me?' Macdonald closed his eyes.

Before he could say anything else, the curtain was pulled back. 'Okay, lad, we'll take it from here,' said a voice.

Macdonald opened his eyes. Two men in suits were standing at the end of the bed. The older one was wearing the cheaper outfit, an off-the-peg blue pinstripe that had obviously been acquired when he'd been a few pounds lighter. He was in his early fifties and had the world-weary look of a policeman who'd carried out more than his fair share of interviews in A and E departments. His hair was receding and swept back, giving him the look of a bird of prey. He smiled at Macdonald. 'I gather you're fit to talk.'

The armed cop glared at Macdonald and walked away, muttering.

'I've nothing to say,' said Macdonald.

'That's how I like it,' said the detective. 'Short and sweet. I'm Detective Inspector Robin Kelly, Crawley CID.' He nodded at the younger man. 'This is Detective Constable Brendan O'Connor. Don't let the Irish name fool you, young Brendan here is as English as they come. Product of the graduate-entry scheme he is, and sharp as a knife. Isn't that right, Detective Constable?'

O'Connor sighed, clearly used to Kelly's teasing. 'Yes, sir. Sharp as a knife.' His accent was pure Oxbridge – obviously destined for greater things than riding shotgun to a detective approaching retirement.

'How about getting us a couple of coffees?' said Kelly. 'Mine's black with two sugars. What about you?'

Macdonald turned to look at the detective constable. He was in his mid-twenties with jet black hair and piercing blue eyes that suggested there was more to his Irish heritage than his name. 'White, no sugar.'

'Sweet enough, as my grandmother always used to say,' said

Kelly. He sat down and crossed his ankles as the detective constable left them. 'I hope I retire before he gets promoted above me.' He sighed and rubbed the bridge of his nose. 'I'm missing my beauty sleep, I can tell you that much. Still, no point in brandishing shotguns in broad daylight, is there?'

'No comment,' said Macdonald.

'And if I was in your situation that's what I'd be saying. No comment until you're lawyered up and then it's "No comment on my solicitor's advice." But unless you take the initiative here, you're going to go down with the rest of the scum.'

'No comment,' said Macdonald.

'You see, the civilians are saying that you were the best of a bad bunch. You tried to stop the flaming-kebabs routine. You said it would be better to call it a night and go out with your hands up. And, bugger me, you only went and poleaxed Ted Verity, gangster of this parish. For which you have the thanks of Sussex Constabulary.'

'How is he?' asked Macdonald.

'Like a prick with a sore head,' said Kelly. He chuckled. 'He's in a better state than you, actually. You didn't do much in the way of damage.'

Macdonald stared up at the ceiling. 'No comment.'

'If I was you, and obviously I'm not because you're the one with the handcuffs on, I'd be wanting to put as much distance between me and the rest of them as I could. A cop was shot. Prison isn't particularly welcoming to people who take pot-shots at law-enforcement officials.'

'I didn't shoot anyone,' said Macdonald.

'Which is another point in your favour,' said Kelly. 'But it's going to take more than that to keep you out of a Cat A establishment for the next twenty years.'

O'Connor returned with three plastic beakers on a cardboard tray. He handed the tray to Kelly, then unlocked the handcuff on Macdonald's left wrist. Macdonald smiled at him gratefully, shook his hand to get the circulation going, then took his beaker of coffee and sipped it.

'So what's it to be?' asked Kelly. 'Can we bank on your co-operation? Or shall I book you a cell with Verity?'

'No comment,' said Macdonald.

Kelly sighed and got to his feet. 'That's that, then,' he said.

The curtain was pulled back and a young woman in a dark blue jacket looked expectantly at him. 'Jennifer Peddler,' she said. 'I'm here for the forensics.' She jerked her head at Macdonald. 'This the shooter?'

'I didn't shoot anyone,' said Macdonald.

'Strictly speaking, that's true,' said Kelly. 'He's a blagger rather than a shooter.'

Peddler put a large case down on the floor, opened it, took out a pair of surgical gloves and put them on. She was a good-looking woman, with high cheekbones and long chestnut hair tied back in a ponytail.

Kelly chuckled. 'Not going to give him the full monty, are you?' he asked. 'We don't think he's got a shotgun up his back passage. We found his weapon at the warehouse.'

The woman flashed Kelly a bored smile. 'Contamination of evidence,' she said. She pointed at the handcuff on Macdonald's left wrist. 'You'll need to take that off so he can remove his clothes.'

'What?' said Macdonald.

'Guns were fired, we need to examine your clothing for particles.'

'I didn't fire a gun,' said Macdonald.

'It's procedure,' she said. 'As these gentlemen will tell you, I don't need a warrant.'

'It's true,' said O'Connor.

'Then what am I supposed to wear?'

Kelly smiled. 'Tell us your address and we'll send round a car for a change of clothes.'

'This is madness,' Macdonald said, annoyed.

'You can wear a hospital robe,' said O'Connor.

'I'm not going into a bloody cop-shop with my arse hanging out,' said Macdonald.

'I've a forensic suit you can wear,' said Peddler. She leaned down and took a plastic-wrapped package from her case, tore it open and removed a one-piece suit made from white paper.

'You're joking,' said Macdonald.

'It's that or the hospital gown.'

'What about my human rights?'

'What about the cop you shot?' said O'Connor.

'I didn't shoot anyone,' said Macdonald.

'We'll start with your footwear,' said Peddler. She removed his trainers and socks, and placed them in individual brown paper bags with polythene windows. Then she helped him off with his jeans and put them into a bag. She took a marker pen from her jacket pocket. 'Name?' she said.

Macdonald said nothing.

'He's not saying,' said Kelly. 'But we'll get the full story once we've run his prints through NAFIS.'

Macdonald took another sip of coffee. A check through the National Automated Fingerprint Information System wouldn't help them identify him. His prints weren't on record. Neither was his photograph. But there was no point in telling them that. There was no point in telling them anything.

Peddler scribbled on the bags, then put down her pen. She took off Macdonald's leather gloves and bagged them, then O'Connor undid the cuff so that she could take his shirt and jacket. She put them in separate bags, sealed them, picked up her pen and scribbled on them. 'You can keep the underwear,' she said, handing him the paper suit.

Peddler swabbed his hands and put the swabs in separate plastic tubes, each of which she labelled. She also took his wristwatch. 'You haven't printed him, then?' she asked Kelly.

'He was brought straight here. We'll scan him at the factory.'

'I'll take my own set now,' said Peddler. 'Give me a head start.' She inked Macdonald's fingers and took a set of his prints. Then she handed him a cloth to wipe off the surplus. 'I need a DNA sample for comparison purposes,' she said. 'It's a simple mouth swab. As you haven't been charged, I need written permission from a superintendent before I can insist.

23

You can give me a sample willingly now or I can catch up with you later.'

'Take what you need,' said Macdonald. His DNA wasn't on file.

Peddler wiped a swab inside his mouth and sealed it in a plastic tube. 'Right, that's me finished,' she said. She went off with the case in one hand and the bags of clothing in the other.

'What happens now?' asked Macdonald.

'We take you back to Crawley for more questioning,' said Kelly. 'You're charged, we bring you in front of a magistrate and then you're banged up until trial, assuming you don't get bail. And I think it's pretty unlikely that any judge is going to let you back on the streets.' Kelly stood up. 'You finished your coffee?'

Macdonald drained his cup and the two detectives escorted him through A and E. Nurses, doctors and waiting patients craned their necks to get a glimpse of him, then quickly looked away. The paper suit rustled with every step and his bare feet slapped against the linoleum floor. Macdonald had a throbbing headache but he didn't know if it was as a result of the blow to his head or the tension that had cramped the muscles at the back his neck. Police, court, then prison. He smiled grimly. This was definitely not how he'd been planning to spend the next few days.

Macdonald was driven to the rear entrance of Crawley police station and taken into a reception area where a bored uniformed sergeant asked a series of questions to which Macdonald replied, 'No comment.'

The sergeant, a big man with steel grey hair and horn-rimmed glasses, seemed unperturbed by Macdonald's refusal to answer any questions. He asked Kelly if he was going to interview the prisoner immediately and Kelly said that they'd talk to him in the morning.

'What about a solicitor?' asked the sergeant. 'Is there someone you want us to call?'

Macdonald shook his head.

'Do you want to see the duty solicitor?'

'No, thanks,' said Macdonald. He knew that the sergeant wasn't offering out of the goodness of his heart, simply following police procedure. Macdonald was in the system and everything that happened from now on would be covered by the Police and Criminal Evidence Act. They'd play it by the book, one hundred per cent.

A young constable removed Macdonald's handcuffs and took him over to a desk where there was a machine like a small photocopier without a lid. The constable made him place his right hand on the screen and pressed a button. A pale green light scanned Macdonald's palm and fingers. Then the constable scanned Macdonald's left hand. The Livescan system would run his prints through NAFIS within minutes, but they would come back unmatched.

Then Macdonald was taken into another room where the constable took photographs, front and side profiles, and returned him to the reception desk. Kelly and O'Connor had gone.

The sergeant asked Macdonald if there was anyone he wanted to phone. Macdonald knew of at least half a dozen people he should call, but he shook his head.

'You do understand why you're here?' said the sergeant.

Macdonald nodded.

'You're going to be charged with some serious offences,' said the sergeant. 'I don't owe you any favours but you really should talk to a solicitor. The duty guy can advise you without knowing your name.'

'Thanks,' said Macdonald, 'but no thanks.'

The sergeant shrugged. 'I'll need your watch and any jewellery.'

'Forensics took my watch, and I don't wear jewellery,' he said. He'd taken off his wedding band two months earlier.

'You were examined by a doctor?'

Macdonald inclined his head.

'Did he say you needed any special attention, anything we should know about?'

'No. But I could do with shoes.'

'There's a bell in the cell. If you feel bad – dizzy or sick or anything – ring it. We can get the duty doctor out to see you. Had a guy die a few years back after being hit on the head. Bleeding internally and nobody knew.' He called the constable over. 'Cell three,' he said, handing him a card on which was written 'NOT KNOWN, ARMED ROBBERY' along with the date and time. 'I'll see what I can do about footwear,' he said to Macdonald.

The constable took Macdonald down a corridor lined with grey cell doors. He unlocked one and stood aside to let Macdonald in. The room was two paces wide and three long with a glass block window at the far end, a seatless toilet to the right, and in the ceiling, protected by a sheet of Perspex, a single fluo-rescent light. There was a concrete bed base with a thin plastic mattress. Two folded blankets lay at the foot. The walls were painted pale green. Probably Apple White on the chart, thought Macdonald. The paint was peeling off the ceiling and dozens of names and dates had been scratched into the wall, along with graffiti, most of which was along the lines of 'All coppers are bastards.'

The constable slotted the card into a holder on the door. 'Don't put anything down the toilet that you shouldn't,' said the constable. 'The sergeant gets really upset if it backs up. And if he gets upset, we get upset.'

'Any chance of some grub?' asked Macdonald.

The constable slammed the door without replying.

'I guess not,' said Macdonald. He picked up one of the blankets. It stank of stale vomit and he tossed it into the corner of the cell. He sat down on the bed. The floor was sticky and he swung his bare feet on to the mattress, then sat with his back against the wall. He'd slept in worse places. At least no one was shooting at him. The light went out and he sat in the darkness, considering his options. He didn't have many. He was in the system now and all he could do was ride it out.

Without a watch, Macdonald quickly lost track of the time. Light was streaming in through the window when the door was unlocked and a constable, a different one from the previous night, handed him a plastic tray that contained a bacon sandwich and a paper cup of tea with the bag still in it.

'Sarge said I was to ask what size your feet are,' said the constable. He was in his late twenties, tall and thin with a slight stoop. He looked more like a librarian than a policeman.

'Ten,' said Macdonald.

The constable started to leave. 'I could do with a shower and a shave,' said Macdonald.

'We don't have any washing facilities,' said the constable. He left, slamming the cell door.

Macdonald took a bite of the sandwich. The bread was stale and the bacon was fatty and cold but it was the first thing he'd eaten in twelve hours so he wolfed it down. The tea was lukewarm and sweet.

The next time the cell door opened a uniformed female sergeant came in, a thick-set woman with tightly permed hair. She was holding a pair of old training shoes. 'These are elevens but they're all we could find,' she said.

Macdonald thanked her and tried them on. There were no laces so he had to shuffle as he walked, but they were better than nothing. He sat down on the bed but the woman jerked her thumb towards corridor. 'You're to be interviewed,' she said.

She escorted him across the reception area. Several uniformed officers stared at him with hard faces. Word must have got round that a cop had been shot. Macdonald looked straight ahead. The sergeant opened a door and gestured for him to go in.

Kelly and O'Connor were already seated at a table with note-books in front of them. A tape-recording deck with spaces for two tapes stood on a shelf and in the corner of the room above Kelly's shoulder there was a small CCTV camera.

'Sit down,' said O'Connor, pointing at a chair facing the camera.

Macdonald did as he was told. By now the detectives had probably discovered that neither his prints nor his photograph were on file. The DNA profile would take longer.

O'Connor switched on the recording machine and identified

himself. He gave the date, looked at his wristwatch and said the time, then looked at his boss. Kelly seemed tired: there were dark patches under his eyes, and the shoulders of his suit were flecked with dandruff. Kelly spoke his name, then sat back to let O'Connor do the talking.

'So, you've had chance to sleep on it,' said O'Connor. 'Are you ready to be a bit more co-operative today?'

'No comment,' said Macdonald.

'You were arrested leaving a warehouse at Gatwick airport late last night,' said O'Connor. 'Would you care to tell us what you were doing there?'

Macdonald knew he hadn't been arrested, he'd been knocked unconscious, but maybe O'Connor was hoping for an argument over the facts that would lead Macdonald to incriminate himself. If that was his intention maybe he wasn't destined for greater things.

'No comment,' he said.

'At this point I'm asking you if you want to be legally repre-sented,' said O'Connor. 'Either by a solicitor of your choosing or by the duty solicitor.'

'I decline legal representation,' said Macdonald, folding his arms across his chest.

'Because?'

'No comment.'

'We understand that the raid was planned by Edward Verity.'

'No comment.'

'And that you were just a hired hand on the job.'

'No comment.'

'We understand that you hit Mr Verity before he could take actions that would have led to the hostages being hurt.'

'No comment.'

'If you explained why you did that, it might make things easier for you.'

'No comment.'

'We discovered a shotgun in the warehouse, close to the emer-gency exit you ran out of. Can you confirm that it was yours?'

'No comment.'

O'Connor reached under the table and brought out an evidence bag containing a pair of leather gloves.

'We removed this pair of gloves from you in hospital in the early hours of this morning.' O'Connor read out the serial number on the bag for the benefit of the tape. 'Can you confirm that you were wearing these gloves?'

'No comment.'

O'Connor bent down and picked up a second evidence bag, this one containing a black ski mask. 'You were wearing this mask when you broke out of the warehouse,' he said.

'No comment.'

'And you were wearing the overalls belonging to the employee of the pest-control company you were impersonating. All of which leaves us in no doubt that you were a member of the gang who broke into the warehouse, assaulted the employees and later shot a policeman.'

'No comment.'

'Refusing to answer our questions isn't going to get you anywhere,' said O'Connor.

Macdonald shrugged.

'The lad's right,' said Kelly. 'This isn't me playing good cop, bad cop either. You're not on file but all that means is that you haven't been caught before. You're a pro, that's as obvious as the wart on my arse. But just because it's a first offence doesn't mean you won't go down for a long time. If the Crown Prosecution Service goes for attempted murder plus kidnapping you could get life.'

Macdonald shrugged again.

'But if you throw in your lot with us, we could persuade the CPS to drop your case to attempted robbery. A few months behind bars. You might even get probation if you can come up with a few character witnesses and an invalid mother.'

'No comment,' said Macdonald.

Kelly leaned forward and placed his hands on the table, palms down, fingers splayed. 'This is a once-only offer,' he said.

'I can't help you,' said Macdonald.

'If you can't, there's others that will,' said Kelly. 'You know

Conrad Wilkinson? Of course you do. He was wearing the same outfit as you.'

Macdonald said nothing.

'Young Conrad's scared shitless about going back to Brixton. Seems he left a debt behind when he got early release. Plus his record is minor – car theft and demanding money with menaces. It's all we can do to shut him up. Trouble is, he doesn't know anything.'

Macdonald remained silent.

'Now Jeff Owen, he does know what time it is. All sorts of bells went off when we ran his prints through NAFIS. Owen wants to do a deal, but as he was the one splashing petrol about, the CPS isn't happy about cutting him any slack. So I'm going to ask you one last time. Do you want to help us with our enquiries, or shall we get ready to throw away the key?'

Macdonald stared sullenly at the detective. Kelly stood up. 'This interview is over,' he said.

O'Connor read the time off his wristwatch, then switched off the recorder. He took out the two cassettes, signed his name on them, and fixed seals over them. 'One of these is for you if you want it,' he said to Macdonald.

'No need,' said Macdonald.

Kelly threw open the door to the interview room and walked out. 'He's all yours,' he said, to the female sergeant. O'Connor hurried after the detective inspector.

The female sergeant took Macdonald back to his cell. On the way he asked if he could have some shoelaces because it was difficult to walk in the oversized trainers. She told him that he was a suicide risk so shoelaces and anything else he might use to kill himself were prohibited. Macdonald smiled to himself as she closed the cell door on him. Killing himself was the last thing he wanted to do.

Macdonald was interviewed three times over the rest of the day, but he didn't see Kelly or his sidekick again. The questioning was handled by a detective chief inspector and a detective sergeant, two men with more than fifty years of police experience between them. They tried every trick they knew but Macdonald said only 'No comment.'

He was fed once, in the early evening. A watery spaghetti Bolognese on a paper plate and a sickly treacle pudding with fluorescent yellow custard. Neither was especially appetising but Macdonald cleaned both plates with the same plastic fork, and washed down the food with another cup of sweet tea.

There was no sink in the cell but he was given a washing-up bowl of warm water and a towel. His request for a razor was refused.

He slept uneasily on the thin plastic mattress and had to drape one of the foul-smelling blankets over his head to blot out the light.

He was woken by the uniformed male sergeant who informed him that his case had been reviewed by a superintendent and the twenty-four-hour grace period had been extended by eight hours; before the eight hours were up he would be charged and taken to Crawley magistrates' court.

Macdonald asked for some clothing and if he could shave before his court appearance. 'If you give us the name of a relative, we can get them to bring some things in for you,' the sergeant said. Macdonald knew there was no point in arguing with him. Besides, even if he appeared in court wearing an Armani suit and an MCC tie he wouldn't be granted bail. A short while later he was given another bacon sandwich, this time with a congealed fried egg inside it, and a cup of instant coffee. He ate the sandwich hungrily and sipped the coffee slowly.

He sat on the bed until they came for him. He was handcuffed to two police officers and taken into a small room where the uniformed sergeant formally charged him on one count of armed robbery. It was a holding charge, Macdonald figured, until they had finished their investigation. Kelly had seemed serious when he'd said that the gang members were all going to be charged with attempted murder and kidnapping.

As he was led through the reception area he caught a glimpse of Jeff Owen through a half-open door. He was sitting at a table, talking quickly. Macdonald couldn't see who was interviewing him but he had the feeling it was Kelly and O'Connor. Owen looked up and saw Macdonald. He said something to the interviewing officers and the door was closed.

The two police officers took Macdonald out through the rear entrance where a large white truck was waiting. A dark blue saloon car was parked behind it: four armed police officers were sitting in it wearing bullet-proof vests. Behind them two police motorcyclists were revving their engines.

The officers took Macdonald inside the van. There were separate stalls, each with its own door. They pushed him into one, attached one of his cuffs to a chrome rail and removed the other, then locked the door.

Macdonald sat down on the moulded plastic seat and stared out of a square window of reinforced glass. He heard more prisoners being brought into the truck, and doors slamming. Then the engine started and the truck edged out of the car park into the street. The two motorcycles roared round it and took the lead; the car of armed police followed behind.

Through the window, Macdonald saw mothers pushing prams, young men in suits striding along purposefully with briefcases, old people standing at bus stops. Normal people leading normal lives. Civilians. Several turned to stare at the truck as it rumbled along the road – wondering, no doubt, which hardened criminals were being taken to get the retribution they deserved. Rapists? Child molesters? Murderers? Only twenty-four hours earlier he'd been on the outside, leading a normal life. Macdonald smiled tightly. No, that was wrong. His life was far from normal. It had been a long time since his life had been anything other than extraordinary.

He saw a young couple embracing, kissing each other full on the lips, then parting and waving goodbye. His stomach lurched. He'd been trying not to think of his wife and son and how they'd be feeling, not knowing where he was or what was happening to him. But there was nothing he could do about that just now. There was no way he could contact them – not until he'd figured out what was going on and why his life had been turned upside-down.

★   ★   ★

The magistrate was a man in his fifties with unfashionably long hair that Macdonald felt was probably tied back in a ponytail when he wasn't on the bench.

Macdonald sat in the dock, a uniformed policeman at each shoulder. He had no idea if anyone else from the gang had already appeared, or if anyone else would follow him. When he'd been taken out of the truck the doors to the rest of the stalls had been locked and there was no one else in the waiting room where he'd been kept for half an hour before his court appearance. Two armed policemen stood guard while he was in the waiting room and two more were in the court. The magistrate read a file through half-moon reading glasses, then looked over the top of them at Macdonald. 'You're refusing to give your name?'

'Yes, sir,' said Macdonald.

'That's a little pointless, isn't it?' He had the vestiges of a Scottish accent, as if he'd been born north of the border but had spent most of his life in London.

'It's my decision, sir,' said Macdonald.

'They'll put you on *Crimewatch*,' said the magistrate, and chuckled at his joke. 'And you're refusing legal representation?'

'I am, sir.'

'Equally pointless,' said the magistrate. 'Your case will be heard at the Crown Court, possibly the Old Bailey, and you will not be allowed to represent yourself there. Unless you have formal legal training.' He smiled patronisingly at Macdonald. 'Do you have any formal legal training?'

'No, sir.'

'Then I suggest you hire yourself a solicitor immediately and, in view of the charges, get yourself a decent barrister. From the look of the evidence against you, you're going to need all the help you can get.' The magistrate glanced at the two CPS lawyers who were sitting at a desk on the opposite side of the court. One was in his late forties, with a tan so perfect it could only have come from a sunbed or a bottle; the other was two decades younger, with an eager-to-please demeanour that suggested he hadn't long been in the job. Behind the lawyers were the two detectives who had taken over Macdonald's questioning. The younger CPS lawyer had done most of the talking while the older one had occasionally turned in his chair to whisper to the detectives. 'Do we have any idea when the further charges you mentioned might be laid?' the magistrate asked the lawyers.

The younger lawyer got to his feet. 'Investigations are continuing, sir,' he said. 'Statements are being taken from employees of the pest-control company who were held prisoner and we would expect charges of kidnapping and assault to be filed shortly. We are awaiting the results of forensic tests before charging the defendant with grievous bodily harm and attempted murder.'

The magistrate looked back to Macdonald. 'In view of the seriousness of the charges, compounded by your refusal to co-operate with the police, I have no alternative but to remand you in custody. And because of the nature of the crime and the fact that firearms were involved, you are to be held in a Category A facility.'

Macdonald stared stonily at the magistrate. It was what he had expected.

'It seems to me that, these days, the criminal fraternity is all too keen to carry firearms in the pursuit of their activities, and I hope that the full weight of the law is brought against you when the case comes to court,' the magistrate continued. Macdonald could see that the man was enjoying his moment of glory. He would spend most of his time dealing with motoring offences and shoplifters: the appearance of an armed robber and potential police-killer in his court would give him lots to talk about at his next dinner party. But the speech meant nothing: Macdonald hadn't even applied for bail.

He was handcuffed again, taken to the van, put back into the stall and the door locked. A few minutes later, the vehicle drove out of the court car park, escorted by the two motorcyclists and the car of armed police.

Macdonald gazed out of the window, trying to work out where they were taking him. At some point they drove over the Thames, which meant they weren't taking him to Belmarsh, but his restricted view meant that he had no clear idea of which direction they were heading.

Macdonald sensed they weren't taking a direct route to the prison. That, and the armed escort, suggested the police believed he was an escape risk. He craned his neck and searched the sky for a helicopter, but saw nothing.

The sun was dropping towards the horizon so it must have been late afternoon when he saw the prison wall in the distance. There was no mistaking its nature: it was over thirty feet high and made of featureless brown concrete topped by a cylindrical structure like a large sewage pipe that ran its full length. There was no barbed wire, so presumably the cylinder was an anti-climbing device. If he was going to get out of the prison, Macdonald reflected, he wouldn't be climbing over the wall.

The van slowed and Macdonald glimpsed a sign: HM Prison Shelton. Then it turned right and headed towards a gatehouse. A uniformed guard raised a barrier, and the van drove through, then stopped in front of a large gate. It rattled back and, a moment later, Macdonald saw three prison officers standing at a doorway, big men, with barrel chests and weight-lifters' forearms, in short-sleeved white shirts with black epaulets. As the vehicle came to a stop another guard appeared, holding a large Alsatian on a tight leash.

The engine cut out. The Alsatian barked. The three guards folded their arms across their chests and waited. Macdonald heard footsteps outside his stall. A prison officer was standing in the doorway, in full uniform with a peaked cap. He undid the handcuff, took it off the rail, then fastened it to his own wrist. 'Welcome to Shelton,' he said, deadpan.

He nodded for Macdonald to stand up, then led him down the van and out into the courtyard. The Alsatian barked again, and struggled to get close to Macdonald, but his handler held him back. The prison officer took Macdonald through a door which led to a reception area. Off to the left there was a glass-walled holding cell lined with wooden benches, and to the right a waist-high desk of dark wood. A prison officer in shirtsleeves was standing behind a line of metal trays. He reached for a clipboard as Macdonald was brought in front of him. He took a form from one of the trays, picked up a pen and looked at Macdonald expectantly as the escorting officer removed the handcuff from his wrist. 'This is the shooter,' he said. 'Be gentle with him.'

The officer behind the desk grunted. He was in his thirties with long sideburns and a drinker's paunch that hung over his belt, like a late pregnancy. 'Name?' he asked Macdonald.

'I'm not giving my name.'

The officer frowned. 'What?'

'I'm not giving my name.'

A uniformed policeman came in and placed a stack of files on the reception desk. 'There you go,' he said. 'Five bodies.'

The officer kept his eyes on Macdonald. 'You can't not give your name,' he said.

Macdonald shrugged. The prison officer waved two officers over. They took Macdonald into a side room and professionally strip-searched him. They checked his open mouth, behind his ears, and made him squat. Then they took him back to the reception desk.

'Name?' repeated the prison officer, as if it was the first time he'd asked the question.

Macdonald shook his head.

'Look, it's no skin off my nose,' said the officer. 'You get a number anyway.' He tapped the form in front of him. 'This number will follow you for the rest of your sentence whether or not there's a name to go with it.'

'I haven't been sentenced,' said Macdonald. 'I'm on remand.'

The prison officer flicked through the files and pulled out Macdonald's, which contained only a few sheets of paper. His photograph was clipped to the inside cover.

The officer's eyes narrowed. 'Have you been in prison before?'

Macdonald said nothing.

The officer read through the papers. 'No fingerprints on file so this is your first time in the system,' he said, as he continued to read. Once he'd scanned the final sheet he looked at Macdonald and sneered. 'Right, then, you being a new boy and all, let me explain something to you. Your time on the remand wing can be relatively painless, or it can be a bloody misery, and the way you get treated depends one hundred per cent on how you treat us. Time out of your cell, the amount you can spend on canteen, recreation, association, the clothes you wear, it's all down to how much co-operation you show us. Do you get my drift?'

Macdonald stared at him, his face blank. The Alsatian barked again, and another prisoner was led into the reception area, handcuffed to a policeman. Macdonald turned to look at the new arrival but it wasn't a face he recognised.

'Name?' repeated the prison officer. He waited for a few seconds, then pushed Macdonald's papers to the side. 'Have it your way,' he said. He turned to a computer terminal and tapped on the keyboard. He looked at the screen, then wrote down a number on a manila file: SN 6759. Next to the number were spaces for Macdonald's surname and forenames. 'You are now in the system, prisoner SN 6759,' said the officer. 'Everything that happens to you will be noted in your F2050 here and it doesn't give a toss whether you've got a name or not.' He gestured with his chin at the holding cell. 'Take a seat.' He beckoned to the new arrival to approach the desk. The prisoner was a teenager in denims, who looked close to tears. Macdonald wondered what he'd done to justify being sent to a Category A facility.

Macdonald shuffled into the holding cell and sat down. A clock on the wall above the door told him it was three thirty. Macdonald hadn't had anything to eat since his sandwich in the police station and his stomach growled. He knew there was no point in asking for something. Besides, it wasn't the first time he'd gone without food and water. He'd survive.

Another prisoner was ushered into the holding cell, a big man with a badly bruised face and a freshly stitched wound on his shaved head. He nodded at Macdonald. 'How's it going, mate?' he asked, in a whining Liverpudlian drawl. He was wearing an England football shirt, Adidas tracksuit bottoms and Nike trainers, but his physique suggested it had been a long time since he'd chased after a ball.

'Great,' said Macdonald.

'What's with the gear?' asked the man, indicating the forensic suit.

'Cops took my stuff,' said Macdonald.

'Bastards,' said the man. He pointed at his bruised face. 'They did this to me. Resisting arrest.' He chuckled.

Two more prisoners were brought into the holding cell, black men in their twenties wearing designer sportswear and expensive trainers. They sprawled on one of the benches, looking bored.

'So, what are you in for?' the bruised guy asked Macdonald.

'Armed robbery,' he said.

'Bloody hell, premier division,' said the man.

'Yeah, well, I would be if we'd got away with it. Why are you here?'

The man laughed. 'Retailing.'

'Retailing?'

'Tried to sell a couple of watches. Turned out they were nicked.'

'That's a pity.'

'My own fault, really. It was me what nicked them.' He rubbed his square chin with his palm. 'Serves me right.'

Macdonald heard the van start up, then drive away.

'Did we have the same magistrate?' asked Macdonald. 'Guy with the long hair?'

'Yeah, recognise him, did you?'

Macdonald frowned.

'He was with that pop group, back in the seventies, the guys who dressed up with the makeup and everything. Right ponces. New fucking Romantics. What the hell were they called?'

A prison officer opened the door to the holding cell. 'Barnes,' he said.

'That's me,' said the man. He flashed Macdonald a thumbs-up. 'Catch you later.'

Macdonald sat and waited. Barnes was processed and taken away. Then another load of prisoners arrived, six this time. They had all been in the system for some time because each man was carrying his belongings in a large, tagged clear-plastic bag. Five were sent into the holding cell. Two were black and young, with

38

the streetwise arrogance of the earlier pair. They stared sullenly at Macdonald and ignored him when he acknowledged them with a nod. He couldn't have cared less whether they were friendly or not – they were obviously dispersal prisoners who had been moved from another institution and he wouldn't see them on the remand wing. Of the three white prisoners, one was a stooped man in his late sixties with thinning grey hair and a smoker's cough. He smiled at Macdonald, showing that half his teeth were missing. His right arm trembled constantly and the hand was curled into a tight claw. 'Got a smoke?' he asked, and Macdonald shook his head.

The other two were similar to Barnes, with shaved heads and logo-covered sportswear. They nodded at Macdonald and point-edly ignored the two black prisoners. 'Nice outfit,' said one, but Macdonald closed his eyes and stretched out. He could see what game the prison officers were playing: he would be pro-cessed last.

The clock on the wall showed five thirty when Macdonald was alone in the holding cell. There had been three more deliveries, including another truckload of remand prisoners. Macdonald had watched them all being interviewed, given forms to sign, then escorted away.

Some were clearly familiar with the system, while others were confused and kept looking around as if hoping they were going to wake up and discover it was all a bad dream. One middle-aged man in a blue pinstriped suit and gleaming black shoes was wiping away tears as he answered the officer's questions.

It was just after six thirty when a female officer opened the door to the holding cell and told Macdonald he was to go back to the reception desk. Macdonald stood with his feet shoulder-width apart, his back ramrod straight. The officer looked at him coldly. 'Bad news,' he said. 'By the time we've finished processing you, they won't be serving food.'

Macdonald shrugged.

'And we seem to have run out of breakfast packs. For the morning.' He pointed at Macdonald's forensic suit. 'Normally we'd be able to get you out of that and into some clothes, but we've left it a bit late. We might be able to get something sorted tomorrow. No promises.' He scratched his sideburns.

'I get the drift,' said Macdonald.

'Good. So let's run through the questions again, shall we? Name?'

Macdonald said nothing.

'Prisoner refuses to give his name,' said the officer, writing slowly on the form. 'Date of birth?'

Macdonald said nothing.

'Prisoner refuses to give his date of birth,' said the officer. 'Address?'

Macdonald sniffed, but said nothing.

The officer smiled to himself. 'Care of HM Prison Shelton,' he said. 'Remand wing.' He finished writing, then looked up at Macdonald. 'Next of kin?'

Macdonald stared back at him.

'Prisoner refuses to identify his next of kin.' In all there were more than two dozen questions on the induction form, and the officer insisted on putting each one to Macdonald before noting that he had refused to answer.

Eventually he turned the form round and pushed it across the desk. 'Sign at the bottom,' he said, slapping down in cheap Biro.

Macdonald picked it up. 'Can I put a cross?'

'Put what you like,' said the officer.

Macdonald made a mark at the bottom of the last page of the form.

The officer pointed at a curtained-off area. 'Go in there and strip,' he said.

'We hardly know each other,' said Macdonald drily.

The man stared at him without speaking. Macdonald stared back, then walked over to the curtain. He pulled it back. There were two metal chairs. He slipped off the training shoes, unzipped the forensic suit and draped it over one of the chairs.

'Pull the curtain back. We don't want to see your spotty arse!' the officer shouted.

Macdonald did as he was told, then removed his underwear and sat down. There was another clock on the wall. It was just before seven. It had been less than thirty hours since he'd run into the warehouse with a sawn-off shotgun. Thirty hours and his life had been turned upside-down. Macdonald put his head in his hand and rubbed his eyes. He was dog-tired. And hungry.

The curtain swished back and a beanpole-thin man in a white coat walked into the cubicle holding a clipboard. He looked like a nervous supply teacher about to get to grips with a problem class in an inner-city school. He had black-framed spectacles with rectangular lenses, and a mop of brown hair that kept falling over his eyes. He sat down on the chair opposite Macdonald and put the clipboard on his lap, then patted the pockets of his white coat, looking for a pen. 'Any health problems I should know about?' he asked.

Macdonald shook his head.

'Are you on any medication?' Before Macdonald could answer, the doctor leaned forward. 'How did that happen?' he asked.

'It's nothing,' said Macdonald.

The doctor stood up and bent over him, examining the old bullet wound just below his right shoulder. 'Stand up, please.'

'It's nothing,' repeated Macdonald. He stood up and stared at the clock on the wall as the doctor prodded the scar tissue.

'What did this?'

'A bullet.' Macdonald was being sarcastic but the doctor was so intent on examining the wound that he didn't appear to notice.

'What calibre?'

'I don't know.' That was a lie. Macdonald knew exactly what it was. He still had it somewhere, a souvenir of the night he'd nearly died. It was a 5.45mm round from a Kalashnikov AK-74. Macdonald didn't usually go into details because when he said it was an AK-74 most people assumed he meant AK-47, the Russian weapon beloved of terrorists and freedom-fighters around the world. Macdonald had got tired of explaining that the AK-74 was a small-calibre version of the AK-47, initially developed for parachute troops but eventually the standard Soviet infantry rifle.

But the weapon that had shot Macdonald hadn't been in the hands of a Russian soldier.

The doctor walked round him and studied his back. 'There's no exit wound,' he mused.

'They dug it out from the front,' said Macdonald.

'Unusual.'

'It hit the bone and went downwards. Missed the artery by half an inch.'

'You were lucky.'

'Yeah, well, if I'd really been lucky I wouldn't have stopped a bullet in the first place.'

The doctor studied Macdonald's chest again. 'Who did the operation?'

'I forget the guy's name.' Another lie. He would never forget the man who'd saved his life, digging out the bullet and patching up the wound before he could be helicoptered to hospital.

'It's . . . messy,' said the doctor, running his finger along the ridges of scar tissue.

'Yeah, well, that's what you get on the NHS,' said Macdonald.

'It's not a hospital scar,' the doctor said. 'This wasn't done in an operating theatre.'

When the doctor saw that Macdonald wasn't going to explain the origin of the wound, he pulled out a stethoscope and listened to his breathing. He examined his throat, then had him sit down while he checked his reflexes with a small metal hammer. The brief physical examination over, he asked Macdonald a dozen or so medical questions, ticking off boxes on a chart on the clipboard. Macdonald answered all in the negative: he was in perfect health.

'Drugs?' asked the doctor.

'No, thanks.'

The doctor smiled thinly. It was obviously a joke he'd heard a thousand times. 'Do you have a drugs problem?' he said.

'No,' said Macdonald.

'Alcohol?'

'The odd pint.'

'Ever been treated for depression? Anxiety?'

'I find a five-mile run usually gets me sorted.'

The doctor stood up. 'That's the lot,' he said. 'You can get dressed now.' He pulled back the curtain and walked away. A prison officer Macdonald hadn't seen before was standing by the cubicle holding an armful of bedding.

As soon as Macdonald had pulled on his forensic overall, the officer thrust the bundle at him. 'These are yours, then,' he said, in a lilting Welsh accent. 'I'll take you to the remand block.' He was a small, balding man with a kindly face.

Macdonald looked down at his bedding. There was a thin pillow, a pale green pillowcase, a green sheet and a brown blanket.

'Don't hang about,' said the officer. He already had his key in his hand and unlocked a barred door with the minimum of effort. He stood to the side to let Macdonald through, then followed him and relocked the door. Macdonald glimpsed the key. It was like no other he'd seen before, no rough edges, just small discs set into the metal strip, which he guessed were magnets, impossible to copy.

The officer walked him through another barred door that led on to a corridor covered by CCTV cameras. It stretched for several hundred yards and was deserted. Their footsteps echoed off the cream-painted walls as they walked towards a door at the far end. The officer unlocked another barred door and took Macdonald up a flight of metal stairs to the first floor. There, two guards were standing in a glass-sided cubicle. One was tapping at a computer terminal; the other was drinking a can of Coke.

The Welshman pointed for Macdonald to stand where he was, then walked into the cubicle. 'Got a mystery man for you,' he said, handing over the file to the guard with the Coke, a tall, broad-shouldered man with bulging forearms.

He scanned the file. 'Okay, thanks, Taff,' he said. He dropped it next to the computer. 'I'll take it from here.'

The Welshman walked away, whistling softly.

Macdonald gazed into the glass cubicle, the administration centre for the block. Along one wall there were half a dozen CCTV monitors. The guard put down his Coke and came out of the cubicle. 'My name's Tony Stafford, and I'm in charge of the block,' he said. 'You've been told how the prison is laid out?'

Macdonald shook his head.

'There are four blocks. This is block B, the remand block. It's made up of three wings, and each wing has three floors. You'll spend all of your time on your wing, unless you're going to the gym, the hospital or the education unit. An exercise yard is attached to the block, your meals are taken on your wing. Any problems, you talk first to the officers on your wing. Any problems they can't handle, they'll bring to me. I talk to the governor. That's the system and you work within it, right?'

Macdonald nodded.

'This your first time inside?'

'Yes.'

'You call me Mr Stafford. Or sir. Or boss. Some of the older lags call the officers "guv" but we'd rather you didn't. Causes confusion. I presume it's been explained what will happen if you continue to refuse to identity yourself?'

'Several times,' said Macdonald. 'Mr Stafford,' he added.

'Right, then, I'll show you to your cell. Come on.' Stafford walked towards a barred door, his rubber-soled shoes squeaking on the polished floor. Macdonald followed.

Stafford unlocked the door, let Macdonald through followed him and relocked it. A second barred door led on to the wing. Stafford went up a flight of metal stairs. A female guard was walking down them, swinging her key chain. She had blonde hair, tied back in a ponytail, and a trim figure.

Macdonald could hear music. An Eagles song, 'Hotel California.' The pounding beat of rap. Jazz. Then the muffled commentary on a football game.

They reached the first-floor landing. There were twenty metal doors around the landing, all closed. A chest-high railing ran round the hole in the middle. A wire-mesh net had been spread across it, presumably to deter anyone wanting to jump. Macdonald looked up: there was a similar net below the second landing.

Stafford took Macdonald along the landing, unlocked a cell

door and pushed it open. 'We'll have a Listener for you tomorrow.'

'A Listener?'

'They're like the Samaritans. You can talk through any problems with them.'

'The only problem I've got is being here,' said Macdonald. 'I don't need to talk to anyone.'

'It's prison policy,' said Stafford.

Macdonald walked in. The cell was about four paces long and three wide, with pale green walls. A bunk bed was pressed against one wall and a small metal desk stood under a barred window. There was a small portable colour television on the desk. It was switched on, a travel show, but the sound was muted. The wall by the desk was plastered with photographs of semi-naked women torn from magazines and newspapers. The door closed behind him with a dull thud. To his right was a small toilet with a white plastic seat.

'Fuck me, I knew it was too good to be true,' said a voice from the lower bunk. A man sat up. He was squat with a shaved head and a swastika tattooed on his neck. He could have been the twin of the man in the holding cell, Barnes, except Macdonald hadn't seen any tattoos on Barnes. 'I told 'em I wanted a cell on my own.'

He stood up and put his hands on his hips. A small vein pulsed in his forehead as he glared at Macdonald. 'I'm as thrilled as you are,' said Macdonald. He nodded at the photographs on the wall. 'Any of those the wife?'

The man's eyes narrowed, then he grinned. 'In my dreams,' he said. 'I supposed I should be glad they didn't put a nig-nog in with me. You're not a smoker, are you?'

Macdonald shook his head.

'That's something I'm Jason. Jason Lee. What's your name, then?'

Macdonald threw his bedding on to the vacant bunk. 'Bit of a problem there,' he said. 'I'm not telling them who I am.'

'That'll only piss 'em off.'

'Yeah, well, I can live with that. Okay if I take the top bunk?'

'You're not a bed-wetter, are you?'

45

'I fart a bit after a few lagers and a curry but I don't expect that's a problem in here.'

Lee slapped Macdonald on the back. 'You're a laugh, you are,' he said. 'Look, what do I call you? I can't keep saying, "Hey, you", can I? Not polite.'

'Thing is, Jason, if I tell you, you might tell someone else . . .'

Lee shot to his feet and took a step towards the bunk. 'You saying I'm a grass?'

Macdonald put up his hands. 'It's not a question of grassing, it's a question of you using my name on the landing. Walls have ears, right?'

Lee's hands had clenched into fists. Macdonald saw HATE tattooed on the knuckles of his left hand.

Lee's brow furrowed. 'Fair point,' he said.

'No offence,' said Macdonald. He wasn't intimidated by his cellmate, but he knew there was nothing to be gained by starting a fight on his first night.

Lee grinned again, showing a gold tooth at the side of his mouth. 'None taken,' he said. He sat down again and gestured at the TV. 'Do you want to watch something?'

'I'm not fussed,' said Macdonald. He wasn't a television fan but that might change if the cell became his home for any length of time.

'I've a radio as well, so let me know if you want music or sport. They won't give us Sky in here, bastards, so if you want the footie you have to watch the radio.' He grimaced as he realised what he'd said. 'You know what I mean,' he said. 'You want music? Or sport? Arsenal are playing tonight but I couldn't give a shit. Chelsea man, me, through and through. You into football?'

'Not really.'

Both men looked at the door as a key was inserted into the lock. The door was opened by a female officer carrying a small plastic tray, the blonde who'd been on the ground floor. She was in her late twenties and wore matching coral pink lipstick and nail varnish. 'You making the new man welcome, Lee?' she asked.

'Yes, ma'am,' said Lee, getting to his feet in a show of manners that took Macdonald by surprise.

The prison officer placed the tray on Macdonald's bunk. It held a metal Thermos flask, a small packet of cornflakes, a carton of milk and a plastic spoon. There was also a plastic cup and a polythene bag, containing tea bags and sachets of coffee and sugar. She handed him a paper bag. Macdonald opened it and smiled when he saw a bacon sandwich inside. It had been his staple diet since he'd been in custody.

'That's all I could get at this time of the night,' she said. 'I'm Principal Officer Lloyd-Davies. I gather you're not introducing yourself at the moment.'

'I'm sorry,' said Macdonald, and he meant it. He knew that she could have let him go hungry.

'Don't worry about Lee here, his bark's worse than his bite.'

'We're getting on fine,' said Macdonald.

'Are those the only clothes you've got?'

'Yes, ma'am.'

'They didn't give you any at Reception?'

'Apparently I was too late.'

'There's not much I can do, this time of night,' she said. 'Are you okay sleeping in that thing?'

'I've slept in worse, ma'am.'

'I'll get you another set tomorrow. Good night, then.'

Lloyd-Davies locked the door and Lee sat down. Macdonald took the sandwich out of the paper bag. He held it up. 'You want half?'

Lee shook his head.

Macdonald took a bite. The bacon was cold but he was ravenous. 'She seems okay,' he said.

'Lloyd-Davies? Yeah, she's fair.'

'Didn't realise they had women in men's prisons.'

'Equality, innit? Most of them are pig-ugly dykes, though.'

'Not her. She's a looker.' Macdonald took another bite of his sandwich. He gestured at the light. 'When does that go off?'

Lee laughed. 'You haven't been inside before, have you? There's

47

no lights-out any more.' He pointed to a switch by the cell door. 'You turn it off yourself. They don't even tell us to turn off the TV, so long as we don't make too much noise. Not that there's much on after midnight. When are you back in court?'

'I'm not sure.'

'No way you'll get bail if you don't tell them your name.'

'Doubt I'll get bail anyway,' said Macdonald.

'Bastards,' said Lee.

'Yeah,' agreed Macdonald.

Macdonald woke to the sound of Lee crunching cornflakes. He was sitting at the metal table by the window, reading a paperback book propped up against the wall. Down the landing, Macdonald could hear rap music.

'Rise and shine,' said Lee, through a mouthful of cereal.

'What time is it?'

'Seven thirty.'

'When do they let us out?'

'Assuming they're not short-staffed, we can use the showers some time between eight and eight thirty. That's if you've booked it with an officer. You've got to run to get there first, though.'

Macdonald sat up. His neck ached from the wafer-thin pillow. He rubbed his face with his hands and felt the stubble on his chin and cheeks. 'What happens then?'

'Labour. That's what they call work in here. Dinner at twelve. More labour. Tea at five. Association, gym and stuff at six. Back in the cells at eight. That's the routine during the week. Varies at weekends. Proper breakfast, for a start.'

There was a rattle of a key chain outside the cell. Lee pulled a face and continued to eat his cornflakes.

First Macdonald caught a glimpse of a male prison officer, then a big man in a blue sweatshirt and baggy linen trousers appeared, a plastic bag in one hand. He was in his fifties with receding hair that he'd grown long and tied back in a ponytail. 'All right if I come in, lads?' he asked.

'Aye,' said Lee. 'You're here to see the new boy, yeah?'

48

The man stuck out his hand for Macdonald to shake. 'Ed Harris, I'm one of the wing's Listeners.'

Macdonald took the hand. Harris had a strong grip and he looked into Macdonald's eyes with a measured gaze. Macdonald knew he was being assessed. Harris handed him the carrier-bag. 'They said you needed a wash pack,' he said. 'Courtesy of the management.'

Macdonald looked inside it. There was a yellow Bic razor, a bar of shaving soap, a shaving brush, a toothbrush and a small tube of toothpaste. 'Thanks,' he said. 'I could do with a towel.'

'I'll get you one,' promised Harris. He gestured at Macdonald's forensic suit. 'Is that all the clothes you've got?'

'Lloyd-Davies said she'd get me something else today.'

'I'll remind her,' said Harris. He leaned against the wall by the door and folded his arms across his chest. 'Did they tell you about the Listeners?'

'Like the Samaritans, they said.'

Harris nodded. 'We're trained by them, but we're not just for people who want to top themselves. We're here if you need someone to talk to. There's four of us on the wing, and you can always find us because we've got orange cards on our cell doors. You need to talk to us any time, day or night, just ask one of the officers.' He gave Macdonald a sheet of paper on which were printed several paragraphs under the heading *The Listeners – Who Are They? How Do I Contact Them? How Do I Know I Can Trust Them?* 'This explains what we do.'

'Thanks,' said Macdonald, though he doubted that he'd ever want to confide his innermost thoughts to a balding man with a ponytail.

'I'm told you're not saying who you are.'

Macdonald didn't respond.

'I know you're angry at being here,' said Harris. 'No one comes into a place like this of their own volition. But there's no point in fighting the system.'

'I'm not fighting anyone, Ed.'

'Call it passive resistance, then. Call it what you want. But you're here and you have to accept that. This place runs on co-operation.

49

If you co-operate, your time in here goes smoothly. If you make waves, you're the one who'll get wet.'

'I've already had the pep talk from the screws.'

'Armed robbery, right?'

Macdonald shrugged carelessly.

'You could get twelve,' said Harris. 'Play by their rules and you could be out in six. Play by yours and you'll do the full twelve. Is it worth an extra six years inside to prove a point?'

'What happened to innocent until proved guilty?' asked Macdonald. 'I'm on remand.'

'The prison is full of innocent men,' said Harris. 'Nine times out of ten the guys I speak to swear on their mothers' graves that they've been fitted up.'

'Some of us were,' said Lee.

'Jason, you were caught with a knife in your hands and a Pakistani shopkeeper bleeding at your feet.'

'I was provoked,' said Lee.

Harris raised an eyebrow incredulously, then turned his attention back to Macdonald. 'The point I'm making is that we all choose our own paths in here. Guilty or innocent, you're inside until the system has finished with you. All I'm saying is that you have to think about what you're doing.'

'I know what I'm doing, Ed.'

Harris pushed himself off the wall. 'I'll drop by again in a couple of days, see how you're settling in. Has Jason here explained the whys and wherefores?'

'Pretty much.'

'You couldn't have a better guide. He's been a guest as half a dozen establishments like this. Take it easy, yeah?'

Harris left, and the prison officer locked the door.

'What's his story?' asked Macdonald.

Lee finished his cornflakes and washed his plastic bowl in the small stainless-steel sink by the toilet. 'Murder, suspicion of,' he said. 'His trial's in a couple of months. Topped his missus.'

'And he's offering advice to me?'

'He's a thief. A good one. Did a three-stretch in the Scrubs and when he came out his wife said she was gonna leave him and take the kids. He snapped. Picked up a bread-knife and damn near severed her head. Provocation, if you ask me. I mean, wives are supposed to stand by their men, right?'

Macdonald lay down on his bunk. 'That's what they say, Jason.' He sighed. He read the information sheet that Harris had given him. '"You can talk to a Listener about anything in complete confidence, just as you would a Samaritan,"' he read aloud. '"Everything you say is treated with confidentiality."' He looked over at Lee. 'Is that right?'

'Supposed to be,' said Lee.

Macdonald stared up at the ceiling. There was only one person he could trust, and that was himself. Everyone else was a potential threat, and that included his cellmate.

It had been light outside for a couple of hours when the cell door was unlocked again. Lee was standing at the ready, jiggling from foot to foot. As soon as it opened he rushed out and hared along the landing. Macdonald heard the pounding of feet as other prisoners rushed to the showers. He felt dirty but without a towel and clean clothes to change into, he didn't see the point of showering.

He climbed down from the top bunk and stared at his reflection in the mirror tiles above the sink. There were dark patches under his eyes and his hair was lank and greasy. He bared his teeth. He looked as if he'd been sleeping rough for a week.

He took the shaving soap and brush, lathered his face, then shaved with the small plastic razor. He cleaned his teeth with the foul-tasting toothpaste. Plastic bristles came off the brush and he spat them out.

As he was rinsing his mouth, the cell door opened. It was Harris, carrying a dark blue towel and a plum-coloured prison-issue tracksuit. 'Lloyd-Davies isn't here until this afternoon but I scrounged these for you,' said Harris. 'Bit worn but they're clean.'

Macdonald thanked him, tossed the clothes on to his bunk and wiped his face with the towel.

'You know you can have clothes sent in from the outside?' asked Harris.

'There's no one I can call,' said Macdonald.

'You can get a change of clothes here once a week, but it'll be the same as you've got there,' said Harris. 'I couldn't get you underwear or socks but I'm on the case. I had a word with the screws and you can use the showers this morning.' He grinned. 'Told them Jason was complaining about the smell.'

He reached into the back pocket of his trousers and handed Macdonald two printed sheets of paper. 'I got you a canteen list, too,' he said.

Macdonald studied the printed pages. It was like a shopping list, starting with half a dozen brands of cigarettes, tobacco and cigarette papers. The bare essentials of prison life, but Macdonald had never smoked. Next on the list were seven different types of battery, stationery, postage stamps, sweets and chocolate, toiletries and groceries.

'You tick off what you want and it'll be delivered tomorrow,' said Harris. 'Providing there's enough money in your account you can spend up to five quid a week as a basic prisoner. If you toe the line they make you an enhanced prisoner and you can spend thirty. Standard is fifteen quid.' He looked pained. 'The bad news is that withholding your details puts you straight on the basic list. That fiver's all you'll have for extra food and telephone calls. It's just one of the ways they can make your life a misery.'

Macdonald tossed the list on to his bunk. 'Nothing there I need,' he said.

A smile flickered across Harris's face. 'Say that after a couple of weeks of prison food,' he said. 'And tobacco gets things done here.' He jerked a thumb at the fresh clothing. 'Better gear, for a start.'

'Thanks, Ed,' said Macdonald, who had realised that Harris was doing what he could to make him feel at home. He wondered if the man really had killed his wife with his bare hands, but decided it would be bad manners to broach the subject.

'You can get money sent in, but it has to come from people on an approved list.'

'I won't be giving anyone a list,' said Macdonald.

'You can bring your own money in, but that'll mean identifying yourself.'

'I figured that much.'

'There's jobs here, and that'll earn you some. If you're available for work but they can't find you a job then you get two pounds fifty a week unemployment rate. Refuse to work and you get nothing.'

'Like I said, Ed, there's nothing on that list I need. And I won't be making any phone calls.'

'And like *I* said, see how you feel after a few weeks. You've got another ten minutes to use the showers.'

As Harris left the cell, Macdonald scooped up the tracksuit and towel and walked down the landing. Two black men in their early twenties, wearing Nike tracksuits and gleaming white Nike trainers, stared at him stonily as they leaned against the railing around the inner atrium. 'Hiya, guys, I'm looking for the showers,' he said.

The men stared at his forensic suit. 'What planet are you from, then?' asked one. He had shoulder-length dreadlocks and a scar that ran the full length of his left forearm.

'Showers, guys, please. I've only got ten minutes.'

The men pushed themselves off the railing and stood in front of him, blocking his way.

'Where's your manners, Smurf?' said Dreadlocks.

His companion snorted. 'Smurf,' he repeated. He was tall and stick-thin, his lanky arms protruding from the sleeves of his tracksuit showing half a dozen beaded bracelets.

Macdonald's eyes hardened and he tried to push past them. Dreadlocks shoved his arm with his left hand and pulled the right back in a fist. Macdonald moved fluidly, tossing his clothes and towel at Stickman, then grabbing Dreadlocks's arm. Macdonald twisted Dreadlocks's arm behind his back and gripped his neck, digging into either side of his windpipe. 'Keep struggling and I'll rip your throat out,' he hissed. Dreadlocks grunted and pushed back, trying to force Macdonald against the railing, but Macdonald's foot was behind his right knee and he pushed down, forcing the man to the ground. He released his grip on Dreadlocks's throat and kicked him in the ribs, savagely.

Stickman kicked out at Macdonald but Macdonald caught his foot and stood up, forcing him to hop backwards. He kept him off balance then kicked him hard between the legs. Stickman's arms windmilled as he fell backwards. His head thudded against the concrete and he slumped to the floor.

Dreadlocks was curled up in the foetal position, his hands at his throat, gasping for breath. Macdonald bent down to pick up his towel and clothing. He looked up and down the landing. Three teenagers in polo shorts and black Adidas tracksuit bottoms stood at the stairs, watching with open mouths. Across the landing, two middle-aged prisoners turned away as Macdonald looked in their direction. Stafford was in the glass-walled administration cubicle, deep in conversation with another male officer. Neither were looking his way. Ahead of him, Ed Harris was standing in the doorway to a cell. 'Winning friends and influencing people already?' he said drily.

'I had no choice,' said Macdonald.

'Watch yourself,' whispered Harris, as he walked by. 'Those guys have friends in here.'

'The more the merrier,' said Macdonald. 'Where are the showers?'

'Along the landing on the right,' said Harris.

Macdonald thanked him and walked away. He could sense Harris watching him, but he didn't look round.

The teenagers scattered, like sheep from a barking dog. 'Nice moves,' said one, but he averted his eyes when Macdonald looked at him.

'Serves the black bastards right,' whispered another.

There were three showerheads, each with a chrome push button set into the wall. Two black men were showering, their hair frothy with shampoo. Macdonald nodded when they looked at him. He took off his laceless trainers. When he turned to hang up his clothes and towel he heard them whisper, then laugh. He was looking forward to ditching the forensic suit. He unzipped it, slipped it off, then hung it on the hook next to his clothes. It was only when he stepped under the free showerhead and pressed the chrome button that he realised he didn't have any soap.

The water kicked out, lukewarm at first but then steaming hot. Macdonald closed his eyes and let the water play over his face and down his body.

'You okay there, man?' one man called.

'I'm fine,' said Macdonald, and opened his eyes.

'Just got in?'

'Yes,' said Macdonald.

The man next to him held out a tube of shower gel. Macdonald hesitated, then took it and thanked him. He squeezed a few drops into his palm, then handed it back.

'Anything you need, I'm your man,' said the guy with the shower gel. 'Name's Digger.'

Macdonald thanked him again.

'Dope if you need it. H. Whatever burns your candle.'

'I'm a man of simple needs, Digger. Plus I've got bugger-all in my account at the moment.'

'Think of me as a credit union,' said Digger. He was well over six feet tall with close-cropped hair and a barrel chest. He ran two shovel-sized hands over his head, then stepped out of the water and wrapped a towel round his waist. 'You can borrow from me, arrange to have me paid back on the outside.'

Macdonald's water cut out and he pushed the button to restart it. 'I'll bear that in mind,' he said.

Digger jerked a thumb at the second black guy. 'He's Needles. You don't see me on the wing, you can talk to him.'

'Will do,' said Macdonald. He turned to let the hot water play over his back. It felt good to wash away two days' sweat and grime.

Digger stood in front of Macdonald, hands on hips, jaw up so that he was looking at Macdonald down his broad nose. 'And your name would be . . . ?'

Macdonald pulled a face. 'I'm not telling anyone,' he said.

Digger chuckled. 'Raging against the machine, huh?'

'Something like that.'

Digger held out a massive fist. Macdonald clenched his own right hand and tapped his fist against Digger's. The black man's was almost twice the size of his own. Digger was well muscled and had the confident swagger of a man who'd never lost a fight. 'Don't forget to wash behind your ears, yeah?' He chuckled.

Digger and Needles dried themselves off. They changed into their clothes – pale blue Nike sweatshirts and Versace jeans – and left Macdonald alone in the shower room. Digger flashed him a clenched fist as he left. Macdonald just hoped they weren't related to the two guys he'd kicked the shit out of. He stretched out his arms, leaned against the wall, and hung his head so that the water cascaded down his face. The rushing water blocked out the noise from the wing and he could have been anywhere. A health club. His own bathroom next to his bedroom, where his son was curled up in bed next to his wife. Standing in the shower with his eyes closed, it was easy to imagine he was only feet from his family. The water cut out and he thumped the button with his fist.

'Shower room's closing,' said a voice.

Macdonald opened his eyes. An officer was standing at the entrance. He was in his late twenties with a shirt collar several sizes too big for his neck and a small patch of red skin over his right eyebrow. His Adam's apple bobbed up and down as he swallowed.

'Just finishing up,' said Macdonald.

'You're the new guy, yeah?' asked the officer. 'The one who won't give his name?'

Macdonald nodded.

'You know we have to identify ourselves? Prisoners have the right to know who their guards are. We're in the wrong if we don't say who we are.'

'I guess you have to follow the rules,' said Macdonald, reaching for his towel.

'So I'm Mr Hamilton.'

'Pleased to meet you, Mr Hamilton.'

'Are you taking the piss?'

56

Macdonald shook his head, then turned his back on the officer and towelled himself dry.

'Had a guy like you on the wing a few years back,' said Hamilton. 'Thought he was hard. Thought he was the bee's bloody knees.'

Macdonald finished drying himself and put on his prison-issue clothes. 'Is it okay if I leave that here?' he asked, pointing at his white paper suit as he slipped on his grubby trainers.

'No, it bloody isn't,' said the officer. 'Take it back to your cell and put it out with your rubbish.'

'Right,' said Macdonald, taking the suit off the hook.

Hamilton stood as if he was glued to the ground, forcing Macdonald to walk round him. 'You can't fight the system,' he said. 'It's broken better men than you.'

Macdonald said nothing. On the way back to his cell, he met Barnes leaning on the rail and looking down at the ground floor. 'See they gave you some gear,' he said.

'Yeah, I'm trying not to think about who wore it before me.'

'Get some sent in,' said Barnes. 'My missus'll be dropping me some stuff off tomorrow.' He took a pack of Marlboro from his pocket and offered it to Macdonald.

'Don't smoke, thanks.'

'Name's Bill,' said Barnes. Macdonald was about to explain his situation but Barnes cut him short. 'I know, I know. Everyone on the wing knows you're playing the strong, silent type.'

'News travels fast.'

'There's not much else to do in here but gossip. They say it's your first time inside.'

'Never been caught before.'

Barnes grinned. 'If you need any tips, let me know.' He nodded at the ground floor. 'I'm on the ones. Bloody triple, but the other two guys are okay.'

'I'm there,' said Macdonald, pointing towards his cell.

'I know. You're in with Jason Lee. He's okay, is Jason. Chelsea fan, but what can you do? Are you sorted for your meals tomorrow?'

'What?'

'Your meals. Dinner and tea. You have to make your choices today for tomorrow. We're given the vegetarian option today unless you've got some pull on the hotplate.'

'You've lost me, Bill. Sorry.'

'You really are a virgin, aren't you?' He put his arm round Macdonald's shoulder. 'Come with me, old son, let me show you a few ropes.'

Barnes took Macdonald down the metal-mesh stairs to the ground floor and over to a large noticeboard. There were several notices that warned of the dangers of drugs and a copy of the Listeners sheet that Ed Harris had given him. At the top of the board was a typewritten menu with a week's meals. There were three choices for each, labelled A, B and C, except for Saturday when there were only two alternatives.

Barnes tapped the sheet. 'You make your choice from this,' he said. To the right of each meal description was a code, and at the bottom of the menu they were explained: ORD was ordinary; MUS was Muslim; V was Vegan; H was the healthy option; VG was Vegetarian. Choice A was always marked ALL DIETS, which Macdonald presumed meant that it was vegetarian, healthy and suitable for Muslims.

Barnes ran his finger down the list. 'So, for dinner we get spicy vegetable bake,' he said. 'Yummy. And for tea we get curried beans.' He chuckled. 'Jason's going to love you,' he said.

There was a table under the noticeboard and a plastic tray containing small forms with spaces for name, prison number, date and meal request. A black Biro hung from a chain, and a cardboard box, with a slot in the top marked 'Meal Slips', stood beside it.

'Make your choice and drop it in there,' Barnes said. 'If you don't show a preference, you get A, and most of the time A is just whatever veg they've got fried, boiled or curried. A word to the wise, don't argue with the guys on the hotplate. They can make your life a bloody misery. Just smile and nod and say thank you. Giving them a bit of puff now and then keeps them sweet.'

Macdonald thanked Barnes. It was just one of a thousand things about the system that he didn't know, and none of the officers seemed keen to inform him of the way things worked. Pretty much all the useful information he'd been given so far had come from fellow prisoners.

'Get yourself a copy of the *Prison Rules*, too. Tells you everything you're entitled to.' Barnes clapped him on the back and went to his landing.

Macdonald chose a cornish pastie for the next day's dinner and the mixed grill for the evening meal and dropped his form into the box. Prison officers walked down the landing shouting, 'Finish off,' and the inmates headed back to their cells. Macdonald hurried up the landing with his paper suit. Lee was already sitting at the desk, reading a book. There was a metal waste-bin under the sink and Macdonald shoved the paper suit into it. 'What happens now?' he asked, sitting on his bunk.

'Work starts at nine. Back here at noon for dinner. Banged up for roll-call, then back to work at one forty-five. Here at five for tea.'

'When do we get some fresh air?'

'After dinner. We get an hour in the exercise yard unless it's raining. Sometimes they let us out during association. Depends how they're staffed.'

Macdonald lay down on his bunk. He had nothing to read, nothing to do, and no idea of what was going to happen to him. 'What sort of work do you do, Jason?'

'I'm assembling electric heaters. Putting the plugs on. Mindless, it is, but you get to talk to the lads. The good jobs are on the hotplate or the cleaning crew, but you need contacts to get them. Or serious money.'

'You mean bribe the officers?'

Lee laughed. 'The screws? Bloody hell, no! They don't run the block. The prisoners do.' He put down his book and jerked a thumb at the door. 'How many screws did you see out there?'

Macdonald rolled over on his bunk. 'Three or four.'

'Right. Two in the bubble. Two on the ones. One on each landing. Maybe one or two floating around if they're fully staffed. Now, how many cons on the spur?'

Macdonald thought about it. A spur was three landings, maybe fifteen or twenty prisoners on each. 'Fifty or sixty.'

'Give the man a goldfish,' said Lee. 'So you've got a maximum of eight screws in charge of fifty cons. No guns, a whole set of rules and regulations they have to follow. Where do you think the power lies?'

'You mean it's anarchy in here?'

Lee grinned. 'More like a bloody dictatorship,' he said. 'Have you met Digger yet? Big black guy?'

'Yeah, he was in the showers. Wanted to sell me some gear.'

'Digger runs the show. Anything goes down on the spur, Digger takes a piece. Nothing happens here without his say-so. If you want to work on the hotplate, you talk to Digger. Cleaning job, he's your man. If you want a single cell, you talk to Digger.'

Macdonald sat up. 'Are you telling me that the prison officers have handed control to him?'

'What do they want?' asked Lee. The question was clearly rhetorical because he continued his argument without giving Macdonald a chance to answer. 'They want what we all want. A nice house, a wife they can shag without putting a paper bag over her head, a flash car, couple of weeks in Spain, good school for the kids. They don't give a toss about rehabilitation – they don't care who does what in here, so long as no one makes any waves. They want an easy life, and that's what they get if they let Digger run the spur.'

'He said I could pay him on the outside. Is that how it works?'

'Has to be that way,' said Lee. 'There's no money on the spur. It's all held on account. Way back when, phone cards were used as currency but the PIN system put paid to that. There's burn and there's gear, but drugs'll get you on a charge and there's a limit to how much tobacco you can hoard, so you either trade stuff on the inside or pay him on the out.'

They heard a noise at the door and looked up. It was Hamilton. 'Come on, Lee, labour.' Lee hurried out of the door. Hamilton reached to pull it shut.

'Mr Hamilton?' said Macdonald. 'How do I get to go to the gym?'

'Gym's a privilege, and prisoners who refuse to co-operate aren't entitled to privileges,' said the prison officer.

'But I'm entitled to a copy of the *Prison Rules*, right?'

Hamilton's eyes narrowed. 'What would you want with that?'

'I'm entitled, so I'd like a copy,' said Macdonald.

Hamilton shut the door.

Macdonald lay back on his bunk and closed his eyes.

Macdonald drifted in and out of sleep. He could hear a television down the landing so he wasn't the only prisoner not working. He lost track of time. He could have switched on the television or radio for a time check, but there was no point. He wasn't going anywhere and he had no schedule to keep.

Eventually the door was unlocked and Lee came in.

'Had a nice day at the office, dear?' asked Macdonald.

Lee frowned, not getting the joke. 'What?'

'Work. Was it okay?'

'Boring as hell. But the guys are all asking about you. They reckon you killed three cops and that SO19 have put out a contract on you.'

Macdonald tutted. 'I didn't shoot anyone. A cop took a few pellets in the chin. And we were out at Gatwick Airport so it was Sussex police and bugger-all to do with SO19. They work for the Met.'

'I know, but it's a better story, innit? Come on, skates on, dinner's ready.' He picked up his Thermos and pointed at Macdonald to bring his. They went down the stairs together. Lee indicated Macdonald's flask. 'Don't forget to fill it,' he said. 'The boiler's by the hotplate. Sometimes they keep us banged up after dinner if they're short-staffed so you need a brew.'

A prison officer Macdonald hadn't seen before was standing at the bottom of the stairs. 'Settling in okay?' he asked. He had a soldier's bearing, his blond hair was cropped short and he had a scar under his chin that looked as if he'd been on the wrong end of a broken bottle.

'Thanks.'

'I'm Mr Rathbone. Craig, if there are no governors around.'

Rathbone seemed more easy-going than Hamilton, so Macdonald thought he'd put in another request for the gym. Rathbone said he'd see what he could do.

Prisoners were hurrying down to the ground floor where a large metal trolley had been wheeled into the association area. Stainless-steel trays of food were being pulled out of cupboards at the bottom of the trolley, which had been plugged into a nearby power socket. A table next to the hotplate supported a basket of bread rolls and a tray of fruit. Three inmates wielded serving utensils and Hamilton was standing to the side, watching them.

Macdonald picked up his Thermos and went downstairs to join the queue. Lee already had his tray of food and was filling his flask at a large chrome water heater.

Barnes was at the front of the line, helping himself to a bread roll. He reached for a second but a server slapped his hand with a spatula. Barnes swore good-naturedly.

As Barnes took his tray to the water heater, another prisoner collected a plastic tray and walked to the front of the queue, a big guy with a shaved head, wearing a mauve Versace polo shirt and black jeans. No one protested as he shoved out his tray. Hamilton was watching, but didn't seem interested. 'Gerry wants sausages,' said the prisoner.

The hotplate man in charge of main courses used a pair of metal tongs to select them.

'He wants them well done,' said the prisoner.

The hotplate man replaced them with two blackened ones. The prisoner kept staring at him. The hotplate man added two more sausages, then the prisoner moved over to the vegetables. 'Just french fries,' he said, and received an extra-large portion. Another prisoner held out his tray. Two sausages were plonked onto his plate. 'I want another,' said the prisoner.

'Yeah, well, I want to share a cell with Pamela Anderson, now fuck off,' said the server.

The prisoner who'd pushed in took his plate towards the stairs.

As he went up he kept one hand on the rail as if he was scared he might spill something.

The spicy vegetable bake seemed to consist of chopped carrots, potatoes, cabbage and beansprouts that had been sprinkled with cheese, then shoved under a grill. Macdonald received a large portion, with a serving of chips and a spoonful of green peas. He took a roll and an orange, then went upstairs to his landing. There, he looked up and saw the prisoner in the Versace polo shirt walking to a cell at the far end of the landing.

Macdonald went into his. Lee wasn't there but he didn't want to sit at the desk. He had the feeling that Lee regarded it and the chair as his own personal territory. The vegetable bake was bland and unseasoned, the chips were greasy and the peas hard. He was peeling his orange when Lee returned. 'They're letting us out in the exercise yard,' he said, and sat down at the table.

Macdonald put his orange on his pillow, took his tray to the ground floor and dropped it into a large plastic dustbin at the end of the hotplate. Prisoners were heading towards the far end of the spur where Rathbone and another officer were searching them before they went go out into the yard. It was a basic pat-down. Arms, waist, legs. The officers carried out the searches on autopilot and the prisoners seemed equally bored by the procedure. Macdonald wondered why they bothered. A blade or a drugs stash could easily be concealed in trainers or underwear.

When it was Macdonald's turn to be frisked he raised his arms and spread his legs as Rathbone patted him down.

Two dozen or so men were already outside, mostly walking round a Tarmac rectangle about the size of a tennis court. A few were standing about, smoking and talking. The exercise area was surrounded by wire mesh three times the height of a man, thick wires criss-crossed the air above their heads, threaded every few yards with dinner-plate sized metal circles. Anti-helicopter cables.

Macdonald walked round slowly, swinging his arms and taking deep breaths. He reached a vacant corner, dropped to the ground and did fifty brisk push-ups. Then he rolled over and did fifty sit-ups, hands clasped behind his neck, relishing the burn in his stomach muscles.

As he got to his feet, Ed Harris ambled over. 'How's it going?' he asked.

'I'm having trouble getting time in the gym,' said Macdonald. He widened his stance and started touching his toes. Left, right, left, right.

'What's the problem?' asked Harris.

'Hamilton,' said Macdonald. 'Says gym time's a privilege and that as I'm not co-operating I don't get any privileges.'

'He's talking bollocks,' said Harris. 'Prison rules say you get an hour a week physical education. That's above and beyond outside time. Two hours if you're convicted. There are privileges they can give and take, but exercise isn't one. I'll talk to him.'

'I don't need anyone to fight my battles, Ed.'

'I can make an approach as a Listener.'

Macdonald straightened up and arched his back. 'It's okay.'

Harris nodded. 'If you change your mind, let me know. Hamilton's got a bit of a chip on his shoulder. He wanted to be a fireman but couldn't pass the physical. Sees this as second best and sometimes takes it out on the prisoners. You've just got to know your rights, that's all. The rules work both ways and if he breaks them it's a black mark on his record.'

'So I can get him into trouble?'

'Let's just say you can make life difficult for him. And if there's one thing a screw wants, it's an easy life.'

Macdonald glanced over at the entrance to the exercise yard. Rathbone was patting down a young prisoner who was wearing a harlequin-type uniform made up of yellow and blue patches. The man said something and Rathbone laughed. He seemed to be taking extra care searching him. 'What's his story?' Macdonald asked Harris.

'The guy in the escape uniform? That's Justin Davenport – he escaped from Brixton a few years back. Managed to get over the wall with a home-made ladder he built in the metal shop.'

Davenport was slightly built and the uniform was several sizes too big for him – the trouser hems scuffed the floor as he walked. He started to circle the exercise yard, prowling like a trapped tiger, his eyes darting from the wire fence to the perimeter wall.

'They caught him last month on the Eurostar heading to France.'

'What was he in for, originally?'

'Believe it or not, TDA – taking and driving away. He'd been stealing cars since he was a kid and eventually a judge lost patience and sent him to an open prison for twelve months. Silly bugger went AWOL. They added a few months to his sentence and put him in a Category C prison. Ran away again. He's been inside now for three times as long as if he'd just done his time and kept his nose clean.'

Macdonald started jogging on the spot.

'I'm getting tired just looking at you,' said Harris, and sauntered away. He joined a group of four middle-aged men from the twos.

Macdonald realised that two black men were staring at him from across the exercise yard. Dreadlocks and Stickman. He returned their gaze. He'd beaten them once and had no doubt he could do it again, but he didn't want to have to keep watching his back on the landing. He had a choice: either beat them so badly they'd never go near him again, or win them over.

Dreadlocks whispered something to Stickman. They continued to glare at him.

Macdonald walked slowly to where they were standing. 'How's it going, guys?' he said.

'What the fuck do you want?' said Dreadlocks, fists clenched. Stickman was looking around but nobody was paying them any attention. There were no officers in the yard.

'We got off to a bad start this morning,' said Macdonald. 'It happens. Sorting out the pecking order and all. But I don't want you thinking that you've got to stick something sharp in my back to get even.'

Stickman was frowning, a faraway look in his eyes. 'What do you mean?' he slurred. Macdonald realised he was doped up to the eyeballs, probably been smoking marijuana.

'I just want to get out of here as quickly as possible. We

clashed heads this morning, and I want to know if that's the end of it.'

'And if it isn't?' said Dreadlocks.

Macdonald stared levelly at him. It was important to show no sign of weakness. The man had to understand that Macdonald was offering a truce, not surrendering. 'Then let's go to it now, two against one,' he said. 'But the way I see it, either I'm going to have to put you in hospital or you're going to have to kill me. Because that's just the way I am. I'm in for shooting a cop. There's not much more they can to do me. Now you two, I'd guess drugs. Probably dope, maybe crack. If you're lucky you'll be out in a few years. But if we go to war and you win, it's life.'

Dreadlocks continued to stare at him. Stickman was swinging his shoulders from side to side. He wasn't a threat: the dope he'd smoked had dulled his reactions to the point at which Macdonald could have pushed him over with his little finger. Dreadlocks was a different matter, though. The scar on his left forearm could have been from a knife fight and he didn't look the sort to back down, even if he wasn't carrying a weapon. But there was sharp intelligence in his eyes and Macdonald could see the wheels turning as he considered what had been said. Macdonald kept his hands loose but he was ready to strike the moment he saw any sign that Dreadlocks was going to get violent.

'Shot a cop, yeah?' said Dreadlocks.

'Didn't pull the trigger but I'll be charged with it,' said Macdonald.

'Dead?'

Macdonald smiled. 'No. He was wearing a vest.'

'Pity,' said Dreadlocks. He wasn't smiling but Macdonald sensed that the tension had gone. He had made his decision.

Dreadlocks pointed at the wound on Macdonald's head. 'They do that?'

'Hit me with the butt of a Heckler.'

Dreadlocks smiled for the first time. 'Ain't that the thing about the white man? Can't even use a gun the way God intended.'

'So, are we okay?'

'We're cool.'

Dreadlocks held out his fist and Macdonald tapped his against it. 'You did look like a Smurf in that paper suit.'

'No argument about that,' said Macdonald. He turned and walked away.

Harris was still deep in conversation with the men from the twos, but he was looking at Macdonald. As he walked past, Harris nodded. He'd obviously seen the confrontation, and Macdonald realised that the nod had been of approval. Not much got past Ed Harris. Macdonald was going to have to be careful around him.

The spur emptied again as the prisoners went back to work. Macdonald was locked up in his cell. He switched on the television but there was nothing he wanted to watch.

A key rattled in the lock and the door opened. It was Lloyd-Davies. 'Your solicitor's here,' she said.

Macdonald sat up, frowning. 'I haven't asked for one,' he said.

'Yeah, well, he's asking for you. I wouldn't go looking any gift horses in the mouth, if I were you. The sort of charges you're facing, you need all the help you can get.'

Macdonald swung his legs off the bunk and slipped on his trainers. Lloyd-Davies stood aside to let him out. She locked the door, then walked down to the ground floor with him. 'How was your first night?' she asked.

'It was okay,' he said. He wasn't sure what she expected him to say. After all, he was banged up in a high-security prison, sleeping on a wafer-thin mattress surrounded by drug-dealers, rapists and other violent criminals.

'At least you got a change of clothes.'

'I could do with new trainers,' he said.

'Ask your brief,' said Lloyd-Davies. 'He can have clothing sent in for you. Money, too.' She unlocked the door on the ground floor and took him along the secure corridor. It was deserted and the clicking of her heels echoed off the walls. 'How did he know you were here?' she asked. 'No one even knows who you are.'

'That's a very good question, Miss Lloyd-Davies. I was wondering that myself.'

'Maybe the guys who were arrested with you sent him.'

Macdonald smiled to himself. He doubted that Ted Verity would have sent him a solicitor. A hit-man maybe.

'You do that a lot,' said Lloyd-Davies, giving him a sideways look.

'Do what?'

'Smile.'

'It's my sunny personality, Miss Lloyd-Davies.'

'The way I hear it, you're on remand for armed robbery and facing charges of kidnapping and attempted murder.'

'I didn't shoot anyone,' said Macdonald. 'The forensic'll bear me out.'

'Even so, I don't see much to smile about.'

'Things have a way of working out for the best,' said Macdonald.

'You believe that?' she asked.

Macdonald grinned. 'No,' he said. He was a realist. He knew that, more often than not, things didn't work out for the best. Bad people did bad things to good people and got away with it. Good people got sick and died. Life wasn't fair, good didn't triumph over evil, and there was no such thing as the Tooth Fairy. 'No, I don't.'

'There's something about you that's not right,' said Lloyd-Davies.

'Yeah, well, if I was completely normal I wouldn't be in here, would I?'

'You don't seem bothered by it.'

'Yeah, well, still waters . . .'

'I've seen thousands of men pass through the remand wing, and they normally fall into two camps.'

'Gay and straight?'

She ignored his attempt at humour. They turned right. More CCTV cameras watched them. Again the corridor was deserted, stretching ahead for almost a hundred yards. Macdonald was bigger than the female officer by a good six inches and probably weighed fifty per cent more than she did. She had no weapons that he could see, and she wasn't wearing a radio. Yet she seemed confident that she could control him.

'Can I ask you a question, ma'am?'

'Fire away.'

'Aren't you concerned that I might turn violent?'

She smiled at him and raised an eyebrow. 'Is that supposed to worry me?'

'It's a serious question. I'm an armed robber, what's to stop me grabbing you and holding you hostage?'

Lloyd-Davies laughed. 'For what? A million quid and a helicopter?'

'The point is, they brought me in here with an armed escort and in handcuffs. Now there's just you and me walking down an empty corridor.'

Lloyd-Davies pointed out the nearest CCTV camera. 'We're watched all the time. If anything were to happen, there'd be a dozen guys in here kicking the shit out of you.'

'And if I had a knife?'

'You haven't. And if I was in any way unsure of my safety, we wouldn't be doing it like this. Is that what you wanted to hear? That I trust you?'

'I guess you get to become a good judge of character, working in here.'

'You've got to know that when you open the hatch in the morning you're not going to have hot water thrown in your face,' she said. 'Or worse. Now was that you changing the subject?'

'What do you mean?'

'I was about to tell you what was wrong about you when you got me on to the dangers of the job. Worried I was going to have an insight into your character that you don't want to hear?'

They reached a barred gate. Lloyd-Davies stood, key in hand, but made no move to unlock it.

'Fire away,' said Macdonald.

'Like I was saying, there's two sorts of guys on the remand wing. There's the new meat, men who've never been in trouble before. It hits them hard the first few days. They walk around in shock. Then there's the men who've been in the system before. Okay, they're not happy to be back behind bars, but they've got a confidence about themselves. The way they treat the officers, the way they react to the other inmates.'

'And?'

'Well, you've got the confidence, but not the experience. You had the confidence to get stuck into two hard nuts on the landing, but you didn't know to order your meals.'

Macdonald wondered how she knew about the fight, but guessed that little happened on the wing without the officers finding out.

'So, what do you think, ma'am?'

She looked at him quizzically, swinging her key chain. 'Either (a) boarding-school or (b) the army. You're not intimidated by institutions. Public-school boys and former soldiers always do well in prison.' She smiled. 'So, which is it?'

Macdonald grinned. 'That would be telling.'

'There's always C,' she said.

'And C would be?'

Lloyd-Davies put the key into the lock and opened the door. '*That* would be telling,' she said.

She let Macdonald through, then followed him and locked the door. She took him along another corridor to a central hallway. For the first time since leaving the remand wing they saw other prisoners escorted by guards.

Lloyd-Davies greeted another female prison officer and stopped to confirm a squash game, then took Macdonald up a flight of stairs. They entered a hallway in which there were four cubicles, each with windows on three sides. She took him to one. The door was unlocked. 'Wait in here,' she said.

Macdonald walked into the room. It was about eight feet square with windows on three sides, a Formica-topped table and four plastic chairs with metal legs. Macdonald sat down and folded his arms. Lloyd-Davies closed the door.

Another officer appeared at the window to Macdonald's right. He was in his fifties, almost bald with wisps of grey hair. He looked at Macdonald, then moved away from the window. Macdonald sighed and settled back in his chair. There were no CCTV cameras in the room, and no obvious signs of listening devices. He recalled that conversations between prisoners and their legal advisers were supposed to be sacrosanct.

The door opened again and the grey-haired officer showed in a middle-aged man in a dark blue pinstripe suit carrying a shiny black leather briefcase. He indicated a bell by the door. 'Ring when you're finished,' he said gruffly.

The man thanked him and sat down opposite Macdonald. He swung the briefcase up onto the table and flicked open its two brass combination locks.

The officer closed the door.

Macdonald leaned forward. 'What the fuck is going on?' he said, his voice a harsh whisper.

'Don't you mean, "What the fuck's going on, *sir*"?' said the man, adjusting his cuffs. He was wearing gold links in the shape of cricket bats. His hair was greying at the temples and it glistened under the overhead lights. Superintendent Sam Hargrove never spent less than forty pounds on a haircut and, whenever possible, visited an upmarket salon in Mayfair for his monthly trim.

'Why the fuck am I here?' said Macdonald.

'If you calm down, I'll tell you.'

Macdonald folded his arms again and leaned back. 'This had better be good.'

'There was a change of plan, after you went undercover.'

'And no one thought of telling me?'

'Spider, I'm as unhappy about this as you are.'

'Plans aren't supposed to be changed, not without a full briefing. Have you any idea how dangerous this is for me? There are six hundred men in here, any one of whom might know who I am. I need a legend that'll stand up to scrutiny. You can't just expect me to wing it.'

'We've run a check. No one here has crossed paths with you. No one will know you are Dan Shepherd. Your Bob Macdonald cover isn't in jeopardy. You continue with that.'

'The legend was set up so I could infiltrate a gang of armed robbers,' said Shepherd. 'We knew exactly who I was going to be pitching to. Now I'm on the remand wing and there are new arrivals every day.'

'We're watching your back, Spider. You have my word.'

Shepherd took a deep breath and forced himself to relax. He had worked in Hargrove's undercover unit for the best part of five years and in all that time he had never seen the superintendent deliberately put one of his operatives in harm's way. Except, of course, that every time an undercover policeman went on duty, his life was on the line.

'I've already spoken to Sue and put her in the picture,' said Hargrove. He held up a hand before Shepherd could speak. 'She's fine – but understandably she's as thrilled about this as you are.'

Shepherd's face tightened. He would have preferred to explain the situation to his wife himself, but the fact that he was behind bars made that next to impossible.

'I'll see what I can do to arrange a visit,' said the superintendent.

'I'm staying here, then?' asked Shepherd.

'I'm hoping to convince you to,' said Hargrove, 'but it's your call.'

That was par for the course, as Shepherd knew. An undercover cop was never forced to undertake an operation. It was always his choice. It had to be because of the nature of the work.

Hargrove opened his briefcase and took out a manila file. He opened it, extracted a glossy ten-by-eight colour photograph and slid it across the table. 'Gerald Carpenter,' he said, 'presently on remand here at Shelton.'

Shepherd didn't recognise the man but that was hardly surprising. There were three floors on his spur, plus two more spurs each with three floors. Out of almost a hundred and fifty men in the remand block, Shepherd doubted that he'd come across more than twenty. Then he remembered the incident at the hotplate. Gerry's sausages.

'He's on the twos,' said Shepherd. 'Gets special treatment.'

'Yeah, well, even in here money talks,' said Hargrove. 'Carpenter has been charged with bringing just over eight hundred kilos of heroin into the country. He's facing up to twenty years. The Drugs Squad have been after him for donkeys.'

Shepherd raised his eyebrows. Eight hundred kilos was worth close to eighty million pounds on the street. Even at wholesale prices, Carpenter wouldn't have got much change from twenty million. The man in the photograph was in his mid-forties, a decade or so older than Shepherd. He had a deep frown lines etched into his forehead and pale blue eyes that squinted suspiciously at the camera. He had thin, almost bloodless lips and bullet-grey hair, parted on the left. Shepherd handed it back. He had photographic recall for faces and a brief glance was all he needed to commit it to memory.

'Carpenter is a millionaire many times over and is very well connected on the outside,' said Hargrove, as he put the photograph back into the file. 'He's pulling all the strings he can to make sure the case doesn't come to court. The yacht that was used to bring in the drugs went up in flames two weeks ago, although it was under the supposedly watchful eye of HM Customs. A CPS solicitor was mugged at Waterloo last week. Two assailants, both white. They ignored the woman's Breitling watch and a wallet full of credit cards, just ran off with her briefcase. Which happened to be filled with papers relating to Carpenter's case.'

Hargrove put the file back into his briefcase. 'Three days ago an undercover drugs officer, who was pivotal to the case, was murdered. Shot twice in the head by two men on a motorcycle.'

Shepherd pursed his lips. There was no need for the superintendent to spell it out. It had been a professional hit – and killing a cop wasn't undertaken lightly. Only a man like Carpenter could afford to have it done.

'Jonathon Elliott. I believe you knew him.'

Shepherd's eyes widened. It had been a good five years since he'd crossed paths with Elliott, but he'd known him as a probationary officer when he was pounding the beat in South London, a lifetime ago. He was a Spurs fan, a fitness fanatic and a first-rate undercover officer. 'Yeah, I knew him.'

'Elliott was one of two undercover operatives preparing to give

73

evidence against Carpenter. The other works for customs and we've got him under wraps.'

'I'm sure that's a great comfort to him,' said Shepherd. 'Why were the agents giving evidence anyway?' Usually undercover agents were protected at all costs. They gathered evidence and helped prepare cases but, as a rule, they didn't appear in court. Once they did, their cover was blown for all time.

'It was the only way to get Carpenter. Until this case he's been untouchable. Like you, he has a photographic memory. Nothing is written down – names, addresses, phone numbers, bank details, all in his head. And, like most of the untouchables, he keeps well away from the drugs. Never goes near the money either. His method of bringing the gear into the country was pretty much infallible.' Hargrove leaned forward. 'He dealt mainly in cocaine and heroin, bought from a Colombian cartel. They fly their drugs out into the Atlantic and drop them into the sea where they're picked up by a tanker that spends most of its life in international waters. Buyers sail out to it. Carpenter had a dozen yachts picking up gear and sailing back to the Scottish coast. It was damn near perfect.'

'Couldn't have been that perfect or he wouldn't be in here.'

'Customs spent almost two million quid,' said Hargrove. 'and they've got him on conspiracy, but for that to stick they'll need agents giving evidence.'

'And the guys are okay with that?'

'Elliott was. And so is the Cussie. Elliott's wife had been wanting him to get out of undercover work for some time and he'd said that the Carpenter job was going to be his last. And the Cussie isn't far off retirement. We'd arranged for them to give evidence via video links with their identities concealed. Best we could do.'

'Best wasn't good enough, was it?' said Shepherd, bitterly. 'Not for Jonathon.'

'There's a bad apple,' said Hargrove. 'Has to be. Elliott is one of the squad's most experienced officers.' The superintendent grimaced. 'Was,' he said. 'We're looking for leaks within the Met, Customs and the CPS.'

'I'm not going to be much good to you in here,' said Shepherd. 'You need me on the outside.'

'Not so,' said the superintendent. 'You're exactly where you're most needed. Close to Carpenter.'

'He can't be doing anything here,' said Shepherd. 'This is a Category A prison. Even on the remand wing they're watched every minute.'

'Carpenter has never trusted anyone,' said Hargrove, 'and he'd never cede control of his organisation – he's too much of a control freak for that. No, he's still running things from behind bars. The question is, how? We know he's not passing anything out on the phone. All conversations are listened to.'

'What about his legal team?' said Shepherd.

'That's a possibility,' said the superintendent. 'We're also watching his family visits. But there's a more likely proposition.'

'A corrupt prisoner officer?'

'It wouldn't be the first time,' said Hargrove. 'A man with as much money as Carpenter wouldn't have any trouble buying help on the inside.'

'And that's why I'm in here? To sniff out the inside man?'

'Assuming you're up for it, yes.'

Shepherd sighed. 'What did Sue say?'

Hargrove shifted in his seat. 'She used a few choice phrases.'

Shepherd could imagine the sort of language his wife would have employed on being told that he was remaining undercover for the foreseeable future. She'd been nagging him to spend more time with their son. 'I'm going to have to see her,' said Shepherd. 'Liam, too. They've been through enough over the past few years.'

'That's not going to be easy,' warned Hargrove. 'Bob Macdonald doesn't have a wife or child, not with the legend the way it is.'

'I'm sure you'll think of something,' said Shepherd. 'There's room for flexibility. Have them separated. She's got the kid. Planning a divorce. It's not rocket science.' Although Shepherd was a detective constable and Hargrove a superintendent, they'd worked together long enough not to worry about speaking bluntly. 'This isn't going to be an overnighter, is it? There's no way Carpenter's going to let me get up close and personal until there's a degree of trust, and that could take weeks. Months.'

'It depends on you,' said Hargrove. 'I doubt that he's ever going to tell you how he's getting his orders to the outside, but you might pick up clues from watching him. That's all we need. Once we know how he's doing it we shut down his lines of communication and let the judicial process take its course.'

'Okay,' Shepherd said. 'I'm in.' He smiled. 'I've just realised that even if I said I didn't want to do it, I don't have much choice, do I? You could just leave me here.'

'You know me better than that,' said Hargrove. 'You always get to choose, Spider. It has to be that way. And the moment you think it's too risky, you bail out. He's already been responsible for the death of one undercover agent so he'd have no qualms about getting rid of another.'

'Who would my contact be?'

'We'll talk to the governor. He'll be the only one who knows who you are.'

Shepherd leaned forward over the table. 'You mean I'm in here alone at the moment? No back-up, no nothing?'

'We don't know who the rotten apple is. Any sort of back-up risks blowing your cover. This way, if you turn down the assignment we pull you out and nothing's lost.'

'What if the governor doesn't co-operate?'

'He won't have a choice,' said the superintendent. 'Besides, it's in his own best interests to find out who's helping Carpenter.'

'And he'll be the only one who'll know what I'm doing?'

'Has to be that way,' said Hargrove. 'We've no idea who Carpenter's using. Chances are it's a prison officer, but it could be anyone in the prison administration. They're not especially well paid, these days. The fewer people who know the better.'

'Until it goes pear-shaped,' said Shepherd. 'What do I do? Rattle my tin mug against the bars and demand to see the governor?'

'Haven't you noticed it's all plastic in here?'

Shepherd smiled grimly. 'You know what I mean. Prisoners don't just get to see the governor. There's six hundred-odd men in here and they've all got grievances. They'd all be in to see the top man, given the chance, but there are procedures in place to stop them. If the shit hits the fan, I won't have time to start filling out forms in triplicate.'

Hargrove reached into his top pocket and took out a white business card, with a handwritten telephone number and a north London address on the back. 'This is a dedicated line and there'll be someone at the end of it twenty-four hours a day. Register the number as your uncle Richard's. He's your mother's brother. If you need to be pulled out, call it and we'll do the rest.'

'And if I can't get to a phone?' Shepherd memorised the number and handed back the card.

'What do you want, Spider? A mobile?'

'I'm just saying, there are only so many hours a day when we're allowed to use the phones and more often than not there's a queue. I can't just push to the front and say, "Sorry, guys, I'm an undercover cop and I've got to call my handler," can I?'

'It's not like you to be so jumpy.'

'Yeah, well, this is the first time I've been undercover in the midst of six hundred Category A criminals. And the cover I've got wasn't set up for the sort of scrutiny I'm going to get here.'

'It's perfect. Career villain, ex-army, parents deceased.'

'But that's as far as it goes. I'm banged up with a guy most of the day. We've got to talk. That's all there is to do. And the way things stand at the moment, I've bugger-all to talk about.'

'So be the strong, silent type. Play the hard man. That fits with your cover. Look, Spider, if this is too much for you just say so and you can leave with me now.'

Shepherd flashed the superintendent a sarcastic smile. 'I've already said I'll do it,' he said. 'It's just that I was in the end phase of the Verity operation, home and dry. I was all geared up for drinks with the lads and a pat on the back, and now I'm having to get used to an open-ended operation with a whole new target. It's going to take me a while to get back into the zone, that's all.' He sat back in his chair and put his hands flat on the table. 'Sue's going to be as pissed as hell.'

'She's a copper's wife, she'll understand.'

Hargrove opened his briefcase and took out half a dozen sheets of paper. He slid them across the table to Shepherd. 'This is a summary of the intelligence we have on Carpenter. I've taken out all the dross.'

Shepherd scanned them and handed them back. He closed his eyes, took a slow breath and forced himself to relax. One by one he pictured the papers in his mind. Ever since he was a child he'd had virtually total recall of anything he read or saw. And he could remember conversations almost word for word. It wasn't a trick or a skill he'd acquired, it was a knack that he'd been born with. It meant he'd had to do the minimum of work at school and university – and it had saved his life several times as an undercover policeman.

'Got it?' asked Hargrove.

'Yes.'

Hargrove took an envelope from his briefcase. He opened it and placed half a dozen black-and-white photographs on the table in front of Shepherd. 'These are Carpenter's associates, the main ones.' He pushed two pictures towards Shepherd. 'These guys are on remand but they're in different prisons. The other four are on the outside.'

'They're all being watched?'

'Best we can, but they're pros.'

'Think they're doing his dirty work?'

'Pretty sure. But thinking and proving are two different things.'

Shepherd turned the photographs over. On the back he read typewritten summaries of their criminal careers.

'So, are we okay about this?' asked the superintendent.

Shepherd passed back the photographs. 'I guess so. What about the money side?'

'The money side?' repeated Hargrove, frowning.

'I'm in here twenty-four hours a day. By my reckoning that's fifteen hours a day overtime. More at weekends.'

'Since when have you been in the job for money, Spider?'

'Have you tried the food in here?' asked Shepherd. 'Have you tried sleeping on an inch-thick mattress with a pillow that's not much thicker? And a cellmate who farts in his sleep.'

'I get the point,' said the superintendent.

'So the money won't be a problem?'

'How about a compromise? Eight hours a day overtime, then take the rest as days off when this is over. It'll give you a chance to spend some time with your family.'

'Deal,' said Shepherd. He sighed and stretched out his legs. 'You might have warned me,' he said.

'There was no time,' said Hargrove.

Shepherd wondered if that was true. Or if Hargrove had wanted him inside before putting the mission to him. It was a lot harder to say no once he was in the system.

'What's happening with Verity?'

'He's in Belmarsh, and that's where he'll stay. Owen's singing like a bird so we'll let the Sussex cops run with him.'

'Any sense that they know I was a cop?'

Hargrove shook his head. 'Owen reckons you lost your nerve. Verity's going to be after your blood, but we've got him under wraps.'

'He'll know I'm here, though. And chances are he'll have mates inside.'

'We'll be watching your back, Spider. Anyone who's associated with you will be kept well away.'

'It was a bloody mess, the whole thing.'

'There was nothing else you could do,' said the superintendent.

The bald officer appeared at the window again. He stood watching Shepherd, his arms folded across his chest.

'Knocked me for six when Owen took the petrol out,' said Shepherd. 'He was going to do it, too. If the warehouse staff find out we knew there was going to be a robbery, they could sue for millions.'

'We didn't have a choice, you know that,' said Hargrove. 'There were too many warehouses at Gatwick to put our own people in every one.'

Shepherd shrugged.

'You did everything you could,' said Hargrove. 'The transmitter on the minibus led us to the right warehouse.'

'Eventually,' said Shepherd.

'We got them. That's what counts.'

'We risked civilians.'

'It was my decision, Spider. It was either that or just do them for conspiracy. I wanted Verity there with his trousers round his knees.' He paused, then leaned forward. 'I'm putting you forward for a commendation. You did a great job.'

Shepherd already had a string of commendations and awards for his undercover work, but he didn't do it for the glory. Or for the money. He did it because he was good at it. And he enjoyed it.

'So, what do you think?' asked Hargrove.

'About Carpenter? He's got people fetching and carrying for him on the wing. The prison officers seem a decent bunch. I presume you've already done financial checks?'

'All clean. But they wouldn't be stupid enough to pay money into their bank accounts.'

'Might not be money,' said Shepherd. 'He could be threatening them. Guy like Carpenter could reach their families any time he wanted.'

'Hopefully you'll hear about it on the wing. That's all we need, Spider. A nod in the right direction. Once we've got a name we can put him under the microscope.'

'Or her,' said Shepherd. 'There are female officers in here.'

'Only two on the remand spur where you are. It's not unknown for female officers to develop crushes on prisoners, which is why they get moved around more than the men. But Amelia Heartfield's married with four kids and, believe me, he's not her type. We had a good look at Joanne Lloyd-Davies' too, but she's got a boyfriend. Several, as it happens.' He adjusted his cuffs. 'And she's very highly thought of. Graduate entrant, studied psychology at Exeter University. She could be running her own prison before she's thirty-five. Not the sort to start taking bungs from a drug-dealer. Don't rule her out on my say-so, but I'd look elsewhere if I were you.' Hargrove pushed back his chair and stood up. 'I'll fix an appointment to see you tomorrow.'

Shepherd got to his feet. Hargrove pressed the bell by the door and the grey-haired officer opened the door and took him down the corridor. A man Shepherd hadn't seen before escorted him back to the remand wing.

By the time he was back on the wing the evening meal was being served. Shepherd wasn't hungry but he joined the queue. He was given the vegetarian option – curried beans – and put a roll and a pot of strawberry yoghurt on his plastic tray with it. As he headed for the stairs he passed Lloyd-Davies and flashed her a tight smile

'How was the meeting with your lawyer?' she asked.

'He agreed with you,' said Shepherd. 'Said I should start cooperating. Would it be possible to speak to a governor some time?'

'About what?'

'About registering, or whatever you call it. I want to start making phone calls, maybe arrange a visit.'

A smile of triumph flicked across her face. 'Decided to face reality, have you?'

'Seems pointless playing the strong, silent type.'

'Cutting off your nose to spite your face – I told you that your first day on the wing,' said Lloyd-Davies.

'I should have listened to you. So I can have a meet with a governor, can I? Run through my details?'

'You don't need to see the governor for that,' said Lloyd-Davies. 'I can take care of it. What do we call you?'

'Macdonald. Bob Macdonald.'

'And this is your first time inside, is it?'

Shepherd nodded.

'I'm sure it won't be your last. Now up the stairs with you.'

'You sound just like my old mum when you say that, ma'am,' said Shepherd. He saw her fighting not to smile as he headed up the stairs to the first-floor landing.

Lee was sitting at the desk, his head down over his plate. He grunted as Shepherd walked in. 'Where'd you get to?' he asked, his mouth full.

'My brief,' said Shepherd. He put the tray down on the table. 'You can have mine, I'm not hungry.'

'Gut trouble?'

'Just not hungry.' Shepherd sat on his bunk.

'The yoghurt, too?'

'Have it all.'

'Cheers, mate.'

Shepherd lay back on the bunk and interlinked his fingers behind his neck. 'Just so you know, I'm Bob Macdonald.'

'No more man-of-mystery, huh?'

'Figured it wasn't getting me anywhere. At least I'll start getting my money and I can register for the phone.'

'Means the screws'll cut you some slack, too.' Lee ripped his roll in half and used it to wipe his plate, then reached for Shepherd's. 'So was it your brief's idea to come clean?' he asked.

'He said they could put me away for just as long even if they didn't know who I was.'

'Makes sense. Is he expensive?'

'I suppose so.'

'It's worth paying the extra, that's what I always say. My brief's a diamond. Worth his weight in gold.'

Shepherd noticed the mixed metaphor but didn't say anything.

'He's the reason I'm in here,' said Lee, digging his plastic fork into Shepherd's beans.

Shepherd rolled on to his side so that he could look at his cellmate. 'Run that by me again, will you, Jason? Your brief's a diamond and he's the reason you're in prison?'

'Not in prison, you soft bugger.' Lee waved his plastic fork around the cell. 'Remand. He's the one who got me in here instead of doing hard time.'

'This is a Category A prison,' said Shepherd, still not following his cellmate's logic.

'It's Cat A, but we're on the remand wing, and remand time is always easier than hard time,' said Lee. He twisted round in the metal chair and wiped his mouth on the back of his hand. 'Look, I'm as guilty as sin, right? So Joe, he's my brief, says we plead not guilty on the basis that there's no way I'm going to get bail whatever happens. I sit here on remand, Joe drags his feet as much as he can before we get to trial, then we put our hands up to it. Judge looks at us favourably because we're saving the taxpayer the expense of a trial and I get a reduced sentence. Any time served here is knocked off the total.' He raised his eyebrows. 'See?'

'Got it,' said Shepherd. He rolled on to his back and stared up at the ceiling.

'He's all right, is Joe,' said Lee, turning back to his meal. 'For a Yid. Always make the best lawyers, Yids do.'

Lee continued to talk, but Shepherd closed his eyes and blanked him out as he went through the information he'd read about Gerald Carpenter. Father of three, married to his wife Bonnie for fourteen years, a keen rugby union fan and an experienced scuba diver. He had a private pilot's licence, a collection of expensive sports cars and a driving licence that had twice been suspended for speeding offences. Educated at Chiswick grammar school, he'd gone on to study economics at Exeter University then dropped out at the start of his second year to spend three years backpacking around the world.

Carpenter was almost fifteen years older than Lloyd-Davies, so there was no possibility of them having met at Exeter, but it might have given him a way to get close to her.

Carpenter had ended up in South East Asia, teaching English in the north of Thailand before coming to the notice of the US Drug Enforcement Administration's office in Chiang Mai. He left the country just days before the DEA and the Thai police swooped on a major heroin consortium. A dozen Thais and two American expats received long prison sentences, but two months later the street price of heroin dropped ten per cent in South London with the arrival of a huge shipment from the Golden Triangle. Carpenter had acquired a large mews house in Hampstead and a Porsche, and was red-flagged by Drugs Squad surveillance teams after he was seen in the company of known drug-importers.

The DEA bust was interesting, thought Shepherd. Undercover operations in the UK, even for Hargrove's special Home Office unit, were tightly monitored and controlled. Every facet of an operation had to be approved and signed for at a high level, but the Americans were often allowed to play fast and loose. He wondered if they'd cut a deal with Carpenter and allowed him to keep his shipment in exchange for information on the Chiang Mai Americans. It wouldn't be the first time that a drug-dealer had prospered under DEA protection.

After the first heroin shipment Carpenter hadn't looked back. He'd moved straight into the premier division of drug-importing and had stayed there. According to Drugs Squad intelligence he was responsible for as much as fifteen per cent of the heroin and cocaine coming into Britain. He had contacts across South America and the Far East, and a daisy-chain network of bank accounts that stretched round the world. He was as adept at money-laundering as he was at shipping drugs, and the National Criminal Intelligence Service could only estimate his wealth. They put a figure of two hundred and fifty million dollars on his net worth, but less than a fifth of that was in the banking system.

According to the file Shepherd had read, Elliott and Roper had spent months getting close to Carpenter, working their way through his organisation, proving themselves, until they were finally admitted to the inner circle. Their evidence would be crucial in putting him away. The recordings Elliott had made, plus the statements he had given to the CPS, would still be admissible, but they were no substitute for a police officer standing in the witness box and swearing on the Bible that he'd tell the truth, the whole truth and nothing but the truth.

According to the intelligence reports, the police and Customs should have expected Carpenter to move against the undercover officers. Over the previous decade three agents had disappeared while investigating his organisation. Two had been Drugs Squad officers; the third was a DEA agent investigating his links with a Colombian cocaine cartel. There was no evidence that Carpenter had had the men killed, but he was as careful to distance himself from violence as he was to keep away from drugs. Jonathon Elliott shouldn't have been out and about, not with the trial so close. Shepherd hoped that the Church was doing a better job of protecting its agent than the Drugs Squad had done with Elliott.

Sandy Roper swung his feet on to the sofa as his wife ran the vacuum cleaner in front of the television. 'Haven't you got anything to do?' she shouted, above the noise.

'I'm fine,' he said.

'You can go down the pub if you want,' she said.

'Alice, I'm fine,' Roper repeated.

Alice switched off the Hoover and faced him. 'Sandy, we've got to talk,' she said.

Roper grimaced and sat up straight. 'I know,' he said. 'This isn't easy for either of us.'

'You're moping around like a wet weekend,' she said. 'If this is what retirement's going to be like then God help us.'

'This isn't retirement,' he said. 'This is gardening leave. Until Carpenter's trial.'

'So go and garden,' said Alice. She looked at the lawn outside the sitting-room window. 'Why don't you get the mower out or clip the hedges? Do something.'

'I will,' said Roper.

'You've been off work for two weeks and you've barely left the house.'

'Orders,' said Roper.

'If the office is so keen on running your life, they should find you something to do.'

'It's not as easy as that,' said Roper. 'Carpenter's going to be hunting high and low for me. Until he's sent down I've got to keep a low profile.'

'But you're a Customs officer. You work for the government. What can he do?'

Roper knew exactly what Carpenter was capable of doing, but he didn't want to worry his wife. Carpenter only knew Roper's cover name and, provided he didn't go anywhere near Custom House, he should be as safe as houses. The head of Drugs Operations, Raymond Mackie, had gone to great pains to reassure Roper that

HM Customs would do everything within its power to ensure that no outsiders, not even the CPS, would know his true identity.

'He might try to intimidate me,' said Roper. He hadn't told his wife about Jonathon Elliott's murder, and he didn't intend to. Roper shared little about his work with his wife. She knew that he'd switched to undercover operations about five years earlier but he'd never gone into detail, letting her believe that most of the time he was working on VAT fraud. She regarded his job as worthy but mundane, and told acquaintances that he was a civil servant.

Roper had barely known Elliott. He hadn't even been told the policeman's real name until after his death. They'd met on the Carpenter operation and had come at it from different angles so they'd only ever been in character. If Roper hadn't been tipped off that Elliott was a cop, he'd never have guessed he wasn't an out-and-out villain. He'd played the part to perfection. That made his murder all the more surprising. Elliott hadn't seemed the type to blow his cover, which meant that someone on the inside must have tipped off Carpenter's people. There was probably a bad apple within SO10, the Met's undercover unit, but as no one in the unit knew who Roper was, he should be safe. That was the gospel according to Mackie, anyway, and Roper saw no reason to doubt his logic. But Roper also knew that a man with Carpenter's resources could just as easily corrupt a Customs officer as he could a policeman. He wouldn't truly be safe until the trial was over.

'If he did, he'd be in even more trouble than he is already,' said Alice.

Roper smiled but didn't say anything. He'd been married to Alice for a little over sixteen years and was used to her naïve view of the world. She'd had a sheltered middle-class upbringing and had been a primary-school teacher until she had given birth to their first boy. Then she'd become a full-time wife and mother, and her perception of the world was based on the evening news and the *Daily Mail*. Roper had done little to disillusion her. He had spent a good part of his working life hunting down men who thought nothing of destroying lives and livelihoods, who saw the law as something to be tested and broken, rather than respected and obeyed. Carpenter would see men like him and Elliott as nothing more than obstacles to be removed.

'You're retiring next year anyway,' said Alice, sitting down on the sofa next to him. 'Why can't they let you go now?'

'My pension doesn't kick in until I'm fifty-five,' said Roper.

'They could make an exception for you, surely.'

Roper smiled at the thought of the Church making exceptions for anyone.

'You *are* going to retire, aren't you,' pressed Alice, 'when this is over?'

'Of course I am. That's what we've planned, right?'

Alice took his hand in hers. 'It's what I want,' she said. 'We've earned some time to ourselves, Sandy. You can spend more time with the boys, we can take holidays. Join the bridge club, like you promised.'

Roper patted her hand. 'We will, love. Once the trial's over.'

Alice leaned forward and gave him a peck on the cheek. 'Cup of tea?'

'Lovely,' said Roper.

Alice went off to the kitchen and Roper stared out of the window at the grass. He didn't want to get out the lawnmower. He didn't want to cut the hedges. He didn't want to join the bridge club. What he wanted more than anything was to continue working for HM Customs and Excise, keep on hunting down men like Gerald Carpenter and putting them away. Roper didn't do the job for money, or his pension: he did it for the thrill of the chase, the excitement of pitting his wits and skills against villains. Sometimes the Church won and sometimes they lost but, no matter what the result, there was always the adrenaline rush and Roper was scared to death of losing it for ever. He sat forward and put his head in his hands. There was no way he would ever be able to explain to Alice that he feared retirement more than he feared a hardened criminal like Carpenter.

Gerald Carpenter leaned on the guard-rail and looked down through the suicide mesh at the ground floor where prisoners were milling around. Association, they called it, but there was no one on the spur with whom Carpenter wanted to associate. He could tolerate the bad food, the smell from his in-cell toilet, even the near constant rap music blaring from the cells on the ones, but having to socialise with men he despised was more than he could bear. Better to sit in his cell and watch television or listen to his stereo.

There was a pool table on the ground floor and two dozen names chalked up. Less than half would probably get a game before it was time for the cells to be locked for the night. Three card tables had been set up. One was a regular bridge group, comprising two businessmen facing fraud charges, a former MP accused of killing his gay lover, and a Pakistani doctor, held under the Prevention of Terrorism Act. Pontoon was being played at the other two tables. The stakes were bits of matchstick but Carpenter knew that debts were paid in tobacco. So did the prison officers, but they did nothing to stop the games. Anything for a quiet life.

Ed Harris walked up the metal steps to the top floor and along the landing. He nodded at Carpenter and joined him at the railing.

'Who are the new arrivals?' asked Carpenter.

Harris nodded at Bill Barnes, who was making short work of clearing the pool table. 'Bill Barnes, second time in Shelton. Calls himself a cat burglar but he's more of a bull in a china shop. Got caught selling a couple of gold Rolexes to an undercover cop in Clapham. Standard con – the cops set up a pawnbroking operation and wait for the gear to surface.'

'Hardly Cat A,' said Carpenter.

'Tried to slash a guard last time he was inside. Did an extra year for that. Word is, he'll be in for a kicking at some point. The guard he tried to nail transferred here and is over on Block D.'

A middle-aged man wearing a white shirt with blue pinstripes, and black wool trousers was standing with his back against the wall.

'See the guy there?'

Carpenter nodded.

'Insurance fraud. Simon Hitchcock. Distant relative of the film director, he says. Sold policies but didn't pass the money on to his head office. Fraud Squad are looking for six million quid.'

'Doesn't look like he'll last long.'

Harris agreed. 'Took his wedding ring off him, and a St Christopher's medal and chain. So much for protecting travellers. Digger's already hit him for protection money.'

Carpenter shook his head. The man was a lost cause. On the outside he was probably a big wheel at his local Rotary Club, played golf with other wheeler-dealers, got special service at the best restaurants and flew business class. On the inside he was easy meat for the sharks. 'Anyone else?'

'Guy by the name of Bob Macdonald, not Scottish. Wouldn't give his name when they first brought him in, but he's seen sense. Armed robbery and they say his crew shot a cop. They've put him in with Jason Lee on the twos. First time inside.'

'He's a pro, though?'

'Handles himself like he's been around, but he can't have been in the system before or they'd have had his dabs.'

'Hard, is he?'

'I can't make him out,' said Harris. 'He gave Austin and his sidekick a thrashing first morning he was in, then bugger me if he doesn't go over to them in the yard and get it sorted.'

'How?'

'Dunno what he said but they're not gunning for him.'

'Threaten them with harm, do you think?'

'He doesn't come over as the threatening type.' Harris pointed down to the ground floor. 'There is he now. Prison sweats. Brown hair.'

Harris was right, Carpenter thought. Macdonald didn't look the threatening type. He was of average height, wiry and seemed relaxed in the prison environment. There was none of the tension of a new arrival, but none of the forced bravado of an old hand. Macdonald walked over to the pool table and stood watching.

'Tell me about the fight, Ed. Did you see it?'

'Yeah, I was on the landing. They started it, but he finished it – bloody quickly, too.'

'Hands, feet, head?'

'Kicked and punched them. Not *kung fu* or anything flash. He was . . .' Harris scratched his nose as he searched for the right word. 'Efficient,' he said eventually.

'Efficient?' repeated Carpenter.

'Like he was matching their violence. Hurt them just enough to stop them.'

'Reasonable force?'

'Yeah, that's it exactly. He was using reasonable force.'

Down below, the man they were talking about folded his arms and leaned against the wall. He looked up and, for a brief moment, had eye-contact with Carpenter. Carpenter was used to hard men trying to intimidate him with cold stares, but Macdonald's expression was more inquisitive, the look a tiger might give an antelope while he decided whether or not it was worth giving chase. Then, just as quickly, Macdonald broke eye-contact and waved at Harris, who waved back.

'Nice enough bloke,' said Harris.

'Well, anyone who shoots cops can't be all bad,' said Carpenter. 'Thanks, Ed. You need anything?'

'Tunnel under the wall and a new identity,' said Harris. 'They're going to throw away the key this time.'

Carpenter pulled a sympathetic face. He was prepared to throw a few home comforts at Harris in exchange for his information, but there was nothing he could do to help Harris out of his predicament. He'd been caught red-handed, literally: the bloody knife that had severed his wife's jugular vein had been in his hands when the police answered a neighbour's 999 call. And he'd confessed all to the sympathetic detectives who'd interviewed him, the tape-recorder running. More likely than not, Harris would die behind bars. Carpenter had no intention of suffering the same fate. He'd do whatever it took to regain his freedom.

Gary Nelson flicked through the files in his in-tray, dropped half a dozen of the most urgent into his briefcase and snapped the lock. His wife had driven up to Newcastle to visit her mother and there was nothing on television that he wanted to watch so he planned on getting some work done. But first he was going to pick up a couple of curries. His wife hated the smell of Indian food, but if he opened the windows and sprayed air-freshener around she'd be none the wiser when she got back.

The office was deserted so he switched off the lights as he left. He took the lift to the ground floor, acknowledged the uniformed security guard and pushed his way through the revolving door. His Toyota Corolla was in an underground car park a short walk from the office. It was starting to rain so he turned up the collar of his raincoat and jogged, clutching his briefcase to his chest.

His car was on the second level below ground. There was a lift but it was claustrophobically small, hardly bigger than a coffin, so Nelson took the stairs.

There were spaces for two dozen cars on the second level, but only three vehicles. Nelson's was at the far end, close to the emergency exit. His footsteps echoed off the bare walls as he walked across the concrete. Overhead there were bare pipes, stark fluorescent lights and the sprinkler system. Two CCTV cameras covered the area but he had never seen a security guard in the building. Nelson took his keys from his pocket. He looked up at the CCTV camera by the emergency exit, then frowned as he saw that the lens had been sprayed with black paint. He stopped walking and looked across at the second camera. That, too, had been spray-painted. It didn't look like the work of vandals, he realised. It was a deliberate attempt to blind the cameras. So that no one would see what was going on. The hairs on the back of Nelson's neck stood up and he shivered. He had a strong feeling that something bad was about to happen. 'For God's sake,' he muttered to himself. 'Get a grip.'

He started walking again, swinging his briefcase and humming. He kept looking round as he approached his car, unable to shake off the dread, but he was alone. He'd been watching too many horror movies. The world was a safe place, he told himself, and he was a thirty-five-year-old male in good physical condition, not the average mugging victim. Not any sort of victim.

Nelson jumped when he heard footsteps behind him. A man in a dark green anorak was running towards him, a black woollen hat pulled low over a pair of impenetrable sunglasses. The door to the emergency exit crashed open and Nelson whirled round. A second man stood there. Leather jacket. Blue balaclava. Sunglasses. Holding a Stanley knife.

Nelson took a step backwards, his heart pounding. He held up his briefcase in front of him, facing the man with the leather jacket. The man was grinning. Totally confident, totally in control. 'I don't want any trouble,' said Nelson, and he could hear the fear in his voice. He took another step backwards.

Anorak was still running towards him. Nelson didn't know what he could say to keep the two men at bay.

'Please . . .' he said. He felt his bowels go liquid and knew he was about to piss himself.

Leather Jacket swished the Stanley knife from side to side. Nelson stared at it in horror. Then Anorak hit him side on and Nelson crashed to the ground. His hand twisted under his chest and he felt his little finger snap. He tried to get to his feet but Anorak kicked him in the stomach and he curled up into a ball.

Anorak kicked him again, his boot catching him under the chin and snapping his head back. Nelson started to black out. Then he was aware that his face was being slapped. He opened his eyes. Leather Jacket had a knee in the middle of his chest. Nelson blinked away tears. He could see his face, his tear, reflected in the black lenses of Leather Jacket's sunglasses.

Leather Jacket leered at him and held the Stanley knife to his throat. 'If I cut you here, you'll bleed to death in less than a minute,' he hissed.

'Please, don't!' Nelson gasped. 'My wallet – my wallet's in my jacket.'

'We don't want your money.'

'My car,' said Nelson. 'Take it. The keys are—'

Leather Jacket pressed the knife to Nelson's cheek and sliced the flesh. Nelson felt a burning sensation, then warm blood spuring down his cheek. 'Shut up and listen,' hissed the man, his mouth just inches from Nelson's ear. 'You know the Carpenter case?'

Nelson nodded. It was a Customs and Excise and Drugs Squad

case, and he had been scheduled to give expert testimony in support of tapes recorded by two undercover officers. He had to show that the tapes hadn't been tampered with, and that the voices on them belonged to Gerald Carpenter and the agents.

'You tell them you can't give evidence,' said Leather Jacket. 'Tell them you're sick, tell them you've had amnesia, tell them what you want, but if you turn up in the witness box we'll be back to finish the job. Understand?'

'They'll know I've been warned off—' The man in the anorak kicked him hard in the ribs. Nelson felt a bone break and pain lanced through his side. He screamed, but the man with the knife clamped a hand across his mouth.

'I'm a nasty piece of work, me, but I've got mates who are ten times worse,' he murmured. 'They'd love nothing more than to spend a few hours in the company of your wife. Pretty woman, Mrs Nelson. Lovely blonde hair. My mates were arguing about whether or not she was a natural blonde, and they'd love the chance to find out. How would you feel if your wife was raped? Take the gloss of your marriage, wouldn't it?'

Nelson didn't say anything. Tears welled in his eyes, not because of the pain but because he felt so helpless. The last time he'd been so powerless was when he was nine, and two teenage bullies at school had taken his dinner money off him every Monday. Nelson had been too scared to tell his parents, too scared of what the older boys would do to him if they found out, so he'd paid them every week. He'd started stealing loose change from the coats in the sixth-form cloakroom and had used it to pay for his lunches. He'd never told anyone. Not his parents. Not his teachers. Not his wife. It was a secret he'd kept buried for years, but lying on the cold concrete floor of the car park with the knife against his throat and blood trickling down his cheek, the shame and self-disgust came flooding back.

'We know where you live, Gary. We know where your wife walks the dogs. Fuck with us and we'll fuck with you.'

Leather Jacket took his hand off Nelson's mouth. Nelson gasped. Every breath was agony – he could feel the fractured ends of his broken rib grating together – but he was grateful that he was still alive, that they weren't going to kill him.

'Just nod to let me know that you understand and agree,' said the man, pushing the blade of the Stanley knife into Nelson's neck.

Slowly, Nelson nodded.

Shepherd woke early. It was a nuisance not having his watch. The forensics investigator still had it, and he had no idea when, if ever, he'd get it back. Lee was snoring softly. Shepherd stared up at the barred window. All he could see was a patch of pale grey featureless sky. It was a strange feeling, knowing that central London was only a few miles away. Pubs, shops, football grounds, all the places he used to take for granted might as well not exist. His wife and son were less than thirty minutes away.

He wondered how it would feel to be a lifer, knowing you were going to be kept behind bars for ever. The confinement would drive him mad, he was sure of it. He'd go the same way as Justin Davenport and devote all his time and energy to breaking out. There was no way he could accept that for the rest of his life he would be told what to do at every minute of every day. Lloyd-Davies had probably been right when she said that a military background prepared a man for prison: the communal food, sleeping and washing arrangements, the requirement to follow orders, the rules and regulations that had to be obeyed, no matter how inappropriate, all brought back memories of Shepherd's time in the army. But there was a big difference between the men with whom he had served and the prisoners in Shelton: choice. Shepherd had wanted to join the army ever since he'd gone into an army careers office with three school friends to shelter from the rain one lunchtime. They'd watched a promotional video, dripping wet and eating packets of Golden Wonder crisps. The others had jeered at the video, but Shepherd had been transfixed. His parents had been pushing him towards university: they wanted him to be a solicitor or a doctor, a professional, someone they could boast about to their neighbours, and they looked horrified when he'd turned up with a stack of army brochures. They managed to persuade him to go to university but he'd left before taking his finals and had signed up as a career soldier.

Once in the army he'd wanted to be the best of the best and had put himself through the SAS selection course twice before he was accepted. It had been harder and more uncomfortable than anything they could do to him in prison, but it had been his choice. Everything he'd done had been his choice, right or wrong, and there hadn't been a day when he couldn't have walked away if that was what he'd wanted. Eventually he had left, and that had been his choice, albeit because it was what his wife had wanted. But the men in Shelton had no choice, and that was what made prison such a terrible punishment. It wasn't the food or the environment or even the people, it was the lack of choice. And when there were choices, they were choices laid down by others. Top bunk or bottom. Tea or coffee. Vegan meal or Ordinary. Choices that were no real choice at all. Even now, Shepherd was in prison by choice. He could have refused the job and woken up in warm double bed with Sue, instead of alone in an uncomfortable bunk with a racist thug beneath him. But if that choice was ever taken away from him, Shepherd knew that the confinement would be more than even he could bear. He'd do whatever it took to get out.

He sat up, not liking where his train of thought was heading. Gerald Carpenter had a wife and family, and he was facing a long prison sentence. Shepherd had been inside only two days but already he had grasped how appalling the prospect of ten or even twenty years was. Carpenter had decided how badly he wanted his freedom, and the price he was prepared to pay to achieve it. He'd kill to get out. Shepherd rubbed the back of his neck where the tendons were as taut as steel cables. Would he be prepared to do the same? He had killed – five times – but in combat, in the heat of battle, the enemy in front of him. Combat wasn't especially clean or honourable, but it was kill or be killed, soldier against soldier. Would he be prepared to kill another human being in cold blood if it meant the difference between life imprisonment and freedom?

Shepherd swung down off his bunk and started doing rapid press-ups. He concentrated on his rhythm and breathing and was soon bathed in sweat. He increased the pace and soon he could think of nothing except the exercise, the burning in his muscles, the pressure on his fingertips, the blood coursing through his veins. Twenty. Thirty. Forty. Fifty. He stopped at sixty, knowing he could do more, and switched to rapid sit-ups, working his left side, then the right, until he rolled over and did another fifty press-ups.

'Bloody hell! Sooner they let you in the gym, the better,' said Lee. He was watching Shepherd with one eye.

'Sorry, Jason,' said Shepherd. The lack of privacy was one of the worst things about his confinement. The only time he could be alone was when he was sitting on the tiny toilet: it had a thin plastic door but even then every bodily function could be heard in the cell. Since he'd been in prison he had always been just a few feet from another human being. He promised himself that the first thing he would do when he got out was go for a long in the countryside. The Brecon Beacons, maybe, where he'd done the SAS selection course. He'd hated the wilderness then, hated the bleak hillsides and the icy, clinging rain that had soaked him to the skin and chilled him to the bone, hated the freezing streams that poured into his boots, hated the wind that froze his cheeks and hands. But now he'd give anything to be out in the open, breathing fresh air that hadn't been through the lungs of a hundred other men. 'What time is it?'

Lee squinted at his watch. 'Twenty past seven. They'll be doing roll-call soon.'

'You okay if I keep exercising?'

'Sure,' said Lee sleepily. He rolled over and put his head next to the wall.

Shepherd carried on doing press-ups, sit-ups and leg raises. He heard boots on the stairs, then inspection hatches.

It was Hamilton who opened theirs. 'Macdonald, you get to shower this morning,' he said.

Shepherd frowned. He hadn't requested a shower and it wasn't like Hamilton to offer him unnecessary privileges. He still hadn't come up with a copy of the *Prison Rules*.

'You've got an appointment with the governor at eight forty-five. RSVP isn't necessary.'

The inspection hatch snapped shut. The governor had obviously been told of his presence, and Shepherd was pretty sure that he wouldn't be happy to have an undercover cop in his prison.

In an ideal world, Shepherd would have preferred that no one knew his true role. But HM Prison Shelton was not an ideal world, and there might come a time when he needed a Get Out Of Jail Free card at short notice. The governor would be his only lifeline, so, whatever his reaction, Shepherd would have to handle him carefully.

The secure corridors were filled with inmates when Hamilton took Shepherd to the governor's office. Prison officers stood at the corners of the corridors linking the various blocks. All the connecting doors were open and they watched the prisoners file past, singly and in groups. The atmosphere was relaxed as a university campus between lectures, and other than the prison uniforms and surveillance cameras there was no real sense that they were in a holding facility for the country's most dangerous criminals.

Most of the prisoners were moving from their blocks to the workshops where they spent three hours each morning. Their jobs were mundane – filling the breakfast packs, assembling Christmas crackers for a high-street chain or electrical goods, putting junk mail into envelopes for financial institutions. Lee had told Shepherd there was a small computer department that did freelance programming work but the only prisoners who could work there had degrees and programming experience. Shepherd had been surprised to hear that half a dozen long-term prisoners fulfilled the requirements; most were in for murder.

The governor's office was on the top floor of the administration block. A small outer office contained two middle-aged women, one working at a computer, the other talking on the phone. One side of the room was lined with metal filing cabinets; flow-charts and posters covered the other walls. Hamilton pointed at a plastic sofa and Shepherd sat down. He'd seen most of the posters in the reception area when he'd first been brought into the prison. How not to get Aids. The penalties for racial abuse. How to contact a Listener.

The woman on the phone put her hand over the receiver and smiled at Hamilton. 'Is that Mr Macdonald?' she asked.

Hamilton nodded.

'Mr Gosden says he's to go in,' she said.

Hamilton gestured at Macdonald to stand up, then knocked on the door to the governor's office and opened it.

John Gosden was a stocky man in his late forties, sitting behind a large teak-veneer desk with two stacks of files in wire trays, a desktop computer and a small laptop, both with modem connections. There was a tropical fish tank by the door. A couple of dozen brightly coloured fish were swimming languidly round a sunken plastic galleon and a diver with a stream of tiny bubbles fizzing out of its helmet.

'Thank you, Adrian,' the governor said to Hamilton. 'You can wait outside.' He waited until the officer had closed the door, then got up. He was a head shorter than Shepherd, but his shoulders were broader. He looked like a bodybuilder who'd given up exercising some years ago.

Shepherd thought the man was going to shake his hand, but Gosden walked over to the fish tank and picked up a container of flaked food. 'Do you keep fish, Shepherd?'

'No, Governor,' said Shepherd. 'Don't mind eating them, though.'

Gosden flashed him a cold smile, then sprinkled a small amount of food on to the surface of the water and bent down to watch the fish feed. 'An aquarium is a delicate balancing act,' he said. 'The mass of fish you can support depends on the volume of water in the tank, the surface area, and the efficiency of your aeration pump. The number of fish determines how much food you put in. If any of the variables is out of kilter, if anything is added that isn't planned for, the whole eco-system can fall apart.'

'I get the analogy, Governor,' said Shepherd. 'I don't intend to do anything to upset the equilibrium of your institution.'

'Your presence does that,' said the governor, straightening up.

'Only if the prisoners work out who I am and what I'm doing here. And they won't.'

The governor's lips were a thin, unsmiling line. 'I'm not just referring to the prisoners. The fact that I have allowed you to go undercover in my prison suggests I don't trust my people. And this place runs on trust, Mr Shepherd. It's all we have standing between order and anarchy.'

Shepherd didn't say anything. The governor must have known there was a good chance that one of his officers was helping Carpenter run his organisation from behind bars.

'I'm not happy about this, Mr Shepherd. Not happy at all.'

'I'm sorry about that,' said Shepherd. He was still standing in the centre of the room. Clearly the governor had no intention of asking him to sit down.

'Have you any idea what a dangerous position this puts me in?' the governor went on. He knocked on the side of the tank and the fish darted to the back. 'If the prisoners find out there's a policeman in their midst, there'll be a riot.'

'I think, of the two of us, I'll be the one in most danger,' said Shepherd.

'You think they'll stop with you?' said Gosden. 'If you believe that, you've no idea how a prison functions.' He snorted, then went to sit behind his desk. 'Your mission is to find out what Gerald Carpenter is up to, is that right?'

'He's sabotaging his case. We have to find out how.'

'And the presumption is that one of my people is helping him?'

Shepherd shrugged. 'I've got an open mind, Governor, but his phone conversations and mail are monitored, so that doesn't leave too many options.'

'His family. His legal teams. He has medical visits.'

'Medical visits?'

'He has a recurring back problem, which means he has a weekly visit from an osteopath. And his dentist has visited twice.'

'I thought the prison had its own medical facilities.'

'Apparently the facilities we have aren't satisfactory in view of the state of his spine or his root canals. He's got world-class lawyers, has your Mr Carpenter, and the 1998 Human Rights Act is full of helpful phrases. At one point it was starting to look as if the great Cherie Booth was going to be representing him so we decided to let him have his own way.' At last the governor waved to a chair opposite his desk. 'Sit down. Please.' He looked suddenly tired. He ran a hand across his forehead and rubbed his eye. 'Look, I'm sorry if I sound tetchy but this is a stressful job at the best of times – and I don't like being told what to do by suits who've never been within a mile of a Cat A facility.'

Shepherd sat down. 'I have to say, Governor, I'm as unhappy as you are about being here. But you've been told what Carpenter's doing – what he's already done?'

'My suggestion was that they move him to another prison. Put him in the secure unit at Belmarsh.'

'And they said?'

'That they wanted it dealt with here. Which I presume means that they suspect the leak is in-house.'

Shepherd nodded. Moving Carpenter wouldn't solve anything. If they kept him in Shelton there was a chance that they would find the bad apple in the prison and identify who on the outside was doing Carpenter's dirty work. 'You were a prison officer yourself?' asked Shepherd. Gosden didn't seen the type to have come into the service at the top.

Gosden smiled. 'Shows, does it? Started off walking the landings in Parkhurst. Six years. Then moved to an open prison and couldn't stand it. Went back to the Isle of Wight, got made Principal Officer and did an Open University degree.'

'It's not a job I could do.' Shepherd was trying to get on the right side of the man, but he was being truthful. Undercover work was stressful but at least he had the adrenaline rush and the satisfaction of putting away the bad guys. Prison officers were at their most successful when nothing happened, when the status quo was maintained. And the job was never-ending. For every prisoner who walked out of the gates, another moved in to take his place. Shepherd doubted he had the stamina or the patience to make a career of keeping people locked up.

'It has its moments,' said Gosden. 'Believe it or not, most prison officers care about what they do. At least, when they come into the service. And a lot of inmates are genuinely remorseful and want to turn their lives round.'

'I sense a "but" . . .' said Shepherd.

'There are enough bad apples to turn even the best-intentioned prison officer cynical after a few years,' Gosden told him. 'Hot water thrown over them, HIV-infected prisoners cutting themselves and flicking blood around, razor blades in soap, ears bitten off. You know all prison officers wear a clip-on tie? That's in case a prisoner grabs it. And these days all the prisoners know their rights, from the *Prison Rules* up to the Human Rights Act. And to make it worse, the officers often feel there isn't enough support from above. If a governor isn't behind his men one thousand per cent, they'll start to think that maybe it's not worth keeping to the straight and narrow. That maybe the rules can be bent.' Gosden stood up and started to pace up and down the office. 'So, if you were to ask me if one of my officers could be on the take, what am I supposed to say? I have to back them.' He stopped. 'Do you understand what I'm saying?'

'Absolutely,' said Shepherd. 'It's the same on the job. Your colleagues come first. They have to, because when the shit hits the fan they're all you've got.'

Gosden nodded.

'But sometimes cops go bad,' said Shepherd.

'We've some in here too. On Rule Forty-five. Couple of Vice cops who were on the take for years.'

'What I'm saying is, when cops go bad you can't turn a blind eye.'

'That's not what I'm doing,' said Gosden, defensively. 'What I'm doing is giving my people the benefit of the doubt. You tell me that one of them's on the take and their feet won't touch the ground, I promise you.'

'That's fine by me,' said Shepherd.

'But if you disrupt my prison, if I think you're putting the safety of my men at risk, I'm pulling you out. I don't care what some Home Office mandarin says, this is my prison.'

Shepherd didn't say anything. He knew that Gosden didn't have the authority to halt the operation, but he could make Shepherd's life impossible. A word in the right ear and his cover would be blown. Once that happened he would have no choice but to bail out.

The two men stared at each other for several seconds, then Gosden relaxed. 'That's my pep talk over,' he said. 'I'm told I have to co-operate with you, so is there anything you want me to do?'

'I need to get close to Carpenter, but I'll have to do that myself. If you were to pull any strings it'd tip him off that something was up. But I could do with a look at your personnel files. Just the officers on the spur.'

Gosden shook his head. 'I'd have a walk-out if I did that. If nothing else they fall under the Data Protection Act.'

'No one would know,' said Shepherd.

'That's not the point. It's a breach of trust.'

'I only need background, just so I know who I'm dealing with.'

Gosden massaged the back of his neck. 'God, this is a mess.'

'Governor, it's as much in your interest as mine to find out who's helping Carpenter.'

Gosden went over to a filing cabinet, opened it and pulled out a dozen files. 'You mustn't make any notes,' he said, 'and I think you should be quick about it. Hamilton's going to wonder why you're in here so long.'

'What reason have you given him for bringing me here?'

Gosden was pacing up and down his office again. 'I told Tony Stafford that I wanted to talk to you about a family matter. I said your wife had written to me saying she was considering divorce. In view of the violent nature of the crime you've been charged with, I said I'd have a talk with you. It wouldn't be unusual, I'm pretty hands-on here.'

Shepherd sat down with the files. He scanned the pages quickly, but his eyes passed over every line. He had to read the words to memorise them. Every name, every date, every fact was recorded perfectly, and would remain in his memory for several years, then begin to fade. Shepherd had no idea how his memory functioned. He could only memorise, not understand.

He went through the files page by page, then stood up. 'There's one other thing you can do for me,' he said. 'I need some phone numbers authorised, and to be able to make calls.'

'I'll set up a pin number for you,' said Gosden, reaching for a pen and a notepad.

'I need money in my account, apparently.'

'I'll get that sorted. I'll put you on "enhanced".'

'Won't that raise eyebrows?'

'Not necessarily,' said Gosden. 'I'll simply say that after our chat I've decided that you're becoming more co-operative and that, as a gesture of good faith, I'm making you enhanced. It's happened before.'

Shepherd gave Gosden his fictitious Uncle Richard's number.

'Do you want to be able to call your wife?'

'There's no way I can risk it from the prison,' said Shepherd.

'You could call her from here,' said Gosden. 'I have a direct line.' He gestured at his desk. There were two phones, one cream, the other grey. 'The grey one doesn't go through the switchboard. The Home Office uses it and I take personal calls on it.'

It had been four days since Shepherd had spoken to his wife, and he had no idea how long it would take Hargrove to get her in as a visitor. He swallowed and realised his mouth had dried.

'It's there if you want it,' said the governor, 'but we're going to have to get a move on. You've already been in here much longer than I'd normally spend with a prisoner.'

Shepherd's mind was in turmoil. He wanted to talk to Sue, to let her know he was okay and missing her. But a call from the prison, even on the governor's direct line, was a risk. If anyone should ever trace the call from his house to the prison it would be the end of the operation. He dismissed the thought. No one knew who he was. As far as the prison population was concerned, he was Bob Macdonald, failed armed robber. No one other than the governor would know that he'd made the call. The benefits outweighed the risks. He nodded.

'I can't leave you alone,' said the governor, apologetically.

'That's okay,' said Shepherd. He picked up the receiver and tapped out Sue's number. His hand was trembling as he put the receiver to his ear. The governor busied himself at the fish tank.

Sue answered the phone on the fourth ring. 'Hello?'

Shepherd closed his eyes, picturing her. Shoulder-length blonde hair, probably tied back in a ponytail. Green eyes. Faint sprinkling of freckles across her nose. She hated her freckles and was forever covering them with makeup. Shepherd loved them. 'Sue. It's me.' Even with his wife, Shepherd rarely identified himself by name.

'Oh, God! Where are you?'

'Didn't Sam tell you?'

'He said you were in prison on a job, but he didn't say which prison. He said that was an operational detail and he couldn't tell me.'

'I'm sorry, love. I don't know why he didn't tell you because he's going to try to fix up for you and Liam to visit. I'm in London, not far away. Did Sam tell you why I was here?'

'Just that you were targeting someone. But he said it was important.'

'It is, love, believe me.'

'How long are you going to be away? Liam's going crazy not seeing you. And Sam said I wasn't to tell him anything, just that you were going to be away for a while.'

'Is he at school?'

'Of course. Life doesn't stop because you're away.' There was a touch of bitterness in her voice. Shepherd wasn't surprised she was upset. She'd expected him home two days ago and now she'd been told that he was on an open-ended assignment that would keep him away twenty-four hours a day.

'I'm sorry.'

'Why didn't they tell us you were going away?'

'They didn't know until the last minute. I was as surprised as you, love. I was in here for a day before they told me what was happening.'

Sue sighed. 'I'm sorry, I don't mean to moan. Sam told me how important it was. And what happened to that other policeman.' Jonathon Elliott, she meant. 'Be careful, won't you?'

'Of course,' said Shepherd.

'Is it horrible?'

'It's not that bad, actually.'

'Really?'

'TV in the cells, food's reasonable, there's a gym and we get out in the fresh air every day. I might bring you and Liam for a week some time.'

'After this you owe us a fortnight in Mallorca, minimum.'

She went quiet. Shepherd couldn't think what to say. He wanted to hold her and kiss her, to smell her perfume and stroke her hair. The phone was a poor substitute. 'I really am sorry about all this,' he said eventually.

'It's your job,' she said. 'It's what you do.'

'Tell Liam I phoned, yeah? Tell him I love him and I'll be home soon.'

'How soon?'

It was a good question. 'I don't know, love.'

'Days rather than weeks?' she asked hopefully.

'If I get lucky, yeah,' he said.

'I love you.' She said it quietly, and he was suddenly ashamed. His place was at home with her and their son.

'I love you, too,' he said. 'I'll make this up to you when I get home. I promise.'

'You'd better.'

'I will.'

'Okay.'

'I've got to go.' The governor had straightened and was looking at a clock on the wall.

'I know.'

'I'm sorry.'

'Stop saying you're sorry. I've been married to you long enough to know how it works.'

'I don't deserve you.'

'That is so true.' She laughed.

'I do love you, Sue. I wish you were here with me now.'

'In prison with a hundred men who haven't had sex for years?'

'You know what I mean.'

'I know.'

'I have to go.'

'I know.'

'I love you.'

'I love you.'

Shepherd closed his eyes. He knew he was behaving like a lovesick teenager, but he couldn't bring himself to hang up on her, not knowing when he was going to have the chance to talk to her again.

'You're going to have to hang up first,' she said, as if reading his mind.

'I don't want to.'

'Can you call later, when Liam's here?'

'I can't, love.' He had no idea when he'd be able to talk to her again.

'Please try.'

'I will.' He hated lying to her but didn't have time to explain why contact was going to be impossible. He didn't know whom he could trust within the prison. Anyone, inmate or officer, could be on Carpenter's payroll. He was taking a big enough risk using the governor's personal phone. 'I've got to go, love. Sorry.'

He put down the receiver and immediately cursed himself for not ending on a better note. 'Sorry,' he'd said. He should have told her he loved her again. If it was the last thing he ever said to her he wanted it to be 'I love you' and not 'Sorry.'

'You're going to have to go,' said Gosden.

Shepherd stuck out his hand. 'Thanks for that,' he said.

'The worst thing about prison is the lack of contact with family,' said Gosden, shaking Shepherd's hand. He had a strong grip with thick fingers and calloused skin. 'They forget that, the people who complain about televisions in cells and education programmes. Being away from your family is the punishment. And it's got to be a hell of a lot worse for you.'

'Yeah, but at least I'll be walking out soon,' said Shepherd. 'Hopefully.'

Hamilton escorted Shepherd back to the remand block. 'So, what did he want?' Hamilton asked, as he unlocked the door to the secure corridor.

'To know what I thought of the prison officers,' said Shepherd.

'What?'

'Home Office is compiling a list of officers who can't do their jobs. The governor's supposed to get the opinions of a random group of inmates. My number came up.'

He stood to the side so that Hamilton could relock the door.

'A survey?' said Hamilton, frowning.

'Home Office.'

Shepherd started to walk down the corridor towards the remand block.

What did you say?' asked Hamilton. 'To the governor?'

'It's confidential,' said Shepherd. 'Sorry.'

They walked the rest of the way in silence. Hamilton unlocked the door to the remand block. 'You're winding me up, you prick,' he said, as Shepherd walked into the spur.

Two prisoners were cleaning the ground floor with mops. They worked slowly and methodically, their heads down. Hamilton took Shepherd up to his cell. It was empty. 'I have to stay banged up?'

'Unless you're on a work detail or education.'

'Can't I go to the gym?'

Hamilton shook his head. 'Don't give me a hard time,' he said. 'Gym is in the afternoon, but you have to be on the list. And you're not.'

'It just doesn't seem fair that I have to stay locked up.'

'Yeah, well, who said life was fair? If it was fair, I wouldn't be in here jingling keys, would I?' He nodded at the cell. 'In,' he said.

'I want a copy of the *Prison Rules*,' said Shepherd.

'I'll get it for you.'

Shepherd stood his ground. 'I want it now.'

'I said I'd get it for you. In the cell, Macdonald.'

'I'm entitled to a copy of the *Prison Rules*. You're refusing to give me what I'm entitled to.'

'You're committing an offence against discipline,' said Hamilton. 'You are disobeying a lawful order. If you don't get into your cell now I'll put you on a charge.'

'In which case I'll be up before the governor and I'll be able to give him my side of the story.' Shepherd put his hands on his hips and stared at Hamilton. There was no way he was going to back down.

Hamilton continued to glare at Shepherd. He was a couple of inches shorter and Shepherd was in better condition. Hamilton couldn't physically make him go into the cell, not on his own. But calling for his colleagues would be an admission that he'd lost control. An admission to his colleagues, and to himself. Shepherd could practically see the wheels turning behind the man's eyes as he considered his options. Hamilton nodded slowly. 'Wait here,' he said.

He walked along the landing swinging his key chain. Shepherd leaned against the railing and watched him let himself out of the spur. The cleaners on the ground floor looked up at Shepherd. One grinned and gave him a thumbs-up.

Hamilton went into the control office and spoke to Tony Stafford. A few minutes later he returned with a booklet and thrust it at Shepherd. On the front it said *The Prison Rules* 1999, and under the title was a list of dates when the rules had been amended. 'Happy now?' asked Hamilton.

'Thank you,' said Shepherd.

'I am now asking you to enter your cell,' said Hamilton. 'If you do not comply with my instruction, I will summon a control-and-restraint team.'

Shepherd smiled easily and stepped inside cell. Hamilton pulled the door shut and Shepherd heard him walk away down the landing. It was a small victory, but he was starting to appreciate how small victories counted when you were in prison. He sat down on his bunk and started to read the rules.

*   *   *

Gerald Carpenter squeezed the excess water out of the mop and swabbed the floor, taking care not to get soapy water on his Bally loafers. Two hundred pounds he'd paid for them and there he was, cleaning a prison floor in them. Sometimes life just didn't go according to plan.

Carpenter didn't enjoy manual work, but the cleaning job was his by choice. It meant that he was out of his cell for most of the day, and was pretty much free to roam the spur. He spent most of his time on the threes, but being on the cleaning crew meant he could go down to the lower floors whenever he wanted. Some of the cleaners worked as go-betweens, ferrying messages and contraband between cells, but the inmates knew better than to ask Carpenter to act as a messenger boy.

The spur was quiet during labour, like a university hall of residence when lectures were on. During association it was bedlam – music blaring, arguments at the pool table, raucous laughter. Even late at night the spur was never completely quiet. There was the murmur of televisions, stereos playing, sometimes prisoners crying or screaming. Constant reminders that another fifty souls were locked up there. A hundred and fifty in the houseblock. But when the men were at labour, there was a peaceful quality to it. Not like a church or cathedral, the surroundings were too ugly for that, but a monastery perhaps – if it wasn't for the barred doors and the suicide nets. But the spur wasn't populated with men seeking spiritual fulfilment, thought Carpenter, with a wry smile. They were about as far from holy men as you could get.

Carpenter's smile widened as he ran the mop from side to side. He'd received some good news that morning. The electronics expert who had been planning to testify for the prosecution had decided that appearing in the witness box wouldn't be conducive to his health. Carpenter knew that Gary Nelson could be replaced, but it would take time for another expert to be brought up to speed, and that was assuming the prosecution could find another expert willing to take his place. The world of the expert witness was small, and word would soon get around. Nelson had been beaten and scarred, a living reminder of what would happen to anyone who threatened Gerald Carpenter.

Bit by bit Carpenter was dismantling the case against him. CPS files had been stolen and destroyed. Jonathon Elliott had been taken care of. The prosecution's prime piece of evidence – the yacht – had gone up in flames. But one major obstacle still had to be removed before Carpenter could be sure of winning his freedom, and that was the Customs officer, Sandy Roper.

Carpenter hated Roper. It wasn't just that the man's evidence threatened to keep him inside for the foreseeable future but because Carpenter had liked him. They'd been drinking together, gone to football matches and lap-dancing clubs, laughed and joked and told stories. They'd almost become friends, and Carpenter didn't let many people get close to him. Roper's betrayal had been personal. Pretty much every word that had left the man's mouth had been a lie. His name, his age, the school he went to, the deals he'd done. It had all been a web of deceit. And half the time Roper had been wearing a wire, recording everything Carpenter had said. Carpenter had let the man into his inner circle and Roper had betrayed him. And it wasn't even for money. Carpenter could have understood that. Sympathised, even. If Roper had been a grass and the cops had been paying him a few grand for the information, Carpenter would have hated the man for being a grass, but he'd have understood his motivation. If the cops had been pressurising him, forcing him to inform, Carpenter could have empathised. He knew that a man under duress was often more reliable than a man working for money. And he knew that cops could bring all sorts of pressure to bear to make a man betray his friends. But Roper had betrayed Carpenter for no other reason than that it was a job. A nine-to-five, dead-end, no-hope, time-serving job. Sandy Roper had been a civil servant with five weeks paid holiday a year, waiting for the day when he got a gold watch and a piss-poor pension. That was what riled Carpenter. He'd been outwitted by a bloody civil servant.

And it wasn't just Roper who'd betrayed him. He'd allowed a copper to get one over on him, too. Jonathon Elliott had been as likeable as Roper. A good-looking guy, always with a story about his latest conquest. Then, after he'd been arrested, Carpenter had discovered that Elliott had a wife and a wall full of commendations for his undercover work. Another civil servant who was trying to put Carpenter behind bars for no other reason than it was the career he'd chosen.

Carpenter hadn't taken any pleasure in having Elliott killed. He'd have preferred to buy the man off, because a cop on the payroll was an asset. But when it became clear that Elliott wasn't corruptible, killing him had been the only way of removing him from the equation. It was a simple one: evidence plus witnesses meant prison. No evidence, no witnesses, and Carpenter was a free man. He would take whatever steps were necessary to ensure that the equation worked in his favour.

He stopped swabbing the floor, leaned on the railing and looked down at the suicide net. One of the cleaners on the ground floor waved at him and Carpenter nodded back. Anton Jurczak, a middle-aged asylum seeker from Eastern Europe, had stabbed an immigration officer in his south London apartment. Like most of the men on the spur, Jurczak's crime made no sense to Carpenter. The immigration officer was unarmed, as was his female assistant and the two uniformed policeman who'd allowed the interview to take place in Jurczak's kitchen. Jurczak had panicked, grabbed a knife and thrust it into the chest of the officer, then tried to throw himself through the kitchen window. A search of the apartment revealed three kilograms of heroin from Afghanistan and over two hundred thousand pounds in cash behind a skirting-board. If he'd kept his nerve the worst that would have happened would have been deportation, a minor inconvenience to a man with Jurczak's money. But now, barring a miracle, Jurczak would spend the rest of his life behind bars. Most men in the remand block had similar stories to tell. Not that many were honest about what they'd done to get sent inside. Everyone lied. Most claimed they were as innocent as new-born babes. Framed. Mistaken identity. A million and one excuses. Not one of the prisoners Carpenter had met had ever admitted to being arrested fairly and squarely. Carpenter knew the truth about the men with whom he shared the spur. He made it his business to know. He paid good money for the information because information was power. Jurczak hadn't told anyone that he was a major player in the drugs industry, but Carpenter knew. There were two rapists and one paedophile on the spur: they wouldn't last a minute if the general population discovered the nature of their crimes. Carpenter knew about their cases, and their secrets were safe with him, as long as they did as he asked.

Carpenter knew that he was different. He wasn't behind bars because he'd lost control or lashed out in anger. He hadn't stolen on impulse or sold drugs on street corners. He'd been targeted, pursued, hunted, by some of the best thief-catchers in the world. And money had been no object. During pre-trial hearings his lawyers had discovered that Customs alone had budgeted almost two million pounds for the investigation. The Drugs Squad's overtime bill had been more than three hundred thousand. The investigators knew that if they put Carpenter away they'd be able to pursue his assets. The day Carpenter was charged they had frozen bank accounts, property and shares worth twenty-eight million pounds. It was less than a fifth of his assets, but Carpenter knew they were still looking. If he was found guilty, all the money would be forfeit.

Carpenter started mopping the floor again. He whistled quietly to himself. It wouldn't be long now before he was back home with his wife and children, where he belonged. All that stood between him and his freedom was Sandy Roper. And, if all went to plan, Roper would soon be as dead as Jonathon Elliott.

Shepherd was lying on his back, staring up at the white-painted ceiling, when he heard the rumble of conversation and the unlocking of the door to the spur. There were shouts and laughter as fifty or so prisoners milled around on the ground floor, waiting for tea.

Shepherd heard footsteps on the landing and then his door was opened. It was a prison officer he hadn't seen before, a huge West Indian with a beaming smile. Shepherd jumped down.

'I'm Hal Healey,' said the officer. 'You settling in okay?' He was a good three inches taller than Shepherd, with huge shoulders that almost blocked the doorway and a thick neck that threatened to burst out of his shirt collar. Shepherd's memory flicked through its filing system and he pictured the file that he'd read in the governor's office. Born 12 April, 1968. Divorced. Child Support Agency taking £450 a month from his wages. Prior to Shelton he'd worked at Belmarsh, where he had twice been accused of assaulting a prisoner. In both cases the prisoner had withdrawn his allegation.

'Fine thanks, Mr Healey,' said Shepherd. He moved to get past the man but the officer stood where he was, blocking his way.

'I heard you were giving Hamilton a hard time,' said Healey, affably.

'I just wanted a set of *Prison Rules*.'

'Disobeyed an instruction, is what I heard.'

'It's sorted now.'

Healey's grin windened. 'It'll be sorted once we've finished this little chat,' he said. 'You've only been in here a day or two, so maybe you don't understand how things work here.'

'I've got the drift.'

Healey ignored Shepherd's interruption. 'This block runs on co-operation. Has to be that way. We can't force you to do anything. Not physically.'

At that Shepherd smiled. Healey was big and strong enough to force practically anybody to do anything.

'The punishments we can impose are basically loss of privileges. We can't all pile in and give you a good kicking. Not officially, anyway.'

There was a touch of cruelty in his smile, and Shepherd wondered why the men in Belmarsh had withdrawn their allegations. 'I don't follow you, Mr Healey.'

'When a prison officer asks you to do something, you do it. We tend to ask nicely, because we like you to co-operate. When you ask us for something, hopefully you'll ask us nicely, too. That way, everybody gets along. But if you don't co-operate . . .'

Shepherd nodded. 'I get it.'

'Well, you didn't this morning, apparently. You insulted Mr Hamilton in front of other prisoners.'

'They were down on the ones,' said Shepherd.

'They heard everything. Now it's going to be that much harder for him to get any prisoner to do anything. And once they used to disobeying him, they might start on me. And I don't want that happening. Not on my spur. Do you understand?'

Shepherd was running through his options, then filtering them through the persona of Bob Macdonald, armed robber and hard man. Dan Shepherd would behave one way but, as far as the world was concerned, he wasn't Dan Shepherd and he had to behave in character. He stared at Healey, then took a step towards him. 'Hamilton is a prick,' Shepherd said quietly. 'And not only is he a prick, he's a cowardly prick, sending you to fight his battles. What was the theory there? Small white guy is scared of big black guy?' Shepherd took another step towards Healey. 'Well, you don't scare me, Mr Healey. You're big all right but most of it is fat, and I've stomped on bigger and fatter guys than you. Hamilton's a prick for sending you and you're a prick for coming in and trying to scare me.'

'Racist insults are an offence against discipline,' said Healey.

'Rule fifty-one, section 20A,' said Shepherd. '"A prisoner is guilty of an offence against discipline if he uses threatening, abusive or insulting racist words or behaviour." But all I did was call you a big black guy, which is what you are. And fat. Which is also what you are. If you want, you can put me on a charge and we can both go before the governor and you can explain why you came into my cell.'

'You called me a prick.'

'And I can justify that to the governor. You called me scum. You started name-calling.'

'Smart arse, huh?' sneered Healey, but Shepherd knew he'd won.

'Rule six, paragraph two,' said Shepherd. '"In the control of prisoners, officers shall seek to influence them through their own example and leadership, and to enlist their willing co-operation."

That's not what Hamilton was doing, and it's not what you were doing by coming into my cell and getting heavy with me. Now, fuck off out. Yes, I know I'm using threatening and abusive words, but that's nothing to what I'll do to you if you don't fuck off.' Shepherd bunched his fists and took another step towards Healey. The prison officer backed away, then hurried off down the landing.

Shepherd took several deep breaths and smiled to himself. Despite his bulk, Healey was a coward. But Shepherd knew that the confrontation wasn't over. He'd won the battle but the war would go on, and Healey would be able to choose his moment. Not that Shepherd was worried about a physical confrontation. He'd meant what he said: he'd hurt bigger men than Healey. Winning fights wasn't a matter of size and strength: technique and commitment counted, and Shepherd had been trained by the best. But Shepherd was on his own and Healey had the backing of his colleagues. He was sure that Hamilton would relish the opportunity of putting the boot in, figuratively and literally.

Shepherd walked out on to the landing and looked down at the ones. Prisoners were already lining up at the hotplate, trays in hand. He looked at the bubble. Healey was talking to Stafford, waving his hands animatedly. It was obvious that he was telling the senior officer what had happened.

Shepherd stretched. The bones in his neck cracked. His wafer-thin pillow offered almost no support. He wondered how Stafford would react if he insisted on being treated by a chiropractor. Under Rule 20, an unconvicted prisoner was entitled to have his own doctor or dentist visit the prison. He rubbed the back of his neck with both hands. As he looked up at the threes he saw the big man with the shaved head walking purposefully down the stairs. He leaned on the railing and watched him to down to the ground floor and the hotplate. Once again, he went to the front of the queue and was served immediately. Craig Rathbone looked on disinterestedly.

Shepherd watched the man carry the tray of food back up to the threes, and lost sight of him as he walked along the landing. Carpenter's cell must be at the far end of the spur. He wondered how easy it would be to get transferred to a cell near him. The governor could probably arrange it but that would mean drawing attention to himself. So far Shepherd hadn't seen Carpenter, either during association or in the exercise yard. And when Carpenter was out of his cell, working, Shepherd was banged up. Carpenter sent his man down to get his food, and Shepherd had no idea when he used the showers, but he doubted that a prison shower was the right sort of place to strike up conversation with a stranger.

Lee walked up the stairs, carrying his lunch on a plastic tray. 'How's it going, Bob?' he asked.

'Bored shitless,' said Shepherd.

'They'll find you a job, now that you're co-operating. Probably put you on breakfast packs.'

'What's that?'

Lee walked along to the cell. Shepherd went with him.

'Those trays we get each night. With the teabag, sugar, milk and cereal. They make them up in one of the workshops. They normally put the new guys on that.'

'Fuck that for a game of soldiers. How do I get on the cleaning crew?'

Lee laughed. 'You don't. Not without influence. Told you before, you'd have to talk to Digger.'

'Who's on the crew at the moment?'

'On the spur, there's six guys. There's Charlie Weston, he's in for VAT fraud. Must have money stashed away because he bought his job in his first week. There's a black guy called Hamster. He didn't pay but he does other stuff for Digger.'

'Hamster?'

'Sold crack in Soho. Kept the balloons in his mouth. Silly bugger had so many in there that his cheeks were always puffed up. Got caught by an undercover squad and couldn't swallow them all.' Lee chuckled.

'Who else?'

'Ginger, the guy down from us, the redhead who always wears Man United gear. He's been cleaning for six months. His wife pays Digger on the outside.'

They walked into the cell. Shepherd stood by the door while Lee sat down at the table and started forking spaghetti into his mouth.

'How do you know that, Jason?'

'No secrets in prison, mate. Ginger tells the guy he shares a cell with, guy tells my mate Jonno in the gym, Jonno tells me. That's all there is to do in here, watch TV and talk. You come in thinking you're going to keep yourself to yourself but after a while you let your guard down. Have to, or you might as well be in solitary.'

'So, Charlie, Hamster and Ginger. Who else?'

'What are you angling for?' asked Lee.

'Just want to know who the competition is,' said Shepherd.

'It's not about competing, you just have to pay Digger.'

'I don't have the money to pay him so I'm going to have to be more creative.'

'Not sure that Digger appreciates creativity,' said Lee.

'We'll see,' said Shepherd. 'Who else?'

'There's a guy called Jurczak. He's Bosnian or something. Stabbed an immigration officer. Nasty bastard, always throwing his weight around. He's up on the threes. Oh, yeah, and Carpenter, he's on the threes as well. Drug-dealer. Supposed to have millions on the outside.' Lee frowned. 'That's five, innit?' He ran through the names in his mind and nodded. 'Yeah, Sledge on the ones is a cleaner, too. He's the one you usually find doing the showers. Big guy, bald as a coot, bulldog tattoo.'

Shepherd had seen him the previous evening, washing the floor after the hotplate had been taken back to the kitchen. 'Doesn't seem the sort of guy who'd have money to spare.'

'He hasn't, but would you want to try to take his mop off him? I don't think Digger does. You know why they call him Sledge?'

'I don't, but I bet you do.'

'Short for Sledgehammer. His weapon of choice. He was on the cleaning crew before Digger got sent here. Digger got the other cleaners to quit, but there's not much he could do to pressurise Sledge. Are you going to get your dinner?'

'I'm not hungry.'

'What did you ask for?'

'Cornish pasty.'

'Do me a favour and get it? If you don't want it, I'll save it for later.'

Shepherd headed for the door.

'Get us a bread roll, too, yeah?'

Shepherd stopped and turned to look at Lee. 'Anything else, Your Majesty?'

Lee put up his hands. 'No offence, Bob. Just a pity to see good food go to waste, that's all.'

Shepherd grinned. 'You should get out more, Jason.'

The next day, Shepherd still hadn't been given any work so he spent the morning locked in his cell. He was let out for dinner, then locked up again. Late in the afternoon, Craig Rathbone opened the door. 'You not been fixed up with a job yet, then?' he asked.

'It's in the pipeline,' said Shepherd. 'What jobs are there?'

'You'll probably be put in one of the workshops,' said Rathbone. 'Or maybe the laundry. I'll speak to Mr Stafford.'

The last thing Shepherd wanted was to go to one of the work-shops. He had to get close to Carpenter, which meant a job on the cleaning crew. And that either meant talking to Digger or getting one of the existing cleaners to give up his job.

'You've got a legal visit,' said Rathbone.

'Yeah, my brief said he'd be back.'

Rathbone stood to the side to let Shepherd out of the cell, then the two men walked down the landing. 'What's your solicitor say?' asked Rathbone.

'Says I should try to get a deal, being caught red-handed and all. But I'm no grass.'

'Honour among thieves?'

'You know what happens to grasses inside.'

'So you'll go down for the full whack? Armed robbery, plus a cop getting shot? You could get life.'

'We'll see,' said Shepherd.

'Good luck,' said Rathbone, and it sounded as if he meant it.

He took Shepherd out of the spur and along the secure corridor to the administration block close to the entrance to the prison. Shepherd had already adopted the rhythm of walking under escort, stopping at each barred gate, standing to the side so that the officer could open it, walking through first, then waiting while the officer relocked it.

Hargrove was already in the interview room. Rathbone told him to use the bell when he'd finished, then closed the door and left them alone.

'How's it going?' asked Hargrove.

'I've only been here two days, and I've been banged up for most of that.'

'Have you seen Carpenter yet?'

'I'm working on it.'

'You're going to have to pull your finger out, Spider.'

Shepherd flushed and he glared at the superintendent. 'Have you any idea what it's like in here? It's a fucking high-security prison, not a holiday camp. I can't just wander along to Carpenter's cell and offer him a cup of tea.' He sprawled back in his chair, exasperated.

Hargrove was clearly concerned at his outburst. 'Are you okay?'

'What do you think?' said Shepherd, his voice loaded with sarcasm.

Rathbone appeared at the window with the bald officer who'd been there during Hargrove's previous visit. Hargrove smiled and nodded, as if he and Shepherd were having a pleasant chat. 'I think you're under a lot of pressure,' he said, 'and I appreciate how hard the task is that you've undertaken. But we're under pressure on the outside, too. One of the Home Office's experts has been attacked. Dr Gary Nelson. He was going to give evidence on the recordings Elliott and Roper made, proving that they hadn't been tampered with.'

'Is he okay?'

'They cut him. Threatened his wife. Threatened him. He's on sick leave, saying he's going to resign. Blames us for not protecting him.'

'He's got a point, don't you think?'

Hargrove sighed mournfully. 'We can't put every person involved on this case under twenty-four-hour guard, Spider. Nelson was just one of a dozen technical experts who've been lined up. There's probably fifty police, Customs, CPS and forensics people working on this case. Round-the-clock protection for them all would mean five hundred men; the Met just doesn't have the resources.'

'Have you told Roper?'

'About Nelson?' Hargrove shook his head. 'If he gets cold feet, the case will collapse. Ditto if anything should happen to Roper. You're our best hope, Spider.'

'I know, I know. I'm sorry.' Shepherd ran his hands through his hair. He felt dirty. He'd only had one shower since he'd arrived at Shelton and no matter how many times he brushed his teeth with the prison toothpaste his mouth never felt clean. 'I haven't been in role twenty-four seven before,' he said. 'I've always been able to go home – or at least somewhere where I can just be myself.'

'Do you want me to get a psychologist in?'

Undercover agents often talked through their problems with police psychologists, but bringing one into Shelton could be Shepherd's downfall. There was no way that a career bank robber would seek psychological help. 'I'll work through it.'

'Let me know if you change your mind,' said Hargrove. The two men sat in silence for a minute or two. 'How much contact have you had with the prison officers?' asked Hargrove eventually.

'I've had dealings with five so far. Tony Stafford runs the block. He's in the bubble most of the time so I don't see how Carpenter could be using him. Lloyd-Davies is on the spur but, like you said, she's a smart cookie and destined for higher things. Hamilton's got a chip on his shoulder and he'd be the one I'd try to turn. The guy who brought me over is Rathbone. Seems okay. And there's a nasty piece of work called Healey who isn't averse to breaking the rules.'

'Is he your main suspect?'

Shepherd shrugged. 'Too early to tell. Carpenter's hardly been out of his cell, at least when I'm around. He's on the cleaning crew, apparently, which means he can move around the spur pretty much as he wants, but when he's out and about I'm banged up.'

'So what's your plan?'

'I'm going to try to get on the cleaning crew.'

'Do you want me to talk to the governor?'

'Hell, no,' said Shepherd. 'Carpenter will see that coming a mile off. Let me see what I can do. Macdonald's a hard man so it wouldn't be out of character for me to start throwing my weight around.'

'Just as long as you don't end up in solitary,' said Hargrove. 'Is there anything you need?'

'My watch – or *a* watch, anyway. It's a pain not being able to keep track of time. And get me some decent clothes. There aren't many status symbols in here and clothing separates the faces from the muppets. Designer jeans. Polo shirts. And trainers – Nikes, whatever the latest model is.'

'I'll get them sent in,' said Hargrove, scribbling in a small black notebook.

'On second thoughts, make the watch a bit flash. And I want to see Sue and Liam.'

'I'm on it.'

'I have to see them,' said Shepherd. 'And I'd be happier talking to Sue without you there. No offence.'

'You'll have to put in an application. Angie Macdonald and Harry. I've had them added to all the computer files on the Macdonald legend. Soon as the application arrives I'll get her in.'

'I was in to see Gosden and he let me talk to her. On the phone.'

Hargrove looked pained but didn't say anything.

'It was a direct line, and if we can't trust Gosden I'm dead in the water anyway.'

Hargrove still looked unhappy.

'Gosden has put it around that I'm having marital problems and that my wife wants a divorce. I'll ask for a visit. Have her driven here by someone you know.'

'I'll make sure she's okay, don't worry.' Hargrove stood up and put away his notebook. 'You're doing a hell of a job, Spider. Don't think it's not appreciated.'

Shepherd stood up and rang the bell. 'Just remember the overtime, that's all.'

The bald officer came for Hargrove, then Rathbone escorted Shepherd to the remand block. 'How did it go?' asked Rathbone, as they walked along the secure corridor.

'He's optimistic,' said Shepherd.

'Yeah, well, they always say that as long as you're paying their bills,' said Rathbone.

'You're a cynical man, Craig,' said Shepherd.

'You get to be in this job,' he said. 'You never meet a guilty man in here. The excuses you hear. Framed by MI5 – get that at least once a week.'

They walked in silence for a while, Rathbone's thick-soled work shoes squeaking on the shiny linoleum floor.

'Can I ask you a question, Craig?' asked Shepherd, as they headed towards the remand block.

'Sure, as long as it's not geography,' said Rathbone. 'I'm crap at that.'

'Who runs the wing?'

Rathbone looked across at Shepherd. 'You mean Tony Stafford?'

'You know what I mean. Who's top dog among the prisoners?'

'You're all equal under the sun,' said Rathbone.

'Yeah, that's great in theory, but it's not how it really works, is it?' said Shepherd. 'You know Digger, right?'

'Ah, the delightful Mr Tompkins. He's got his claws into you, has he?'

'He said he could get me sorted with the canteen until my money comes through.'

'Yeah, well, be careful. Neither a borrower nor a lender be, is the best advice I can give you.'

'Why do they call him Digger?'

Rathbone chuckled. 'He was supposed to have done double murder a few years back,' he said. 'Got rid of two Yardies who were encroaching on his turf. Never got caught and told everyone he'd buried them with a JCB.'

'What's he in for now?'

'A single murder this time. Shot another Yardie point-blank. Did a runner but got nailed by forensics. Seriously, be careful, yeah?'

'Everyone tells me he runs the spur. If not the block.'

'Do they, now?'

'Said that anything I need, he can get for me.'

'I'd like to see him get you out of here.'

'You know what I mean, Craig. Thing is, I don't want to start asking favours of the wrong people.'

'You wouldn't be trying to pull a fast one on me, would you, Macdonald?'

'What do you mean?'

'Maybe you see yourself as top dog and want to know who you have to take out.'

'Furthest thing from my mind,' said Shepherd. 'Besides, what's the point of being the big man on a remand wing? The population's always changing.'

'There's still money to be made, though.'

'If you know what he's doing, why don't you do something about it?'

Rathbone grinned sarcastically. 'Me, you mean?'

'The authorities. The governor.'

'You're not that naïve, Macdonald. You know how it works here.'

'First time inside, remember?'

'Yeah, I wonder about that. You might not have a record, but you've slotted right in.'

'Just because I'm not sobbing into my pillow at night doesn't mean I'm enjoying myself,' said Shepherd.

They reached the door to the spur and Rathbone opened it. He held it so that Shepherd couldn't walk through. 'You seem like a nice guy, Bob, so a word to the wise, yeah? Don't even think about going up against Digger. He's a mad bastard. He'll be Cat A for his whole sentence, pretty much, so he's got nothing to lose. When he's done his time he'll be deported. He doesn't have British citizenship so it's back to sunny Jamaica when he's an old man.'

'I hear what you're saying,' said Shepherd.

Rathbone moved his arm and let Shepherd through.

'How do I apply for a visit?'

'Family or legal?'

'Family. My wife. And kid.'

'I thought your wife was divorcing you.'

Shepherd didn't like the way that everything he said or did in the prison seemed to become common knowledge within hours. 'Yeah, but we've got things to discuss,' he said.

Rathbone frowned. 'With your kid there?'

'I've not seen my boy for weeks.'

'You must miss him.'

'Yeah.' Shepherd wished Rathbone would stop talking about his family, but he thought the officer was just trying to be friendly. Cutting the conversation short might offend him.

'Is she definite about wanting a divorce?'

'That's what the governor said. I'll know more once I've seen her.'

'You should ask for a compassionate visit,' said Rathbone. 'That way the other cons can't hear what's being said. I'm sure the governor'll approve it, under the circumstances.'

Rathbone took Shepherd down stairs to the ones and showed him the visitor application forms. He helped Shepherd fill one out, put it into a box labelled 'Outgoing Mail and Visit Applications', then took him back up to the twos.

'If you need a Listener, Bob, just shout,' said Rathbone.

'Thanks, but I'm not suicidal,' said Shepherd.

'The Listeners aren't just for suicides,' said Rathbone. 'They're there to talk through any problems you have. Any time, night or day.'

'Even when we're banged up?'

'If we think it's serious, we can get you a Listener any time one's needed. It's at our discretion.' Rathbone unlocked the cell door.

'Thanks,' said Shepherd, and he meant it.

Rathbone locked the door and Shepherd climbed up on to his bunk. He was looking forward to seeing Sue and Liam, but what he really wanted was to be on the outside with them, twenty-four hours a day. And the quickest way of achieving that was to put paid to Gerald Carpenter. The sooner the better.

Kim Fletcher looked at the photograph for the twentieth time. 'They all look the bloody same in those uniforms,' he muttered.

Pat Neary tapped his fingers on the BMW's steering-wheel. 'Is that him?' he said. A boy was walking out of the school gates, a mobile phone pressed to his ear.

Fletcher screwed up his eyes. 'I don't think so.'

'Do you need glasses?'

'Fuck off,' said Fletcher, looking at the photograph again.

'We should have waited nearer the house,' said Neary.

'Right, and get picked up by the filth.'

'I said nearer the house. Not near. Sitting outside a school we look like a couple of nonces on the prowl.'

'Speak for yourself,' snarled Fletcher. A black Range Rover driven by a middle-aged blonde pulled up in front of the gates and three boys piled into the back. Fletcher ignored them. The boy they were looking for always walked home.

The Range Rover roared off. A boy with a blue Nike backpack was standing at the school gate, talking to a taller boy with black-framed glasses.

'That's him,' said Fletcher.

Neary put the BMW into gear. Fletcher twisted in his seat as they drove away from the school. There was no mistake. The boy with the backpack waved goodbye to the taller boy and headed away from the gates, his hands thrust deep into his trouser pockets. His tie was at half-mast, the top two buttons of his shirt undone.

They drove a couple of hundred yards down the road, then Neary stopped the car in front of a row of small shops. Fletcher got out, and slipped on a pair of impenetrable Ray-Bans. Neary pulled a tight U-turn, parked on the other side of the road and sat there with the engine running.

Fletcher looked into the window of a cake shop while he waited for the boy. What he was about to do had to be handled right. If he spooked the boy, Fletcher knew he wouldn't be able to run after him: he had just turned forty-five and it was a long time since he'd jogged, never mind sprinted.

He looked to his left. The boy was about fifty feet away, his head down and his shoulders hunched, hands still in his trouser pockets. He was twelve years old.

Fletcher walked slowly towards him, his right hand reaching into his overcoat pocket. The boy looked up and brushed his chestnut hair out of his eyes. He saw that Fletcher was in his way and moved to the side, nearer to the road. His forehead was creased into a deep frown, as if he had something on his mind, but he wasn't looking at Fletcher.

'Ben Roper?' said Fletcher, not because there was any doubt but because he knew that the boy was less likely to run if he was addressed by name.

'Yes?' said the boy, the frown deepening.

Fletcher's hand emerged from his overcoat holding a gleaming white envelope. 'Can you give this to your dad, please?' He held it out.

'What is it?' said the boy, suspiciously.

Fletcher flashed what he hoped was a disarming smile. He was proud of his teeth: they'd cost him several thousand pounds and were the finest dentures money could buy. He hated dentists and years of neglect had meant that, by his late thirties, his gums had receded and the teeth rotted. The pain had been so bad that he had had to seek treatment but his mouth was in such a state of disrepair that the man he'd been referred to had offered only two choices, both of which involved the removal of all his teeth. The surgeon said he could bolt new teeth into Fletcher's jaw or fit him with dentures. Fletcher had gone for the dentures.

'It's a personal letter,' he said. 'It's important, so I don't want to risk posting it.'

The boy took it, but he looked at it suspiciously.

'Just give it to your dad, okay?' said Fletcher.

The boy kept the letter at arm's length as if reluctant to accept ownership. 'I'm not supposed to take things from strangers,' he said.

'It's only a letter,' said Fletcher tersely. He looked left and right but no one was paying them any attention.

'Who shall I say gave it to me?'

Fletcher nodded at the letter. 'It's all in there,' he said. 'Your dad will understand everything when he's read it. Just tell him I gave it to you near the school.'

'I guess that's okay,' Ben said, and put the envelope into his blazer pocket.

'Good lad.' Fletcher patted his shoulder.

Ben headed down the road, towards his home. Fletcher waited until he was well on his way before he crossed the road and climbed into the BMW. Neary gunned the engine. 'Now what?'

'Now we see if Roper gets the message,' said Fletcher, look off the sunglasses and slipped them inside his jacket.

'And if he doesn't?'

Fletcher made a gun with his hand. 'We get ourselves another motorbike.'

Shortly after the men returned from the workshops Shepherd's door opened. It was Lloyd-Davies, holding a white carrier-bag and a clipboard. 'Your solicitor dropped these in for you,' she said, giving him the bag.

'Thanks,' said Shepherd. He tipped the contents out on to his bunk. There were two Ralph Lauren polo shirts, one red, one blue, two pairs of black Armani jeans and a pair of gleaming white Nike trainers, Calvin Klein underwear and Nike socks. Tucked into one of the trainers was a Rolex wristwatch and a gold neck chain. Shepherd studied the expensive timepiece. It wasn't the one that the forensics woman had taken off him, so maybe Hargrove had requisitioned it from a drug-dealer's confiscated property. It was gold and studded with diamonds, a real player's watch.

Lloyd-Davies handed him the clipboard and a pen. 'Sign here,' she said, tapping the bottom of a form, which listed everything she'd given him.

Shepherd scrawled his Bob Macdonald signature and gave the clipboard back to her. 'I'd be careful with that,' she said, nodding at the watch.

Shepherd slipped it on to his wrist. 'It's just a watch,' he said.

'It's five grand, maybe more,' she said. 'There's guys in here would kill for five grand.'

Shepherd dropped the chain round his neck.

'Bob, I have to tell you, wearing jewellery like that is just asking for trouble.'

Shepherd smiled. 'I can take care of myself, ma'am,' he said. He held up the shirts. 'Which do you think?'

'Red,' she said. 'It'll go with your eyes. I'm serious. If your jewellery gets taken off you, there's not much we can do.'

'You could call the cops.'

Lloyd-Davies flashed him a cold smile. 'Suit yourself. I'm only trying to help.'

Shepherd saw that he'd offended her and felt suddenly ashamed. She'd gone out of her way to be friendly and helpful, but Bob Macdonald would see that as a sign of weakness. As Dan Shepherd he wanted to apologise, but that would be out of character. He had no choice but to keep giving her a hard time. 'Anyone tries to take my stuff, I'll give them what for.' He moved towards the cell door. 'Okay if I get my tea?'

Lloyd-Davies tapped the clipboard against her black trousers, then walked out.

Shepherd took off his prison-issue sweatshirt and pulled on the red polo, then changed into the black jeans and Nikes. He went out on to the landing and along to the stairs, looking down at the ground floor where prisoners were lining up at the hotplate. Lloyd-Davies had gone into the bubble and was talking to Stafford. There were no officers on the twos. Shepherd craned his neck. He couldn't see any on the threes either. He hurried up to the top floor and looked around. Still no officers. Three prisoners, all in T-shirts,

Adidas tracksuit bottoms and Adidas trainers, rushed past him and clattered down the stairs.

Shepherd took another quick look down at the ones. Hamilton was at the hotplate. Rathbone was beside by the pool table. Lloyd-Davies was still talking to Stafford. He walked quickly along the landing. There was a white card in a holder to the right of each cell door and he checked the names. He found Jurczak's cell and pushed open the door.

Jurczak was lying on his bunk, watching television. 'What the fuck are you doing in my cell?' he snarled.

Shepherd kicked the door shut behind him. 'I want your job on the cleaning crew,' he said.

'Fuck off,' said Jurczak, getting up from his bunk. 'This is my cell. You don't come into another man's cell.'

Shepherd rushed at Jurczak, grabbed him by the throat and banged him against the wall. Jurczak's tray clattered to the floor. Shepherd was a good three inches taller and at least ten years younger. He blocked all thoughts of Jurczak as a human being. He was no more than a problem that had to be solved. And it had to be done quickly because as soon as tea had been served the prisoners were checked before association. He had less than five minutes to do what had to be done. 'All I want is for you to get off the cleaning crew,' he said.

'Fuck you,' hissed Jurczak. 'I paid five hundred for that job. Why should I give it to you?'

Shepherd head-butted him, his forehead slamming on to Jurczak's nose. Blood streamed down the man's chin, and Shepherd let go of his neck. Jurczak slumped to the cell floor, unconscious. Shepherd knew that a broken nose wouldn't be a serious enough injury to get him taken off the cleaning crew so he pulled out Jurczak's left leg and jammed the foot against the horizontal truss of the chair. Then he took a deep breath and slammed his foot on Jurczak's knee. The joint cracked like a dry twig. Shepherd stared down at the injured man, breathing heavily. Jurczak was a drug-dealer and a murderer, so he felt no sympathy for him but he'd taken no pleasure in crippling him. It had

had to be done, though: Jurczak wasn't the type to respond to threats.

Shepherd opened the cell door a few inches and squinted down the landing. It was clear. He walked quickly to the stairs. The man with the shaved head was walking up from the twos carrying Carpenter's tray. He frowned as Shepherd walked by but didn't say anything.

Tony Stafford was alone in the bubble but his head was down. Lloyd-Davies was nowhere to be seen. Shepherd padded down the stairs and joined the queue at the hotplate. The mixed grill was a burnt sausage, an equally burnt beefburger and a strip of underdone bacon. The vegetable man gave him a scoop of chips and a spoonful of baked beans. Shepherd put a bread roll and a tub of raspberry yoghurt on his tray, then headed back to the cell. As he went he looked up at the threes: no officers on the landing.

Lee was sitting at the desk in the cell. He'd gone for the mixed grill, too. 'New gear?' he asked, as Shepherd sat on his bunk.

'Yeah, my brief dropped them off.'

'Watch too?'

'Yeah. Forensics took it, but I guess there was nothing on it.'

'Nice.'

'Tells the time.'

Lee nodded at Shepherd's tray. 'You going to eat the roll?' Shepherd tossed it to him. 'And the yoghurt?' Shepherd gave him that too.

Lloyd-Davies pushed open the door. 'All right, gentlemen?'

Shepherd held out his tray. 'Want a chip, ma'am?'

'I forgot to tell you, Macdonald, I got you on the gym list for this evening,' she said.

'Thanks, ma'am,' said Shepherd.

She was about to say more when someone shouted from the threes: 'Stretcher! Get me a stretcher up here!'

Lloyd-Davies hurried away. Lee stood up and rushed to the cell door. Shepherd followed him. They'd found Jurczak.

An alarm sounded. Half a dozen officers hurried on to the spur and shouted for the prisoners to get into their cells.

Lee craned his neck to look up at the threes. 'Bet someone's topped themselves,' he said.

Healey came along the landing, checking cells. Doors were clanging shut all over the spur. Two prison officers dashed up the stairs with a stretcher. Healey appeared at the door. 'Inside, Lee,' he said. 'Nothing for you to see.'

'What happened, Mr Healey?'

'Prisoner hurt,' said Healey, and closed the door.

'Topped himself?'

Healey didn't answer. Lee switched on the television and sat down on the chair. 'Shit,' he said. He stabbed his sausage with a plastic fork.

'What?' asked Shepherd.

'They'll keep us banged up until whatever it is gets sorted,' said Lee. 'No association, no exercise, no nothing. Just because some wanker decides to hurt himself.'

Shepherd put his tray down on the bunk. He'd lost his appetite.

Alice Roper frowned when she saw the two cars parked in the road outside her house. As a rule there was just one, with two men from the Church. It had always seemed strange to Alice that the men of HM Customs and Excise were called the Church. The Custom House headquarters by the Thames didn't look in the least like a house of worship and there was nothing religious about the men and women who worked there. The reason, Sandy had once told her, was because of the code used over the radio. Custom House became Charlie Hotel, CH, and then their colleagues at MI5 had begun to use Church instead. The Customs men quite enjoyed the religious overtones of the codename; the honest and true forces of good battling against the powers of evil. They were like children sometimes, thought Alice.

One of the cars, a big black saloon, was empty but she recognised the two men in the other vehicle. Sandy had introduced them, but Alice couldn't remember their names. Over the past weeks there had been more than a dozen taking it in turns to sit outside the house and Alice's only contact with them had been to take out occasional cups of tea. One of the men smiled and waved as she drove by and turned into the flagstoned driveway. She parked the Ford Fiesta by the garage door and carried the shopping into the kitchen. Sandy had refused to go with her to the supermarket: the office was insisting that he go out as little as possible. That didn't make any sense to Alice because Sandy had claimed from the start that no one knew who he was or that he was involved with the court case. If that was so, why was the office so worried that he might be recognised? She hadn't argued as she was fed up being cooped up in the house with him all day and she'd quite enjoyed the time alone, even if all she was doing was pushing a trolley round Sainsbury's.

She walked to the front door, let herself in and heaved the carrier-bags on to the kitchen table. 'Do you want tea, Sandy?' she called, as she switched on the kettle.

Ben and David were in the garden, kicking a football. Alice saw a man at the end of the garden, close to the small greenhouse. He was tall, gangly, in a raincoat with sleeves that were slightly too short for his spindly arms.

She heard footsteps and whirled round, but it was only her husband. 'Who's that in the garden?' she asked.

'Alice, we've got to talk,' said Roper.

Lee had been right: the cell doors remained locked all night. In the morning Lee was due to shower so he was up as soon as he heard doors being unlocked down the landing. He stood at the door with his towel and washbag humming. Shepherd climbed down from the top bunk in his prison-issue sweatpants and a T-shirt. He started to shave at the washbasin. The spyglass clicked open and the door was unlocked. Lee rushed off down the landing.

Hamilton had opened the cell door.

'What's the story, Mr Hamilton?' Shepherd asked.

'What do you mean?'

'The lockdown last night.'

'A prisoner was attacked on the threes.'

'Is he okay?'

'Broken leg. He's in the hospital. What's your interest, Macdonald?'

'I missed out on the gym because we were banged up, that's all. How do I go about getting on today's list?'

'I'll see what I can do,' said Hamilton, but Shepherd could tell from his tone that he wouldn't.

He finished shaving and dried his face, then went out on to the landing and down to the ground floor. Digger's cell was in the corner opposite the door to the exercise yard. Prisoners were milling around but no one paid him any attention.

Digger's door was ajar. Shepherd pushed it open. The cell was empty. Shepherd cursed.

'You looking for something, man?' said a voice.

Shepherd turned. Needles was standing behind him, his hands on his hips. 'I'm looking for Digger.'

'Don't you know you never go into another man's cell until you're invited? Never as in ever.'

'I wasn't over the threshold, but I hear what you're saying, Needles. Now, where is he?'

'Showering,' said Needles. 'What do you want?'

'To talk to Digger.' Shepherd moved to get past him, but Needles put out a massive arm, blocking his way.

'You can talk to me,' he said.

Shepherd looked at the arm. It was the thickness of his leg. 'You spend a lot of time in the gym, yeah?' asked Shepherd.

'Some.'

'Lift weights, yeah?'

'Some.'

Shepherd wasn't sure how much damage he could do to a man as big as Needles. He was huge, but he wasn't fat. It was muscle. That didn't necessarily mean that he was hard, but it did mean that all his vital organs and nerve centres were well protected. If it came to violence Shepherd would have to aim for the unprotected areas – the throat, the temple, the sternum. But the problem with aiming for a vital area was that if he hit Needles too hard he risked killing him. Not hard enough, and Needles would have a chance to retaliate. He was capable, evidently, of inflicting a lot of damage.

'Here he comes now,' said Shepherd.

As Needles turned, Shepherd drove his knee into the man's groin. The breath exploded from Needles's mouth and he bent over, groping for his balls. His eyes were wide and staring as his mouth worked soundlessly. Shepherd stepped round him, then put his foot against the back of the man's left knee and pushed hard. Needles toppled forward. Shepherd started to walk back along the spur. He'd taken three steps before he heard Needles hit the ground with a dull thud. Two black men in tracksuits moved to let him walk by. From the astonished looks on their faces it was clear that they'd seen what he'd done to Needles. He glared at them, then scanned the spur. No prison officers.

He went quickly back up the stairs. There were two officers in the bubble, both men in their mid-thirties whom Shepherd hadn't seen before. He went along to the shower room. Lee was walking out, his hair still wet. 'Is Digger in there?' asked Shepherd.

Lee nodded and hurried away, as if he realised what Shepherd was planning to do. There were two men in the showers, a stocky white guy with a tattoo of the union flag on one shoulder, and Digger.

Shepherd leaned against the wall where two towels were hanging. The white guy glanced over at him and he gestured with his thumb for him to go. The man took his towel and left.

Digger turned to watch him go, then smiled. 'You want something?'

'A word.'

'In here?'

'Not shy, are you?'

'You could have talked to Needles.'

'I did.'

The water stopped running. Digger walked over to Shepherd, his huge feet slapping on the wet tiled floor.

'I want Jurczak's place on the cleaning crew,' said Shepherd.

'There's a queue.'

'Fuck the queue. I want his place.'

Digger loomed over him. He was as big and as hard as Needles, but he didn't seem the type to fall for the behind-you ruse. 'You got money?' asked Digger, thrusting his chin forward.

'I can get you money.'

'A grand.'

'Fuck that,' said Shepherd. 'Jurczak paid five hundred.'

'Inflation.'

'The way I see it, you've already got five hundred from Jurczak so the job's paid for.'

'You did a number on him. Broke the man's leg.'

'I asked him nicely first. Now I'm asking you nicely.'

Digger's eyes narrowed. 'That sounds like a threat,' he said.

'I just want Jurczak's place. He's not going to be walking for a while. Cleaning crew's a man short. I'm that man.'

'Five hundred.'

'Agreed.'

'You pay my sister on the out.' Digger told Shepherd her name and address. A flat in Brixton. 'Five hundred by tomorrow night.'

'Okay. When do I start?'

'Soon as it's okayed with the screws.'

'Who okays it?'

'I fucking okay it. That's all you need to know.'

Shepherd hadn't expected that Digger would tell him who his contact was, but it had been worth a try. 'There's something else.'

'Yeah?'

'Needles.'

'What about Needles?'

'We had a run-in downstairs.'

'And?'

'I had to hurt him.'

Digger chuckled. 'You hurt Needles?'

'A bit.'

'Because?'

'He blocked my way.'

Digger put a hand on the wall and pushed his face closer to Shepherd's. 'What if I block your way?'

Shepherd shrugged but didn't say anything. When a man was that close his options for attack were limited; Digger was too close to kick or punch so that meant a headbutt or a knee in the groin. Digger was several inches taller than Shepherd so headbutting would be difficult and Shepherd kept his hands low so that he could block the knee if it moved. However, Digger was menacing, but his body positioning was wrong for an attack.

'Am I going to have a problem with you, Macdonald?'

Shepherd shook his head. 'It's your spur. I just want to get out of my cell, that's all.'

'That money isn't paid to my sister by tomorrow night, I'll be paying you a visit.'

'She'll get it.'

Digger nodded slowly, then pushed himself away from the wall. Shepherd looked down at the other man's groin and grinned. 'It's true what they say about you guys, then?'

Digger chuckled. 'I don't get no complaints.'

Bonnie Carpenter tossed two containers of spaghetti carbonara into the microwave and slammed the door.

'I don't want pasta, Mum,' moaned Jacqueline. She was sitting at the kitchen table with a science book in front of her.

'Me neither,' said Paul, trying to match his older sister's tone and doing a pretty good job.

Bonnie twisted the dial and the microwave buzzed into life. 'It's Marks and Sparks,' she said. 'It's not as if I cooked it myself.' She picked up a French loaf and began hacking at it with a bread-knife.

'I'm a vegetarian, Mum,' said Paul, pulling a face.

'First of all, you're not a vegetarian,' said Bonnie, tossing chunks of bread into a basket. 'You're just copying Harry and he's only a vegetarian because his parents never grew out of their hippie phase and they won't let him eat meat.'

'Actually, they're too young to have been hippies,' said Jacqueline. 'Hippies were in the sixties.'

Bonnie waved the bread-knife at her daughter. 'I didn't say they were hippies, I said they went through a hippie phase.'

'Harry said they were punks,' said Paul. 'His dad had a safety-pin through his nose. He says there's a picture in one of their albums. And you can see his mum's breast in one of the pictures. Most of it. He says he's going to bring it to school.'

Bonnie transferred the attentions of the bread knife to her son. 'And second of all, there's no meat in spaghetti carbonara, so you won't be breaking any of your new-found principles.'

Jacqueline pushed back her chair and went over to the kitchen worktop as Bonnie emptied a pack of pre-washed salad into a glass bowl. 'Do you want dressing?' Bonnie asked.

'Dressing's fattening,' said Jacqueline, as she studied one of the cardboard wrappers that had been round the ready meals.

Bonnie ripped open the plastic sachet with her teeth and squeezed the dressing over the salad. 'You're a growing girl,' she said. 'You need the essential vitamins and minerals in olive oil.'

'It says here there's ham in the spaghetti sauce.'

'You don't think they use real ham, do you?' asked Bonnie, carrying the bread basket and salad bowl over to the kitchen table. 'It's that artificial stuff. Made from soya beans.' She frowned at her daughter. The last thing she wanted was her son refusing to eat meat. He was picky enough at the best of times.

Jacqueline held up the wrapper so that Bonnie could see the picture. 'Looks real enough to me,' she said.

'Just goes to show how cunning food scientists can be,' said Bonnie. 'It's artificial, trust me.'

'Was Dad ever a punk?' asked Paul.

Bonnie laughed harshly. 'If there's one thing your dad most definitely never was, it's a punk,' she said. 'Jacqueline, while you're on your feet could you get me a bottle of Pinot Grigio out of the fridge?'

'You drink too much,' scolded Jacqueline.

'You drive me to it,' said Bonnie. 'Be an angel and open it for me, will you?'

'I will,' said Paul, and rushed to the drawer where they kept the corkscrew. The phone on the wall rang and he changed direction to answer it.

The microwave pinged and Bonnie took out two plastic dishes of steaming pasta.

'It's Dad!' said Paul.

'Let me talk to him,' said Bonnie, holding out her hand for the phone.

'I want to tell him about my football match,' said Paul.

'Let me talk to him first,' said Bonnie firmly.

Paul gave her the phone reluctantly.

'Hiya, honey,' said Bonnie. 'How long have you got?'

'Six minutes and counting,' said Carpenter. 'Sorry. Should have more credit in a day or two.'

There was a small mechanical timer on the worktop and Bonnie twisted it to six minutes. Paul saw the time and pulled a face.

'You okay for tomorrow?' asked Carpenter.

'Sure, do you need anything?'

'Just clean clothes. See if I've any thirty-two-inch jeans, will you? The thirties are getting a bit tight.'

'Gerry . . .'

'I know, love, but it's the bloody food here. All starch and carbs.'

'Mum . . .' complained Paul. He pointed at the timer, which was down to five and a half minutes.

'Paul wants a word,' said Bonnie.

'Everything okay there?' asked Carpenter.

'There's been a BT van parked down the road for the past three days,' said Bonnie. 'They must think I'm stupid.'

'Ignore them,' said Carpenter. 'If they want to waste their time, let them.'

'The DVD in the bedroom's playing up. Keeps saying there isn't a DVD in when there is. What is it with these machines? They think they're smarter than we are sometimes.'

'Chuck it and buy a new one,' said Carpenter. 'Costs more to repair them than it does to replace them. Repair shops, bloody robbers they are.'

'Mum . . .' whined Paul.

Bonnie handed the phone to Paul. 'Ninety seconds, then give it to your sister.'

Paul grabbed at the receiver and started telling his father about the game of football he'd played the previous day.

Bonnie went upstairs and knocked on the door to Stephanie's room. It bore a sheet of paper with 'PRIVATE – KEEP OUT' printed on it. Underneath were the words 'Especially you Paul!' Bonnie opened the door. Stephanie was sitting in front of her television with her PlayStation 2. 'Steph, your dad's on the phone,' she said.

'So?' said Stephanie, her eyes never leaving the screen. It was some shoot-'em-up game, blowing zombies into dozens of bloody pieces.

'It'd be nice if you said a few words to him.'

'Like what?'

'Like asking him how he is. Like telling him how much you miss him.'

'I'm busy, Mum.'

'Steph, get downstairs and talk to your father. Now.'

'Let me get to the next level.'

'He's only got a few minutes.'

'So I'll talk to him tomorrow.'

Bonnie glared at her wilful daughter. She had half a mind to walk over and pull the plug out of the video game but knew how unproductive that would be. Tears, threats, and probably a week-long sulk. She closed the bedroom door and swore under her breath.

When she got back to the kitchen there were just three minutes left and Jacqueline was standing behind her brother, poking him in the kidneys with a spoon. 'Paul, let your sister talk to your father.'

'I haven't finished yet,' Paul protested.

'Yes, you have.' Bonnie took the receiver from him and handed it to Jacqueline.

She poured the spaghetti on to four plates and put them on the table as Jacqueline chatted to her father. Paul sat down at the table with a sour look on his face. Bonnie picked up the glass of wine, which her daughter had poured for her, and drank half of it in one gulp.

When there was a minute left on the timer, Bonnie took the phone from Jacqueline. 'Where's Steph?' asked Carpenter.

'In the bath,' said Bonnie.

'She was in the bath last time I called.'

'Just be glad she's not like her brother. I can't get him to stand still in the shower long enough to get wet.'

'She's okay?'

'As okay as any ten-year-old can be,' said Bonnie.

'Sorry I'm not there to help out,' said Carpenter.

'Yeah, you and me both,' said Bonnie. 'How much longer are you going to be in there, love?' She regretted the question as soon as she'd asked it. She knew that he was doing everything he could to get out of prison, and that there was nothing he could tell her, not with the authorities listening in to all his calls.

'I'll be back before you know it, honey,' said Carpenter.

'I'm sorry,' said Bonnie. 'I know how tough it is for you in there.'

'Piece of cake,' said Carpenter. 'Got to go, see you tomorrow.'

The line went dead and Bonnie put the receiver back on its cradle. She drained the rest of her wine and refilled the glass. 'It's not your dad's fault,' she said to Paul. 'He only has so many minutes to use the phone.' She ruffled Paul's hair. 'He'd talk to you all day if he could.'

'It's not fair,' he said. 'It's bad enough that he's in prison, what difference does it make how long he uses the phone for?'

'It's part of the punishment,' said Bonnie.

'But it's punishing me and I'm not the one who did anything wrong.'

'Dad didn't do anything wrong either, did he, Mum?' said Jacqueline.

Bonnie took a deep breath, then forced a smile. 'Of course he didn't. Go and tell Steph her food's on the table.'

Shepherd nodded at Carpenter as he replaced the receiver. 'How's it going?' he asked. He'd been waiting in the line for the two phones and had heard most of Carpenter's end of the conversation – 'I'll be back before you know it,' Carpenter had said, and he'd sounded confident.

'Okay,' said Carpenter. 'You're Macdonald, yeah?'

'Bob,' said Shepherd. 'I'm in with Jason Lee on the twos.'

'Gerry Carpenter. I'm on the threes.'

'You've got a single cell?'

Carpenter shrugged.

'How do I go about getting one?' Shepherd picked up the receiver.

'You fed up with Jason?'

'Wouldn't mind some privacy, that's all. Who do I speak to?'

'Put in a request to Stafford. He runs the block.'

'He'll just put my name on a list, won't he?'

'That's the way it works.'

'No short-cut?'

'Wouldn't know,' said Carpenter, and walked away.

Shepherd keyed in his four-digit pin number and got a dialling tone. He tapped in the north London number that Hargrove had given him on their first meeting. It was answered on the second ring.

'This is Bob Macdonald,' said Shepherd.

'Hello, Bob. This is Richard. What do you need?'

Shepherd recited the name and address of Digger's sister and explained that she had to be given five hundred pounds.

'Anything else?'

'That's all,' said Shepherd, and cut the connection.

As he walked away from the telephones, Lloyd-Davies waved him over. She was watching two prisoners play pool. 'Sorry you missed your gym yesterday, Bob.'

'No sweat, ma'am. Any chance of you getting me on the list again?'

She smiled. 'Still got excess energy?'

'I used to run a lot, on the out,' he said.

'From the cops?'

Shepherd laughed. 'You don't run from cops, these days, ma'am.

They never get out of their cars. You've just got to be able to drive faster than them, that's all.'

'I'll see what I can do. Still got the watch, then?'

'No one's tried to take it off me.'

'That wasn't why you had the altercation with Needles, was it?'

Shepherd feigned innocence, but his mind raced. How did she know about Needles? There had been no officers in the vicinity when Shepherd had hit him. And there was no way that a man like Needles would go running to an officer. 'Altercation, ma'am?'

'Butter wouldn't melt, would it, Macdonald? You know what I'm talking about. I heard you kneed him in the balls, then kicked him to the floor.' She shook her head sadly. 'You're going to have to watch your back.'

'Not while I've got you looking after me, ma'am.'

'I'm serious,' she said. 'This is your first time inside. You don't know how it works in here. You make waves, sometimes you get thrown out of the boat.'

Shepherd walked down the spur to the exercise yard and joined the line of inmates waiting to go out. Two officers were doing the searches. One was Rathbone, the other a middle-aged West Indian woman whom Shepherd hadn't seen before. She had a pretty smile and seemed to know all the prisoners by name. It was clear that they preferred a pat-down from her to one from Rathbone, and several pushed their groins forward as she ran her hands down their legs. She took it all good-naturedly.

Shepherd stood in front of Rathbone with his legs apart and his arms outstretched. The officer rubbed his hands along the top of Shepherd's arms, then underneath, around his armpits down his waist to his legs, inside and out. Then he patted his back and chest and waved him through.

As soon as he was out in the open air Shepherd took several deep breaths. He found an empty corner and stood swinging his arms, his head back so that he was looking up at the sky.

'You okay, Bob?' said a voice.

Shepherd turned to find Ed Harris standing behind him. 'Why do you ask?'

'Heard you had a run-in with Needles.'

'Word gets around fast in here.'

'Not much else to do but gossip,' said Harris. He handed Shepherd a sandy-coloured booklet: *Anger Management* and below, in smaller type, *Controlling Your Temper Under Pressure*. 'There are courses you can go on, too.'

Shepherd raised his eyebrows. He flicked through the pages. There were self-assessment quizzes, exercises, and lots of flow-charts. 'You are taking the piss, right?'

'Anger is an understandable reaction to what you're going through,' said Harris. 'What you've got to learn is that it's yourself you're angry with. You lash out at others because you don't want to lash out at yourself.'

'Ed, I'm really not angry,' said Shepherd. That was true. He hadn't been angry when he'd hit Needles and he hadn't been angry when he'd crippled Jurczak. Anger hadn't come into it. He had done what he had to do. What he'd been trained to do. Even when he was with the Regiment and he'd been under fire, he hadn't been angry with the men shooting at him. And he hadn't been angry when he'd fired back and killed them.

'That's denial,' said Harris. 'I hear it all the time. If it's not controlled you lash out at others, or you hurt yourself.'

'I'm not suicidal,' said Shepherd.

'You were in a fight,' said Harris. 'You've only just arrived on the spur and you're lashing out.'

There was no way Shepherd could explain why he'd hit Needles. Or Jurczak. But explaining wasn't the issue. Shepherd knew it was vital that he reacted as Bob Macdonald, career criminal, and not as Dan Shepherd, undercover cop. That was one of the hardest parts of being undercover. He could memorise his legend and all the facts about his targets, but his emotions and reactions had to be faked. He had to filter everything he did so that he was consistent in whatever role he was playing. But it had to be done instantly because any hesitation would be spotted by someone who knew what they were looking for. That was why so many undercover agents ended up as alcoholics or basket cases. It wasn't the danger or the risks: it was

143

the strain of maintaining a role when the penalty for failure was a beating at best or, at worst, a bullet in the back of the neck. 'He got what was coming to him,' he said.

'Do you want to tell me what happened?'

Shepherd flashed him a sarcastic smile. 'No, Ed, I don't. Now, fuck off and leave me alone.'

Harris walked away. Shepherd did a few stretching exercises and then started to walk round the yard. Two middle-aged men in Nike tracksuits nodded at him and he nodded back. One was a hotplate server, but Shepherd knew neither of their names. They were just showing respect. He was making his mark.

The prison officer sighed with relief as he saw that the metal detector wasn't manned. He'd arrived for his shift ten minutes early, assuming he'd be able to slip in without being scanned, but it had still been a risk. The mobile phone was a tiny Nokia tucked into the side of his left shoe.

He let himself into the secure corridor and walked to the remand block. The Nokia was a pay-as-you-go model and he'd put a hundred pounds' credit into its account. Carpenter was paying him ten grand for the phone. And he'd promised a further two grand for each battery and a hundred pounds for every ten pounds' worth of credit. He was a good earner, was Carpenter. It was just a pity that he was a remand prisoner. Within the next month or so he'd either be walking out a free man or off to serve his sentence in a dispersal prison. The gravy train would be over, as Carpenter was concerned. The officer smiled to himself. But there'd be other Carpenters. There always had been and there always would be. Men with the means to pay for the little extras that made their time behind bars just that little bit more bearable.

The prison officer had earned more than thirty thousand pounds from Carpenter over the past month. The money was paid in cash on the outside by a man he'd never seen. There was a small park close to the officer's house in Finchley and he took his dog there for a walk every evening when he wasn't working nights. If he had a message from Carpenter he'd tuck it into a copy of the *Sun* and drop it into a waste-bin near the park's entrance. He'd do a circuit with his spaniel and by the time he got back to the bin the *Sun* had been replaced with a copy of the *Evening Standard* with an envelope full of used banknotes inside it. The officer kept the money in a safety-deposit box in West London under an assumed name. He wasn't stupid: he knew that the Home Office ran regular checks on prison employees to ensure that they weren't living beyond their means. He had no intention of touching it until long after he'd left the service.

He had no qualms about taking money from Carpenter or prisoners like him. It was one of the perks of the job. Like the unquestioned sick days. And the regular overtime. Backhanders from prisoners were just another way to boost his income. And if it meant that Carpenter was causing trouble on the outside, then it was the fault of the cops for not doing their job in the first place.

Shepherd had booked a shower so as soon as he heard the doors being unlocked he picked up his towel. Lee was sitting at the table, eating cornflakes and drinking tea.

An eye was pressed to the spyglass, then a key jangled. Rathbone pushed open the door. Shepherd started down the landing towards the showers but Rathbone called his name.

Shepherd stopped. Rathbone went over to him, swinging his key chain. 'You're on the cleaning crew as of today,' he said.

'That's good to hear,' said Shepherd.

'Not for Jurczak it's not.'

'Yeah, terrible what happened to him, wasn't it?'

'He was barely off the spur before your application for the job hit the bubble,' said Rathbone.

'I needed work,' said Shepherd. 'I was going stir-crazy locked in all day.'

'It was working its way through the system,' said Rathbone. 'I was pushing to get you into one of the workshops.'

'No need now,' said Shepherd.

Rathbone's eyes narrowed. 'I hear you gave Needles a going-over, too.'

'He's a big boy, I'm sure he won't go crying to the governor.'

'You putting in an application to be the hard man on the spur, Macdonald?'

'Didn't know there was a vacancy,' said Shepherd.

'I thought you were better than this.'

'Better than what?'

'Throwing your weight around. Playing the hard man.'

'Do I look hard to you, Mr Rathbone?' Shepherd smiled amiably.

'All I know is that one prisoner's in hospital, another's limping around the ones, and you've got one of the prime jobs on the spur.' Rathbone jerked his head towards the shower room. 'Off you go, then.'

When Shepherd got there three prisoners were already showering and another half-dozen waiting. He joined the queue. He was surprised at the speed with which he'd been given the cleaning job. It had taken less than twenty-four hours for Digger to get fixed him up as Jurczak's replacement. Tony Stafford ran the block, which presumably meant that he must have approved the placement. Did that mean Stafford was taking backhanders from Digger? And if Digger could get jobs approved through Stafford, what else could he do? Maybe Carpenter wasn't bribing an officer, maybe he had just plugged into Digger's contact. Carpenter paid Digger, and Digger paid his man. But did that mean Stafford was also passing messages to Carpenter's men on the outside? If so, he was an accessory in the murder of Jonathon Elliott.

Shepherd washed quickly, then headed back to his cell. A prison officer he hadn't seen before stopped him, a man in his early fifties with greying hair. 'You've a visitor this afternoon,' he said. 'Your wife and boy.'

'What time?'

'Two o'clock.'

'Where do I go?'

'Wait at the spur entrance just before two. Prisoners move to labour at one thirty, then you'll be taken to the visitors' centre.'

Shepherd thanked him, then went back to his cell.

Lee had dressed and was cleaning his teeth. He rinsed his mouth and spat as Shepherd laid his towel over the end of his bunk. 'How did you get the cleaning job, then?' asked Lee.

'Paid Digger on the out,' said Shepherd. 'Like you said.'

'How much?'

'A monkey.'

'Five hundred quid? Bloody hell.' Lee grinned. 'Still, you rob banks so I guess cash isn't a problem, right?'

'I'd have paid anything to get out of this bloody cell,' said Shepherd. 'No offence.'

Lee threw on an England football shirt to go with his Adidas tracksuit bottoms, and Shepherd went with him to the bubble where the prisoners were assembling to so to the workshops. Craig Rathbone was there with a clipboard, ticking off names. 'Macdonald, down on the ones. Mr Healey'll show you where the cleaning supplies are.'

Shepherd went down stairs.

Healey glowered at him. 'I knew you'd be trouble, Macdonald,' he said. 'You step out of line and you'll be straight off the crew and back in your cell.'

Another prisoner walked up to Healey and nodded. Then held out his hand to Shepherd. 'Charlie Weston,' he said.

They shook hands. 'Bob Macdonald,' said Shepherd.

Weston was in his sixties with white skin and bloodless lips. His receding hair was almost white and he looked as if he hadn't seen the sun in years. Healey unlocked a cupboard containing mops, metal buckets and bottles of cleaning fluid. Plastic baskets of cloths and brushes stood on a shelf. 'Start down here,' said Healey. 'Someone was sick by the pool table yesterday evening.' He walked up the stairs to the bubble.

'That's it?' asked Shepherd.

'We're left pretty much to ourselves,' said Weston.

'There's six on the cleaning crew?'

'That's right.'

'So why are only you and me doing any work?'

Weston laughed drily. 'Sledge is in the showers. Hamster's cleaning the kitchen with Ginger.'

'There's a guy up on the threes supposed to be helping us, right?'

'Don't know, mate.'

'Carpenter, right?'

'Suppose so.'

'Why isn't he here, then?'

Weston moved over to Shepherd and put his head close. 'Gerry Carpenter does what he wants,' he said, out of the side of his mouth.

'He bought his job, right? Same as you and me.'

'Him and Digger have got an arrangement.'

'Like what?'

'Hear no, see no, mate,' said Weston, tapping the side of his nose.

'You've lost me, Charlie. Does he work with us or not?'

'Sometimes he cleans up on the threes. Sometimes he's down here. He chooses where he works. None of my business. I just do as I'm told. If I were you, I'd do the same.'

Shepherd and Weston cleaned the floor of the ones, then went up and did the twos. There was no sign of the other cleaners. At eleven forty-five they heard the buzz of returning prisoners and by midday the ground floor was packed again. The floor that Shepherd and Weston had cleaned was soon scuffed and dirty.

Shepherd picked up his dinner – a tired lamb chop, mashed potatoes and carrots, with an orange – and ate it in his cell. Lee came in with his food.

The cell doors were locked and the roll-call was taken, then the doors were unlocked again.

Shepherd and Lee went down the landing to the bubble. Craig Rathbone shouted for all those expecting a visit to go over to him and checked names against a list on his clipboard. One prisoner was missing. Carpenter. He looked up at the stairs. Carpenter was walking down slowly. He was wearing a white linen shirt and pressed chinos, and his hair was neatly combed. Bill Barnes was there and nodded at Carpenter. Carpenter nodded back, but said nothing as he joined the group.

Rathbone unlocked the barred door leading out of the spur and held it open. The prisoners filed through. There were more prisoners in the secure corridor, escorted by officers, men from the other two spurs on the block.

Shepherd fell into step beside Carpenter. 'How's it going?' he asked.

'Yeah, fine,' said Carpenter.

'My first visit, this. The wife.'

'Good luck.'

'I think it's tougher for her than it is for me.'

'That's the punishment,' said Carpenter. 'It's not about bars on the windows and crap food, it's about keeping us away from our families.'

'Yeah, but we're not even guilty. That's what so shit unfair.'

Rathbone drew level with Shepherd. 'You got your compassionate visit,' he said. 'You'll be in a private room.'

'Thanks, Mr Rathbone.'

'Good luck,' he said, and walked ahead of the group.

'Compassionate visit?' said Carpenter.

'Yeah. The missus is threatening to divorce me,' said Shepherd. 'I didn't want her mouthing off in front of everyone.'

'You having problems?'

Shepherd looked at him. He didn't want to tell Carpenter anything about Sue. Even though she was coming in as Angie Macdonald, it was still a risk. But Carpenter was interested, and he was also a husband and father so it might be a way of getting closer. 'You know what wives are like,' he said.

Carpenter frowned. 'How did you know I was married?'

'That's what visits are for, right? For the wives? Plus you're wearing a wedding ring. Elementary, dear Watson.'

Carpenter pulled a face. 'Mothers come sometimes,' he said.

'My mother's written me off.'

'Can't understand where she went wrong?'

149

'You know what I gave her for Christmas last year?' said Shepherd. 'Five grand in readies. Told her to buy herself something nice. My dad told me she gave the money to the RSPCA. Go figure.'

They turned right. More prisoners joined the crowd. Several new arrivals began to chat to prisoners from other blocks. Shepherd figured it was one of the few occasions when prisoners from different blocks could mix.

'How's your wife taking you being inside?' asked Shepherd. He asked the question lightly, knowing that he was crossing a line. It was a personal question and the way that Carpenter reacted would determine which way the investigation went from that moment on.

'She's not happy,' said Carpenter, 'but she blames the filth, not me.'

Shepherd's heart pounded. It was an offhand remark, but it was a confidence shared. A sign that a bridge was being built. 'My wife says it's my own stupid fault. She wants the house, the car, everything. And my kid,' he said.

'Get yourself a good lawyer,' said Carpenter. 'You've got to fight for what's yours.'

'Your wife's not giving you grief?'

Carpenter smiled. 'She knows I won't be here long.'

'You're not tunnelling, are you? I think that's the only way I'll be getting out.'

Carpenter chuckled. 'You need a better plan than that.'

'Is that what you've got? A plan?'

'I'm not going to let them send me down for fifteen years, that's for sure.'

'Bastard judges.'

Carpenter shook his head. 'Don't blame the judges. All they're doing is following the rules. It's like blaming the referee because your team lost. The way I look at it, it's your own fault for getting caught. And the cops' fault for catching you.'

'Yeah, that's the truth,' said Shepherd. 'If I ever found out who grassed me up, I'll kill them.'

Carpenter flashed him a sidelong look. 'You were grassed?'

'Must have been,' said Shepherd. 'Everything was sweetness and light and then suddenly the cops are everywhere. Armed cops, too, so they knew we were tooled up.'

'Any idea who set you up?'

'I was the new guy on the team. Could have been anybody. I'll find out, though. If it takes me for ever, I'll have the bastard.'

'Won't get you out of here any faster.'

'So what's your plan, then?'

Carpenter tapped the side of his nose. 'Need to know,' he said.

'And I don't,' Shepherd said. 'Right.'

The prisoners were escorted into a waiting area. There was a door at the far end where two male officers searched them, then handed each a yellow sash and ushered them through the door. Shepherd and Carpenter joined the queue.

The search was far more thorough than it was for going into the exercise yard. Every inch of Shepherd's front, back and sides was patted down, and he had to open his mouth and stick out his tongue, then flick his ears forward to show he had nothing concealed there. The officer made Shepherd run his hands through his hair, then handed him a bright yellow sash.

'Going cycling, are we?' Shepherd asked, and grinned over his shoulder at Carpenter. 'See this, Gerry? I'm off for a bike ride with the wife.'

The unsmiling prison officer nodded at Shepherd to go in. The visiting room was huge, the size of a tennis court. There was a balcony above the door from where an officer with a bored expression looked down on the rows of chairs and tables. There were already more than a hundred visitors, some sitting, some standing, waiting for their loved ones. Most were women and almost half had children with them. The tables were lined up in five rows, A to E, and each had four plastic chairs round it. The chairs could be moved but the tables were screwed to the floor.

A young red-headed woman, with a small baby strapped to her chest, was jumping up and down and waving. Her husband, who seemed barely out of his teens in a prison-issue tracksuit, waved back, then went over to a raised desk where a female officer checked his name against a list. Shepherd went over to her and gave her his name and number. 'I'm supposed to have a private visit,' he said.

She ran her pen down her computer printout. 'Room five,' she said, and pointed to the far end of the room.

As Shepherd walked between the tables he saw CCTV cameras in the four corners of the room. They were moving, focusing on individual tables, watching silently as husbands embraced wives, fathers cuddled small children and kissed babies. Several men were crying unashamedly, tears streaming down their faces as they held their wives.

Three officers were walking among the tables, their faces impassive as they watched the prisoners take their places. If they saw a man getting too passionate they'd tap his shoulder and tell him to sit down. The prisoners had to sit on the right-hand side of the table, the visitors on the left.

In one corner of the room a booth sold soft drinks and sweets, and there was a play area for young children, minded by a couple of cheery middle-aged women.

The door to room five was open and Sue was already sitting at the table, Liam saw Shepherd first and ran towards him, arms outstretched. 'Daddy, Daddy!' he shouted.

Shepherd picked him up and squeezed him. 'Hiya, kid,' he said, and kissed him.

'When are you coming home, Daddy?' asked Liam.

Shepherd kissed him again. 'Soon,' he said.

'Today?'

'No, not today, but soon.'

He put Liam down and held out his arms for Sue. She smiled, but he could see how tense she was. He held her and she slipped her arms round his waist. 'God, I've missed you,' he said.

'It's your choice, being here,' she said, and he heard resentment in her voice.

'I'm sorry,' he said.

'I didn't realise how horrible it was.'

'It's prison,' he said, trying to smile. 'What did you think it'd be like?'

'Your hear stories, don't you, about them being like holiday camps?'

'That's open prisons,' said Shepherd.

'What's this, then?'

'Category A. It's high security.'

'But you haven't had a trial or anything. What happened to innocent until proven guilty?'

'It's the system, love,' said Shepherd.

'Why are you in prison, Daddy?' asked Liam. 'Were you bad?'

Shepherd knelt down and put a hand on his son's shoulder. 'I've not been bad, Liam, but you mustn't tell anybody about Daddy being here.'

'It's a secret?'

'That's right.'

'I won't tell, Daddy.'

Shepherd ruffled his hair. 'Good boy.' Sue took a colouring book and some crayons out of her bag, put them on the table and Liam sat down with them. Shepherd stood up. 'Thanks for coming,' he said to his wife. 'Did Sam Hargrove bring you?'

'He sent a driver. He's waiting for us outside. How long is this going to take, Dan? How long are you going to be in here?'

The room had a glass window so that prison officers could see inside, but no one seemed to be taking an interest in Shepherd.

'A few weeks, maybe.'

'Isn't it dangerous?' she whispered, not wanting Liam to hear. She sat down at the table. She was wearing her ten-year-old sheepskin jacket, the one she always wore when they went out walking, faded blue jeans and scuffed boots. Prison casual. But she'd taken care with her makeup and was wearing her long blonde hair loose, the way he liked it.

Shepherd shook his head. 'It's a remand wing,' he said. 'Everyone's on their best behaviour because they want to get out.' He wouldn't tell her about his run-in with Needles. Or about breaking Jurczak's leg.

'Some of the women waiting to come in were saying that there was a suicide last week.'

'Not on the remand wing, love,' said Shepherd.

'What's it like?' Sue asked.

'Boring, most of the time.'

'Do you have a cell of your own?'

Shepherd smiled. 'I wish. But it's got a television.'

'You're joking!'

'It's no big deal,' said Shepherd. 'Keeps the inmates quiet.'

'And are there fights and things?'

Shepherd laughed. 'Of course not. It's not like the movies. We don't hang out in a yard having knife fights. We only get to exercise for forty-five minutes a day and we're searched every time we go in and out.'

He sat down opposite her and they watched Liam colour a pirate ship, his brow furrowed in concentration.

Sue frowned. 'Where did you get that watch?'

Shepherd glanced at the flashy Rolex. 'Hargrove.'

'It's horrible.'

'I know. It's part of the cover.' He showed her the thick gold chain round his neck. 'This too.'

'You look like a . . . I don't know what you look like.'

'It's not for long.'

'You owe me for this, Dan Shepherd. You owe me big-time.'

'I know.'

'I miss you.'

'I miss you, too.'

'I mean it, Dan. They're not just words.' Her eyes moved to Liam. 'He's not sleeping either.'

'This is important, love.'

'It's always important, though, isn't it? It's always the big one. The guy who's got to be put away. And then, once he's gone, there's another. And another.'

'That's why it's important. If they're allowed to get away with it, what sort of world would it be?'

'But it's always you, isn't it? It's always you taking risks. First

154

with the Regiment and now with Hargrove and his have-a-go heroes.' She leaned across the table. Shepherd could see that she was close to tears. 'You're an addict, Dan. That's what it is. You're an adrenaline junkie.'

A prison visiting room wasn't the place for a discussion about his career, or his psyche, Shepherd knew. And he didn't want to argue with her, especially not in front of Liam. There was another reason, too: in his heart of hearts he knew she was right.

Shepherd ruffled Liam's hair. 'You okay, kid?'

Liam nodded.

'We'll go fishing, when I come home.' He turned back to his wife. 'Your mum and dad okay?'

'They're fine.'

'You haven't told them . . .'

'Give me some credit, Dan. How long have I been a policeman's wife?' She sighed, then answered her own question. 'Too long.'

'Do you want anything? A drink? Biscuits?'

'No, thanks.'

'I'm going to have to ask you to do something,' said Shepherd.

'I don't like the sound of that.'

'The reason we got the private visit is because everyone thinks you want to divorce me.'

Liam's jaw dropped. 'You and Mummy are getting divorced?'

'Oh, God, no!' said Shepherd. He picked up his son and cuddled him. 'It's just a joke. Like a play at school. Pretending.'

Liam frowned. 'You're pretending to get a divorce?'

'That's right.'

'But you're still coming home, aren't you?'

Shepherd kissed him. 'Of course.'

'What's going on, Dan?'

Shepherd put his son down in front the colouring book and waited until the boy was absorbed again before he answered. 'Carpenter's outside.'

'The man you're after?'

Shepherd nodded. 'He's got a visit from his wife.'

'So?'

'So if you and I fake an argument, it gives me a chance to get closer to him.'

'How?'

Shepherd could see she wasn't happy with the idea, but it was too good an opportunity to miss. He leaned across the table and took her hands in his. 'If he sees us argue, it gives credence to my legend. My cover story,' he whispered. 'If you go out cursing me, I can start spilling my guts to Carpenter. Husband to husband.'

'And what about . . . ?' whispered Sue, gesturing at Liam.

'We'll say it's a play,' he said.

'I like plays,' said Liam.

Shepherd tapped the colouring book. 'You've missed a bit,' he said.

'I can't believe you want to use us like this.'

'I'm not using you,' said Shepherd, but even as the words left his mouth he knew it was a lie.

'Isn't it bad enough, you being away like this?'

'The sooner I get what we need, the sooner I'll be back home.' An officer walked by the window, picking his nose. 'Please, just do this one thing for me.'

'But it's not one thing, is it? It's always like this. Out all night, whispered phone calls when you're home, you coming back battered and bruised. Now you're dragging me and Liam into it.'

Shepherd sat back in his chair and sighed. She was right. 'I'm sorry,' he said.

'Did you know he'd be having a visit today?'

'No,' said Shepherd.

'So it's just a coincidence that you've both got visitors at the same time?'

'Absolutely.' As soon as the word left his mouth, Shepherd wondered if it was the truth. Hargrove had fixed up Sue and Liam's visit to Shelton. Had he known that Carpenter's wife was due today? Hargrove knew that Shepherd was having a compassionate visit in a private room visit so he wasn't putting Sue and Liam at risk, but he had given Shepherd the chance to get closer to Carpenter.

'He's got children?'

'Three. Boy and two girls.'

'Why would a family man do what he does? Doesn't he know the damage drugs do?'

'He knows, he just doesn't care.'

'But everything he has, everything his family has, is based on the misery of others.'

'I don't think guys like him give it a second thought,' Shepherd told her. 'When you talk to them, they regard drugs as just another commodity. It's like they're running an import-export businesses. They buy product, move it from place to place and make a profit on each deal.'

'So he's no conscience? No sense of right and wrong?'

'If you talk to guys like him, they usually say they're no different from cigarette companies. They say that nicotine is addictive, and that cigarettes kill far more people than any class-A drug.'

'They should just legalise everything and have done with it.'

Shepherd grinned. 'Yeah, but what would I do then?'

'Spend some time with your family, for a start,' said Sue. She reached across the table and stroked his cheek. 'You should be at home. With us.'

'Soon,' said Shepherd. 'I promise.' He pressed her hand to his cheek.

'What do you want me to do?' she asked.

Shepherd took her hand and kissed it. 'Are you sure?'

'If it gets you out of this hell-hole quicker, I can hardly say no, can I?'

'Thanks, love.'

'You haven't told me what you want me to do yet.'

'I need Carpenter to think we're on the rocks,' Shepherd said. 'You can storm out and through the visitors' room. Curse me something rotten. Tell me you'll set your solicitor on me.'

'Oh, Dan! I *can't.*'

'I'll know you won't be serious.' Shepherd ruffled his son's hair. 'What about you, Liam? Do you want to play a game?'

'What game?'

'When you go Mummy's going to shout at me. We'll say goodbye and then when we open the door Mummy's going to pretend she's angry with me.'

'And she'll be acting?'

'That's right. Like in a play. Is that okay?'

'Sure.'

'Chip off the old block, isn't he?' said Sue, but Shepherd could tell she didn't think it was a particularly good thing.

'You're definitely putting on weight,' said Bonnie playfully. She was sitting with Carpenter in row E, close to the wall. She had been to the canteen, run by volunteers from the Women's Voluntary Service, and got them Diet Coke and KitKats.

'I told you, it's the food in here,' said Carpenter, 'and I'm lucky if I get to the gym four times a week.'

'You said they let you use it every day.'

'Yeah, but if they don't have enough staff they don't open it. And the screws here are forever taking sickies. One of the perks of the job.'

Bonnie patted his stomach. 'Sit-ups,' she said. 'You don't need a gym to do sit-ups.'

Carpenter laughed. 'Soon as I'm out you can put me on a diet,' he said. He pushed the two KitKats towards her. 'These won't help.'

'You think I'm joking?'

'Honey, I'll be so glad to be out I'll eat anything you give me.' He sipped his Diet Coke. At the table next to him a West Indian prisoner was cuddling a baby, smothering its tiny face with kisses. His right hand slid inside the child's nappy. A couple of seconds later he coughed and he used the same hand to cover his mouth. It had been done so subtly that Carpenter doubted that any of the officers would have seen the drugs transferred even if they'd been watching. Carpenter looked up at the CCTV cameras. None was pointing in the West Indian's direction. The baby started to cry and he handed it back to the mother.

'I wish you'd let the kids come and see you,' said Bonnie.

Carpenter shook his head firmly. 'No way. I'm not letting them see me in here.'

'They're not stupid, Gerry. They know what's going on.'

'It's one thing to know I'm in prison, it's quite another to see me in here.' He flicked his yellow sash. 'Wearing this thing, sitting at a table that's screwed to the floor, goons in uniforms watching every move we make. I don't want them seeing that.'

'What if they sentence you?' asked Bonnie. 'What if you get sent away for fifteen years? Does that mean you won't see them for fifteen years?'

'That won't happen,' said Carpenter flatly.

'It might.'

'Trust me,' said Carpenter.

'What are you up to, Gerry?'

'You don't want to know.'

'Yes, I do.'

'No, Bonnie. Because if I tell you what I'm doing you become an accessory and there's no way I want you in the firing line.' He reached over and held her hand. 'It's bad enough there's one of us behind bars.'

'Bloody cops,' said Bonnie. 'If they'd played fair this would never have happened.'

'They're worse than the criminals,' laughed Carpenter. 'Don't worry, love, it's being sorted. I promise.'

They heard a commotion at the far end of the room and turned to see what was happening. A blonde woman with a small boy in tow had thrown open the door to one of the closed-visit rooms. 'I hate you!' she shouted. 'I hope I never see you again, ever! You can rot in here for all I care!' She stormed towards the exit, dragging the child after her.

Carpenter saw Macdonald rush to the doorway and call after his wife, but she ignored him. Macdonald cursed and kicked the door. A guard walked over and told him to calm down. Macdonald put his hands in the air. 'Okay, okay,' he said.

'Who's that?' asked Bonnie.

'New guy,' said Carpenter. 'Bob Macdonald. He's in for armed robbery. That was his wife just walked out on him. She wants a divorce.'

'I know how she feels.' She reached over and took his hand. 'Joke,' she said.

'It better had be a joke,' he said.

'They say it's harder for the families than it is for the men in prison,' said Bonnie. 'And they're right.'

'That's why most wives walk away, if it's a long sentence. "Stand by your man" just doesn't come into it.'

'Don't think you're going to get away from me that easy,' said Bonnie. 'Till death do us part, remember.'

She looked into his eyes and he could see that she meant it. But Carpenter knew that if he was locked up for fifteen years her fierce intensity would gradually die away. Eventually visits to him would become a chore, and no matter how much she loved him now there'd come a time when she wanted, or needed, a warm body beside her at night. She'd get a new husband, the kids would have a new father. And Carpenter would join the ranks of the sad old lags with no lives on the outside to look forward to. He shivered. No way was he going to allow them to keep him inside. 'I'd wait for you, too, if you were in prison,' he said, and laughed.

There were still five minutes to go before visiting time was over and Carpenter and his wife chatted about their children. From time to time Carpenter looked across at Macdonald, who was leaning against the wall with his arms folded, glaring at anyone who made eye-contact with him. The prisoners weren't allowed to leave until all the visitors had gone, so Macdonald had to stay where he was until the end. Carpenter sympathised with the man, having to stand there after his wife had hurled abuse at him in front of everybody.

Eventually, over the Tannoy, a disembodied voice announced that all visitors had to leave. Some of the women groaned. Carpenter stood up and held his wife, kissed her cheek, then hugged her. 'Won't be much longer, love,' he said.

Children were crying and officers moved through the tables, telling visitors they had to go. Several of the younger prisoners were crying too, clinging to their wives and swearing undying love.

Bonnie kissed Carpenter's lips, then headed for the visitors' exit.

He went over to join the line of prisoners waiting to be searched. Bonnie gave him a final wave as she reached the door, then blew him a kiss. He blew one back.

Macdonald joined him in the line.

The search on the way out was even more thorough than it had been on the way in. Two West Indians were taken away, protesting loudly.

'What's the story with them?' Macdonald asked Carpenter.

'Caught on camera, probably,' said Carpenter.

'Doing what?'

'Kissing their wives,' said Carpenter. 'Bit too long, bit too deep. Probably transferring drugs. Didn't go well, then, your visit?'

'You heard, yeah?'

Carpenter grinned. 'Bob, everybody heard her parting shot.'

'She's well pissed off at me.'

'Sorry,' said Carpenter.

'Not your fault,' said Macdonald. 'But thanks.'

Carpenter reached the front of the queue and Rathbone patted down his arms and legs, then sent him out into the secure corridor to wait for the rest of the men from the remand block. Two minutes later Macdonald joined him. 'She's set on divorce. There's something going on, something she's not telling me about.'

'Another man?'

'Maybe. Could just be her mother winding her up. It'd be different if I could talk to her on the out, but being here just makes it worse.'

'That was your boy?'

'Yeah. Says she's going to file for custody.'

'She'll probably get it, you know that.'

'Fuck.'

'It's just the way it is,' said Carpenter. 'Cons don't rate highly when it comes to parental rights.'

'Yeah, well, until I'm found guilty I'm not a con. I'm a remand prisoner.'

Carpenter wasn't sure what to say. Macdonald had been caught red-handed and a policeman had been shot. They'd throw away the key. But he knew how Macdonald felt. Angry. Hurt. Betrayed. And Carpenter knew how he'd react if Bonnie ever threatened to leave him and take the children with her. His reaction would be quick, vengeful and permanent.

Net curtains fluttered at the sitting room of the house next door. It would be Mrs Brennan, a spinster in her eighties, the road's resident busybody. Alice looked across at her husband. 'Can't we even tell Mrs Brennan what's going on?' she said. 'She's going to think we've been arrested.'

'It doesn't matter what anyone thinks,' said Roper, swinging a suitcase into the back of the van.

Through the sitting-room window he could see Ben and David playing with their Gameboys. All he had told them was that they were going on holiday. The time for explanations would be later, once they were safe.

There were four Church cars parked on the road outside the house, and there was a white Transit van in the driveway, its rear doors open.

'Where are we going?' asked Alice.

'A safe-house,' said Roper.

'Our own home was supposed to be safe,' said Alice. 'That's what you said – they'd never find out who you are or where you live.'

'And I was wrong,' admitted Roper. 'What do you want me to do, Alice? Open a vein? I'm trying to fix this as best I can.'

'You're not fixing anything. We're just running away and you won't even tell me where.'

'Because I don't know,' said Roper, exasperated. He was being truthful. As soon as he'd opened the envelope Ben had given him he'd phoned his boss in Drugs Operations. Within thirty minutes there had been a dozen men in and around his house. The envelope contained three photographs. One of Ben arriving at school. One of David leaving school. And one of Alice taking out the rubbish, wearing the faded pink housecoat she'd had for years. There was no note. There was no need for one. The meaning was crystal clear.

Raymond Mackie, the head of Drugs Operations himself, was

on Roper's doorstep less than an hour after Roper had made the call, promising him the earth. Roper would be protected, so would his family, and Mackie would make sure he found out how Roper's cover had been blown. First things first, Roper and his family would be moved to a Customs and Excise safe-house. Roper hadn't asked where, it wasn't important. All that mattered was to get as far away from the family home as possible. Mackie had brought a bouquet of flowers with him and presented them to Alice as if he were there to celebrate her birthday. Alice had dropped them into the dustbin as soon as Mackie had left in his chauffeur-driven Rover.

'What about the children's schools?' asked Alice.

'For God's sake, Alice. Carpenter knows where they go to school.'

'So their education is put on hold? For how long?'

Roper felt a surge of anger towards his wife. He wanted to shout at her, scream at her, shake her until she saw sense, but he fought to control himself. He knew it wasn't really Alice he was angry with. She hadn't let the family down. She hadn't put their lives on the line. Sandy Roper was angry with himself.

Two men in anoraks came out of the house with black bin-liners filled with clothing and threw them into the van. 'We've put boxes in the kitchen, Mrs Roper,' said one. 'Can you fill them with any kitchen stuff you want?' he said.

'What about the stuff in the freezer?' asked Alice.

'I'd leave it,' said the man. 'I'm not sure if there's a freezer at the new place.' Roper didn't know his name but Mackie had sworn on his mother's grave that the only personnel involved in the transfer to the safe-house were men he knew personally and that he would trust with his own life.

'What about the children's bikes?' asked Alice.

'I wouldn't recommend that the children be outside, frankly,' said the man.

Alice turned to her husband. 'See? They're going to be prisoners. We're all going to be prisoners.'

The Customs men went back into the house. Roper put his arms round his wife. She was trembling. 'I'll make this up to you, Alice. I promise.'

'Damn this Carpenter,' hissed Alice. 'How dare he ruin our lives like this? How dare he?'

Roper stroked the back of his wife's head. The photographs had been a warning, but Carpenter must have known there was a good chance that Roper would report the contact immediately and that the Church's reaction would be to close ranks and protect him and his family. Roper knew Carpenter better than almost anybody: the man was meticulous in his planning. The photographs had been Carpenter's first attempt to stop him giving evidence in court, and Roper was sure it wouldn't be his last. 'It'll be okay,' Roper whispered, as he stroked his wife's hair. 'Once the case is over and he's behind bars for good, it'll all be back the way it was, I promise.'

A man in a grey suit was standing at the front of the car in which the children were playing. He hadn't offered to help carry any of their belongings out of the house and had acknowledged Roper with nothing more than a curt nod as he'd climbed out of one of the Church cars. He stood at the gate with his hands at his sides and his eyes never left the road outside the house. A gust of wind tugged at his jacket and Roper saw the butt of a semi-automatic in a shoulder holster. He hugged his wife closer so that she wouldn't spot it. Roper was beginning to wonder if things ever would be back to the way they were before he'd helped bring down Gerald Carpenter. For the first time he realised he was scared of what Carpenter could do to him and his family. And for the first time he was doubting that the Church would be able to protect them.

Shepherd was mopping the ones when Hamilton came up to tell him that his lawyer was there to see him. The officer escorted him to the visitors' centre and showed him into the soundproof room, where Hargrove was waiting.

They shook hands as Hamilton closed the door. Shepherd could see from Hargrove's expression that something was wrong. He sat down and waited for the bad news.

Hargrove wasted no time. 'We've lost the tapes that Elliott and Roper made,' he said, sitting down opposite Shepherd. 'They've been wiped.'

'What?'

'Someone got into the evidence room and ran a high-powered electromagnet over them.'

'How the hell could that have happened?' said Shepherd.

'If we knew that, we'd have the guy in custody,' said Hargrove.

'I thought anyone who went into an evidence room was logged.'

'They are. But we don't know when it happened.'

'For God's sake,' said Shepherd, exasperated, 'what's the point of me putting my head in the lion's den if you lot can't even take care of the evidence you've got?' He pushed himself out of his chair and paced the room. Hamilton was watching through one of the windows. 'This is fucking unbelievable, it really is. He's killing off agents, threatening witnesses and destroying evidence, and you lot are sitting around with your thumbs up your arses.'

'That's not quite the position, Spider.'

'It looks to me like it's exactly the position,' said Shepherd. 'How the hell could someone get into a locked evidence room and destroy tapes?'

'We only found out yesterday because the CPS wanted to check part of Roper's transcript. The tape was blank so we checked the rest. All blank.'

'And you don't know when it happened?'

'The last time they were used was when Gary Nelson had them for his authenticity check. That was four weeks ago. There have been hundreds of officers in and out of there since. We're on the case, Spider. The room was covered by CCTV so we're going through every minute of tape. Plus we're interviewing every officer who logged into the room. We'll find out who did it, but it's going to take time.'

'Nelson's the forensics guy who was threatened, right?'

'That's him. He's now in the Algarve with his wife and says he isn't coming back until Carpenter's behind bars.'

'Sounds like he's the only one with any sense,' said Shepherd. He rubbed his face. 'So where does that leave us?'

'Elliott's evidence is now useless. The transcripts alone aren't worth anything. Losing Roper's tapes isn't the end of the world because we have the transcripts and Roper can back them up.'

'Unless Carpenter gets to Roper.'

'That's not going to happen,' said Hargrove.

'You know, I'd have a lot more faith in that if Elliott wasn't dead and the tapes hadn't been wiped.' Hamilton was still watching through the window so Shepherd sat down with his back to him.

'I've got something I want you to think about,' said Hargrove. 'Totally up to you but it might make things a bit easier, case-wise.' Shepherd looked at Hargrove expectantly but didn't say anything. 'You could wear a wire,' said the superintendent quietly.

Shepherd's jaw dropped. It was the last thing he'd expected to hear Hargrove say. 'You are joking, right?'

Hargrove shook his head. 'If you could nail Carpenter on conspiracy, we'd have him on your evidence alone.'

'You know where I am, right?'

'Yes, Spider,' said Hargrove patiently. 'I know.'

'The guys in here are Cat A. They're professional criminals, most of them. They'd spot a wire a mile off.'

'Not necessarily,' said Hargrove. 'We could get something special from the technical boys. A recording device that looks like a CD player or a Walkman, maybe.'

'And if someone finds out what I'm doing?'

'Then we pull you out.'

'If I got caught in here with a wire you wouldn't have time.'

'Just give it some thought,' said Hargrove. 'I'm not forcing you to do anything you don't want to.'

'What's the state of play on Carpenter's case?'

'He's got another court appearance next week, but his case won't be heard for another two months, and that's without his lawyers playing silly buggers. Could be four months.'

'So he's got four months to get to Roper.'

'That's one way of looking at it. The other way is that you've got four months to nail him.'

'I'm not going to be in here for four months!' said Shepherd.

'As soon as you've had enough, all you've got to do is say.'

Shepherd sat back and folded his arms. He knew that the superintendent was right. He was in Shelton by choice, and it was his decision how long he stayed there. But that didn't make him feel any more comfortable. 'I think you should have a closer look at Tony Stafford,' he said.

'Because?'

'Because that five hundred quid you gave to Digger's sister bought me a place on the spur's cleaning crew.'

Hargrove took his black notebook from his jacket pocket and started scribbling.

'The guy's name is Tompkins,' said Shepherd. 'Everyone calls him Digger. He's in for another murder, shot a Yardie. The Operation Trident guys should have the full SP on him. I went to see Digger to tell him I wanted a place on the cleaning crew and he told me to get five hundred pounds to his sister. Next day I was on the crew. Tony Stafford runs the block so any jobs have to be approved by him.'

'He could have rubber-stamped someone else's request, couldn't he?'

'Sure. We need a look at the paperwork. Gosden should be able to do that for you.'

'We'll put the sister under surveillance. If Digger's paying off a prison officer, she might be acting as a conduit.' Hargrove scratched his ear with his pen. 'Does Digger have much to do with Carpenter?'

'I haven't seen them together, but Carpenter keeps himself to himself.'

'Stafford could be Digger's man, Carpenter could have someone else.'

'Yeah, I know.'

Hargrove closed his notebook and put his pen away. 'Are you okay?'

'So far. But it's hard work.'

'I never thought it'd be easy, Spider.'

'You know what worries me most?' Hargrove raised his eyebrows. 'If I talk in my sleep,' said Shepherd. Hargrove smiled, but Shepherd was serious. 'I can control what I do and say when I'm awake, but I could say anything while I'm dreaming. What if I dream I'm talking to you? Or Sue? I've no control over my dreams.'

'Have you ever talked in your sleep before?' asked Hargrove.

'There's a first time for everything.'

'What about moving to a single cell? I could talk to Gosden.'

'Absolutely not. If I move I'll have to make it happen myself. There's too much status attached to a single cell. If I get it *gratis* it'll be a red flag that something's up.'

'So you'll ask Digger to fix it?'

'My cellmate says Digger's the one to arrange it. I've already raised it with Carpenter. He said to put in an official request to Stafford. Be interesting to know how Carpenter got a single.'

'I could ask Gosden.'

'Might be an idea. Check the paperwork for his move with the paperwork for my job on the cleaning crew. See if there's a match.'

'I'm on it, Spider.'

Shepherd was tired. The previous night someone on the ones had been crying. The night staff hadn't thought it serious enough to intervene and they'd just let him get on with it. It had been almost dawn before he'd stopped. Now Shepherd appreciated just how tough prison was. In-cell televisions and a choice of menu didn't make the confinement any easier to bear. No one had shouted at the crying prisoner to shut up, because every man on the spur had known exactly how he felt.

Shepherd woke up and looked at his watch. Seven thirty. It was Saturday, his first weekend behind bars. There was no work at weekends, and no breakfast packs in the cells: breakfast was served at the hotplate. Shepherd had found himself waking at seven thirty every morning, a few minutes before the prison officers started the roll-call. He lay on his bunk, waiting for the spyglass to flick open.

Lee got up and padded barefoot to the toilet. He groaned and urinated. He was in mid-flow when the spyglass flicked open. 'I'm on the bog!' shouted Lee. The spyglass snapped shut.

Shepherd let Lee wash and clean his teeth at the basin before he got down from his bunk. The cell was so poky that there was barely enough room for two men to move around at the same time. Whenever possible he kept out of Lee's way, staying on his bunk. He also let Lee have ownership of the television's remote control, although both of them were paying the weekly rental.

As Shepherd washed and shaved, Lee sat on the chair and flicked through the television channels. News programmes and children's television. 'Why's there nothing on in the mornings?' asked Lee.

'Because most sensible people are lying in,' said Shepherd. He changed into a clean polo shirt. Weekend lie-ins were a Shepherd tradition, when he wasn't away on a job for Hargrove. He'd go downstairs, make a pot of tea and some toast, pick up the papers from the hall, then get back into bed with Sue. Liam would join them, and he and Sue would lie together munching toast and reading the papers while Liam looked as the comics.

The prison regime at the weekends was less restrictive than it was during the week. There was association in the morning and afternoon, but the cell doors were locked earlier, at five fifteen instead of eight o'clock. That meant a full twelve hours banged up.

Shepherd had applied to be on the gym list for Saturday and Sunday, and Lloyd-Davies had told him he'd made it on the Saturday list. Just. Eight prisoners from each spur were allowed to use the gym in each session and Shepherd had been number eight.

The cell door was unlocked at half past eight and Shepherd went down to the hotplate with Lee. There was already a queue of a dozen men there, which they joined. There were three hotplate men, watched over by the middle-aged West Indian female guard, Amelia Heartfield. Everyone used her first name and, even when she was giving prisoners an order, she did the same. She was always smiling and seemed to enjoy talking to them. In return they never gave her any grief. From time to time prisoners would let off steam on the wing but Shepherd had never heard anyone curse or shout at Amelia.

Shepherd picked up two plastic trays and handed one to Lee. The hotplate men worked efficiently, doling out the food: one sausage, two pieces of bacon, a scoop of scrambled egg, a tomato, a spoonful of beans, half a slice of fried bread. Two slices of bread.

Shepherd reached the head of the queue, but as he was about to hold out his tray a figure appeared at his shoulder. It was the prisoner with the shaved head from the threes, Carpenter's man. He nodded at Shepherd and pushed his tray forward. 'Two sausages, well done. Four rashers of bacon, crisp. Four slices of bread.'

One of the hotplate men put the bacon and sausage on the plate and handed him a side plate with four slices of bread. The man nodded again and headed for the stairs.

'Who is that guy?' Shepherd asked Lee.

'That's Gilly,' he said. 'Gilly Gilchrist. He's in for GBH.'

'But he fetches and carries for Carpenter?'

'He's not a butler,' said Lee. 'He's muscle. Haven't you noticed that he's never far away from Carpenter on the spur? When Carpenter goes out into the exercise yard, Gilly goes with him. During association Gilly goes wherever Carpenter goes.'

'Did Carpenter pull a thorn out of his paw?'

Lee frowned, not understanding. 'What?'

'Why does he work for Carpenter? It's not a gay thing, is it?'

'Don't let Gilly hear you say that, he'd rip your lungs out. He's got five kids, has Gilly. He's short of readies so Carpenter pays him on the out.'

They carried their trays into the cell. Lee sat at the table while Shepherd climbed up on to the bunk. The scrambled egg was rubbery and the beans were cold, but he ate them anyway.

At nine o'clock Shepherd heard doors clanging. 'Now what?'

'Lock-up,' said Lee, slotting sausage into his mouth. 'It's just for an hour while the screws get on with their paperwork. They'll unlock the gym list at ten fifteen and it's all doors open at ten thirty for association and exercise.'

Shepherd wiped his plate with a piece of bread. 'Why don't they give us a schedule, tell us what happens when?'

'That'd be too logical,' said Lee. 'Anyway, you soon get into the swing of it.'

'Who told you, though?'

'Guy who was in the cell before you had been here five months.'

Rathbone appeared at the door. 'Okay, lads?'

'Fine, Mr Rathbone,' said Lee, raising a forkful of beans.

'You're on gym list, Macdonald. Friends in high places?'

'Miss Lloyd-Davies put my name down,' said Shepherd.

'Just so long as you didn't break anybody's leg.' Rathbone closed the door.

Lee switched on the television and flicked through the channels. 'Can I ask you something?' he said.

'Sure.'

'Jurczak. Did you really break his leg?'

'He fell,' said Shepherd. 'We were having a chat and he fell.'

'But his knee was all smashed up.'

'He fell awkwardly,' said Shepherd, and laughed. It was important that he played the hard man with Lee. Lee was clearly a blabbermouth, so anything Shepherd said to him would be common knowledge on the spur. 'Let me ask you something,' he said. 'Who really runs the spur? Everyone says Digger, but they tug their forelocks when Carpenter's around. And at least Digger goes to the hotplate himself.'

'Different strokes,' said Lee. 'Digger's got muscle, right. If Digger wants you to do something, he tells you. He says jump, you say how high, right?'

'I've gathered that.'

'But Carpenter's got money. More money than you can shake a stick at. He doesn't have to threaten anybody. He just buys what he wants.'

'Through Digger?'

Lee's brow furrowed. 'What's your interest in all this?' he asked.

171

Shepherd held up his hands. 'Hey, just want to know who does what, that's all.'

'You're not thinking of taking him on, are you?'

'Digger? Or Carpenter?'

'There's got to be a daddy on the block. Always is. But Digger'll fight for what he's got.'

'What about Carpenter?'

Lee grinned. 'Carpenter doesn't have to fight.'

'Yeah, he doesn't look hard.'

'That's the point. He doesn't have to be hard. But he can have you sorted, inside or out. Cross him, and there's half a dozen guys in the spur who'd stick you for what he can pay them on the out. The screws know it too, which is why he's allowed to take liberties. You know he's on the gym list most days?'

'How does he manage that?'

'Buggered if I know.'

'What about his single cell? Did Digger get that for him?'

'No idea, mate. Why don't you ask him?' He frowned. 'Hey, I'm not getting on your tits, am I?

Shepherd laughed. 'Nah, you're fine. I could just do with some privacy, you know?' He cleaned his plate, put it on top of the wall cupboard and lay back on his bunk. Other than the odd titbit from Lee, time spent in his cell was wasted time as far as his investigation was concerned. The only occasions when he could talk to Carpenter were on cleaning duties, out in the exercise yard, in the gym, or walking down the secure corridor. But the difficulties were compounded by the fact that his quarry spent much of his time in his cell, even when he was free to move around. It was all very well getting block gossip from the likes of Ed Harris and Lee, but if Shepherd was going to put a stop to Carpenter's wrongdoing he was going to need hard evidence. Soon.

Rathbone opened the cell door at ten fifteen and told Shepherd to wait at the bubble. Shepherd had changed into his prison-issue tracksuit, but when he got to the bubble he could see that he was underdressed. Bill Barnes was there in a brand new Reebok tracksuit and trainers. Three other prisoners, all West Indians, wore pristine sportsgear and thick gold chains round their necks. They grinned at Shepherd's attire. He flashed them a tight smile. He didn't care what he looked like: he just wanted to get rid of some of the energy that had been building up over the past few days.

He looked up at the threes. Carpenter was coming down the stairs, wearing a red Lacoste shirt with white shorts, socks and trainers. He was carrying a bottle of Highland Spring and a small white towel. He looked like a well-off businessman on the way to his local fitness centre.

Rathbone came up to the group as Carpenter arrived. The prison officer ticked off the eight names on his clipboard, then took them out into the secure corridor.

Shepherd hoped to talk to Carpenter on the long walk to the gym but before he could get next to the man, Barnes fell into step beside him. 'How's it going, Bob?'

Shepherd looked over his shoulder. Carpenter was walking at the rear of the group, talking to Rathbone.

'When's your next court appearance?'

'Not sure,' said Shepherd.

'You've got to appear before a judge every two weeks when you're on remand,' said Barnes. 'At least it's a day out. You okay for puff?'

'I'm still not smoking, Bill. Not tobacco and not wacky-backy.'

'What about booze?'

'You can get booze in here?'

'Sure, home brew. I've got a couple of pints on the go at the moment.'

Shepherd laughed, thinking Barnes was joking.

'I'm serious, mate,' said Barnes, earnestly. 'I've got a mate in the kitchen who pinches yeast for me. You put it with a bit of fruit and water in a Ziploc bag, throw in some sugar, and Bob's your mother's brother. I've got some cider that'll be ready in a few days, and orange and pear that's ready to go. Once it's fermented we put it in 7-Up bottles and sell it. Get me two packs of Marlboro and I'll let you have a bottle.'

Shepherd wasn't that desperate. He liked a drink, sure, either beer with the lads or a good bottle of wine with Sue, but it wasn't the alcohol he enjoyed so much as the company.

'Suit yourself,' said Barnes. 'After you've been inside for a few months you'll want to get high, one way or another.'

They reached the gym. Rathbone searched the prisoners one by one, a perfunctory pat-down of their arms and legs. Shepherd followed Barnes in. A couple of dozen prisoners from the other blocks were already there. It was a big room, packed with equipment – half a dozen bikes and four good-sized treadmills along one wall, four rowing machines, two multi-gyms, and in one corner a weights section with half a dozen benches.

The West Indian prisoners immediately went over to the weigths area where half a dozen others were standing around talking. They were greeted with high fives and clunked fists. No one seemed interested in lifting any weights.

Carpenter was still outside so Shepherd went over to the multi-gym and started doing some gentle stretching exercises. A balcony ran the length of one wall and a bored prison officer stared down at nothing in particular.

Carpenter came in and went over to one of the treadmills. Shepherd didn't want to appear too obvious so he stayed on the multi-gym, working on his arm and chest muscles. Rathbone and another officer stood at the entrance, chatting. Barnes was on a bike, pedalling for all he was worth.

Shepherd revelled in the exercise. He'd been doing sit-ups and press-ups whenever Lee was in his bunk but there was something therapeutic about working against the machine with its steel-grey weights and chrome pillars. He worked his upper and lower arms, his shoulders, then did a series of leg stretches.

He looked over at the treadmills. Carpenter was still there, running fluidly, his breathing regular and even, his towel draped round his neck and his bottle of Highland Spring in his right hand. There was an Arab on the machine next to him, an obese man with a thick moustache who was bathed in sweat even though he could barely manage a fast walk. As soon as the Arab climbed off, Shepherd went over to take his place.

He nodded at Carpenter and started off at a slow jog, giving his muscles a chance to get used to working.

Carpenter upped the speed of his machine but he was barely breaking sweat. He took a swig from his water bottle. He was staring straight ahead as he ran. Shepherd figured he was probably imagining green fields ahead of him, not a blank white wall. Shepherd increased the pace. It had been over a week since he'd last been on a run and his muscles were burning already. It felt good to be moving again, though. His trainers thumped down on the machine's rubber tread and he increased the pace again. He glanced across at the control panel of Carpenter's machine. Carpenter was running at almost twice Shepherd's speed. And while Shepherd was running on the level, Carpenter's was set at an incline of ten per cent. He didn't seem aware that Shepherd was running alongside him.

Shepherd altered the incline so that it matched Carpenter's. The machine whirred and he had to drive himself harder to maintain the same speed. The adrenaline kicked in and he stopped being aware of his feet hitting the treadmill. He increased the speed again, to match Carpenter's machine, and the two men ran in synch.

Carpenter glanced at Shepherd's control panel, then jabbed at his speed button. The pace picked up and he started breathing heavily. Shepherd smiled to himself. Carpenter was clearly competitive, and he was more than happy to take him on. He increased his speed again to match Carpenter's, and fell into the other man's rhythm. They ran together for ten minutes. Then Carpenter increased his speed. His mouth was open, his arms pumping as he ran.

Shepherd matched his speed and settled into the new rhythm. He knew he was close to his maximum; he was a distance runner, not a sprinter. But Carpenter was also close to his limit, and he seemed to be tiring quickly.

Shepherd knew he could outlast Carpenter – stamina was his strong point, always had been – but he was trying to win the man's confidence, not humiliate him. Sweat was pouring down Carpenter's face, and his Lacoste shirt was soaked. Shepherd let his own breath come in unsteady gasps, and faked a stumble. He powered on, but let his feet slap on to the rubber tread and his knees go weak. He reached out and slowed down his machine, panting. He stole a glance at Carpenter, who was smiling grimly.

Shepherd slowed his treadmill to a walk, wiped his face with his hands, still faking exhaustion, then stopped his machine and climbed off.

Carpenter ran for another full minute, then slowed to a jog.

Shepherd bent over, then dropped into a crouch. Carpenter grinned and stopped his machine. He stepped down, wiping his face with his towel.

'You're fit, all right,' said Shepherd.

'Just practice,' said Carpenter, stretching his legs.

'You know, in the old prisons they used treadmills as hard labour. Nowadays they're a privilege. Progress, huh?'

Carpenter chuckled.

'You're in the gym every day, pretty much, aren't you?' asked Shepherd.

'Pretty much.'

Shepherd straightened up. 'How do you manage that?'

Carpenter took a long drink from his water bottle but his eyes never left Shepherd's. Shepherd didn't look away, but kept an amused smile on his face, knowing that Carpenter was weighing him up. Carpenter wiped his mouth with his towel. 'You know how I manage it,' he said.

'Digger?'

'That and a broken leg should do it,' said Carpenter.

'There's only eight on the spur allowed at any one time, right?'

'That's the rule.'

'And Digger can get me on the list every day?'

Carpenter grinned at him. 'You'd have to ask him about that. Just don't try to get my slot.'

Shepherd pulled a face. 'Wouldn't want to screw things up for you.'

'You won't,' said Carpenter. He went over to a bike and climbed on. As he started pedalling, Shepherd climbed on to one next to him.

Both men cycled in unison, but this time there was no competition.

'Heard from your wife?' asked Carpenter.

Shepherd shook his head. 'I reckon it'll be her solicitor I hear from.'

'She seemed pretty angry.'

'Be different if I was outside,' said Shepherd. 'If I could just talk to her without the bloody screws looking on. The whole thing is bound to turn her against me, isn't it? The wall, the bars, the searches, the drugs dogs.'

'I've told my kids not to come,' said Carpenter. 'No way I want them seeing me in here.'

'Yeah, I wish mine hadn't brought my lad in. Especially if that's the last time he sees me. Hell of a memory. His dad behind bars with that stupid yellow sash.'

'You'll see him again,' said Carpenter. 'Fathers have rights.'

'Not if I'm sent down for twenty,' Shepherd said. 'By the time I get out, he'll have forgotten me.'

Carpenter didn't say anything. He took a drink from his bottle.

'You seem pretty calm about your situation,' said Shepherd.

Carpenter shrugged. 'No point in letting off steam in here,' he said. 'Throw a tantrum and they'll either drug you up or put you in a cell with cardboard furniture.'

'If it looks like I'm going to do twenty, I'll top myself.'

'You adapt,' said Carpenter.

'Fuck that,' said Shepherd.

'How would killing yourself make it any better?'

'Now you sound like Ed Harris. I mean it, I'd be better off dead.'

They pedalled in silence for a while. Shepherd wanted to keep Carpenter talking but without appearing over-eager. The West Indians had split into two groups and were lifting heavy weights.

'Your wife seemed okay,' said Shepherd, eventually. 'About coming to see you in here, I mean.'

'She knows it won't be for ever,' said Carpenter.

'But what if you don't get off?'

Carpenter snorted softly. 'It's not about getting off. If I get in a courtroom, I'm buggered.'

'So what's your way out?'

Carpenter flashed him a sideways look. 'Why are you so interested?'

'Because if I don't come up with something, I'm fucked.'

Carpenter looked at him, his eyes hard. Then he nodded slowly, as if he'd decided he could trust Shepherd. 'How much money have you got on the outside, tucked away?'

'A fair bit.'

'You'll need more than a fair bit. Getting out from an open-and-shut case costs.'

'I've got a few hundred grand offshore. Even the wife doesn't know about it.'

'How good is the case against you?'

'I was caught red-handed. I wasn't carrying but there was a shotgun inside the warehouse.'

'Witnesses?'

'I think one of the guys is grassing.'

'That's where you start,' said Carpenter. 'You have to get him out of the equation.'

'Buy him off, you mean?'

'Whatever it takes.'

Shepherd's heart was racing. This was what he'd been working towards. It was why he was behind bars. 'Are you talking about something else?'

'Like I said, whatever it takes.'

'And what about the evidence?'

'You make it go away.'

'What – like abracadabra?'

'Like paying someone to make it go away.'

'You can do that?'

'Anyone can do it, providing you've got the money and the right person to give it to.'

Shepherd was pedalling slower now. 'The cops have got the shooter,' he said.

'So a cop can make it go away.'

'And you've got people who can do that?'

'We're not talking about me,' said Carpenter, 'we're talking about you. You find out where the shooter's kept and then you get to someone in the station. Or an officer on the case.'

'Oh, come on,' protested Shepherd. 'That's Fantasy Island.'

Carpenter put his hands on the bike's handlebars and concentrated on pedalling. Shepherd realised he'd offended him. 'I mean, do it wrong and I'll end up on corruption charges,' he said.

'So don't do it wrong,' said Carpenter. 'Put out feelers. You don't do it yourself, obviously. You get someone on the out to make the approach.'

'What do you reckon it would cost? To get rid of evidence?'

'Hypothetically?'

'Yeah.'

'Thirty grand. Forty, maybe.'

Shepherd stopped pedalling. 'Forty thousand quid?'

'That's why I was asking if you had ready money. You can't piss around, Bob. And buying off a cop has to be a hell of a lot cheaper than buying off a judge.' He grinned again. 'Hypothetically.'

Shepherd carried his lunch tray back to the cell. Cottage pie, chips and baked beans. Chocolate pudding and custard. It was no wonder that so many men on the spur were overweight.

Lee was still in the queue down on the ones, but Shepherd sat on his bunk and toyed with his food. The conversation he'd had with Carpenter had been a big step forward. He had been far more forthcoming than Shepherd could have hoped. He'd practically admitted to paying off cops on the outside, and come close to suggesting that Shepherd bribe a policeman and kill a witness. Shepherd's word on its own wouldn't be good enough to get a conviction, though. He'd have to do what Hargrove wanted and wear a wire. But that would be taking one hell of a risk.

He ate a forkful of cottage pie. It was greasy and tasteless, the potato lumpy and cold.

Another problem was getting on the gym list regularly. That would mean persuading Lloyd-Davies to put him on it or paying off Digger again. Shepherd had to know when and where he'd be talking to Carpenter: it would be far too dangerous to wear a wire all the time. And what would he do with the wire when he wasn't wearing it? There was hardly any space in the cramped cell, and it would be next to impossible to keep it hidden from Lee. Hargrove had suggested he use a recorder made to look like a CD player or Walkman, but it had to be functional or Lee would be suspicious. And Shepherd was all too well aware of how often equipment malfunctioned. He'd experienced everything from leaking batteries to microphone feedback. Usually on an undercover operation he'd have back-up close by so that if something went wrong he could be pulled out, but that wasn't possible in Shelton.

Shepherd had confirmation that Carpenter was killing witnesses and destroying evidence, but he didn't know yet how he was doing it and who was helping him. Shepherd suspected it was Tony Stafford, but Hargrove was going to want proof. Hargrove knew exactly how dangerous it would be for Shepherd to wear a wire, but he'd still asked – because he knew that if Carpenter wasn't stopped more people would die on the outside until he got what he wanted. His freedom.

Healey appeared at the door to Carpenter's cell. 'Got your papers here, Carpenter,' said the prison officer.

'Thanks, Mr Healey,' said Carpenter. He went to the door and took them. The *Daily Mail*, the *Daily Telegraph* and the *Guardian*. 'What was the hold-up?' As a rule the papers arrived before dinner.

'Short-staffed today. We didn't have anyone to check them. The post's running late too.'

Carpenter took his papers over to the table and flicked through the *Guardian*. The spur always seemed to be short-staffed on Saturdays. The officers didn't like working weekends. The envelope was in the City section. He ripped it open and took out a single sheet of paper. The tapes had been wiped. Now only Sandy Roper stood between him and freedom. And Kim Fletcher was on the case.

A prisoner appeared at the door. It was Andy Philpott.

'Got your papers, Mr Carpenter.' He handed Carpenter *The Times* and the *Mirror*.

'Thanks, Andy,' said Carpenter.

'Got your cappuccino, too,' said Philpott. He put a box of sachets on Carpenter's bunk.

Philpott was in his early twenties, remanded on burglary charges. Fifty-seven offences. Despite being a prolific housebreaker he had little in the way of money to show for it. His savings had soon gone to pay his lawyers, and now his wife and small child had to rely on family income support. He used his prison allowance to purchase items Carpenter wanted from the canteen, and Carpenter paid his wife on the out, ten pounds for every pound spent inside. It was an arrangement that suited them both. Philpott wasn't a smoker and didn't have a sweet tooth, and he was prepared to survive on prison food if it meant his family had an easier life.

'Appreciate it,' said Carpenter. As Philpott left, Digger arrived at the cell door.

'Okay if I come in, Gerry?' asked Digger.

'Sure,' said Carpenter. He waved at the chair. 'Please.'

Digger sat down. 'Drink?' Carpenter had a selection of bottles and cans on his table including Fanta, Coca-Cola, 7-Up, orange juice and sparkling water. He also had tea-bags, coffee, the cappuccino sachets and two flasks of hot water.

'OJ's fine,' said Digger. Carpenter poured him some and handed the glass to him.

'How's things?'

'Fine,' said Digger. 'There's a new guy on the ones bringing in crack next week. He's done hard time before so he knows the score. His girlfriend can regurgitate at will, he says.'

'More detail than I needed.' Carpenter laughed. 'How much?'

'He says twenty grams but I'll check he's not pulling a fast one. We're taking thirty per cent but if it becomes regular we'll take more.' Digger reached into the pocket of his tracksuit and gave Carpenter a gold band. 'There's the ring you wanted.'

Carpenter took it, pulled a face, then placed it on his pillow. 'What happened to Jurczak?'

'Got stamped on. The new guy, Macdonald. He wanted to be on the cleaning crew.'

'Sounds like he got what he wanted.'

Digger shrugged. 'Macdonald came through with five hundred. Someone had to get the job, seemed easier to give him what he wanted.'

'Is he going to be a problem?'

'I can handle him.'

'Is that what Needles thought?'

'He caught him by surprise.'

Carpenter laughed.

Digger's face hardened. 'He hit him while he wasn't looking.'

'Is Needles letting bygones be bygones?'

'It's personal so I'm not interfering. If he wants to stick Macdonald, that's his call.'

'I don't want the spur locked down because there's blood on the floor,' said Carpenter. 'If it turns into a gang war, we'll all suffer.'

'Macdonald's a loner, he won't have anyone backing him up. But I hear what you're saying, Gerry.'

'What do think of him, this Macdonald?'

'Keeps himself to himself unless there's something he wants. Then he goes for it.'

'Is he into you for anything?'

'Doesn't smoke, doesn't do drugs. Isn't interested in betting. Hardly ever uses the phone. Doesn't even spend at the canteen.'

'The man's a saint?'

'It's like he's not even here.'

'Doesn't look like a hard man, but Needles is no pushover.'

'Macdonald's hard, all right, even if he's not big.'

'But you can handle him?'

'I won't be fighting him. What he wanted wasn't unreasonable.

182

And he paid the fine hundred straight away. Needles was taking liberties, so more fool him.'

'Who paid?'

'Some guy on the out. Said he was his uncle. Turned up at my sister's with the readies in an envelope.'

'Notes okay?'

'Do me a favour, Gerry, I wasn't born yesterday.' He drained his glass and placed it on the table. 'Thanks for the juice.'

'Thanks for dropping by.'

Carpenter picked up the wedding ring and examined it as Digger left. It was a simple band, twenty-four-carat gold. Inside was an inscription: 'Simon and Louise. For ever.'

Alice Roper popped her head round the sitting-room door and told her two boys to get ready for bed.

'What's the point, Mum? It's not like we've got school tomorrow, is it?' moaned David. 'It's Sunday.'

'It's almost ten,' said Alice. 'Do as you're told.'

'When can we go back to school?' asked Ben.

'Soon.'

'When's soon? Monday?'

Alice didn't know what to say to her children. They'd been kept away from school since the day Ben had been approached in the street and they'd had to move away from the family home. She didn't want to worry her children, but obviously they knew something was wrong. No school. Moving to a strange house. She didn't want to lie to them, but how could she tell them the truth, that men were trying to kill their father? 'I don't know, Ben. As soon as I do, so will you. Believe me, it's no fun having you under my feet all day.'

'I hate this house,' said David.

'You and me both,' responded Alice. 'Now bed. Both of you.'

Her husband was sitting at the kitchen table, his hands round a mug of tea that she'd made almost an hour earlier. The kitchen was tiny, about a third of the size of the one in that own home. Everything about the so-called safe-house was small, And there were only two cramped bedrooms so the boys had to share a double bed.

'Sandy, we can't go on like this,' said Alice. She sat down opposite him.

Roper looked up, his eyes blank, as if his thoughts were a million miles away. 'What?'

Alice waved a hand round the kitchen. 'This place. It's just not suitable.'

'It's temporary. And it's safe.'

The house was in the middle of a sand-coloured brick terrace at the end of a small cul-de-sac in one of the older areas of Milton Keynes, the anonymous new town some fifty miles to the north of London. The Church had also arranged to use a room in a house at the entrance to the cul-de-sac. The owners were being paid handsomely and had been told that the men in the room were Drugs Squad officers on a surveillance operation. From their position they could monitor everyone who entered and left the dead-end street. There were only two ways into the house: the front door, which was approached across a small paved courtyard separated from the road by a low brick wall, and the rear door, which opened on to a walled garden. Beyond the garden there was a school playing-field. Anyone approaching the rear of the house could easily be seen from the upstairs bathroom window, where a man from the Church was permanently stationed with binoculars and night-vision goggles. Roper could see the advantages of being in the house, but the rooms were small and, other than the garden, there was nowhere for the children to play safely.

'They won't even let me out to buy food,' complained Alice. 'I have to give them a shopping list, like I was an invalid or something. Half the potatoes they came back with this morning were rotten.'

'I'll speak to them about the potatoes,' said Roper. His shoulders were slumped and his eyes had dark circles under them. Neither had slept much the previous night. The man on bathroom duty had a smoker's cough and an irritating sniff, and the walls had little in the way of soundproofing.

'This isn't about potatoes, it's about living like animals,' said

Alice. 'It's like we're the ones in prison here. Every time we want to use the bathroom we have to ask permission. I bet Carpenter has more freedom than we do.'

'It won't be for ever.'

'It feels like we've been here for ever already,' she said. 'This isn't fair on the children.'

'I know.'

'Why can't they go and stay with my parents?'

'Because if Carpenter knows who I am he'll know everything else about us. Every friend, every relative. Nowhere will be safe.'

'I can't even go for a walk.'

Roper leaned back in his chair and stared at the ceiling, exasperated. There was a small damp patch above the kitchen sink. The house had been neglected for many years: the once-white paintwork had yellowed, the door handles on the kitchen units were loose and the gas cooker was caked with burnt grease. Alice had done her best to clean the place, but she was right, it wasn't suitable for a family – although with the best will in the world, Roper didn't see what he could do to remedy the situation. The purpose of the safe-house was protection, not comfort. And, as he kept telling his wife, it wouldn't be for ever. Gerald Carpenter wasn't being vindictive and his attempts to put pressure on Roper weren't personal. All he wanted was to keep his freedom, and once a judge had handed down a sentence that would be an end to it.

Roper's mobile phone rang. He stood up, grateful for the interruption. It was in the hallway, on a glass table with ornate brass legs. There was a regular phone on the table but the Ropers had been told not to use it. The only people who knew the number of the landline were the Church and it would only be used in the event of an emergency. Roper picked up his mobile. The caller had blocked his number. Nothing unusual in that. Most of his Church colleagues routinely withheld their numbers and when he was working undercover virtually every call he received was from a blocked number. He put the phone to his ear. 'Roper,' he said.

'How's it going, Sandy?' someone asked.

Roper frowned. It was a guttural voice with an accent he couldn't quite place. West Country, maybe, but flattened out from years of living in London. It wasn't a voice he recognised. The mobile was his personal phone so the only people who had the number were friends, family, and the Church.

'Who's that?' he asked.

'Someone with your best interests at heart,' said the man. 'What did you think of the pictures, then?'

Roper bit down on his lower lip. The call was almost certainly from a throwaway mobile and therefore virtually untraceable. Even with the full resources of the Church technical boys they'd only be able to pinpoint the general area where the phone was being used. If he could have recorded the conversation then maybe they'd have been able to pick up clues from the background noise but as it was Roper was helpless.

'What do you want?' he asked.

'You know what we want,' said the man.

Alice came out of the kitchen and stood behind him, evidently sensing that something was wrong. Roper turned away from her, not wanting her to hear. 'How did you get this number?' he asked. He didn't expect an answer but he wanted to keep the man talking until he could think of something to say, something that would help him identify the voice.

The man chuckled. 'How's the missus?'

'You can tell Carpenter he's wasting his time,' said Roper. Alice put a hand on his shoulder but Roper went into the sitting room. Through the net curtains he could see two Church bodyguards sitting in a blue saloon, but he knew there was no point in attracting their attention. There was nothing they could do. Nothing anyone could do.

'Tell him yourself when he gets out,' said the man.

Alice followed Roper into the sitting room and stood in front of him, her arms folded across her chest. 'Who is it?' she mouthed, but Roper turned his back on her.

'There aren't many ways you could have got this number,' he said. 'It isn't listed.'

'We've given you every chance to save yourself and your family any grief,' said the man. 'What happens next is up to you.'

'And what is going to happen?' asked Roper.

'Sandy?' said Alice, but Roper silenced her by pressing a finger to her lips.

'You know what happened to the cop. We can get to you just as easily as we got to him.'

'So why the phone call?'

'Last resort,' said the man. Roper could definitely hear a trace of West Country in his accent. 'We were told to look for alternatives. We'd offer you money but the word is that you're one of the untouchables, Sandy. Tell me I'm wrong and we can put six figures in your bank account tomorrow.'

'That's a possibility,' said Roper. If he could persuade them to transfer money into his account it would leave a trail the Church could follow, a trail that would lead, hopefully, to Carpenter.

The man chuckled again. 'Do I sound as if I've got "fuckwit" tattooed across my forehead?' he asked. 'We've had you well checked, Roper, and you've never got your hands dirty, not once. You and that cop are whiter than white.'

It was good to hear that a villain considered him incorruptible, Roper thought, even though that was what had put him in his present precarious position. 'Which leaves us where?'

'We've asked nicely. Now we're telling you. Let it be known that you've had a sudden lapse of memory. That's all you have to do.'

'I can't.'

'We understand how that would be your first reaction,' said the man. 'You're career Customs, worked your way up through the ranks, done your bit for Queen and country. Probably get a minor gong when you hang up your white hat for good. But you've got to understand who you are and who we are, Sandy, what we've got to lose and what you've got to lose. And is what you've got to lose worth what you're going to gain by seeing my boss stay behind bars? What do you win? You get the satisfaction of seeing a family man like yourself sitting in a cell for ten years. Fifteen, maybe. And what have you got to lose? Well, you know exactly what you've got to lose. How old are you now, Sandy? Fifty-three, yeah? Birthday coming up next month. Retirement on the horizon. Those years with your wife and kids, that's what you're going to throw away.'

Roper said nothing. His wife stood in front of him, deep furrows across her brow. 'Who is it?' she mouthed again.

'This is the last time you'll hear from us,' said the man. 'If we don't hear by tomorrow that you're refusing to give evidence, you'll be a dead man. That's not a threat, that's a promise.'

Roper put the phone down.

'For God's sake, Sandy, who was it?' shouted his wife.

Roper wanted to lie to her, to tell her that everything was fine, but he knew it was too late to tell her anything but the truth. So he told her. And when the tears came, he held her tight.

Shepherd had been asked what religion he practised when he was brought into Shelton and he'd answered truthfully: none. But religious services were one of the few occasions when prisoners from the different blocks got together and he wanted to see if Carpenter talked to anyone. Shepherd had asked to be put on the Church of England list. The Catholics were taken from the spur at nine fifteen for their service, and returned to their cells an hour later. Lee was also down for the C of E service so when their cell door was unlocked at ten thirty they both went down to the bubble. More than thirty prisoners were waiting to go to the service. 'Didn't realise we were in with such a religious lot,' Shepherd said to Lee.

Lee wiped his nose with the back of his hand. 'This is the big get-together,' he said. 'It's when you chase up debts, catch the gossip on the other spurs, find out who's been ghosted in.'

'Ghosted?'

'It's when the screws move a troublemaker around at short notice. Shove him in a van and deliver him to another prison across the country.' Lee grinned. 'Carry on the way you're going and you'll maybe get ghosted one day.'

Carpenter came down the stairs from the threes with Gilly Gilchrist.

Lloyd-Davies checked off all their names on her clipboard, then unlocked the barred gate and walked them through to the secure corridor. Hundreds of other prisoners were on the move, all being escorted by prison officers.

At the entrance to the room where the service was to be held, the prisoners were given a thorough pat-down. Shepherd figured that religious services were the main opportunity they had for moving contraband between blocks so the guards had to be extra-vigilant.

He took a seat at the back of the room. There was seating for almost a hundred in front of a small wooden lectern and, in the far corner, a small electronic keyboard where a middle-aged woman in a flowery print dress and a wide-brimmed hat was playing a hymn.

Carpenter walked down the centre aisle and sat next to an overweight man with fleshy jowls, who was constantly wiping his face with a handkerchief. He had a gold earring in his left ear and receding hair cropped close to his skull. He whispered something to Carpenter, who nodded. The two men sat with their heads close together, deep in conversation.

Shepherd relaxed and ran through the thousands of photographs in his memory. He'd seen the man before, in a photograph, though not in person. An arrest picture. Front and side view. Ronnie Bain. A major marijuana importer who'd been imprisoned for eight years after one of his gang turned supergrass. He was less than half-way through his sentence and had been labelled Cat A after two jurors had been offered bribes to bring in a not-guilty verdict.

Two prisoners gave out hymn books, which were passed from hand to hand along the rows. Shepherd settled back in his seat, folded his arms and looked round the room at the murderers, drug-dealers, paedophiles and terrorists. There were huddled conversations going on everywhere, and despite the body searches Shepherd saw notes and small packages being transferred from mouth to hand and from hand to mouth.

The elderly minister announced a hymn and the congregation shuffled to its feet. A Welsh prison officer standing at the door led the singing, his deep baritone echoing round the room. Shepherd did his best to keep up but he wasn't familiar with the hymn. Bain and Carpenter were singing. So was Lee, who was sitting among a group of men in their twenties, all wearing the England football strip and sporting a variety of tattoos, predominantly bulldogs, the cross of St George, and blood-tipped daggers. They were all singing at the tops of their voices, heads tilted back, mouths wide open. They made Shepherd think of wolves howling at the moon.

There was no work on a Sunday but Shepherd was let out of his cell after lunch to help clean the floors on the spur. He worked with Charlie Weston and met Hamster and Ginger for the first time. Hamster was a lanky West Indian with a speech impediment that made him sound as if he was talking with his nostrils pinched together. Ginger was dressed from head to foot in Manchester United gear, including a baseball cap, team strip, wristbands and trainers with the team's logo on them. It was Ginger's sole topic of conversation as he worked. There was no sign of Carpenter.

Shepherd spotted Lloyd-Davies walking along the spur, her head down, deep in thought. 'Ma'am?' he said.

She looked up, frowning.

'Sorry to bother you, ma'am, but is there any chance of me getting on the gym list this afternoon?'

'Bit short notice,' said Lloyd-Davies.

'I keep asking but I'm told the list is full.'

'Everyone wants to go to the gym. You have to take your turn. Anyway, you all get three hours of association today and the exercise yard is open. Do a few laps of it.'

'Some people don't seem to have a problem getting on the gym list every day.'

Lloyd-Davies squinted at Shepherd. 'What are you trying to say?'

'Just that some guys are in the gym every day but I'm having to get down on my knees for one session a week.'

'You've only been here a few days,' said Lloyd-Davies. 'These things take time. And under prison rules you're only entitled to an hour a week in the gym. Anything above that is a privilege, not a right.'

'Yeah, well, it looks to me as if some prisoners are getting more privileges than others.'

'That's the whole point of the privilege system,' said Lloyd-Davies. 'Carrot and stick. Gym time is one of the carrots we offer.'

'So, how do I go about getting more carrots from you, ma'am?' said Shepherd, grinning.

'Stop giving me grief, for a start.' She grinned back. 'I'll see what I can do.' She pointed down at the floor. 'You've missed a bit.' When he looked down she chuckled. 'Made you look,' she said, and walked away.

Carpenter finished his cappuccino and placed his cup and saucer on the table. The coffee was a pale imitation of what Bonnie made for him at home but, then, she had a two-grand state-of-the-art coffee-maker that Carpenter had had shipped from Italy. He'd put in a request to have a coffee-maker in his cell but the governor had turned it down as a safety risk. It was a nonsense ruling, but so many prison rules owed nothing to logic. Prisoners weren't allowed kettles, but they were allowed Thermos flasks of hot water. From an electrical point of view, a coffee-maker was no more of a danger than the television sets the prison supplied. Carpenter had applied to buy a larger model for his cell but that application had been refused – another nonsense ruling – but a DVD player had been approved. Now all he had to do was to accumulate enough money in his account to buy it. He was on enhanced status, which meant he had thirty pounds a week to spend. There was nothing he could do about his phone calls, which had to be paid for from his account, but he could reduce all the other drains by getting other people to make purchases for him. All the food and drink in the cell came from other prisoners. Carpenter placed orders and they brought it to his cell. He reimbursed them on the out, at a rate of ten to one.

Carpenter strolled out of his cell and leaned over the rail. Prisoners were lining up to be searched before going out into the exercise yard. Carpenter hated the yard. It reminded him of his schooldays. Turfed out of the classrooms for an hour to burn off excess energy so they'd be good little boys when lessons resumed.

Carpenter pushed himself off the rail and walked down the stairs to the ones. Several inmates nodded at him – anyone who'd been on the spur for any length of time knew who he was. Carpenter didn't plan to be behind bars long enough to have to build relationships. He'd bought Digger, and that was all he needed.

Hitchcock's cell was opposite the pool table. The door was open, but Carpenter knocked. 'Okay if I come in?' he asked.

Hitchcock was lying on his bunk. 'What do you want?'

'A chat,' said Carpenter.

'I just want to be left alone.'

'Difficult objective to achieve in here,' said Carpenter. He walked in and closed the door. It was a double cell and Hitchcock was on the top bunk: he rolled over so that he was facing the wall. Carpenter took the ring out of his pocket. 'I think this is yours,' he said.

Hitchcock twisted round. His mouth opened when he saw the wedding band. He rolled over again and took the ring from Carpenter, staring at it as if he feared it might disappear at any moment. 'Where did you get it from?' he asked.

'Thought you might want it back,' said Carpenter.

Hitchcock slipped on the ring. 'That was the first time it's been off my finger since I got married,' he said. 'Are you married?'

'Fourteen years,' said Carpenter.

'Why are you in here?' asked Hitchcock.

Carpenter wagged a finger at him. 'Prison etiquette. You never ask a man what he's done. If he tells you, that's fine. But you never ask him.'

'I'll remember that. Sorry.'

'There are other rules,' said Carpenter. 'Like you never step into another man's cell without being invited. And you always repay a favour. Nothing comes free in here.'

Hitchcock looked at the ring. Realisation dawned on his face. 'How much do I owe you?' he asked.

Carpenter smiled. 'Money isn't a currency in here, Simon.'

'But you want something from me?'

'You're a quick learner. Don't worry, Simon, I don't want anything major, just the *FT*.'

'The *FT*?'

'The *Financial Times*. Monday to Saturday. And *The Economist* every week. You place an order with the office and they'll have it delivered from the local newsagent. Soon as it arrives you bring it up to my cell. I'm on the threes. The top floor.'

'How do I pay for it?'

'Comes out of your allowance,' said Carpenter. 'Can't see you getting into trouble so you'll be enhanced, which means you get thirty quid a week to spend.'

'But I need that money to call my wife.'

'You'll have enough for that. You need anything else Digger can get it for you and you pay him on the out.'

Tears welled in Hitchcock's eyes. Carpenter knew his demands were unfair but he felt no sympathy for the man. In prison you were either a sheep or a wolf. Carpenter and Digger had come in as wolves and recognised it in each other. Even the new man, Macdonald, had shown his strength within days of arriving at Shelton. But men like Hitchcock had vulnerability stamped on them. Victim. Soft target. And if Carpenter didn't take advantage of him, others would.

'This is a nightmare,' said Hitchcock. He sat on the edge of his bunk with his head in his hands.

'You've got money outside, right?'

Hitchcock nodded.

'So use it. Digger's the man to help. You want a single cell, Digger can arrange it. You want a decent job, you see Digger.'

'He's the big black guy, right? He's the one who stole my ring. And my St Christopher.'

'He runs the spur. He can take pretty much what he wants.'

'Why don't the prison officers do something?'

'This isn't nursery school. You can't go running to the teachers.'

'I spoke to one of the officers. He said he could write up a report saying what had happened, but that if he did Digger would . . .' He tailed off. 'This is a bloody nightmare.'

'Which officer?'

'Hamilton. The young guy.'

'He was giving you good advice. If he'd taken a report it would have gone to the governor and you'd have been branded a grass. Grasses don't last long in prison.'

'So I just have to do what he says. Whatever Digger wants, he gets?'

'You can try standing up to him, but he's big and he's got a lot of muscle. Or you pay him for what you want. You're lucky, Simon. You've got money. The guys who've got nothing still have to pay him. One way or another.'

Carpenter headed for the door.

'Gerry?' Carpenter stopped and turned. 'Thanks,' said Hitchcock. Tears were running down his cheeks. Carpenter felt a rush of contempt for the man. 'Just remember the *FT*,' he said.

Shepherd was watching two prisoners, in yellow and green Jamaican football strips, play pool when he saw Carpenter come out of Hitchcock's cell and head for the stairs. He caught up with him as he reached the twos. 'Gerry, can I have a word?'

'What's up?'

They stood together at the railing, looking down on the ones. It was just before four thirty, which meant that tea would be served soon. Lock-up would start at five fifteen, which meant another fifteen hours stuck in their cells. Another fifteen hours with Lee, watching mindless television. Fifteen hours during which Shepherd's investigation remained in limbo.

'What we were talking about yesterday – in the gym?'

'What about it?'

Shepherd looked about him to check that no one was within earshot, and lowered his voice to a whisper: 'I've got to get out of here, it's doing my head in.'

'There's none of us in here by choice,' said Carpenter.

'I'm going crazy. I couldn't do a year inside, never mind a ten-stretch.'

'You adapt,' said Carpenter calmly.

'Fuck that!' spat Shepherd.

'Don't get pissy with me, Bob. I'm just telling you how it is.'

Shepherd gripped the rail so tightly that his knuckles whitened. 'I'm sorry,' he said. 'I've just had as much as I can take, that's all.'

'That's why we go to the gym. Burn off the excess energy.'

'That's okay if you know you're heading out. I'm going down for a long time, Gerry. Unless I do something about it.'

Carpenter shrugged. 'I've got problems of my own.'

'But you're dealing with them, right?'

Carpenter's eyes were icy. 'How do you know?'

Shepherd looked back at him, keeping his breathing regular, suppressing all the tell-tale signs of nervousness. He looked him right in the eyes, smiling slightly. Just a regular guy, shooting the breeze, not an undercover cop interrogating a suspect. He hadn't made a mistake. Bob Macdonald didn't know for sure that Carpenter had been killing witnesses and destroying evidence, but after the conversation they'd had in the gym it was a fair assumption. 'You're too laid-back,' said Shepherd. 'You know you're out of here.'

'Maybe I've just got a good lawyer.'

'If you had a good lawyer, you wouldn't be on remand. No, you're making it happen, right? Like you said yesterday, you're taking care of it on the out.'

'If I am, that's my business.'

'You've got to help me, Gerry.'

'I don't have to do anything.'

Shepherd put a hand on Carpenter's arm. 'Look, I've got people on the outside who can help me, but it's getting to them that's the problem. My lawyer's as straight as they come, he won't pass on messages – not the sort I'm going to need to send – my wife wants nothing to do with me, and they listen in to all phone calls. I'm fucked, unless you can help me.'

Down below, two men in aprons wheeled in the hotplate and plugged it into a power point. According to Lee, Sunday tea was the major meal of the week: roast beef or roast turkey and all the trimmings.

'Why would I help you, Bob? Where's the up-side for me?'

'I can pay.'

'I don't need your money.'

'But I need your help. I just need you to get a message out for me. A note to the guys who can get things sorted.'

Carpenter rubbed his chin. 'Let me think about it,' he said.

'You'd be doing me one hell of a favour. I'd owe you.'

'That's for sure,' said Carpenter. He headed up the stairs to the threes and his cell.

Shepherd leaned on the railing. A queue was already forming at the hotplate. One of the West Indians playing pool cheered and slapped the hand of his opponent. Shepherd realised that Needles was propped against the wall close to the pool table, staring up at him. Shepherd stared back. Needles pushed himself away from the wall and folded his arms. His lips curled back in a contemptuous snarl. Shepherd straightened, but continued to stare back at him. He wasn't worried by the show of aggression. He'd beaten the man once and he'd beat him again, if necessary. And the fact that Needles was being so up-front about his hostility meant that Shepherd could be prepared. He could feel hatred pouring out of the man and he knew that whatever Needles had planned wouldn't be long in coming.

'Don't tease the animals,' said a voice.

Shepherd turned to see Ed Harris behind him. 'He started it, miss,' he said, grinning.

'You didn't bother with the anger-management booklet, I take it.'

'This isn't about anger,' said Shepherd. 'It's about Needles down there wanting to do me harm and me not letting him.'

'Needles works for Digger, and Digger can pull together a dozen guys on this spur alone,' said Harris.

'Digger's not the problem,' said Shepherd.

'He'll back up his man if he has to.'

'We'll see.'

'Fighting on the wing makes life difficult for everybody. We all get banged up and that causes resentment.'

'Is that a threat, Ed?'

Harris smiled genially. 'I don't make threats, Bob. I'm a Listener. I help where I can.'

'I don't need help.' Shepherd gestured at Needles, who was still glaring up at him. 'You should talk to him. If anyone needs lessons in anger management, it's your man down there.'

Harris leaned on the rail, his back to the suicide mesh. 'This isn't racial, is it?'

'Give me a break,' said Shepherd.

'They come down on it really heavily in here, racial attacks.'

'You mean, has Needles got it in for me because I'm white?'

Harris snorted. 'It doesn't work that way. They'll see it as you picking on him because he's black and you'll be back on basic, maybe even removed from association, which means twenty-three hours a day in your cell.'

'It's nothing to do with his colour,' said Shepherd. 'It's about power and status. He wants everybody to know he's a big man.'

'And that upsets you?'

'Don't bother trying your amateur psychology on me, Ed,' said Shepherd. 'There's no power struggle going on. He doesn't have anything I want. He got heavy with me, I retaliated. That hurt his pride so now he wants to stamp on me. It'll make him feel better and show everybody how hard he is.'

'Just be careful, that's all I'm saying.' Harris headed down the stairs towards the hotplate.

Shepherd looked back at the ones. Needles was still glaring at him. Harris was right about one thing: if his quarrel with Needles erupted into open warfare the officers might well react by locking down the whole spur. Or, even worse, they might try to transfer Shepherd to another. If that were to happen then the only way for him to stay where he was would be for the governor to intervene and that sort of special treatment would only raise eyebrows among officers and inmates. There was no way Shepherd could allow that to happen, and the only way to prevent it would be to get in his retaliation first. He smiled down at Needles and made a gun of his right hand. He pointed it at the man: 'Bang,' he whispered to himself.

It was stifling inside the hood, and sweat was trickling down the back of Hargrove's neck. The car made a right turn and he took several small breaths, trying to quell the gag reflex.

'Are you okay, Sam?' asked Raymond Mackie. He was sitting next to Hargrove in the back of the Rover.

'I'll be a darn sight more okay when this bloody hood's off,' said Hargrove. The Rover made another turn and his stomach lurched. He had a throbbing headache and his mouth had filled twice with acidic vomit that he'd had to swallow. It wasn't how he'd planned to spend his Sunday afternoon.

'I'm sorry about the cloak-and-dagger,' said Mackie. 'It's as much for Roper's peace of mind as anything.'

'It's not a problem, Ray,' said Hargrove. 'I'd probably do the same if it was my man under siege.'

The car accelerated suddenly and Hargrove's stomach churned. He breathed in. The hood was made of black cotton and loose at his throat but, even so, the air he took into his lungs was hot and stifling. The Customs and Excise Head of Drugs Operations had handed it to him as they drove through north London and had requested apologetically that he put it on. Hargrove hadn't had to ask for a reason: he'd already been told that Roper's life had been threatened and that the location of the safe-house was known to only a handful of men from the Church. A more sensitive man might have taken the request as an insult, but Hargrove knew that the murder of Jonathon Elliott meant the police no longer held the moral high ground. He'd put on the hood and suffered in silence.

The Rover slowed and turned again, then braked and came to a halt. 'I'd be grateful if you'd keep the hood on for a little longer,' said Mackie. 'I'm sure you understand.'

Hargrove understood exactly. The procedure wasn't so much to keep him from seeing the safe-house, it was more to reassure Roper that all precautions were being taken to ensure his safety. Hargrove smiled, despite his discomfort. If there was ever a case of rushing to shut stable doors after horses had bolted, this was it.

The car moved as the driver climbed out, then the rear passenger door opened and Hargrove felt a light touch on his arm. 'Mind your head,' said the driver, and helped the superintendent out of the car.

Mackie walked with Hargrove to the front door, knocked, then guided him over the threshold. As soon as the door was closed, he removed the superintendent's hood.

Hargrove blinked in the hall light, then ran his hand over his hair. A man in his fifties was standing in a doorway, a woman with a tear-stained face behind him.

Mackie smiled amiably. 'Sandy, Alice, can I introduce Super-intendent Sam Hargrove? I hope he will able to allay some of your fears.'

'Are you with the Drugs Squad?' asked Roper.

Hargrove shook his head. 'No, Sandy, I'm not.' He smiled at Alice. 'I don't suppose I could have a cup of tea, could I, Mrs Roper? I've been wearing that hood for the best part of an hour and I'm parched.'

Alice hurried off to the kitchen. Roper went back into the sitting room. A small colour television was on in the corner, the sound muted. Mackie and Hargrove followed him and sat down on the cheap red plastic sofa. Roper stood with his back to the television, his arms folded across his chest. 'With all due respect, I'm not happy about police involvement, not after what happened to Jonathon Elliott,' Roper said to Mackie.

'Superintendent Hargrove is not involved in your protection, nor will he be,' said Mackie. 'He's here only to offer you some reassurances. Just hear what he has to say.'

Roper looked as if he was about to argue, but then the fight went out of him and he sat down on an armchair, made of the same red vinyl as the sofa. It produced a soft farting noise as he settled into it and he looked pained. 'My wife hates this suite,' he said. 'Hates the whole house.'

'I can understand why,' said Hargrove. 'But it won't be for much longer. I gather you had a phone call?'

Roper nodded, then related what Carpenter's man had said. Hargrove listened in silence until he had finished. 'I'm not in the business of teaching anyone to suck eggs, but you realise that all he did was call your mobile? They've no idea where you are.'

'It was my personal mobile,' said Roper.

'Which means the number would be in general circulation,' said Hargrove. 'I agree that it is a worry how they got it, but it's not the end of the world.'

'They photographed my wife and children.'

'Gerald Carpenter doesn't hurt families,' said Mackie. 'He's a nasty piece of work but he's old school and, to the best of my knowledge, he's never hurt a woman or a child.'

'Other than by selling them drugs, you mean,' said Alice.

Hargrove nodded, conceding the point. 'What I mean is that the photographs and the threats to your family are just a way of intimidating you. I don't believe for one minute that he would actually carry them out.'

'My husband tells me that Carpenter has already killed a police officer. I have to say, if he'd told me that sooner I'd never have let him get into this.'

'The undercover agent he killed was in his way. And the shooter made sure that the agent's wife wasn't in the line of fire. Mrs Roper, I want to reassure you that your family are not in danger.'

'As far as you know.'

Hargrove nodded again. 'Agreed, but I doubt that anyone knows Gerald Carpenter as well as I do.'

'You've only met him since he was arrested,' said Roper. 'I was close to the man on the outside. I drank with him, broke bread with him. I know very well how dangerous he is.'

'There was always a risk that he'd identify you. It's a risk you take every time you go undercover.'

Roper shook his head. 'This is different. Carpenter's getting help from someone, either within the Church or within the Drugs Squad. I don't mind going in to bat against a demon bowler, but

'I'm damned if I'm going to put my life on the line if members of my own team are helping to threaten my family.'

'We don't know for sure that there's a bad apple,' said Mackie.

'They know my date of birth,' said Roper. 'They know I'm due to retire. They have my mobile number. They know my home address. Someone's leaking, sir.'

'And because of that you're threatening to walk off the case?' said Mackie.

'I don't see I've any choice, sir. You can see the state my wife's in. The boys are like caged animals. I asked to be put in a safe-house and, fine, that's happened, but then I get a call on my mobile and it's all up in the air again. I don't know who I can trust any more.'

'Let's not get ahead of ourselves here, Sandy,' said Mackie. 'I know this is tough for you, but refusing to give evidence will just get you into even more trouble.'

'Is the job threatening me now, too?'

Mackie put up his hands as if trying to soothe a nervous horse. 'We've invested a lot of time, money and manpower on this case,' he said. 'We can't afford to have it go down the toilet. It's bigger than you, Sandy. It's bigger than all of us.'

'So you'd let a judge send me down for contempt, is that what you're saying? I don't believe I'm hearing this.'

Alice appeared at the doorway with a tray of tea-things and and some biscuits. She seemed to sense the tension and frowned. Hargrove stood up and took the tray from her. 'Let me help you with that,' he said.

Alice pulled a small coffee-table in front of the sofa and Hargrove put the tray down on it. 'The biscuits are shop-bought,' she said. 'The oven is a mess.'

'They're fine,' said Mackie. He picked one up and took a bite. 'Delicious.'

Alice looked around the room. Mackie's ample frame took up most of the sofa and her husband was in the only armchair. Hargrove waved at his place on the sofa. 'Sit there, please, Mrs Roper.'

Alice sat down and poured milk into the cups. They were all chipped.

'I was just telling your husband what a terrific job he's doing, and how we do understand the stress you're all under,' said Mackie. 'I know that this house isn't the most comfortable of places, but it is secure, and at the moment that's what counts. How are the children bearing up?'

'They're upset. They're missing their friends and their school.'

'Where are they now?'

'In their room.' Alice's hand shook and milk dribbled on to one of the saucers. 'I don't want Sandy testifying,' she said.

She'd been watching too much American television, thought Hargrove, but he didn't say anything. Witnesses in UK courts gave evidence, they didn't testify.

'I understand your fears,' said Mackie, looking around for somewhere to put the uneaten half of his biscuit. Hargrove handed him a plate. It was scarred from years of washing. 'What you've been through so far is more than we could ever have asked from you. It's above and beyond the call of duty.'

'It's not me I'm worried about,' said Alice. Her hand shook even more and she put down the milk jug and sat with her fingers entwined in her lap. 'It's the children.'

'I've been explaining to your husband that they are absolutely not at risk,' said Hargrove. 'The man we're dealing with doesn't hurt women or children, certainly not civilians.'

'He sent us photographs,' said Alice.

'To intimidate your husband,' said Mackie.

'He's not testifying,' said Alice. She was staring at her fingers.

'Can I just ask you both to hear what Superintendent Hargrove has to say?' said Mackie. 'He's come a long way and I made him wear a ghastly hood most of the time he was in the car.'

Alice smiled and wiped her eyes with the back of her hand. Hargrove pulled a crisp white handkerchief from his top pocket and gave it to her.

Mackie looked up at Hargrove and nodded. Hargrove moved over to the door so that he could see Roper and his wife. He waited until they were both looking at him before he spoke. 'First let me reinforce what Mr Mackie has said. You've both been through far more than we could reasonably have asked of you. And do sympathise with your desire to put the matter behind you. But please do believe me when I say that you and your family are under the best possible protection. I know you're upset about the death of the Drugs Squad undercover officer, but he was out in the open, going about his daily business. He wasn't being protected, he wasn't taking anything more than normal precautions.'

'Why weren't you protecting him?' asked Alice.

'He wasn't one of my officers,' said Hargrove. 'I don't work for the Drugs Squad. Nor do I report to the Metropolitan Police. I'm not passing the buck by saying that. Even if he had been working for me, I doubt that we'd have handled things any differently. Jonathon Elliott didn't realise he was in jeopardy. No one did. He assumed his cover was intact and that no one knew his true identity. The attack came out of the blue.'

'They didn't threaten him first?' asked Roper.

'Not as far as we know,' said Hargrove. 'But I'm not here to talk about the measures taken to ensure your safety. That's in the hands of the Church. I'm here to let you know that we haven't finished with the Gerald Carpenter investigation. Far from it. We have a man undercover as we speak, trying to get close to him.'

'But he's in prison . . .' said Roper. His voice tailed off as he grasped the implications of what the superintendent had said.

'As a rule I wouldn't be discussing operational matters with you,' said Hargrove, 'and certainly not with a civilian,' he nodded at Alice. 'But under the present circumstances, coupled with the fact that you are now effectively isolated from the outside world, we've decided to bend the rules.'

Roper leaned forward in his armchair, his head tilted to one side as he stared at Hargrove.

'I head up an undercover unit that reports directly to the Home Office,' said Hargrove. 'We are a police unit, but separate from all police forces. If and when a chief constable requires our assistance, a request is made to the Home Secretary. If it is approved, our unit is seconded to a particular case. More often than not it involves the positive targeting of a named individual, someone who has been able to evade conventional police operations. A request was made last week for my unit to move against Gerald Carpenter, and an operation to that effect is now in place.'

'You've got a guy undercover in a Category A prison?' said Roper, astonishment on his face. 'He must have balls of steel.'

Hargrove smiled. That pretty much described Spider Shepherd. 'His mission is two-fold,' the superintendent continued. 'We are trying to find out how Carpenter is continuing to run his organisation from behind bars, and we hope our man will be able to gather evidence that Carpenter was responsible for ordering the killing of Jonathon Elliott. Our man is risking a lot – everything, in fact – and I wanted you to be aware of that. He's undercover twenty-four hours a day in horrendous conditions that I wouldn't wish on my worst enemy. And if you do pull out and the case against him collapses, Carpenter walks and our man will have risked his life for nothing.'

'This man, he's a policeman?' asked Alice.

'He's a former soldier but he's a policeman now. He's been undercover for most of his police career, but this is the most dangerous mission he's ever undertaken.'

'And does he have a family?' Alice looked anxiously at Roper.

'Yes, he does,' said Hargrove. 'And his wife is as fearful for his safety as you are for your husband's.'

Roper was smiling now. 'You're going to get him, aren't you? Carpenter's going down?'

'We're going to get him,' said Hargrove. 'You and my team. Together we'll put him where he belongs. Hopefully for most of the rest of his life.'

'Sandy . . .' said Alice.

'You heard the man, Alice,' said Roper. 'This isn't just about us now. It's not as if the whole case rests on my evidence.' He looked up at Hargrove earnestly. 'Conspiracy to murder, right?'

'At the very least,' said the superintendent.

'That's life,' Roper said to his wife. 'He'd be away for life. And this time it wouldn't all be hanging on my evidence.' Alice's shoulders slumped. Roper got up and stood next to her. Then he knelt beside her and took her hands. 'What if it was the other way round?' he said. 'What if it was me in prison, putting my life on the line, and he was at home with his family? Wouldn't you want him to do what was right?'

Alice looked at him. A tear ran slowly down her cheek, but as he was holding her hands she couldn't wipe it away. 'It's not about what's right and what's wrong,' she said. 'I know that what you're doing is right, but I'm not a child. I know that sometimes bad people get away with doing evil things, and good people get hurt. I don't want our family hurt, Sandy.'

'You won't be hurt, I promise.'

'That's not a promise you can make,' she said. She took a deep breath, then looked across at Mackie. 'My husband can do what he wants,' she said, her voice suddenly stronger, 'but the children and I are not staying here.'

'Mrs Roper—' began Mackie, but Alice continued to speak.

'We're leaving now. I have a sister in Bournemouth. We'll go and stay with her.'

'Mrs Roper, that's really not wise,' said Mackie.

'You can have men watching the house there, but if what you say is true we'll be in no more danger there than we are here. It's Sandy who's in the firing line, so it makes sense for us to be as far away from him as possible.'

Mackie and Hargrove exchanged a look. Roper stood up. 'It's probably for the best,' he said to Mackie. 'It's a guest-house near the seafront. The Church could put people in there without attracting suspicion.'

'And you're still with us on this?'

'One hundred per cent,' Roper said. He smiled reassuringly at his wife, but she looked away, stony-faced.

Shepherd dropped to the ground in the corner of the exercise yard and started doing slow press-ups. He did twenty on the flat of his hands, then another twenty on his fingertips. He rolled on to his back and did a hundred crunches, then leg-raises.

As he stood up he saw Needles in the far corner, deep in conversation with Dreadlocks. Both West Indians turned to look at him and he knew they were talking about him. He had the feeling that whatever truce there had been with Dreadlocks following the fight on the landing was about to be rewritten. He'd already assumed that Needles wouldn't come for him one-on-one.

Shepherd knew that as long as he was in the yard he was safe. When the attack came it would be out of sight of the officers and CCTV cameras, in a cell or the showers. And this time Needles wouldn't be fighting empty-handed. It would start with a mug of boiling water thrown into his face or a plastic toilet-brush handle carved into a spike and thrust between his ribs. Needles wouldn't be fighting fair because nothing in prison was fair: all that mattered was winning.

Shepherd started touching his toes, swinging his arms and building up a rhythm. It was four o'clock in the afternoon so the inmates were allowed another forty-five minutes out of their cells before the evening meal was served and they were locked up for the night. If anything was going to happen that day, it could only happen within the next forty-five minutes.

Shepherd straightened up and started to walk round the perimeter of the exercise yard. He went clock-wise – everyone did, even though there was no rule that prevented them going the other way.

Lee and his football cronies were leaning against the wire fence, deep in conversation. Lee nodded at Shepherd as he walked by. He nodded back. He had to walk past Needles and Dreadlocks to get out of the yard. He didn't look at them, although he could feel them staring at him. He had gone past the stage of sour looks and menacing stares: he'd made his decision. All he needed now was the opportunity.

He walked out of the exercise yard, back on to the spur, and slowly towards the stairs. Half a dozen of the older inmates were sitting at a table playing dominoes, and four Jamaicans were playing pool. One of them was Stickman, the tall, thin guy that had attacked Shepherd with Dreadlocks on his first morning. Shepherd sensed no hostility from him as he walked past the pool table. No sullen look, no hard stare.

He reached the bottom of the stairs. Out of the corner of his eye he saw Needles and Dreadlocks emerge from the exercise yard. They'd been searched when they went into the yard so Shepherd knew they wouldn't be carrying weapons. He went up to the twos. Needles and Dreadlocks walked along the ones and into Needles's cell, which he shared with another West Indian who was still in the exercise yard. Shepherd leaned over the rail. Rathbone was at the entrance to the exercise yard, patting down prisoners who wanted to go outside. There were no other officers on the ones.

There were two in the bubble, drinking coffee and talking.

Shepherd turned and hurried down the stairs. The Jamaicans were intent on the pool game. The old lags were bent over their dominoes. He walked towards Needles's cell. Charlie Weston was at the water-boiler, filling his metal Thermos flask. A middle-aged prisoner in a prison-issue tracksuit was filling out a visitor application.

Shepherd reached Needles's cell. The door was ajar. He took a final look round and pushed it open.

Ray Mackie waited until the Rover was within a mile of the City, then told Hargrove he could remove the hood. He took it off and ran a hand across his hair and down the back of his neck. 'I look forward to taking you on a clandestine meet one day, Ray,' he said.

Mackie chuckled. 'You're lucky we didn't get the rubber gloves out.'

Hargrove settled back in the plush leather seat and looked out of the window at the passing traffic. The Rover's rear windows were tinted so other motorists wouldn't have been able to see that he was hooded. 'I didn't like having to lie to them like that,' he said quietly.

'We didn't have a choice,' said Mackie.

'Even so.'

'Are you saying your people don't bend the truth?' asked Mackie, rhetorically. 'How far would an undercover agent get if he never lied?'

'There's lying to the villains, and there's lying to your own,' said Hargrove.

'And if we'd told Alice Roper that Gerald Carpenter would kill his mother if it meant his freedom, how would that have helped our present situation?' asked Mackie. 'You saw how close to the edge she is.'

'She'd be better off in the safe-house,' said Hargrove. 'Wherever it is,' he added drily.

'The further away from her husband she is, the better,' said Mackie. 'She's making him nervous. If he thinks she and the kids are out of harm's way, he's less likely to have any thoughts of pulling out.'

'And what about this guest-house?'

'She's probably right. We can screen any guests as and when they make bookings, and we can put our own people in.'

'This is one hell of a mess, isn't it?' said Hargrove.

'It was never going to be easy,' said Mackie. 'There was no way Carpenter was going to go down without a fight.'

'With Roper in the witness box and the evidence that hasn't gone up in smoke, Carpenter's going away, isn't he?'

'CPS says so.'

'And the Crown Prosecution Service has never been wrong in the past, has it?' said Hargrove, his voice loaded with sarcasm.

'Which is why your man Shepherd's in play,' said Mackie. 'How's he bearing up?'

'He's the best I've got,' said Hargrove.

'Like Roper said, he must have balls of steel. Twenty-four hours a day among some of the hardest bastards in the realm.' Mackie peered out of the window. 'I'm heading south of the river to Wimbledon,' he said. 'Can I drop you anywhere?'

It was a warm, sunny day and Hargrove wanted some fresh air. He needed thinking time too. 'Here's fine,' he said.

'Pull over, Stan,' said Mackie. The driver indicated and brought the Rover to a halt at the herb. Mackie looked earnestly at Hargrove. 'I do appreciate what you did today, Sam,' he said.

'I know you'd have done the same,' said Hargrove. The two men shook hands and Hargrove climbed out of the car. He turned up the collar of his overcoat and started to walk westwards, his hands deep in his pockets.

Needles was on his knees by the two-tier bunk, reaching under the mattress. Dreadlocks was standing by the table. He was holding a blue toothbrush into which two razor blades had been set. The were a couple of millimetres apart so that no surgeon could repair damage done to the skin.

'What the fuck—' said Needles. Shepherd kicked the door closed behind him.

Dreadlocks raised the home-made cutter – a mistake because the weapon was designed for slashing, not stabbing. Shepherd moved quickly. He grabbed the steel Thermos flask from the sink with his right hand and stepped forward. As Dreadlocks brought down the blade, Shepherd smashed the Thermos against his hand. Dreadlocks grunted and the weapon clattered to the floor. Shepherd backhanded the Thermos into Dreadlocks's mouth. Blood and bits of tooth splattered across the wall and Dreadlocks fell back, his arms flailing. He stumbled over Needles and crashed into the bunks.

Shepherd punched him twice, right and left, a blow to each kidney, then grabbed him by the scruff of his football shirt and slammed his head against the wall. Dreadlocks sagged to the ground, on top of Needles.

Needles struggled to get to his feet. In his right hand he was holding a piece of broom handle that had been sharpened to a point. He pushed Dreadlocks away with his left hand. 'You're fucking dead meat!' he spat.

Shepherd said nothing. There was no point in talking: all that mattered was the fight. And winning it. He still had the Thermos. Needles had his left hand out, fingers splayed. He kept the sharpened stick close to his body, the point angled up. It was a killing weapon, sharp and long enough to drive up through Shepherd's ribs and into his heart, or through his eye deep into his skull. He was breathing heavily, his eyes were wide and staring, gearing himself up to attack, making small jabbing movements with the stick.

Shepherd stared into the man's eyes and not at the stick. The eyes were the key to seeing where the attack would come. The stick could be faked, a jab down and then a thrust up, but the eyes never lied, unless the man was a professional, but nothing Needles had done suggested he was anything more than a violent amateur. Shepherd unscrewed the top of the Thermos as he continued to stare at Needles. It was half full of hot water.

Needles swallowed, then his lips curled into a snarl. He took a deep breath and his eyes flicked towards Shepherd's stomach. Before Needles could stab him, Shepherd threw the hot water into his face, blinding him, then slammed the Thermos flask against his throat, not hard enough to shatter the voicebox but enough to stop him screaming.

Needles lashed out with the stick but it was a slashing motion and Shepherd easily blocked it with his left arm, pushing the weapon up into the air and exposing the big man's stomach. There were kilos of fat and massive blocks of muscle to absorb the strongest blows, Shepherd slashed his open palm across the man's neck.

Needles staggered back and his left hand went to his injured throat. His breath was coming in ragged gasps and his chest was heaving. His eyes were still filled with anger and hate and the sharpened stick was pointing at Shepherd's chest.

Shepherd was treading a dangerous line. He couldn't kill Needles – his undercover role wasn't a licence for that – but he had to injure him badly so that he'd be moved off the wing. And he had to do it with a minimum of noise. If the officers broke up the fight Shepherd would be moved to solitary and the operation would be over.

Needles stabbed at Shepherd's face with the stick but Shepherd swayed back, avoiding the blow, then lashed out with his foot and caught Needles between the legs. Needles bent forward and Shepherd punched him on the side of the chin, hard. The big man's head snapped to the side and his eyes rolled back in the sockets. He slumped on top of Dreadlocks.

Shepherd stood looking down at the two unconscious men. He wiped his lips with the back of his hand. Neither man was seriously damaged, certainly not enough to be taken off the wing. He went to the door and eased it open. The Jamaicans were still playing pool, giving each other high-fives after each shot.

Shepherd shut the door. He looked at his watch. Ten past four. He picked up the makeshift knife Dreadlocks had been using. The two blades had been taken from a plastic safety razor. The bristles had been shaved off the toothbrush and the plastic melted over a flame until it was soft enough to push in the two blades. It was a nasty weapon whose only purpose was to produce a wound that would never heal properly.

Needles was lying face down on top of Dreadlocks. Shepherd pulled him off. He put the toothbrush handle into Dreadlocks's right hand, then ran it across Needles's arm. Blood flowed in two parallel lines. Then he pulled up the T-shirt Needles was wearing and made two long cuts across his stomach. They spurted blood. Shepherd cut Needles again, from side to side. The wounds were in no way life-threatening but they would need careful stitching and Needles would have to remain immobile while the wounds healed. Any movement would rip the double cuts apart.

Blood dripped down on to Dreadlocks's tracksuit bottoms. If Shepherd did this right, it would look like the two men had been fighting. He doubted they would tell the authorities what had happened. No matter how badly injured they were, they were unlikely to grass. Plus there was the embarrassment factor of admitting that one man had put them both in hospital.

Shepherd undid the laces from Dreadlocks's trainers and tied them together, then used them as a tourniquet around the man's right thigh. Then he picked up the sharpened stick and put it into Needles's hand. He pulled up the right leg of the man's tracksuit bottoms then stabbed at the calf with the pointed stick in Needles's fist. It pierced the flesh and skewered the calf muscle. Blood spurted over Needles's fingers and the leg twitched. Shepherd slowly withdrew the stick. Blood pooled in the wound, then dribbled down the leg towards the trainer. It was a slow, steady flow so he hadn't ruptured any major vessels – a serious wound but not a fatal one.

Shepherd stood up. He washed his hands in the sink, then

checked in the mirror for blood spots on his shirt. He looked down at his black Armani jeans and white Nike trainers. No blood.

Needles was groaning. His stomach glistened wetly and blood was pooling around Dreadlocks's leg.

Shepherd slipped out of the cell, leaving the door ajar. He walked slowly up the stairs, went into his own cell and lay down on his bunk. A few minutes later he heard three loud blasts on a whistle, then shouts.

Shepherd climbed off the bunk and went to the door. Prisoners all over the landing were rushing to the railings and looking down at the ones. Shepherd joined them – to have stayed in his cell while all hell was breaking out would only have drawn attention to him.

Four prison officers rushed in from the bubble carrying two metal stretchers. The prisoners on the twos and threes cheered and yelled obscenities. Rathbone came out of Needles's cell, his face pale.

Two officers went into the cell with a stretcher, and two minutes later they came out carrying Needles. He was shivering, his eyes wide open, his stomach covered in blood. The other two officers went inside with for Dreadlocks.

More officers came on to the spur and started to usher the inmates back into their cells. 'Come on, there's nothing to see,' said one.

'What happened, boss?' asked Lee. The officers were applying dressings to the wounds on Needles's stomach.

'Nothing,' said the officer.

'We're supposed to be getting our tea,' said Lee.

'Get back in your cell or you'll be on a charge,' said the officer. 'I'm easy either way.'

Down on the ones, Dreadlocks was carried out on the second stretcher. They took him straight to the stairs and up to the twos. His leg was drenched in blood, despite the tourniquet. More prisoners were crowding against the railings, trying to get a better look. The officers were shouting for them to get back into their cells.

'Would you look at all that blood!' said Lee.

The officer put a hand on Lee's arm. 'In your cell, laddie, or you're on a charge.'

Lee backed away from the railing, complaining, but headed for his cell. Shepherd followed him. He glanced up and saw Carpenter staring down from the threes. Carpenter wasn't watching the action on the ground floor, he was gazing thoughtfully at Shepherd. Then he pushed himself away from the railing and Shepherd lost sight of him. He followed Lee into the cell and the prison officer clanged the door shut behind them.

At five o'clock the prisoners were shouting and banging on their cell doors. Tea should have been served at a quarter to but the doors had remained locked after the injured men had been carried out of the spur.

'This is a bloody liberty,' said Lee. 'We're entitled to our food.'

Shepherd lay on his bunk and stared at the ceiling.

'What do you think happened down there?' asked Lee. 'Did you see all that blood?'

'Dunno,' said Shepherd.

'Looked to me like Needles and Bunton had a set-to with shivs.'

Bunton must be Dreadlocks, Shepherd realised. He hadn't known his name. Hadn't cared.

'Thought they were tight, those two,' Lee went on.

'You never know,' said Shepherd.

Down below they heard cell doors being unlocked. Lee started banging on the door again. 'Come on, we're starving here!' he yelled.

At five thirty Rathbone unlocked it. 'What's going on?' Lee asked.

'We're doing the landings one at a time.'

'You can't,' said Lee.

Rathbone grinned. 'Jason, we can do what we like.' He gestured for Lee to go and get his meal. 'You too, Macdonald.'

'I'm not hungry,' said Shepherd.

'If you don't eat, it's got to go down on your report,' said Rathbone. 'Save me the paperwork and get your tray, will you? You can always give it to Jason.'

Shepherd climbed down and went to the ones with his flask. The doors there were already locked.

He had chosen the roast turkey option, and had it with mashed potatoes and carrots, then a raspberry yoghurt. He filled his Thermos with hot water and headed back to his cell. Lloyd-Davies was by the bubble. She waved over at him. 'Bob, I got you on the gym list for tomorrow.'

'Thanks, ma'am,' said Shepherd.

'No need to thank me, your name was next on the list,' she said.

As Shepherd walked back to his cell he realised what had happened: Needles or Bunton, possibly both, must have been on the gym list. Two birds with one stone.

Shepherd and Weston were supposedly under the supervision of Hamilton while they cleaned the twos, but he was in the bubble talking to Tony Stafford. Weston worked in silence, humming, as they moved methodically along the landing with their mops and buckets.

Shepherd heard footsteps behind him. It was Carpenter, holding a mop and bucket. He smiled at Weston. 'Give us a moment, will you, Charlie?' he said.

Weston picked up his bucket and headed to the far side of the landing.

Carpenter put down his bucket and began to mop the floor. 'What's your game, Bob?' he asked.

'It's not a game,' said Shepherd.

'That's three men you've put in hospital now,' said Carpenter. 'Are you taking on Digger, is that it?'

'I don't want to run the spur, I just want out of here.'

'And how does crippling cons achieve that?'

'Needles started it.'

'This isn't the fucking playground,' said Carpenter.

'If I hadn't given it to him, he'd have given it to me,' said Shepherd.

'You carry on this way you'll fuck it up for everyone.'

'How does me taking care of myself fuck it up for you, Gerry?'

Carpenter stopped cleaning. 'If cons start fighting each other we're going to be banged up twenty-three hours a day. That's one. We're going to have the cells turned over every day for weapons. That's two. And if the governor thinks Tony Stafford's lost control of the block, he'll be moved. That's three. Any one of those fucks up my life, and I'm not going to stand for it.'

'That'd be a threat, would it?' asked Shepherd.

'You want to fight me now, do you?' asked Carpenter.

'I don't want to fight anyone. Like I said, I just want out of here.'

Carpenter started mopping again. 'You carry on like this, they'll put you in segregation.'

'The only way they'll know what happened is if someone grasses,' said Shepherd. 'And if someone grasses, they'll have me to deal with.'

'Now you're the one making threats.'

Shepherd looked across at him. 'It's only a threat if you're planning to grass me up,' he said.

'I don't have to grass anyone up,' Carpenter sneered. 'I'm perfectly capable of taking care of business myself.'

'So I don't have a problem. I wanted out of my cell, so I had to take care of the Bosnian. Needles was planning to cut me up, so I took care of him.'

'And what next?'

Shepherd shrugged. 'Like I said, I need someone on the out to get my case sorted. One way or the other.'

Carpenter leaned on his mop. 'What if I help you get a message out? Will you stop sending inmates to hospital?'

Shepherd grinned. 'I'll be as good as gold.'

'Let me think about it.'

They heard the buzz of prisoners arriving back from the workshops. Carpenter picked up his bucket and headed for the stairs.

Shepherd smiled to himself. He'd just picked up two nuggets of gold from Carpenter. He had a vested interest in Tony Stafford running the block. And there was something in his cell that he didn't want found.

*　　*　　*

215

'You're going to be late for school,' said Sue Shepherd, ruffling her son's hair. 'You're always like this on a Monday.'

'This toast's burnt,' said Liam. He was sitting at the kitchen table, his backpack on the chair next to him.

'It's not burnt. It's fine.'

'It's black.'

'It's brown.'

'It tastes burnt.'

'Well, put more jam on it.' Sue looked at her wristwatch. It was a Cartier, a present from Dan. He'd given it to her as she lay in her hospital bed with newly born Liam in her arms.

'Just because I put jam on it doesn't mean it's not burnt,' said Liam slowly, as if she was a simpleton.

'I know that,' said Sue. 'If you don't want to eat it, leave it. I've got things to do, Liam, don't make life difficult for me. Please.'

Liam sniffed at his toast, then put it down and drank his milk.

Sue picked up her bag and a handful of bills that needed paying. 'Ready?' she asked. She looked out of the kitchen window. The grass needed cutting. Just one of a hundred jobs Dan had been promising to do. She mentally cursed her husband.

'What?' asked Liam.

Sue realised she must have spoken aloud. 'Nothing,' she said. 'Come on, let's go.'

Liam grabbed his backpack and rushed into the hallway. He stood at the front door as Sue set the burglar alarm, then opened it for her. She double-locked the door and waited for the alarm to stop bleeping.

She opened the door of her black VW Golf and Liam climbed into the back and fastened his seat-belt. The school-run was a necessary evil, the price of living in London. Sue had been pestering her husband for years to move to the countryside, but his job with the Met meant he had to be in the city. It was her own fault, she thought ruefully, as she slotted in the ignition key and started the car.

Shepherd had acceded to her demand that he quit the SAS, but she hadn't been specific enough about his replacement career. When he'd told her he'd been offered a job as a policeman she imagined him in a uniform, driving a police car, manning a desk, maybe, working shifts, but at least spending most of his time at home with her and Liam. She'd never imagined that his job as a policeman would be every bit as dangerous and demanding as his military career, and that she'd see even less of him than when he was a soldier.

'What's wrong, Mummy?' asked Liam.

'Nothing,' said Sue.

'Were you thinking about Daddy?'

Sue twisted around in her seat. 'Why do you say that?'

'You look sad.'

Sue forced a smile. 'I'm not sad,' she said. 'Ready for blast-off?'

'All systems go!' Liam laughed.

Liam's school was half an hour's drive away and the main roads were packed with early-morning traffic but, like most hard-pressed mothers, Sue knew several rat-runs to the school, weaving in and out of narrow streets. At one point she drove across a filling-station forecourt to cut out a set of traffic lights. She'd made the journey so many times that she drove on auto-pilot, her mind running through all the household tasks she had to get done before she picked up Liam.

'Mummy, I can't get my bag.'

'What?' A black cab braked in front of her. Sue pounded on her horn then pulled round it. The driver scowled at her as she drove by.

'My bag, Mummy, it's on the floor.'

Sue glanced over her shoulder. Liam's backpack had fallen off the seat and he was reaching for it.

'Leave it, we're nearly there,' said Sue, blipping the accelerator and crossing a traffic light as it turned red.

'I want my book!' whined Liam. Sue heard him unclip his seat-belt.

217

She glared at him in the rear-view mirror. 'Just behave, will you?' she shouted. 'Do that seat-belt up *now!*'

'I want my bag.'

'Seat-belt. Now!'

Liam muttered under his breath but did as he was told.

'You can get it when we stop,' said Sue.

'I want it now.'

Another set of lights turned amber. Sue's foot instinctively pressed on the accelerator but she realised she'd be cutting it too close so she braked instead, so hard that the seat-belt cut into her shoulder.

'Ow!' squealed Liam. 'That hurt.'

Sue unclipped her seat-belt and twisted round to reach for the backpack. It was heavy with books and sports equipment and she felt a stab of pain in her back and swore.

'What's wrong, Mummy?' asked Liam.

'Nothing,' said Sue. She grunted as she heaved the bag on to the seat next to Liam. A car behind her sounded its horn. 'All right, all right,' she muttered.

She turned back, put the car in gear and stamped on the accelerator. It was only as the car leaped forward that she saw the lights were still red against her. She swore and took her foot off the accelerator. Then saw the truck, and time seemed to stop as if all her senses were in overdrive. It was a Tesco truck, white with the supermarket's logo across the side. She could see the driver, his mouth open, his eyes fearful and staring. He had a shaved head and was wearing wire-framed spectacles. The horn of the car behind her was still beeping. But not beeping at her, not telling her that the lights had changed. She could see the sky overhead, pure blue and cloudless. She could hear Liam screaming. Then time speeded up as she stamped on the brakes and swung the steering-wheel hard to the right. It was too late and she knew she was going to hit the truck – and hit it hard. She wanted to turn round and tell Liam she was sorry for shouting at him, sorry for swearing, sorry for what was about to happen, but there was no time. She screamed as the car ploughed into the side of the truck.

*   *   *

Shepherd waited until after dinner before he went down to use the phone. He'd changed into his prison-issue trackshirt and was carrying a blue prison towel. As he headed down the stairs Lloyd-Davies called, 'Macdonald, gym list!'

'I just want to make a phone call, ma'am,' Shepherd shouted. 'Won't be a minute.'

'If you're not right back we go without you,' said Lloyd-Davies.

Shepherd passed Digger on the stairs. He was wearing a Nike tracksuit and spotless white trainers. He glared, and muttered something under his breath that Shepherd didn't catch.

One of the phones was being used by Simon Hitchcock but the second was free. Shepherd tapped in his pin number, and then Uncle Richard's. His call was short and to the point. He said he wanted his Walkman to be sent in. As soon as possible. He replaced the receiver. He knew he was taking a risk, but it was a calculated one. Carpenter had opened up to him, and his offer to pass a message to the outside was a huge step forward. Shepherd was ready to take advantage of it. Carpenter had as good as admitted that he was being helped on the inside. Shepherd's next step was to try to get him to talk about his plan to kill Sandy Roper. If he could get Carpenter talking about it on tape then he'd stay behind bars for the foreseeable future, no matter what happened to the drugs charges. The downside? Shepherd didn't want to think about it. He just wanted to be on the out. With his wife and son.

As he walked up to the gym group Gerald Carpenter smiled at Lloyd-Davies. 'Sorry I'm late, ma'am,' he said. He was wearing shorts and a Reebok sweatshirt, and carrying his towel and a bottle of Highland Spring.

'You're not the last,' said Lloyd-Davies, ticking off his name on her clipboard.

Digger was standing by the barred gate doing stretching exercises. He nodded at Carpenter, who went over and stood next to him. 'How's Needles?' he asked.

'All cut up,' said Digger. He grinned at his own joke.

'He'll be okay, yeah?'

'The cuts were tramlines, almost impossible to stitch. He's going to have to lie in bed for a couple of weeks.'

'Do you know why Bunton went for him?'

Digger looked at Carpenter. He was still smiling but his eyes were hard.

'What?' asked Carpenter innocently.

'Don't fuck me around, Gerry. You know as well as I do what went down.'

'I heard that Bunton laid into Needles with a shiv and that Needles gave as good as he got.'

Digger chuckled, but his eyes had narrowed to slits.

Carpenter held up his hands. 'Fine, whatever.'

'Nothing happens in this houseblock without you knowing,' said Digger, 'and mostly it happens because you say it happens.'

'You saying that I put Needles in hospital?' asked Carpenter.

'No profit in you doing that,' said Digger, 'but you know as well as me that it was Macdonald done the dirty deed.'

'Anyone see him?'

'He was seen going in and he was seen coming out. Did anyone see him cut Needles? No. But I don't need no calculator to add two and two.'

Carpenter leaned on the rail. Down below, Macdonald was walking away from the phones. 'It ends here and now,' he said quietly.

'Needles isn't going to be on his back for ever,' said Digger. 'And he's going to come after Macdonald, big-time.'

'Didn't you hear what I just said? I said it ends now. You tell Needles that if he moves against Macdonald, I'll destroy his life, inside and outside.'

'Is Macdonald your man now? Is that it?'

'If he was, that'd be my business, not yours,' said Carpenter. 'But it's nothing to do with him working for me. It's to do with wanting a quiet life. You do what you have to do to keep Needles quiet, okay?'

'Okay,' said Digger.

'I mean it, Digger,' said Carpenter. 'I'm holding you responsible.'

'I hear you.'

Carpenter patted Digger on the back. 'Tell him, I'll take care of any expenses. And I'll put a couple of grand his mother's way, too.'

'He'll appreciate that,' said Digger.

'Come on, let's go and burn off some of that excess energy.'

Shepherd upped the speed on the treadmill. On the outside he tried to run at least five kilometres a day, ideally on grass, and he was determined to take full advantage of whatever gym time Lloyd-Davies could get for him.

There were more than two dozen prisoners in the gym. Most of the West Indians had gathered at the weights area where Digger was holding court. A prison officer watched them from the balcony with a look of disdain. Carpenter was on a bike, his legs pumping furiously. The machine next to him was unoccupied, but Shepherd didn't want to seem too eager to approach him. Carpenter's routine never varied. He did thirty minutes' running on the treadmill, ten minutes on bike, and whatever time was left he spent on one of the multi-gyms. The only variation came on the multi-gym when he'd work either his arms or his legs. He never went near the weights area, and he rarely spoke to anyone. He never had to ask for a piece of equipment to be vacated: prisoners always moved away as soon as he approached. He'd acknowledge them with a tight smile and a nod, but never a word of thanks, accepting the deference as his right.

Shepherd upped the speed of the treadmill and increased the incline. His calf muscles burned but he ignored the pain. He fixed his eyes on the wall and concentrated on maintaining his rhythm. A couple of minutes before Carpenter was due to finish cycling, Shepherd got off the treadmill and went over to one of the multi-gyms. He was working on his pecs when Carpenter came over. He got off and nodded for Carpenter to take his place.

'Can I ask you something, Gerry?' said Macdonald, as Carpenter pulled the metal bar down to his chest.

'What?' Carpenter grunted.

'It's just that you're smarter than the average bear, right, so why are you inside?'

'I was set up. Undercover cops. Got me on conspiracy.'

'Bastards.'

'I was so bloody careful. Followed the golden rules. Never went near the drugs. Never went near the money. Never wrote anything down.'

'What – nothing? Not even phone numbers and stuff?'

'Especially phone numbers. Never write them down, never store them in your phone's memory.'

'Yeah, but I can't remember my own, never mind anyone else's,' lied Shepherd. His memory, of course, was infallible. 'If it wasn't for the phone book in my mobile, I'd never be able to call anyone.'

'Recipe for bloody disaster. You know the cops can access them whenever they want?'

'If they get hold of the phone, you mean?'

'Nah, that's the point. They don't need it. They can access all the info on the Sim card over the airwaves. Every number you've called, every number that's called you, every number in the phone book.'

'Bloody hell,' said Shepherd. It was old news to him. Getting access to a suspect's phone records was one of the first things the police did when they had a target under surveillance. All they needed was the number and the technical boys did the rest.

'I've known half a dozen guys go down because of info on their phones,' said Carpenter. 'They're a liability. Stick to landlines or throwaway mobiles, and never write *anything* down.'

'That's what I was asking,' said Shepherd. 'How do you remember everything? Is it a photographic memory?'

Carpenter stopped working on his arms and wiped his neck with his towel. 'It's a technique,' he said. 'Anyone can do it. You have to remember images instead of numbers. Say the first digit is five. You represent it with a five-letter word. Like tiger. Then say the next digit is three. Use dog for that. So you have a tiger, followed by a dog. Easy to remember, right? Five then three. You just do that for every number.'

The technique made sense, and Shepherd could see how an image would be easier to remember than a string of numbers. It wasn't the way his own memory worked – he simply remembered the numbers.

'How many numbers have you remembered that way?' Shepherd asked.

'Couple of hundred. It's virtually foolproof.'

'And what about bank-account numbers and stuff? It works for that?'

Carpenter looked at him and for a moment Shepherd thought he'd pushed it too far. He shrugged. 'Just interested, that's all. I have to write down all my pin numbers and I'm buggered if I know my bank-account number.' The lie came easily. He had spent several months being coached by actors and psychologists before he'd gone on his first undercover operation and he knew how to mask the tell-tale signs of dishonesty.

'What the hell? It's not as if it's a secret,' said Carpenter. He started working his arms again. 'Memory experts do it all the time. You know *pi*, right? From school. The circumference of a circle divided by whatever. The number never ends.'

'Sure.'

'Well, there's a guy in Tokyo who can rattle of the value of *pi* to more than forty-two thousand places.'

'Sounds like he should get a life,' said Shepherd.

'Macdonald!'

Shepherd turned his head. It was Hamilton, standing at the door to the gym. 'Stop nattering,' Hamilton shouted, his Adam's apple bobbing up and down. 'Your brief's here.'

Shepherd walked away from the multi-gym, frowning. 'Have I got time to change, Mr Hamilton?' he asked.

'He's waiting for you,' said Hamilton, 'and I've got work to do.' He waved at the officer on the balcony. 'Macdonald's brief is here,' he shouted. 'I'll take him back to the wing when he's done.'

The prison officer flashed Hamilton a thumbs-up but his face remained impassive.

Shepherd followed Hamilton out of the gym. When they reached the administration block, the officer showed him into one of the private interview rooms. Hargrove was sitting behind the Formica table and stood up awkwardly. Shepherd could tell that something was wrong.

'Press the bell when you're done,' Hamilton said to Hargrove.

Shepherd wondered what had happened. His first thought was that the operation had been blown and that he was about to be pulled out, but if that was the case there'd be no need for a conversation in the interview room. His second thought was that Hargrove was there to tell him Roper had been killed. The superintendent's face was like granite and he was avoiding Shepherd's eyes.

It was when Hargrove asked him to sit down that Shepherd realised he was there for personal reasons and that could only mean Sue or Liam. 'What is it?' he asked. 'What's happened?'

'Sit down, please,' said Hargrove, folding his arms across his chest.

'What's happened?' repeated Shepherd, his voice shaking. 'Is it Liam?'

Hargrove put his hands up, fingers splayed, and when he spoke it was with the measured tones that a trainer might use to calm a restless horse. 'There's no easy way to say this, Spider. It's Sue. There's been an accident. She's dead.'

Shepherd stared at Hargrove, unable to say anything. He felt light-headed, as if all the blood had drained out of his brain. He wanted to to tell Hargrove that there must have been a mistake, that there was no way Sue could be dead.

'I'm sorry, Spider. I'm so, so sorry.'

Shepherd's mouth was bone dry. He saw movement out of the corner of his eye. It was Hamilton, watching from one of the observation windows. He sat down and put his hands on the table, palms down.

Hargrove sat opposite him. 'It was a car accident. She died instantly, Spider. It was nothing to do with Carpenter.'

Shepherd put his head into his hands, clenched his fists and pulled at his hair, wanting to feel the pain, trying to use it to blot out the reality of Sue's death. Images flashed through his mind. The first time he'd set eyes on her, walking down the main street in Hereford, one of half a dozen girls out on the town. She was wearing a bright yellow dress, cut low to show lots of cleavage, the hemline mid-thigh, a thin gold chain and crucifix round her neck, a cheap plastic watch on her left wrist, a gold charm bracelet on the right. The bracelet had belonged to her grandmother.

Shepherd had been with three of his friends from 22 SAS and they'd stopped and chatted with the girls. Shepherd hadn't been able to take his eyes off Sue. She'd had a couple of drinks and kept insisting that she'd never go out with a soldier, that she knew what they were like, how they broke hearts wherever the went. She'd walked away and called for her friends to follow her, but Shepherd had hurried after her and begged her to go for a drink with him. He could remember every word of their first conversation in the snug of a smoky pub. How she hated her job, how her boss had body-odour, how she was bored with Hereford and how she wanted more than anything else to travel the world. How she didn't want kids because kids only held you back, and wanted to live her life to the full before she thought about settling down. They'd married six months later in a small stone church on the outskirts of Hereford and Liam had been born the following year. She'd never got to travel the world. Then, images of the last time he had seen her flashed through his mind. 'I hate you!' she'd shouted. 'I hope I never see you again, ever! You can rot in here for all I care!' and she'd dragged Liam out of the visitors' room. The last thing she'd said to him was that she hated him. She hadn't meant it, it had been a lie, but the words had hurt then and the hurt was a million times worse now. Now that she was dead.

'Spider?'

Shepherd opened his eyes. 'How's Liam?'

'He's fine.'

'Where is he?'

'Sue's mum's taking care of him.'

'I've got to see him.'

'Absolutely. We're arranging it as we speak.'

Shepherd pushed back his chair and stood up. 'Now,' he repeated. 'I want to see him now.'

'Spider, sit down and listen to what I have to say.'

'It's over,' said Shepherd firmly. 'This operation is over. My son needs me. I'm out of here.'

'Hear me out,' said Hargrove. 'Listen to what I've got to say and then we'll get things sorted.'

Shepherd glared at him, then slowly sat down.

'Liam is with Sue's mum, and he's fine. He was wearing his seat-belt, Sue wasn't.'

'He was there when she died?' asked Shepherd. 'For God's sake, what the hell happened?'

'She was taking him to school. Jumped a red light. Hit a truck. It was an accident, pure and simple.'

'Sue always wore her seat-belt,' said Shepherd. 'She had a thing about it. Wouldn't even start the car if everyone wasn't buckled up.'

'The front of the car went under the truck, Liam was in the back. The emergency services were there within minutes. He was shaken but physically he's fine.'

'Oh, Christ,' said Shepherd, putting his head in his hands again. 'He saw what happened? He saw her die?'

'He was in shock, Spider. He doesn't remember the accident.'

'He's blocking it out. He needs me.'

'No question. And we're going to take you to see him. Soon as we can arrange it.'

Shepherd leaned back in his chair. Hamilton had walked away from the observation window. 'Sue's mum came down from Hereford?'

'The Regiment sent a helicopter. You've still got friends there.'

Even a career policeman like Hargrove wouldn't understand the bond that linked the men of the Special Air Service, Shepherd thought. Once you joined the Regiment you were part of it for ever, and it remained a part of you. It was a bond as strong as blood. Stronger, sometimes. Walking away from the SAS had been the hardest thing Shepherd had ever done, but he'd done it for Sue.

'She's moved into your house, and we've fixed up a psychiatrist to talk to Liam.'

'He doesn't need a psychiatrist,' said Shepherd. 'I'll talk to him.'

Hargrove nodded sympathetically. 'We've spoken to the school, and they'll do everything they can,' he said.

'I'm not staying here,' said Shepherd. 'This operation is over.'

'We're entering the end phase, Spider. We're almost there. Just a few more days.' He held up his right hand, his thumb and first finger almost touching. 'We're this close to getting Carpenter. His men are putting the frighteners on Roper. All we have to do is tie them together and we put the lot of them away.'

'My son is more important than a shit like Carpenter.'

'Of course he is. And of course he needs you. But if you pull out now, we don't have time to get anyone else close to Carpenter. He'll finish what he's started and he'll walk. He'll *walk*, Spider. He'll be out on the streets bringing in heroin and cocaine and more kids are going to die.'

'That's not my problem.'

'And what about Elliott? Carpenter had him killed. Is that going to be for nothing?'

Shepherd's eyes hardened. 'You can't lay that on me,' he said quietly.

'I'm not laying anything on you,' said Hargrove. 'But Carpenter's evil and he needs to be stopped. The only person who can do that is you. There is no one else, Spider. If you pull out now, Carpenter's home, free, and everything we've worked for turns to shit.'

'It's just a job,' said Shepherd. 'Liam is my son. Carpenter is an assignment.'

'Carpenter ruins lives. God knows how many die from the drugs he brings into the country. And he kills people. Let's not forget that. Elliott wasn't the first undercover agent he's killed, and if he gets out he won't be the last.'

'It's not fair to dump that on me.'

'I'm not dumping anything on you. If you decide you want to pull out, I'll respect that. Hell, I don't have any choice. No one can force you to do what you do, Spider. I, of all people, know that.'

Shepherd sighed. His mind was still whirling through memories of Sue. The way she'd rubbed his backside as they stood in front of the altar and prepared to say their vows. The first time they'd made love in her bedsit, her on top, her long blonde hair round her shoulders, the way she'd kissed him afterwards and whispered his name. The look of pride in her eyes when the nurse handed Liam to him, his face all red and puffy, wrapped in a soft white towel and crying as if he hated the world and everyone in it.

'We'll get you together with Liam, you have my word on that. But hold fire on making a decision about the operation a while longer.'

'You're asking me to go back on the wing after what's happened?'

'If you leave with me now, you won't be able to come back. Too many people will know. But if you let me arrange it, we can get you out of here for a few hours, then get you back in.'

'A few hours isn't going to cut it. Liam has lost his mother. I've lost . . .' Shepherd couldn't bring himself to finish the sentence.

'I know,' said Hargrove.

'I can't believe you're asking me to do this. Anyone else would have taken me straight to see my son.' He paused. 'I've never asked you, but have you got kids?'

'Two. Girl and boy. Charlotte's married with a daughter of her own and James is off to university next year.'

'Liam is seven,' said Shepherd.

'I know.'

'He needs his father.'

'And you need time to grieve. I know that.'

'It's not about me. It's about my son.'

'It's about both of you. You need each other. I know what I'm asking, Spider, and I wouldn't if I didn't think it was absolutely necessary.'

'He's one man. We put him behind bars and someone else will take his place. Just because Gerald Carpenter goes down it doesn't mean the drugs business will grind to a halt.'

'He's a murderer.'

'He's not charged with murder, though, is he?'

'If you stay undercover, he might be.'

Shepherd cursed.

'I am sorry about your wife,' said Hargrove.

Shepherd closed his eyes and more images of Sue flashed through his mind. Curled up on the sofa, watching *EastEnders* as if her life depended on it. Testing the heat of the iron by patting it with her fingers, then yelping when she burned herself. The expression in her eyes when she told him she wanted him to leave the Regiment because he was going to be a father and a father's place was with his family, not fighting wars in distant lands. Her pride the first time she'd seen him in his constable's uniform. And the despair when he'd told her that he was being seconded to the undercover unit. From a soldier's wife to the wife of an undercover policeman. Out of the frying-pan into the fire, she'd said. That he'd never be happy until he'd been shot again. That he had a death wish. It wasn't fair, he thought bitterly. He'd put his life on the line time and time again after joining Hargrove's unit, taking risks he'd never told Sue about, but she was the one who'd died in a stupid, meaningless accident.

'Okay,' he said. 'Let me think about it.' There was something he'd meant to tell Hargrove. Something about Carpenter. Then he remembered. 'Carpenter's pally with Ronnie Bain,' he said. 'Marijuana importer who got eight years a while back. They were pretty tight in the prison chapel. Bain's in another block but he might be helping Carpenter get messages out.' He felt disloyal to his wife. He'd just been told she was dead and now he was talking shop with Hargrove.

'We'll check him out, Spider. Thanks. And we got your message about Stafford.' The superintendent hesitated, then stood up and came round the table to put a hand on Shepherd's shoulder. 'One more thing,' he said. 'I know this is shit timing but we've got the Walkman ready. Do you want me to send it in?'

Shepherd didn't know what to say. All he could think about was that his wife was dead.

Hargrove stood up and pressed the button by the door. Hamilton opened it and stood to the side to let Hargrove out. The superintendent's feet echoed on the tiled floor, then faded. Shepherd heard the rattle of keys and a door being opened, closed, and locked. Then silence.

'Chop-chop, Macdonald,' said Hamilton. 'We haven't got all day.'

Shepherd stood up slowly and walked out of the room. Hamilton sneered at him. 'Bad news, I hope,' he said.

Shepherd stopped and turned. He took a step towards the officer, his mouth a tight line, his hands tensing into claws. He was barely breathing as he stared at Hamilton. He knew of a dozen different ways he could kill him. The heel of his hand into the nose. A chop to the bobbing Adam's apple. A finger-strike into the eyes. A back-fist to the throbbing vein in his temple. A foot-sweep to the floor followed by a stamp on the neck. Shepherd had been trained by experts, and had followed up his training with on-the job experience that few men could match. He knew what it was like to kill and knew, too, that he could take the officer's life without a moment's regret or guilt. Hamilton swallowed and took a step back, his right hand clutching for his radio. Shepherd took a deep breath, his eyes still boring into the other man's. All he had to do was make the decision. The second he decided that Hamilton should die, the training would take over and the man would be dead before he hit the ground.

There was panic in Hamilton's eyes and his hands were shaking. The colour had drained from his face and his Adam's apple was bobbing up and down as if it had a life of its own. He took a step back.

He wasn't worth it, Shepherd decided. If he killed Hamilton he'd spend the rest of his life behind bars, undercover cop or not. No man was worth that. He turned away and headed back to the wing. By the time they reached the barred door to the main corridor, Hamilton had recovered some of his composure but he still kept

230

a watchful eye on Shepherd as he unlocked and locked the doors on the way back to the remand block.

Hamilton took Shepherd along to his cell and unlocked the door. Lee was sitting at the table, writing a letter. 'I heard they pulled you out of the gym,' said Lee, as Shepherd lay down on his bunk.

Shepherd waited until Hamilton had locked the cell door. 'My brief wants more money,' he lied. 'I've got to get it transferred from overseas.'

'Leeches, all of them,' said Lee. 'How do you spell miscarriage?'

Shepherd told him, then rolled over and turned his back. Lee took the hint and wrote the rest of his letter in silence.

The prison officer threw the stick high into the air. The spaniel yelped and gave chase, its stub of a tail wagging furiously. The man loved being out in the open, breathing fresh air, grass under his feet, hearing the wind blow through the trees.

The mobile phone in his pocket warbled. He took it out and looked at the caller ID. It was Carpenter's man. Not that the officer was surprised. The phone was a pay-as-you-go and only Carpenter's man used it. The officer had insisted that the phone was the only way that Carpenter's man contacted him. If the shit ever hit the fan he could dump the mobile and no one would be any the wiser.

'Yeah?'

'Where are you?'

'Walking the dog.' The officer had never met the caller and had often wondered what he looked like. The voice had a trace of West Country in it and a slight lisp. It was deep and resonant, which suggested he was a big man. Possibly in his forties.

'When are you inside again?'

'Tonight. Night staff.'

'Can you get a message to the boss?'

'Not until the morning.'

'Fuck that.'

'The cells are locked by the time I get there and they're not opened until seven forty-five.'

'You've got a fucking key, haven't you?'

The spaniel came running back with the stick in its mouth. The officer pulled it from the excited dog and threw it as far as he could. 'I can't just go opening cell doors at night. I need a reason.'

'Well, find one.'

'If I open a door it's got to go on the incident sheet.'

'You're going to have to do what you've got to do. I have to get a message to the boss – and soon.'

The officer cursed under his breath. 'If you want me to get the message to him tonight, it'll cost you a monkey.'

'Fine,' said the man. 'Tell him he has to call me. Urgently.'

'Okay. When do I get the money?'

'Tomorrow. When he's called me.'

The line went dead. The officer smiled to himself. Five hundred quid for passing on a message. Easy money.

Shepherd heard the cell door open. It was Lloyd-Davies. Lee was standing at the washbasin as jittery as a racehorse waiting for the off. 'Association,' she said. Lee slipped out of the door.

Lloyd-Davies entered the cell and stood looking at Shepherd. He lay on his back, his hands behind his neck. 'What's wrong, Macdonald?' she asked.

'I'm fine,' said Shepherd.

'Legal problems?' she asked.

'Everything's fine.' Hamilton must have told her how he'd reacted after the visit from Hargrove.

'Do you want to talk to a Listener? I can send Ed Harris along.'

'I'm fine,' said Shepherd. 'Really.'

'Everyone has their ups and downs,' said Lloyd-Davies. 'The trick is not to bottle up the bad stuff. Talk it through with someone. No one expects you to open up to us, but the Listeners are on your side.'

'Nobody's on my side,' said Shepherd, but he regretted the words as soon as they'd left his mouth. Far better to say nothing.

'Do you want to see the doc?'

'I'm fine, ma'am. I just want to be left alone.'

Lloyd-Davies stood at the end of his bunk for a few seconds more, then left the cell.

Shepherd closed his eyes. All he could think about was Sue. Memories whirled through his mind. Holidays they'd taken. Meals they'd eaten. Arguments they'd had. Films they'd watched. And alongside the memories was the aching certainty that they were in the past and that he'd never hold or talk to her again. They were constant reminders that everything to do with Sue was in the past. Finished. Over.

His future now lay with his son. So why was he still in a cell, surrounded by scum who didn't care whether he lived or died? Why hadn't he just walked out with Hargrove? Even now all he had to do was walk down to the phones and play his Get Out of Jail Free card. One call and he'd be out with his son, where he was needed. Where he belonged.

'Shit, shit, shit.' He clenched his fist and pounded the side of his right hand against the cell wall, relishing the pain. He deserved to be hurt. He'd failed Sue: he hadn't been with her in the car. When they were together she always let him drive, and if he'd been at the wheel maybe the accident wouldn't have happened. Maybe she'd still be alive. 'Shit, shit, shit.'

He sat up and swivelled round so that he was sitting with his back to the wall. Lee had stuck pictures from magazines on the wall opposite – landscapes, forests, desert scenes, a sailboat on an ocean, all the vistas that were denied him on the inside. They were denied to Shepherd, too, but he was keeping himself behind bars. He knew why he hadn't bailed out, why he hadn't told Hargrove that the operation was terminated. Because he wanted to beat Carpenter. It was war, and he was going to do whatever it took to win.

Shepherd heard an officer shouting that association was over, and a few minutes later Lee appeared at the open cell door. 'You're wanted at the bubble,' he said.

'For what?' Shepherd asked.

'Didn't say. Stafford told me to get you down there now.'

'Tell them to go and fuck themselves.'

'What's up with you today?'

'I just want to be left alone.'

'Yeah, well, telling Tony Stafford to go fuck himself is going to get you all the peace and quiet you want,' said Lee. 'They'll send up the mufti squad and you'll be dragged off to solitary. Cardboard furniture and no toilet seat and they put stuff in your food to keep you quiet.'

Shepherd sat up and took a deep breath. He had to get back into character. No matter what had happened on the outside, as far as the Shelton population was concerned he was Bob Macdonald, career criminal and hard man, and if he strayed outside that role he risked blowing the operation.

He walked slowly along the landing. Healey was standing by the door and opened it as Shepherd walked up. He gestured for him to step out of the spur. 'What's up?' asked Shepherd.

'Don't you mean "What's up, Mr Healey"?' said the prison officer. Stafford was watching from the bubble.

'Forget it,' said Shepherd.

'Any more of your lip and I'll put you on report, Macdonald.'

Shepherd ignored him and walked over to the entrance of the control office. 'Mr Stafford, Prison Officer Healey is refusing to tell me why I'm being taken from my cell.'

'Just do as you're told, Shepherd,' said Stafford.

'Prison rule six paragraph two,' said Shepherd. '"In the control of prisoners, officers shall seek to influence them through their own example and leadership, and to enlist their willing co-operation." Seems to me that as a way of enlisting my co-operation, I should be told where I'm being taken.'

Stafford sighed. 'Governor wants to see you.'

'Because?'

'That's for him to tell you.' Stafford turned his back.

'Come on, Macdonald,' said Healey. 'I don't have all day.'

Shepherd figured that the governor wanted to talk to him about Sue's death. It was the last thing he wanted to discuss, but he knew he had no choice. Lee was right: refusing to comply would mean he'd be thrown into solitary.

234

Healey escorted Shepherd along the secure corridor to the governor's office, and waited outside while one of the secretaries took him in. The door had barely closed behind him before the governor was out of his seat, pointing an accusing finger at him. 'Just what the hell are you playing at?' asked the governor.

'What?' said Shepherd. He'd expected empty words of comfort, not a verbal attack.

'I thought going undercover meant adopting a low profile. Blending in. Now I find you've put half the bloody spur in hospital.'

Realisation dawned. The governor was talking about Jurczak, Needles and Dreadlocks.

'Nothing to do with me,' said Shepherd. He had no choice but to lie. If he admitted he'd assaulted three prisoners the governor would have the perfect excuse to call an end to the operation. And even if he didn't have the authority to have Shepherd taken out of Shelton, he could make his position untenable with just a word in the wrong ear.

'Please don't insult my intelligence, DC Shepherd,' said Gosden. 'I've a man with a broken leg, another who's been cut to ribbons, and a third with broken teeth, kidney damage and a punctured leg. Any one of those cases could get you seven years in here for real.'

'Has any of the men said I attacked them?'

'Don't play games with me, DC Shepherd. You've been in here long enough to know how it works. But the word is out. You're the new hard man on the spur.'

Shepherd shook his head. 'That's not what happened.'

'Then perhaps you'd care to enlighten me.' Gosden sat down behind his desk and picked up a pencil. He tapped it against a metal filing tray.

Shepherd stared at him. The man was presiding over an institution in which the inmates appeared to be in charge, where jobs were allocated by prisoners rather than officers, and where a drug-dealer was able to run his operation unhindered. 'I haven't done anything that hasn't been necessary to resolve this case,' said Shepherd.

'I doubt that your orders include assaulting prisoners,' said Gosden.

Shepherd took a deep breath. There was no way he could explain to the governor that his sole reason for hurting Jurczak was to get the man's place on the cleaning crew. Or that his attack on Needles and Dreadlocks had been a pre-emptive strike and that he'd been in no immediate danger. The governor was a career civil servant, and while he had once worked at the sharp end of the prison service he now dealt with inmates from behind a desk. He'd read the file on Gerald Carpenter, but that didn't mean he knew the man or understood what he was capable of. And that sometimes the end really did justify the means.

'Please don't give me any bullshit about not being able to make an omelette without cracking a few skulls,' added Gosden.

'You have my word, Governor, that any force I've had to use has been necessary and controlled.'

'Jurczak is lying in the hospital wing with a broken leg.'

'That's as may be, but he's a drug-dealer who tried to kill an immigration officer,' said Shepherd. 'He deserved what he got.'

'Unless it's slipped your mind, this is a remand wing,' said Gosden. 'Innocent until proven guilty. And even if he'd been found guilty and sentenced, what right do you have to cripple the man?'

Shepherd felt a surge of anger and fought to quell it. He wanted to tell Gosden that Jurczak had paid for his job on the cleaning crew, that the spur was so corrupt that inmates could buy themselves an easy life and that the only way they could do that way because there was at least one corrupt officer on his staff. But Shepherd knew that the time to reveal the level of corruption in Shelton was after Carpenter had been dealt with. 'Governor, you have my word on this. I had nothing to do with whatever happened to Jurczak. Or the other two men.' Outright denial was the only option available to him. There had been no witnesses to any of the attacks, nothing caught on CCTV. All he had to do was stick to his story and there was nothing the governor could do.

236

'So, it's just coincidence that a few days after you arrive, three other prisoners are in hospital?' said Gosden.

'It's a violent place.'

Gosden stared at Shepherd for several seconds. 'I could have you pulled out of the block,' he said eventually.

'I doubt it would be as simple as that, sir,' said Shepherd quietly. 'My boss reports direct to the Home Office. I might be a bog-standard DC but this operation was sanctioned at a level way above your pay scale.'

'Having you here risks a major riot. I can't be held responsible for what the prisoners do if they find out there's an undercover cop on the spur.'

'And how would they find out, sir?'

The two men stared at each other, neither prepared to look away.

'The way I see it, the only man in here who knows my true role is you,' said Shepherd.

'And let's hope it stays that way,' said Gosden.

'I wouldn't want to think that I didn't have your full support,' said Shepherd, his voice barely above a whisper. 'If my cover should be blown, my superiors would be looking very carefully in your direction.'

'That sounds like a threat,' said the governor.

'No more than your suggestion that the inmates might discover I was an undercover police officer,' said Shepherd. 'Neither of us has anything to gain by threatening each other.'

'I want your word that no more prisoners are injured.'

'I'll do my best,' said Shepherd.

Gosden rubbed the back of his neck. 'I'm going to talk to your boss. I've no choice. I have to make my reservations clear in case this all goes wrong.'

'I understand that, sir. You have to cover yourself. It's what I would do if I was in your position.'

'Do you have any idea yet if any of my officers are helping Carpenter?'

'No, sir,' lied Shepherd. 'As soon as I know, so will you.'

'I wish I could believe that, DC Shepherd,' said the governor. 'I really do.'

That night Shepherd didn't sleep. He lay on his back and stared up at the ceiling. His mind wouldn't give him a moment's peace. All he knew of Sue's death was what Hargrove had told him. 'She jumped a red light. Hit a truck. It was an accident, pure and simple. The front of the car went under the truck.' That was all the information he had, but his subconscious kept playing it back in a thousand variations. Different trucks. Different crashes. But the ending was always the same. Sue in the wreckage, covered in blood, her eyes wide and staring. Liam in the back of the car, crying.

At seven thirty Lee woke up, washed and ate his cereal while watching breakfast television. The spyglass clicked open and closed at seven forty and the cell door was opened at eight. Lee must have sensed that something was wrong because he said nothing to Shepherd before he disappeared on to the landing.

Twenty minutes later, Amelia Heartfield appeared at the doorway. She was wearing a black pullover with epaulettes, and black trousers that were slightly too small for her. 'What's wrong, Bob?' she asked.

'Just leave me alone,' said Shepherd. He knew he was out of character. Bob Macdonald wouldn't lie on his bed sulking: he would express his rage. He'd lash out, verbally and physically, make someone pay for what he was going through. 'I don't want food, I don't want to watch television, I don't want to clean floors or weave bloody baskets. I just want some peace and quiet.'

'Swearing will get you on report, Bob,' she said, almost apologetically. 'You know that. Don't give me a hard time.'

'I don't think "bloody" counts as swearing any more,' said Shepherd. 'Just leave me alone.'

'You've got visitors,' said Amelia. 'Police.'

'From where?'

'Glasgow.'

Shepherd swung his legs off the bed. They must be Hargrove's way of getting him out of prison. 'What do they want?'

'You know the police, Bob. They treat us like mushrooms. But I think they're taking you up north for an ID parade.'

Shepherd wanted to rush down the landing because the sooner he was off the spur the sooner he could be with his son, but it was vital to stay in character. Bob Macdonald wouldn't want to be driven up north by Scottish detectives. 'Shit,' he said, and grimaced.

'Bad news?'

'I've had better.'

'Is that what the chat with your brief was about?'

'He didn't mention it.'

'If it is an ID parade, you've got the right to have your solicitor there. Word to the wise.'

Shepherd was surprised at her concern for his welfare and smiled gratefully. 'Thanks,' he said.

Amelia gestured with her chin. 'Come on, let's not keep them waiting longer than we have to,' she said.

She walked him along the landing and down to the ground floor. Lee was there, playing pool with one of the West Indians. 'What's up, Bob?' he called, as Shepherd walked by.

'Jocks are trying to pin something on me,' Shepherd called back, loud enough for several prisoners to hear him. He wanted the wing to know why he was being hauled out.

Amelia walked Shepherd out of the remand wing and down the secure corridor to the reception area. Two men were waiting there, big men in dark raincoats. Shepherd recognised one but blanked him as Amelia dealt with the processing paperwork. He was Jimmy 'Razor' Sharpe, a twenty-year veteran of the Strathclyde Police who had worked with Shepherd on several undercover cases. Hargrove must have sent him so that Shepherd would see a friendly face.

'When will you be bringing him back?' asked Amelia.

The man Shepherd didn't know shrugged. He was over six feet tall with broad shoulders and a boxer's nose. 'We're running him to Glasgow, and then we've got to put him in front of a little old lady in intensive care. It'll take as long as it takes.'

'If he's out overnight we have to ensure that the arrangements are in place for him to be fed.'

The man walked up to Amelia and looked down his nose at her. 'There's a seventy-year-old woman up in Glasgow who got shot in the legs when three men held up her local post office with sawn-off shotguns. She's a grandmother who just happened to be in the wrong place at the wrong time and I think your sympathies would be better with her than with a scumbag like Macdonald.'

'You're saying he shot her?' asked Amelia.

'I didn't shoot anyone,' said Shepherd. 'This is a fit-up.'

The man pointed a warning finger at Shepherd. 'You speak when spoken to, Macdonald,' he said.

'Macdonald is here on remand,' said Amelia. 'Until his court case, he's innocent until proven guilty.'

'Yeah, yeah, yeah,' said the man, 'and the Tooth Fairy gives me a blow-job every night.'

'What did you say?' said Amelia, her eyes hardening.

'Just do the paperwork,' said the man. 'We run him by the witness, and if he isn't our man we'll have him back in his cell before his sheets are cold.'

Amelia looked as if she wanted to argue, but she countersigned two sheets of paper, put one into a file and closed it. She handed the other to the detective.

'Are we all done?' he asked, folding it and putting it into his coat pocket.

'He's your responsibility now,' said Amelia.

Sharpe took out a pair of handcuffs and fastened his left wrist to Shepherd's right.

'Remember what I told you, Bob,' said Amelia, as Sharpe took him towards the exit.

'Will do, Ma'am, and thanks,' replied Shepherd.

There was a blue Vauxhall Vectra in the courtyard, its engine running. Sharpe opened the rear door and let Shepherd slide in, then joined him. Even in the car Sharpe stayed in character, his face impassive, his body language suggesting that there were a million things he'd rather be doing than babysitting an armed robber.

The other detective got into the front passenger seat and pointed towards the gate. The driver, a small, balding man with the collar of his leather jacket turned up, put the car into gear and pressed the accelentor.

Shepherd twisted in his seat. Amelia was standing outside the reception centre, a clipboard in her hand, watching them drive away.

The Vauxhall stopped at the gate. A prison officer in a padded jacket walked over to the driver and checked the paperwork through the open window. He stared at Shepherd. 'Date of birth?' he asked.

Shepherd gave him the date in the Macdonald legend.

'Prison number?'

Shepherd told him.

The officer asked to see the three detectives' IDs and one by one they held up their warrant cards. He checked their faces against their photographs, then stepped back from the car and waved at a colleague. The huge gate rattled back and the driver wound up the window. 'The sweet smell of freedom,' he muttered, under his breath.

Sharpe waited until the car was on the main road, driving away from the prison before he said, 'Sorry about your loss, Spider.'

Shepherd nodded, but didn't say anything. Sharpe introduced his two associates. The big man with the boxer's nose was Tim Bicknelle, a new addition to Hargrove's squad, and the driver was Nigel Rosser. 'We call him Tosser 'cos he once tossed a caber,' said Sharpe. 'That's what we tell him, anyway.'

Rosser grinned good-naturedly and flashed a V-sign at Sharpe.

'Just keep your eyes on the road and your foot on the pedal,' said Sharpe.

'Thanks for putting the word out that I shoot little old ladies,' said Shepherd. 'That'll put me one step above the nonces.'

'Don't worry. When we take you back we'll make sure the screws know you're not in the frame for the Glasgow job,' Sharpe told him.

Bicknelle opened the glove compartment and took out a stainless-steel flask with two plastic-wrapped Marks and Spencer's sandwiches.

He handed them back to Shepherd. 'Coffee,' he said. 'The boss said you liked it black with no sugar.'

Shepherd put the flask between his legs. 'Thanks.' He studied the sandwiches. One was beef on brown bread, the other chicken salad on white.

'Thought you might like a change from prison food,' said Sharpe.

'Bloody right,' said Shepherd. He used his teeth to rip open the pack of beef sandwiches and bit into one.

'Plan is to run you round the M25 and up the motorway, checking for tails,' said Sharpe. 'Assuming we're clear, we'll take you home. Liam and his grandmother are there. We've got a change of clothes and a washbag in the boot. We can stop at a service station and spruce you up.'

Shepherd continued to chew. He was still wearing his burgundy prison tracksuit, which he'd been wearing when he was pulled out of the gym to see Hargrove, and he hadn't showered recently.

'Story we've spun is that we're taking you to Glasgow so we'll have to stay overnight,' continued Sharpe. 'Figure we'll get you back inside by tomorrow evening. Gives you the best part of a day with your boy.'

A day, thought Shepherd. Twenty-four hours. Sue had died and that was all Hargrove could give him with Liam.

'I know that's bugger-all, Spider, but any longer than that and it's going to raise red flags.'

Shepherd said nothing.

Sharpe leaned over and undid the handcuffs. 'What's it like inside?' he asked.

'Ninety per cent boredom, ten per cent on a knife edge,' said Shepherd. 'The inmates run it, pretty much. If anything were to kick off, there's nothing the officer can do except call for reinforcements, so they're given a fair bit of leeway.'

'And how's the target?'

'He's a hard bastard. I'm walking on eggshells.'

'Rather you than me,' said Sharpe. 'I'd go stir-crazy.'

'You get used to it.'

Bicknelle offered Shepherd a bottle of Jameson's whiskey. 'Do you want a stiffener in your coffee?' he asked.

Shepherd was tempted but he didn't want to turn up at home smelling of drink so he declined it. He unscrewed the top of the Thermos and poured himself some coffee.

'Got it from Starbucks,' said Sharpe. 'None of that instant crap.'

It smelt rich and aromatic, a far cry from the insipid brew Shepherd had got used to on the wing. Ahead of them were two big motorcycles were parked at the roadside. One peeled away from the kerb and drove in front of the Vauxhall. The rider was dressed from head to toe in black leather with a gleaming black full-face helmet. The second waited until the Vauxhall had passed, then followed.

'They're with us,' said Bicknelle. He took a small transceiver from his coat pocket and spoke into it. 'Bravo One, check?'

The transceiver buzzed. 'Bravo One, loud and clear.'

'Bravo Two, check?'

The transceiver buzzed again. 'On your tail,' said the rider behind.

Bicknelle put the whiskey into the glove compartment and settled back in his seat.

'It's Elliott's funeral day after tomorrow,' said Sharpe.

'I didn't know that,' said Shepherd.

'He was good guy, was Jonathan,' said Bicknelle. 'For a Spurs fan.'

'You worked with him, didn't you?' Sharpe asked Shepherd.

'Drugs bust, five years back. He was my introduction to a Turkish gang in north London, but we went back a long way. We were probationers together. You going to the funeral?'

'Hargrove's vetoed all attendance,' Sharpe said. 'Carpenter'll probably have the funeral staked out.'

'How did he die?' asked Shepherd.

'Two guys on a motorbike pulled up next to him at a red light. Bang, bang, thank you and good night. Bike was trashed, a totally professional job.'

'How's his wife bearing up?'

'Sedated to the eyeballs. She was in the car with him when it happened.'

'Christ,' whispered Shepherd. Hargrove hadn't gone into details, which was typical. He must have reckoned that Shepherd didn't need to know the manner of Elliott's murder. 'No kids, though, right?'

Sharpe grimaced. 'She's pregnant. Two months. He didn't even know. She was planning to surprise him.'

Shepherd shuddered. He hadn't opened the chicken-salad sandwich and he'd lost his appetite. He offered it to Sharpe, but the detective shook his head.

'If that's going spare, I'll have it,' said Rosser.

Shepherd passed it to him. 'Who's representing the squad?' he asked.

'There'll be plenty of uniforms,' said Sharpe, 'but Hargrove isn't going.'

'So the answer's no one?' said Shepherd. He hated the idea that none of Elliott's associates would be there to say goodbye but he understood the logic behind it. One of Carpenter's men with a long lens would be able to blow the cover of any undercover cop who turned up.

'We're sending flowers, and Hargrove has been to see her,' said Sharpe. 'But we've got to make sure that bastard Carpenter spends the rest of his life behind bars.'

'Amen to that,' said Rosser.

The sun was high in the sky when the Vauxhall Vectra pulled in front of the three-bedroom semi-detached in Ealing. It was a warm, sunny day. As Sharpe opened the car door and climbed out, Shepherd heard birdsong. He looked out of the passenger window at the house. It had been their home for almost six years. They'd moved into it when Liam had been crawling. There were so many memories of so many good times. Shepherd got out of the car. He'd washed at a service station on the M1 and changed into a denim shirt and blue jeans. He hadn't shaved because he couldn't afford to return to Shelton clean-shaven. Scottish cops wouldn't have bothered to let Bob Macdonald shave.

'We'll leave you to it, Spider,' said Sharpe. 'We'll pick you up tomorrow. Give us a call if you need us.' He told Shepherd his mobile number.

Shepherd continued to stare at the house as Sharpe got back into the car and it drove away. He looked up at the roof. There was a slate loose near the chimneys. He had promised Sue he would fix it. The gutters needed painting, another job she had been nagging him about. He felt a sudden urge to apologise to her for all the jobs he'd failed to do, the times he hadn't been there for her.

He walked towards the front door, his feet crunching on the gravelled path. The door opened and, for a wild moment, Shepherd thought it was Sue standing there, that it had all been a terrible mistake and she was still alive. But it wasn't: it was her mother, Moira, in her late fifties, tall and striking, with Sue's high cheekbones and full mouth, her greying hair dyed a rich auburn. She wore no makeup and was wearing jeans and a floppy dark blue pullover. She forced a smile and kissed his cheek.

Shepherd didn't know what to say to her. They hugged on the doorstep.

'Where the hell have you been, Daniel?' she asked. His mother-in-law was the only person who called him by his full Christian name. At home and through his schooldays he'd been Danny. When he'd joined the army he'd decided Danny was juvenile and told his fellow recruits he was Dan. When he'd joined the SAS his troop had rechristened him Spider after a training course in the jungles of Borneo. It had all been down to a bet as to which of them could eat the most disgusting insect without throwing up; Shepherd had wolfed down a tarantula. Now everyone called him Spider, except Moira: to her he would always be Daniel, the soldier who'd stolen her daughter. Sue had always called him Dan.

'Where's Liam?' Shepherd asked, ignoring her question.

'In the sitting room, playing with his video game.'

'How is he?'

Moira wrapped her arms round herself. 'He wasn't hurt, he was strapped in. But he was there when Sue—'

She couldn't finish the sentence.

'Has he said anything?'

'Only that he doesn't want to talk about it. The doctor said he's dealing with it in his own way. He'll talk when he's ready.'

Shepherd hugged her. 'Thanks for coming, Moira. Thanks for taking care of him.'

'He's my grandson, Daniel,' she said flatly.

Shepherd released her and stepped into the hallway. The sitting room was on the right. He could hear electronic gunfire, and screams. Moira closed the front door.

Liam was sitting cross-legged on the floor in front of the television, his thumbs flashing over the PlayStation handset. On the screen, soldiers were exploding as machine-gun bullets ripped through their bodies. Liam didn't look up as Shepherd walked in.

'Hi,' said Shepherd.

'Hi,' said Liam, his eyes still on the screen.

Shepherd stood where he was. This wasn't what he'd been expecting. He'd assumed that his son would rush at him in tears to be hugged and picked up and told that everything was all right.

'Are you okay?'

Liam shrugged and carried on with his game. Shepherd sat down on the floor next to him. 'That looks fun,' he said.

Liam went on playing with his left hand but handed Shepherd the second control pad with the right. Shepherd looked at its coloured buttons as Liam continued to shoot make-believe soldiers with make-believe bullets.

Shepherd started to play the game with his son. Bang, bang, you're dead. Make-believe blood. Make-believe gore. No regrets, no conscience.

'Do you want coffee, Daniel?' asked Moira, from the door.

'No thanks,' said Shepherd.

'Liam? Lemonade?'

Liam shook his head.

'Say, "No, thank you,"' said Shepherd.

'No, thank you,' repeated Liam.

'Jaffa cakes?'

'No, thanks.'

Shepherd looked over his shoulder. Moira was close to tears, her hands clutched together. He smiled reassuringly, but she turned away and went into the kitchen.

'Do you want to go to the park?' asked Shepherd. 'Kick the football around?'

'Okay,' said Liam.

Liam kicked the football and ran after it. A red setter chased it, too, but Liam got there first and kicked it high into the air. The dog ran after it, barking. Liam still hadn't talked about his mother's death. He'd barely said anything. Shepherd had tried to start a conversation several times, but all Liam did was grunt or answer monosyllabically. Shepherd knew that he was bottling up his emotions and that eventually it would all come tumbling out. But just then all he wanted to do was run with the red setter.

Shepherd saw a man on the other side of the football field, walking in his direction with his hands in his overcoat pockets. It was Sam Hargrove.

Shepherd watched his son play with the dog as Hargrove walked up to him. 'Nice day for it,' said Hargrove. The evening wind tugged at his immaculately styled hair.

'Any day out of prison is a nice day,' said Shepherd.

'How is he?' asked Hargrove, nodding in Liam's direction.

'His mother just died, how do you think he is?' said Shepherd, and realised how churlish that sounded. He tried to apologise, but the words caught in his throat.

Hargrove put a hand on his shoulder. 'I'm so sorry about what's happened,' he said. 'If there's anything I can do, you just have to ask.'

'I know.'

For a few moments they were silent.

'This isn't just social, is it?' asked Shepherd.

'If you don't want to talk about the job, that's fine by me,' said the superintendent.

'I'm okay,' said Shepherd. At least if he was thinking about the case he wasn't thinking about Sue.

'Tony Stafford is Digger's man,' said Hargrove.

'I can't say I'm surprised. Carpenter told me as much.'

Hargrove took a manila envelope from his overcoat pocket and handed it to Shepherd. Inside were half a dozen surveillance photographs of Stafford meeting a pretty black girl and taking an envelope from her, then walking away with a smile on his face.

'We've found an offshore building-society account with fifty-eight grand in it.'

'Stupid bugger.' Shepherd recalled Stafford's file. Married with three children, one at university. Wife worked as a nurse. Two incomes, so money shouldn't have been a problem. Maybe it was greed. Or resentment. The same reasons that turned criminals into informers.

'Thing is, he's Digger's man. I don't think he's Carpenter's man. We've had Digger's sister under surveillance and she hasn't gone within a mile of any of Carpenter's people. Neither has Stafford. We've been through all their phone records. Nothing. No connection between either of them and Carpenter.'

'So Carpenter has someone else?'

'That's the way I read it. He uses Digger to fix up the perks on the spur, but someone else is running errands to his people.'

'Shit,' said Shepherd.

'Yeah,' said Hargrove.

'What about Bain?'

'We've checked Bain's phone calls and visitors. No connection with Carpenter's men. Also, Bain is pretty much finished. His wife took most of the cash and she's shacked up in Málaga with a Turkish waiter. A couple of his gang set up on their own using the contacts he'd made. He's a spent force. We'll keep tags on his calls and visits, but it doesn't look like he's the conduit.'

'So now what?'

'That's the thing, isn't it?' said Hargrove. 'If we pull in Stafford, we show our hand.'

'So you let him run?'

'Until we find out who else is on the take.' Hargrove paused. 'If you're up for it.'

Moira was waiting with the front door open as Shepherd and Liam walked down the road, hand in hand. 'I don't like Gran's cooking,' said Liam. 'She uses too much salt.'

'Well, tell her.'

Moira waved at them and Shepherd waved back.

'Dad, are you home for good now?'

Shepherd stopped. 'Let's talk about it tomorrow, yeah?'

'You're not going away again, are you?'

'It won't be long, Liam.' Shepherd made the sign of the cross over his heart. 'Cross my heart.'

'You're always going away.'

'It's my job.'

Tears welled in Liam's eyes. 'Don't leave me with Gran. Please.'

Shepherd scooped up his son and held him tight, burying his face in his son's hair. Liam was racked with sobs. 'I miss Mum.'

'So do I.'

'It's not fair.'

'I know.'

'It was my fault, Daddy.'

'No, it wasn't. Don't be silly.'

'She was trying to get my bag and she died.'

Shepherd kissed his son's cheek, wet with tears. 'It wasn't anybody's fault,' he said. 'It was an accident. But your mummy loves you more than anyone else in the world and she's in Heaven looking down and watching over you. She'll be watching over you for the rest of your life.'

'Are you sure?' asked Liam, blinking away tears.

'Cross my heart,' said Shepherd.

'You have to do it to make it count,' said Liam.

Shepherd cradled him in his left arm and crossed his heart with his right hand, then carried Liam to the house. He took him into to the sitting room, half expecting to see Sue lying on the sofa watching TV or reading one of the trashy celebrity magazines she loved, ready to bite off his head for working late yet again.

Shepherd put Liam down on the sofa. 'Do you want to watch TV?' he asked.

'I want to play with my PlayStation.'

'Go on, then,' said Shepherd, and left him to set it up. He went into the kitchen, where Moira was busying herself over a casserole. 'It'll be ready in an hour or so,' she said. 'Do you want mash or chips?'

'Anything's fine,' said Shepherd. He sat down at the kitchen table and poured himself a cup of tea. He didn't take sugar but he stired it round and round, with a teaspoon, staring into the vortex. 'I can't believe it's happened. It's not sunk in yet.'

Moira bent down and put the casserole into the oven. When she straightened up there were tears in her eyes. Suddenly it hit Shepherd that Moira had lost her only daughter. He'd been so tied up with his own and Liam's pain that he hadn't considered how Moira must feeling. She only had two children – Sue, and a son who was in Australia and whom she was lucky to see once a year. Her lower lip was trembling.

Shepherd stood up quickly and went over to her. 'Oh, God, Moira, I'm sorry,' he said, and put his arms round her.

'I'm not going to cry, I'm not,' she said.

'It's okay,' said Shepherd, stroking the back of her head. 'Really, it's okay.'

'It's not fair.' She sniffed. 'She never did anyone any harm, she loved everybody, she didn't deserve to die like that. Damn it, damn it, damn it.'

It was the first time Shepherd had heard his mother-in-law swear. Tears sprung into his own eyes but he fought them back.

'I never thought I'd be burying my daughter,' said Moira. 'Children aren't supposed to die before their parents.'

A tear escaped, and trickled down Shepherd's right cheek; he brushed it away on Moira's shoulder.

'A stupid car accident,' said Moira. 'A stupid, stupid accident. If she'd driven another way to school, if the truck hadn't been there, if she'd seen it sooner – there are so many "ifs" that it tears me apart. She shouldn't be dead. It's not right. It's not fair.'

She sobbed into his chest and Shepherd stood there, his arms round her. It was the first time he'd ever held his mother-in-law. The first time he'd ever seen her cry. There were so many firsts. But with Sue there'd be no more. They'd had their last meal together. Their last sex. Their last fight. Everything to do with Sue was now in the past.

Shepherd helped Moira to a chair and poured her a cup of tea. He gave her a piece of kitchen towel to dry her tears.

'I never wanted her to marry you,' she said.

'I know,' said Shepherd. Moira and her bank-manager husband had made that clear from the start. They had regarded Shepherd as unsuitable, both because of his working-class background and his profession. There was nothing they could do about his parentage, but they did all they could to persuade him to leave the Regiment. He'd steadfastly refused, and it was only when Sue had threatened to elope that Moira and Tom had caved in and agreed to a full church wedding. All Shepherd's Regimental friends were told to dress in civvies, but he was delighted that they had worn small SAS pins in their lapels.

'She loved you so much, you know that?' said Moira.

'Yes,' said Shepherd.

'We told her, marrying a soldier leads to nothing but heartbreak.'

Shepherd put his hands round his cup of tea. Sue had kept the cups for best and they usually drank from mugs, but Moira didn't have a mug in her house. It was always cups and saucers. Tears streamed from his eyes and he put his head down so that his forehead rested on the edge of the table.

Carpenter nodded at Lloyd-Davies as he walked along the landing. 'How's it going, Miss Lloyd-Davies?' he asked.

'Hunky-dory, thanks for asking,' said Lloyd-Davies.

'Your hair looks good like that,' said Carpenter.

Instinctively her hand went up to touch it.

Carpenter smiled. 'It shows off your cheekbones.'

Lloyd-Davies was half flattered and half annoyed. She knew he was only trying to press her buttons: Carpenter could turn the charm on anybody and it just happened to be her turn. But it was the first time she'd tried wearing her hair tied up and not one of her colleagues had noticed.

Carpenter leaned against the railing, looking down at the prisoners congregating on the ground floor. The evening meal was about to be served. Usually one of his men fetched his food for him, but today he had reason for mingling with the general population.

He headed down the metal stairs. The food had arrived and inmates were lining up with plastic trays. A couple of guys at the head of the line motioned for Carpenter to cut in front of them, but he shook his head. He saw Lee at the pool table, practising his stroke, and went over to watch him. 'How's it going, Jason?'

Lee straightened and put his cue back in the rack. 'Same old, same old.'

'Your cellmate's got a pass, then?'

'Glasgow cops have taken him up north for an ID parade.'

Lee moved to get past him, but Carpenter gripped his elbow. 'Hang on a minute, Jason, I want to pick your brains.'

Lee looked uncomfortable, but stayed where he was, shifting his weight from foot to foot.

'What's he like, Macdonald?' asked Carpenter.

'Keeps himself to himself. Doesn't say much.'

'Listens a lot, does he?'

'Just stays quiet.'

'Hard or soft, would you say?'

'He's civilised, that's for sure, but if push came to shove he'd shove back.'

Carpenter nodded thoughtfully. 'Has he said much about the job he was done for?'

'Armed robbery, some warehouse out at Gatwick. Silicon chips, he said. State-of-the-art stuff. Went in with shotguns and it all went tits-up.'

'What about the guys with him?'

'Hasn't said a word about them.'

'He was in to see his brief this morning, wasn't he?'

Lee nodded. 'Yeah, said he was looking for more cash. You know what lawyers are like. Bloody leeches.'

'They pulled him out of the gym, like the meeting wasn't expected.'

'Yeah, that's what I heard.'

'Did he say anything about it back in the cell?'

'Like what?'

'Like, was the visit by the cops a surprise? Did his brief tell him the Jocks were on their way?'

Lee's brow furrowed as he concentrated. 'Nah, he didn't say nothing. Just lay on his bunk.' He chewed the inside of his mouth. 'He was upset. Really upset. Maybe he did know they were coming to get him.'

'You saw him being taken out, yeah?'

'Yeah. Amelia took him.'

'How did he seem then?'

Lee rubbed his chin. 'Okay. Called to me to tell me what was happening.'

'Did he now?'

'Yeah, but it was kosher. Hamilton was having a laugh about it later. Little old lady took pellets in the leg when he was knocking over a post office. She's in intensive care so Macdonald gets a day out.'

Carpenter patted Lee's shoulder. 'Do me a favour, Jason.'

'Anything, Gerry.'

'Keep an eye on him when he gets back. Ear to the ground, yeah?'

'You want me to go fishing?'

'No need for that. Just keep a watching brief.'

'No problem. Whatever you want's fine by me.'

Carpenter winked at him and went over to the food line. Eric

253

Magowan was standing behind a tray of lasagne with a metal spatula in his hand. He was a tall, cadaverous man in his fifties who'd been accused of poisoning three old women at the nursing-home where he'd worked as a care assistant. He'd been given the hotplate job on the basis of his catering experience, but Carpenter reckoned that the screws got a sadistic pleasure from having a poisoner, albeit an alleged one, serving meals. Magowan saw Carpenter and said something to the men in the line. They parted to allow him space. A prisoner handed Carpenter a tray.

'How's it going, Eric?' said Carpenter. 'What's least likely to make me ill, huh?'

Liam was engrossed in a video game, his thumbs almost in spasm over the control pad of his PlayStation, his eyes fixed on the screen where a shotgun was blowing away Russian soldiers.

'You know they're illegal,' said Shepherd, as he dropped on to the sofa next to his son.

'What are?' asked Liam, still watching the screen.

'Shotguns. Can't use them in war. They're against the Geneva Convention.'

'What's that?'

'The rules of war.'

'That doesn't make sense,' said Liam. 'You can use rifles but you can't use shotguns?'

'Them's the rules,' said Shepherd.

'Guns are supposed to kill people, right?'

'Sure.'

'So why can't soldiers use shotguns? They do more damage than regular guns.' On screen he blasted away at a Russian trooper, whose head dissolved in a cloud of red mist. 'Look at that!' he said.

'Yeah. Doesn't this game have some sort of parental guidance warning?'

'Mum always lets me play it.'

Shepherd smiled to himself. From the age of three Liam had tried to play him off against Sue, and vice versa. 'Your dinner's ready.'

'I'm not hungry.'

Shepherd didn't feel hungry either, but he knew they both had to eat. 'Your gran's gone to a lot of trouble,' he said. 'Try to eat something to make her feel better, okay?'

'Okay.' Liam went on playing his game.

'Now,' said Shepherd.

'Okay.'

Shepherd picked up his son and shook him until he dropped the control pad, then carried him, giggling, into the kitchen. Moira had set the table for three, using Sue's best china.

Liam frowned at the plates. 'Mum doesn't let us use those, they're for best,' he said.

'It's okay,' said Shepherd.

'I didn't know . . .' said Moira.

'It's fine, really,' said Shepherd.

'Mum always lets us eat in front of the TV,' said Liam.

'Well, we're eating here tonight,' said Moira, using a ladle to pour helpings of beef stew on to the plates.

Shepherd sat down. Moira had put mashed potatoes and boiled carrots into two bowls. He heaped vegetables on to Liam's plate, then helped himself.

Moira sat down, smiled at them, then closed her eyes and put her hands together in prayer. Liam looked at his father, who nodded at him to follow suit and they put their hands together as Moira said grace. The prayer was short and to the point, but Shepherd barely heard the words. He didn't believe in God. His time in the SAS had destroyed whatever religious beliefs he might ever have held, and his police career had done nothing to convince him that a higher power was taking care of things. The world was a mean, vicious place where the strong devoured the weak and where bad things happened to good people. Shepherd wanted nothing to do with any god that countenanced such unfairness.

Carpenter lay on his bunk, staring out of the small barred window above his desk at a sliver of the moon. Along the landing he could hear spyglasses clicking as a member of the night staff did the hourly visual check. Carpenter could never understand its purpose: if an inmate was serious about suicide, they'd simply wait until it had been done before they went ahead. An hour was more than long enough to fashion a noose from a torn pillowcase or cut a wrist.

Carpenter's spyglass flicked open. He didn't react. Then it closed. He was still staring at the moon. The inspection hatch below the spyglass opened. That was unusual. He sat up. A hand appeared and tossed a folded piece of paper into the cell. The hatch was shut. Carpenter rolled off his bunk and picked up the note. The spyglass clicked open. An eye winked and the spyglass closed. Carpenter switched on his light and opened the note: 'Phone me.'

He took his CD player off its shelf and used the metal clip from his ballpoint pen to unscrew the back. He laid the four screws on his blanket, then eased off the plastic casing. The tiny Nokia phone was tucked behind the left speaker and the battery behind the circuit board. Carpenter's cell was rarely turned over, and even when it was he was usually given plenty of notice. Any search was generally cursory, but that didn't mean there was any point in taking risks so the mobile was always well hidden. He always kept the battery out of the phone to minimise the risk of it accidentally discharging. He clipped the battery into place, switched on and tapped out a number. The phone rang for some time and Carpenter cursed. 'Come on, Fletcher, you lazy bastard,' he muttered.

Just as he was convinced that the answering-service was going to kick in, Fletcher answered. 'Yes, boss?'

'What's happening, Kim?'

'We've found Roper.'

'Where?'

'Milton Keynes.'

'Safe-house?'

'Seems so. We're taking a run up today.'

'Softly, softly, yeah? If they know that we know, they'll bury him so deep we'll need a submarine to get to him.'

*   *   *

Shepherd tucked the duvet under his son's chin and kissed his forehead. He smelt of spearmint: Shepherd had made sure he'd cleaned his teeth for a full two minutes, despite Liam's protests that his mother never made him do it that long. Now Liam mumbled something in his sleep, then started to snore quietly.

Shepherd closed the bedroom door and went downstairs. There was a bottle of Jameson's in the kitchen cupboard over the fridge and he poured himself a large measure. He added a splash of tap water and took it through to the sitting room where Moira was sitting on the overstuffed sofa in front of the television. She frowned critically at the drink in his hand but didn't say anything. Moira was a confirmed teetotaler and always had been.

'Straight off to sleep,' said Shepherd, and sat in an armchair. There was something hard under the cushion and he pulled out a paperback book. Philip Roth. *The Human Stain*. She'd folded down the corner of the last page she'd read, about midway through. Shepherd sniffed the book, wondering when Sue had last held it. He wondered if she'd enjoyed it, and if she'd planned to give it to him to read. She'd always done that when she found a book she enjoyed. She'd loved to sit down with him and talk for hours about something they'd both read. She'd drink white wine, he'd have his whiskey, and truth be told it was Sue who did most of the talking. Most of the time Shepherd would just sit and listen to her, loving the enthusiasm in her eyes, the excitement in her voice. He'd kept telling her she should try writing herself, maybe do a course or join a book group, but she'd always insisted that it was reading she loved, not writing.

'I've spoken to the school,' said Moira. 'They said he can stay off as long as he needs to.'

'Good,' said Shepherd, sipping his whiskey. 'Thanks. Dinner was lovely.' He took another sip of whiskey, then put the glass on the coffee-table. 'How's Tom?'

'It's hit him hard,' said Moira. 'His deputy's away on holiday so he has to stay with the branch. He'll be here at the weekend.'

'I should phone him.'

'I'd leave him be,' cautioned Moira, 'for a day or two. The doctor's prescribed something.' She grimaced. 'He wanted to give me something, too, but I said I didn't need it.' Tears were in her eyes again and she dabbed at them with a white handkerchief. 'It's been twenty-six years since I've been to a funeral, and that was my father's,' she said. 'I've been so lucky. My brother's family all well, Tom's relatives seem to go on for ever. It was like we were blessed. But now this . . .' She sobbed into her handkerchief.

'What do we do? About the arrangements?' Shepherd had never had to organise a funeral, and didn't know where to start.

'I've spoken to a local firm already. They'll arrange everything. I gave them my credit-card number. They said . . .' Moira dissolved into tears.

Shepherd looked around the sitting room. Sue's presence was everywhere. The book she'd been reading. The *TV Times* on the coffee-table, open at the listings for two days earlier. The video she'd rented was still on the sideboard, in its box ready to be returned. A scribbled note to herself – a reminder of shopping she had to do: shampoo, rubbish bags, tea. Sue's memory wasn't a patch on his, he thought, and she was forever making lists of things she had to do. He'd always teased her about it. When they'd gone shopping together he'd taken a brief look at her list and wouldn't have to refer to it again. She had a Filofax and an electronic organiser for her phone numbers, but Shepherd had never forgotten a number in his life. Other husbands might forget birthdays and anniversaries but not Shepherd. He could recall the date of every event in his life, important or otherwise.

'This job you're doing, what is it exactly?' asked Moira.

'I can't tell you,' said Shepherd. 'I'm sorry, but it's a sensitive operation.'

'It was tearing Sue apart, you being away so much.'

'I know,' said Shepherd, 'but there wasn't anything I could do about it.'

'Well, whatever it is, it's over now.'

'Moira!' protested Shepherd.

'He's your son,' said Moira emphatically. 'He comes first.'

'Of course he does. You don't have to tell me what my priorities are.'

'Maybe somebody has to,' said Moira. 'Your family always played second fiddle to your army career and things weren't much better when you joined the police.'

'I gave up the army for Sue,' said Shepherd quietly. He didn't want an argument with his mother-in-law, especially one that he'd had a thousand times with his wife.

'Sue wanted you to have a regular job. She didn't expect you to start working as an undercover policeman doing who knows what.'

'She shouldn't have told you what I was doing,' said Shepherd. 'There's no point in my being undercover if people are shouting it from the rooftops.'

Moira looked at him scornfully. 'The thing you don't seem to realise, Daniel, is that family comes first. Sue had no secrets from me.'

Shepherd knew that Sue had kept dozens of secrets from her mother. The time they'd made love in the bathroom while Moira and her husband had been downstairs watching *EastEnders*. The lump he'd found in her breast, which had kept her awake for weeks with worry until the specialist had pronounced it benign. Shepherd knew that family was more important than anything, but what Moira didn't seem to understand was that *he* had been Sue's family. Him and Liam.

'This job's important, Moira.'

'I knew it. You're not coming back, are you?'

'It's more complex than that.'

'No, it isn't!' hissed Moira. 'You've got a simple choice to make. Your job or your son.'

Shepherd put his head in his hands. 'Moira . . .' he said.

'Sue's not even buried and all you can think about is your pathetic little job. You're an adrenaline junkie, that's what you are. We warned Sue that nothing good would come of getting involved with a trooper. You're all the same. You thrive on danger, on putting your life on the line. That's what you did in the SAS and that's what you're doing now. You're like a junkie who needs his fix of heroin and you put that fix ahead of everything else in your life.'

'That's not fair.'

'You're right it's not fair. You're putting your job ahead of your son's welfare – and for what? It's not as if it pays well, is it? The amount of hours you're away from home, you'd get more working in a factory.' She waved her hand around the room. 'Look at this! It's the same furniture you had in Hereford. Tom and I bought your bed and the wardrobes. And look at the state of the carpet – you can almost see through it. Whatever it is that you get from your job, it's not money.'

'It isn't about money,' said Shepherd.

'Exactly. It's about you getting your kicks, that's what it's about.'

'It's about making a difference,' said Shepherd. 'It's about making the world a safer place.'

Moira laughed harshly. 'Oh, the world's a safer place now than it was twenty years ago, is it? I don't think so.'

'It'd be a darn sight worse if it wasn't for the work we do,' said Shepherd, but even as the words left his mouth he wondered how true they were. Much of his undercover work involved putting away drug-dealers and traffickers, yet the volume of drugs entering the country had consistently increased year after year. For every dealer that Shepherd had helped put behind bars, another two had taken their place. But Gerald Carpenter had to be dealt with. It didn't matter who replaced him, there was no way he could be allowed to get away with what he'd done. Moira opened her mouth to speak but Shepherd held up his hand to silence her. 'There's a man in prison,' he said, 'who deserves to stay behind bars for the rest of his life, but the way things are going he's going to get away scot-free. He brings millions of pounds' worth of drugs into the country every year, and he kills anyone who gets in his way.'

'If he's in prison, that's the end of it, isn't it?'

'It's not as simple as that. He's been caught red-handed, but there's a world of difference between being caught and being sentenced. He's on remand while he waits for his trial. And he's killing witnesses, destroying evidence, doing everything he can to make sure that he never gets to trial. I'm the last line of defence, Moira. If I pull out, he walks.'

'Would that be so bad?'

'He killed an undercover policeman, a friend of mine. Shot him dead in front of his pregnant wife.'

'That's not your problem.'

'Then whose problem is it, Moira? If I don't do something about it, who will?'

'You're not the only policeman in the country. Let someone else put themselves in the firing line for a change.'

'There isn't time. Look, I can't tell you exactly what I'm doing, but it's something only I can do. There isn't time for someone else to get close to this guy. If I pull out, he gets a clear run. He gets away with murder.'

'You keep saying that. You keep saying he's done this and he's done that and he's having people killed. If you know that, why don't you just charge him with it and have done with it?'

'Because life isn't like that any more,' said Shepherd. 'This guy's got the most expensive lawyers in the country. Any wrong move, any mistake, and they'll get him off. The case against him has to be one hundred per cent watertight.'

Moira's shoulders slumped. She suddenly looked a decade older than her true age.

'I need your help, Moira,' said Shepherd. 'I need you to take care of Liam for a while.'

'He needs his father,' said Moira, but Shepherd could tell that the fight had gone out of her.

'And he'll have me,' said Shepherd. 'Just let me get this thing out of the way.'

'How long?' asked Moira.

'Weeks rather than months,' said Shepherd. 'As soon as his case goes to trial, my job's over. And if I can find out how he's getting his orders to the outside, I'll be done even sooner. Can you stay here? There's no one else I would trust to be with Liam.'

Moira studied him. 'I hope you're less obvious with the criminal fraternity,' she said. 'What do you think, Daniel? That you can soft-soap me with a few sweet words? That might have worked with Sue but I find it an insult to my intelligence.'

'It's the truth,' protested Shepherd. 'There's no one on my side of the family close enough to Liam. He barely sees my brother and I've never been close to my parents. He thinks the world of you and Tom. I know that sounds like I'm trying to sweet-talk you again, Moira, but, hand on heart, I mean it.'

'I'm not sure I can leave Tom on his own.'

'He can stay here.'

'He's got his job. Same as you have.'

'Why not take Liam back with you?'

'What would his school say about that?'

'You said they were okay with him taking some time off, and there are schools in Hereford. In a way it might be better to get him out of this environment for a while.'

'You mean it might make it easier for you to be away?' Moira sighed. 'I'm too tired to argue any more,' she said. 'You do what you want. Tom and I will take care of Liam until you're prepared to accept your responsibilities.' She pushed herself up off the sofa. 'I'm going to bed. What time are you away tomorrow?'

'I don't know. Early afternoon, I guess.'

'I'll do lunch,' she said. 'I was going to do a roast but Liam said he wanted fish fingers.'

'Fish fingers is fine.'

Moira went out, leaving Shepherd nursing his whiskey and water. He stretched out his legs and groaned. Prison felt a million miles away, and there was no doubt he wanted to walk away from the job and let someone else bring Carpenter down. It was true that there wasn't time to get someone else in place, but Moira had been close to the mark when she'd accused him of being an adrenaline junkie. A big part of him wanted to pit his wits against Carpenter's, to put his life on the line as he had a hundred times before. If he was truly honest with himself, Shepherd had to admit that he never felt more alive than when he was in combat, facing an enemy with a gun, knowing that it was his life or the life of his adversary, that there could be only one winner and one loser, and that more often than not the loser's life was forfeit. Undercover work wasn't the same as combat, but the thrill was similar. And nothing compared with the elation of winning the game, of seeing a target led away in handcuffs wondering where it had all gone wrong, while Shepherd knew it had been down to him, that his skills and maybe his luck had made him the better man on the day. There were men, and women, sitting in prison cells around the country because Shepherd had put them there, a living roll-call of victories.

Shepherd drained his glass, then went into the kitchen and refilled it. He wondered what Carpenter was doing. Probably lying on his bunk, listening to the radio. Reading, maybe. Planning his next move. Planning what he'd be doing when he got out, how he'd spend his millions. 'The best-laid plans . . .' he said, and raised his glass in tribute. If Shepherd had his way, Carpenter's plans would come to nothing and he'd spend the rest of his life behind bars, never knowing who had betrayed him.

Jason Lee was sitting at the table when he heard his door being unlocked. He frowned. It was half an hour early. Then he remembered that his cellmate was due back and twisted in his wooden chair, expecting Macdonald. He was surprised to see Eric Magowan, one of the hotplate men, standing in the doorway, holding a plastic canteen bag. A prison officer was standing just behind him but Lee couldn't see who it was.

'Not me, mate, I'm spent up,' said Lee. He leaned back in his chair but he still couldn't see the officer's face, just a black-trousered leg and a glimpse of white shirt. He couldn't even tell if the officer was male or female.

'Don't look a gift-horse in the arse,' said Magowan, tossing the bag at him.

Lee caught it. He was about to argue with Magowan when he saw what was in it. Three Pot Noodles. Two bars of chocolate. A jar of coffee. He hadn't ordered the treats. They were a pay-off – from Carpenter.

Magowan walked away and the prison officer slammed the door

and locked it. Lee stared at the bag. He knew that Carpenter never gave anything for nothing. He would be expected to keep a close eye on his cellmate. God help him if Macdonald was up to something and Lee didn't come up with the goods.

Shepherd woke up and rolled over, half asleep. He could smell Sue's perfume and reached across the bed for his wife, murmuring her name, but before his hand touched the pillow he snapped back to reality. The cold emptiness returned and he curled up into a ball as the memories of everything he'd lost washed over him. Shepherd had lost people before, and he'd seen more than a handful of his friends killed, but nothing compared with the loss of the woman he loved.

He'd been splattered with the blood of an SAS captain whose head had exploded in the Afghan desert, and he'd been cradling the man in his arms when a sniper's bullet had slammed into his own shoulder. He'd seen a young trooper die of a snakebite in the Borneo jungle on a survival training course, a stupid mistake because the medic had brought the wrong anti-venom pack with him. The trooper had died in a helicopter just ten minutes away from hospital, his spine curved like a bow, bloody froth at his lips, while Shepherd held his hand and hold him to hang on, that everything would be okay. He'd watched from a cliff-top on the Welsh coast as a trooper laden with gear fell to his death during a training exercise, another stupid mistake that had cost a life. But the death of friends and colleagues at least made some sort of sense: they were fighting for their country or pushing themselves to their limits, and it was the occasional price to be paid. Like any member of the armed forces, Shepherd accepted death as a possible outcome of his career choice. And as a policeman, he accepted that from time to time he'd be confronted with violence and possibly death. But Sue's death had been so unnecessary. A simple road accident, two vehicles colliding, and Shepherd was without the wife loved, Moira and Tom had lost their daughter, and Liam his mother.

Shepherd rolled on to his front and buried his face in the pillow. Images of the last time he'd spoken to Sue filled his mind. Sitting in the visitors room, he in his stupid fluorescent sash, her in her old sheepskin jacket and blue jeans, the small gold crucifix at her neck, arguing about what the hell he was still doing in prison. He remembered every word she'd said to him, every grimace, every flash of her eyes, the way she'd tapped the table with the nail of her wedding ring finger, the way she'd glared at the prison officers as if they were to blame for his confinement. It was a lousy memory, one that filled him with guilt and self-loathing. If he hadn't been inside, if he'd been with Sue and Liam, maybe he'd have done the school run that day, maybe he'd have seen the truck, maybe he'd have braked sooner, but even if he hadn't and he'd hit the truck full on, then better that he'd died instead of Sue. Moira was right. Shepherd was just a policeman, one of many, and there were dozens who could take his place at a moment's notice, but Liam had only one mother and she was irreplaceable.

He cursed into the pillow, he swore and blasphemed, but even as he did to he realised the futility of his anger. There was no one to blame, no one to wreak vengeance on.

He turned on to his back and stared up at the ceiling. What was done was done. All he could was make the best of the hand he'd been dealt, no matter how shitty it was.

He showered and went downstairs. Moira was in the kitchen wearing Sue's white towelling bathrobe and nursing a cup of coffee. She gestured at the robe. 'You don't mind, do you?' she asked. 'It's just . . .'

She couldn't find the words, but Shepherd knew what she meant. It smelt of Sue, her perfume, her sweat, her essence, and wearing it allowed Moira to hold on to her just a little longer.

'I know,' said Shepherd. 'It's as if she's just popped out for a while, as if she's going to be back at any moment.'

'I dreamed about her last night,' said Moira. 'I hardly slept but when I did I dreamed she was back, that it had all been a terrible mistake and that someone else had been in the car.' She smiled ruefully. 'Stupid, isn't it?'

It wasn't stupid. Shepherd had dreamed about Sue, too, and in his dream she'd told him she'd had to go away on a job for Sam

Hargrove, a job so secret she couldn't tell him about it, but it was over now and she'd never be working for him again. Even asleep he'd known that what she was saying didn't make sense and he found the dream slipping away from him. He'd fought to keep her, even though he knew it wasn't real, but he'd woken up calling her name, wanting her back.

'I'll go down to the shops, get what we need for lunch,' said Moira.

'I'll take Liam to the park.'

'Aren't you going to shave?' she asked.

'I can't. It's part of the role.

Shepherd went back upstairs and sat on the bed next to his son. Liam's face was stained with dried tears and he was hugging one of his pillows. Shepherd stroked his forehead. 'Time to wake up, kid.'

Liam rolled over sleepily. 'You're home?' he said.

'Of course I'm home,' said Shepherd. Liam's eyes widened, and Shepherd saw that on waking he'd forgotten what had happened. Now it was all flooding back. Shepherd lay on the bed and wrapped his arms round his son. 'It's all right,' he whispered into Liam's ear. 'It's going to be all right.'

'Mummy's dead.'

'I know. But she's watching over you.'

'In Heaven?'

'That's right.'

'I want to be with her in Heaven, too.'

'It's not your time to go to Heaven,' said Shepherd. 'You have to stay here with me and your gran.'

'It's not fair.'

'I know. I know it's not.'

'Is she really in Heaven, Daddy?'

Shepherd gave his son a small squeeze. 'Of course,' he said. 'She's with Jesus, and Jesus is taking care of her.' Shepherd didn't believe that. Sue was dead. A body on a slab somewhere, being prepared for burial or cremation. She wasn't sitting on a cloud playing a harp and she wasn't looking down on Liam. She was dead,

266

and one day Shepherd would be dead, too. But what Shepherd believed and what he wanted his son to believe were two different things. He'd had an argument with Sue when Liam was three and he had wanted to tell the child that there was no Father Christmas. Father Christmas was nothing more than a marketing exercise, Shepherd had argued, and telling Liam otherwise was tantamount to lying. Sue had disagreed and insisted that children needed their fantasies. Shepherd had asked her if that included God and she'd given him a frosty look. She'd won the argument, and it had only been when schoolfriends had put him straight that Liam stopped believing in the fat man in the red suit. Shepherd rated God on a par with Father Christmas, but he had no wish to add to his son's despair by telling him there was no such place as Heaven and that he'd never see his mother again.

'I love you, Mummy,' Liam shouted. 'Don't forget me!' Then he said, 'Did she hear me, Daddy?'

'Of course she did,' said Shepherd. 'And she loves you.'

Liam snuggled up to him. 'I love you, too, Daddy.'

Gerald Carpenter turned up the volume of his personal stereo. He was listening to a news programme on Radio Four, but even with his headphones on he could still hear pounding rap music from one of the cells below, the click-click of balls on the pool table, the clanging of doors closing, raised voices, forceful rather than angry, sarcastic laughter – all the sounds of association, when prisoners were let out of their cells to socialise. But even when everyone was banged up there was never a time when the wing was silent. Even in the middle of the night radios played, there were muttered conversations, snoring, the squeak of boots on the landing as an officer walked by, the rattling of keys. Even with his eyes closed there were constant reminders of where he was. His inability to control his environment was one of the worst things about being in prison. At least he had the money and contacts to ensure that his confinement would only be temporary. He could think of nothing worse than to be behind bars on a long sentence, knowing that for the next ten or twenty years everything you did was controlled by people who thought you were no better than an animal to be caged, fed and occasionally exercised.

Carpenter took several deep breaths and forced himself to relax. He filled his mind with images of his wife and son, on their motor launch at Málaga, soaking up the sun and enjoying the envious looks of the tourists on the quayside; Bonnie riding her horse, looking damn good in her jodhpurs and boots; himself walking into his local pub and buying a round, talking football with guys who had no idea what he did for a living. If everything went to plan, it wouldn't be long before Carpenter was on the outside enjoying those things for real. He'd already spent the best part of two million pounds on destroying the case against him, but if it took another twenty million it would still be a small price to pay for his freedom.

After breakfast – scrambled eggs and cheese on toast, Liam's favourite – Shepherd took his son for a walk on the local common. Liam was talking about his mother. Mostly he started with 'Remember when . . .' then relate a story from start to finish. The time she'd locked herself out of the house and had to break a window to get in. The time she'd taken him to hospital thinking he'd broken his collarbone after falling off his bike. The time they'd eaten oysters on holiday on the Scottish coast. He told the stories happily, and Shepherd listened, ruffling his hair.

They kicked the football around, then took it in turns to be in goal and had a penalty competition, which Liam won. They walked to a copse and Liam said he wanted to climb an oak tree with spreading branches. Shepherd stood underneath anxiously, but Liam was surefooted and fearless. He sat on a branch and waved to him. 'Come on, Daddy!'

Shepherd climbed up and joined him. Liam pointed off into the distance. 'Our house is there, isn't it?'

'I guess so.'

'Can you see it?'

'No, I can't.'

'Mum never let me climb trees,' said Liam.

'She was scared about you falling, that's all.'

'But I won't fall,' he said.

'I know,' said Shepherd.

'Will we live in the same house?'

'I don't know.'

'I don't want to live anywhere else,' said Liam firmly.

'You can stay with Gran for a bit, though, can't you?'

'Do I have to?'

'It'd be a help for me. There are some things I have to do.'

Liam nodded seriously. 'But when you've finished, we can live at home, right?'

'Sure.'

'Can I sleep in the big bed?'

'Of course you can.'

As Shepherd walked back along the road to the house with his son, he saw the blue Vauxhall Vectra parked at the end of the driveway. Jimmy Sharpe climbed out of the back and waited, his hands in his overcoat pockets.

'Who is that man, Daddy?' asked Liam.

'A friend,' said Shepherd, putting his hand on his son's shoulder.

'He looks like a policeman,' said Liam.

Shepherd smiled. Sharpe had spent a good ten years working undercover and would have been most put out to learn that he'd been rumbled by a seven-year-old. 'Why do you say that?' he asked.

Liam looked up at him. 'He's got cold eyes. Like you.'

His son's words cut Shepherd to the core. Was that how his son saw him? A policeman with cold eyes? 'He's a good guy,' said Shepherd. 'His name's Jimmy Sharpe.'

'Sharp like a knife?'

'Yeah, but with an extra *e* at the end.'

'Are you going to go with them?'

'I think so. Yes.'

'Okay.'

'But we'll have lunch first. Your gran's doing fish fingers. Your favourite, right?'

Liam shrugged but didn't say anything.

When they reached the Vectra, Sharpe nodded at Shepherd. 'Hargrove wants a word,' he said.

Shepherd patted his son's head. 'Go and tell your gran I'm on my way,' he said.

As Liam ran up the driveway to the house, Sharpe tapped out a number on his mobile phone and handed it to Shepherd. Hargrove answered within a couple of rings. 'Have you decided what you're going to do?' he asked Shepherd. He sounded tired.

Shepherd looked at Sharpe. Sharpe looked back at him. Shepherd turned to the house. Liam was standing at the front door, watching him, still holding the football. Moira was behind him. 'I'm going back,' said Shepherd.

'Thank you, Spider,' said the superintendent. 'I know you're doing the right thing.'

'Just make sure there are no screw-ups on the outside.'

Hargrove thanked him again and Shepherd handed the phone to Sharpe. 'I'm going to have lunch, then we'll head back,' said Shepherd. 'I can't ask you in. The mother-in-law's a bit anti-police at the moment.'

'That's okay,' said Sharpe. 'Tim's got more M and S sandwiches. And another bottle of Jameson's. We'll be fine.'

'Liam's going to stay with my in-laws in Hereford. Look in on him now and again, will you?'

'It'll be a pleasure.'

'You know there could be a few bad apples we don't know about?'

'Carpenter's a shit-stirrer, that's for sure. With enough money to stir a whole lot of shit.'

'Have you got a pen?'

Sharpe gave him a ballpoint and a small notebook. Shepherd wrote down a telephone number and a name. 'This guy's SAS,' he said. 'Any hint that there's a problem, call him and explain the situation.'

Sharpe slipped the notebook and pen into his overcoat pocket.

When Shepherd walked into the house Moira was placing food on the table. Fish fingers, chips and frozen peas. Shepherd had barely any appetite and Liam only played with his food. They made small-talk as they ate, but Shepherd was already back in prison, entering the end game. He forced himself to chew, swallow and nod as Moira talked about the work that needing doing in the garden in Hereford, how peas never tasted as good as they used to, and how she hoped her husband had remembered to unload the washing-machine.

When they'd finished, Shepherd hugged Liam and kissed him. 'Be good for your gran,' he said.

Liam said nothing. There were no tears, no recriminations, no pleading for him to stay. He just looked at his father blankly.

'I won't be away for long,' Shepherd promised.

'I want to play with my PlayStation,' said Liam, looking away so that he didn't have to meet his father's eyes.

'Okay,' said Shepherd.

The child walked out of the kitchen, his hands limp by his sides.

'He'll be all right,' said Moira.

Shepherd nodded slowly. All it would take was one phone call to Hargrove and he'd be out, able to spend as much time as he wanted to with his son. One phone call. He closed his eyes and took a deep breath.

'You've made your decision,' said Moira, softly. 'Don't make it worse by hesitating now.'

It was only with his eyes closed that Shepherd realised how alike Moira and Sue sounded. He wanted to freeze time, to hold the moment, because standing in the kitchen with the sound of Moira's voice, it was as if none of the bad things had happened, as if Sue was still with him, about to nag him to do the dishes and, afterwards, lie with him on the sofa watching a movie on television, falling asleep in each other's arms.

'Daniel . . .' said Moira.

Shepherd opened his eyes and the spell was broken. He pecked Moira on the check, then rushed out of the house. He hurried over to the Vectra and climbed into the back. 'Drive,' he said to Rosser. 'Just get me away from here before I change my mind.'

★   ★   ★

Hamilton escorted Shepherd from the reception area back to the remand block, swinging his keys like an aeroplane propeller. 'Word is that you shot a little old lady,' he said.

'A case of mistaken identity,' said Shepherd. 'Sorry to burst your bubble.'

'No skin off my nose,' said Hamilton. 'The Gatwick robbery's going to mean you doing a twelve-stretch, minimum.'

'You do understand how the British trial system works, don't you, Hamilton?' said Shepherd. 'Innocent until judged guilty by my peers.'

'That's the theory, Macdonald. But I can count the number of innocent men in here on the fingers of one hand.'

Hamilton unlocked the gate to the remand block and ushered Shepherd through. Lloyd-Davies was in the bubble and she smiled when she saw Shepherd. 'I was worried that the Jocks might not let you back, Macdonald,' she said.

'Mistaken identity, apparently,' said Hamilton.

'Just in time for tea,' said Lloyd-Davies.

Shepherd was about to say he wasn't hungry, but that would have been a mistake: as far as the prison staff were concerned, he'd been in the custody of cops who wouldn't have given him much in the way of food and drink. Not when he had been involved in the shooting of one of their own. 'Thanks, ma'am,' he said.

Hamilton unlocked the door to the spur and Shepherd walked through. It was association time. Down on the ones four prisoners were playing pool, and there was a card game going on. Shepherd stood at the stairs, looking for Carpenter. No sign of him. He walked back to the bubble and asked to have Jimmy Sharpe's name and telephone number on his approved list.

'Who is he?' asked Lloyd-Davies. 'Family?'

'He's the cop who took me to Glasgow,' said Shepherd. 'Said he might have something to help with my case.'

As Shepherd walked away from the bubble, Lee came over to him, his hands in his pockets. 'How did it go, Bob?' he asked.

'Blind as a bat, she was,' said Shepherd.

'Couldn't identify you?'

'I doubt she'd recognise herself in the mirror,' he said. 'Much happen while I was away?'

'You weren't away long.'

'What do you mean?'

'Traffic must have been good to get to Glasgow and back so quick.'

Shepherd frowned. 'We drove to King's Cross and got the train from there. Bastards wouldn't even let me have a hot meal on the journey.'

'Where did they take you?'

'Some hospital.'

'What about the cop shop?'

Shepherd frowned, not understanding the question.

'They must have taken you to a cop shop for questioning, right? Craigie Street, was it?'

'Not much to question me about. It was a waste of time. She said it wasn't me. Not by a mile.'

'Still, you got a day out, didn't you? Raining, was it?'

'What?'

'Raining in Glasgow, was it? Always rains in Glasgow, it does.'

Shepherd's eyes narrowed. 'Why the sudden interest in the weather, Jason?'

'Just making conversation.'

'Sounds more like the third degree. What's going on? You planning on writing my biography?'

Lee put his hands up and took a step backwards. 'Fine, I'll keep my gob shut,' he said. He pushed past Shepherd. 'It's teatime, anyway.' He joined the queue at the hotplate.

Shepherd hadn't selected his meal so he was given the vegetarian option – mushroom pizza. When he got back to the cell, Lee was sitting at the table. Shepherd apologised for snapping at him. 'It's been a shitty couple of days,' he said.

'Gave you a lot of grief, did they?'

'You know what cops are like.'

'Was your brief there?'

'Phoned him to put him in the picture, but I'm a big boy, Jason.'

Lee chuckled. 'Good to have you back, anyway. It was too quiet without you. Nobody got their legs broken.'

Carpenter waited until one o'clock in the morning before he got out of bed and took the Nokia phone and battery from their hiding places. He slotted the battery into the phone and switched it on. About a quarter of the power had already gone.

He went over to the door and listened. There'd been a check at a quarter to one so there shouldn't be another for at least forty-five minutes. He tapped out a number. Fletcher answered on the second ring.

'How's it going, Kim?'

'He's there,' said Fletcher. 'We've eyeballed Roper.'

'Much in the way of security?'

'A couple of Cussies. No guns, as far as we can see.'

'I need him taken care of, Kim.'

'I'm on it, boss.'

Carpenter massaged the bridge of his nose with his fingertips. He had a headache. 'Wait a mintue. Kim.'

'What's up, boss?'

Carpenter took a deep breath. He had a bad feeling about Roper, but couldn't put his finger on what was troubling him. 'Get in a couple of freelancers,' he said.

'I can take care of it myself,' said Fletcher.

'I don't doubt that. But just in case, yeah? Get blacks. Muddy the waters.'

'Okay, boss.'

'Soon as you can. If there's a grass inside, I could get turned over at any moment. And if I lose this phone, we're back to passing messages.'

'Tomorrow night, boss. On my life.'

'We've given him plenty of chances to back out, anything that happens from now on is his own bloody fault.'

'What about the wife and kids?'

'Unless they get in the way, leave them be,' said Carpenter. He had no wish to hurt the man's family. In fact, he had no wish to hurt the man. He wasn't killing Roper out of anger or hatred, simply removing the last remaining obstacle to his freedom.

Hal Healey opened the cell door at a quarter to eight. Shepherd had put in an application to shower and he was on the way out when Healey stopped him and handed him a plastic bag. It contained a Walkman and a set of headphones. 'Your lawyer sent this in,' said Healey. He thrust a clipboard at Shepherd. 'Sign for it.'

Shepherd did so and put the bag on his bunk.

He went along to the shower room, and after he'd changed into a clean polo shirt and jeans, he waited until Lee had left for labour before checking the Walkman. It was a device he'd used before. It functioned as a cassette-player and radio, but the pause button activated a separate recording system that could store up to twelve hours of audio on a hidden chip.

He clipped it to his belt and hung the earphones round his neck. All he had to do now was to get Carpenter talking and activate the recorder.

He went downstairs to collect his cleaning equipment. Weston and Ginger were already cleaning the ones. Amelia Heartfield was standing by the supplies cupboard. 'Come on, Bob, the early bird . . .'

'Sorry, Amelia,' said Shepherd. She grinned at him and winked.

Shepherd took out a mop and a bucket, which he filled from the tap by the boiler. He looked up at the threes. Carpenter was at the head of the stairs, working with his mop. Shepherd pressed the pause button, activating the recorder, then headed up the stairs. He nodded at Carpenter and began to swab the floor. 'Never thought I'd be grateful to have a mop in my hand,' he said.

'Beats being in the workshops with the muppets,' said Carpenter.

Shepherd moved closer to Carpenter. 'What you said about getting a message out for me . . .'

'I'm a bit pushed at the moment,' said Carpenter.

275

'But you can do it, right?'

'I've got a few problems need sorting.'

Carpenter moved away and Shepherd followed him. 'Are you okay?'

Carpenter leaned on his mop. 'Look, Bob, I'm not your nursemaid, right?'

'Yeah, but you said you'd help me out, right, get a message out for me?'

'I said I'll think about it. And I'm thinking about it.' Carpenter looked around, but there were no prison officers within earshot. 'Let me take care of my business, then I'll help you with yours, okay?'

'Anything I can do?'

'I've someone taking care of it for me as we speak.'

'On the out?'

Carpenter nodded. 'Until that's done, I'm keeping my head down.'

'Getting rid of witnesses, yeah?' Carpenter frowned, and Shepherd realised he'd pushed him too far. 'None of my business,' he added.

'That's right,' said Carpenter.

'Best of luck with it, anyway,' said Shepherd. 'Just don't forget the shit I'm in, that's all.'

Shepherd moved away. Carpenter had said nothing that could be used to build a case against him, but the hint had been clear enough: he was getting ready to move against Roper. He got an with mopping the floor, keeping to the far side of the landing, away from Carpenter, not wanting to crowd him.

He waited until the prisoners returned from the workshops before he went down to the ones and stood in line for the phones. Lee was standing near the hotplate with half a dozen other prisoners, holding a plastic tray. He grinned and flashed him a thumbs-up.

Shepherd looked up through the suicide mesh. Carpenter had gone back to his cell. If he knew where Roper was being kept, he had to have a source high up in the Church or in Sam Hargrove's unit. And if the source could locate Roper, he might also identify Shepherd. Shepherd could feel the muscles tightening at the back of his neck. If Carpenter discovered he was a cop, he could have him killed inside the prison just as easily as out. Shepherd forced himself to relax. There was no point in worrying about what might be. There'd been nothing in the conversation to suggest that Carpenter suspected anything.

A hand gripped Shepherd's shoulder and he whirled round.

'Hey, I'm cool,' said a man, his hands up. 'I was just asking if you want to use the phone.'

Shepherd apologised. He'd been so deep in thought that he hadn't noticed one of the phones was unoccupied. He tapped out his pin number, then Uncle Richard's. It was answered on the third ring. 'What do you need?' said a male voice. Shepherd couldn't tell if it was the man he'd spoken to last time he'd called.

Two West Indians were waiting to use the phone, close enough to overhear everything he said. 'Hiya, Richard, it's Bob,' he said cheerily.

Use of the names meant the man at the other end of the phone realised that the conversation was non-secure.

'What do you need?' said the voice.

'How's Sam doing?' said Shepherd.

'Do you want me to get a message to him?'

Shepherd laughed for the benefit of the West Indians. 'Yeah, that's right. It's been ages since I talked to him.'

'Are you requesting a meeting?'

'No, visiting hours are a pain in the arse here. It takes for ever to put a visiting order through.'

'Is this a matter of urgency?'

'Absolutely. Has he seen Sandy?'

'Sandy Roper?'

'I know, they're perfect for each other, aren't they? It's about time they went on holiday, isn't it?'

'Has Roper's location been compromised?'

'Tell Sam I said they should go away. The sooner the better. The rest will do them good.'

'I'll pass that on immediately,' said the voice. 'Do you need anything else?'

277

'I'm fine. Bored out of my skull.'

'You're in no immediate danger?'

'Shit, no. Everything's fine. I'm just looking forward to getting out. Look, I'd better go, there are people waiting to use the phone.'

'Good luck,' said the man.

Kim Fletcher pulled on a pair of night-vision goggles and pressed the on switch. They buzzed, then flickered into life. 'They work?' asked Lewis from the back seat.

'Of course they do,' sneered Fletcher. 'They cost a grand.' He took off the goggles and handed them to Lewis. Lewis was nineteen and had already killed five men, four for money. Sitting next to him was Jewel, who had just turned sixteen. Lewis had taken on Jewel as his assistant and was teaching him the tricks of the trade. He was learning fast.

Jewel screwed a bulbous silencer into the barrel of his pistol, a Swiss-made SIG-Sauer P-220, not that he cared about the make of the weapon: to him, a gun was a gun. As long as it fired bullets, that was all that mattered. Fletcher took a second pair of goggles from the BMW's glove compartment and handed them to him.

Lewis checked the goggles, nodded, then took them off. He checked the safety on his gun. It was also a SIG-Sauer but, unlike Jewel's 9mm, it was the more modern P-232, chambered for 7.65mm Browning cartridges. Like Jewel, Lewis didn't care what the gun was. They'd bought the weapons from an underworld arms dealer in Harlesden, a Yardie who had been prepared to sell them on a return-if-not-fired basis, but Fletcher had told Lewis he was to buy them outright. Fletcher was paying him twenty thousand pounds for the job. It was up to him how much he gave Jewel.

'Okay?' Fletcher asked Lewis.

Lewis nodded. He had been paid half the money in advance and would get the rest when Roper was dead. He took a deep breath. The adrenaline always kicked in when he had a loaded gun in his hands. Not fear, not even excitement, just a gearing-up of all his senses for what lay ahead. The taking of a human life.

'Call me when it's done,' said Fletcher.

Lewis jerked his chin at Jewel and the pair climbed out of the BMW.

They had left their Suzuki jeep in a supermarket car park, behind the BMW. They climbed in and drove for half an hour to the house where Roper was being held.

They parked outside the school that bordered the housing estate and clambered over its railings. They slipped on the night-vision goggles, switched them on, checked their guns and ran across the playing-field. They vaulted the garden wall and stood staring at the rear of the house. They waited for a full ten minutes until they were satisfied that no one was watching from any of the windows, then crept towards the kitchen door, their guns at the ready.

Lewis attached a small suction cup to the glass panel in the kitchen window and used a glass cutter to scratch out a hole big enough for his hand to go through. He tapped the glass and it cracked cleanly. He pulled it out and placed it on the ground, then reached through and unlocked the door.

They moved through the kitchen. There was a stack of dirty plates in the sink, and half-drunk mugs of coffee on the worktop. They stood for a while in the doorway, listening, then moved slowly up the stairs, keeping close to the wall to keep the noise to a minimum.

The bathroom was at the back of the house, the door closed. Lewis put his hand on the handle and nodded at Jewel. Jewel held his gun with both hands and Lewis opened the door. During the day there had been a man in the bathroom keeping watch on the garden, but now he'd gone. Lewis frowned, then pointed towards the master bedroom. That was where Roper and his wife were sleeping. They moved down the hallway towards the bedroom. They passed the children's room and ignored it. Fletcher had been insistent that they were not to be hurt. The same went for the wife. Roper was the target.

They reached the master bedroom. Lewis took the handle. Jewel nodded, and he opened the door. Jewel took three quick steps into the middle of the room and aimed his gun at the bed. It was empty. Lewis moved to the wardrobe and opened it. No clothes. Nothing.

'Fuck,' he said.

'What's going on?' asked Jewel. He still had his gun aimed at the bed, his finger on the trigger.

'The birds have fucking flown,' said Lewis.

'We're getting paid, though, yeah?' said Jewel.

'Fucking right we're getting paid,' said Lewis.

'Why don't you just arrest them?' asked Roper. He was watching a CCTV monitor that showed a night-vision view of the bedroom window of the safe-house. He could see two men standing in the middle of the room, holding guns.

'It'd tip Carpenter off that we know what he's up to,' said Hargrove.

'The fact the house is empty will tell them that,' said Roper.

'Not necessarily,' said Hargrove. 'They might just think we've moved you.'

'Bit of a coincidence. They must have staked the place out, and then, just as they move in, the place is abandoned.'

'Give me a break, Sandy,' said Hargrove. 'We got you and your family out, didn't we? If we pull those two in Carpenter's going to suspect we've got someone on the inside. At least this way there's some confusion. There they go.'

On the monitor, the two men moved out of the bedroom. Hargrove flicked a remote-control button and another view flickered on to the screen. This time it was from a camera inside the house. The two men moved down the stairs. They were both wearing night-vision goggles.

'Do you know who they are?' asked Roper.

'Not yet, but we've put a tracking device in their car so we soon will. And we'll keep an eye on them from now on.'

'None of his crew are black. None of the ones I met, anyway.'

'They might be hired help.'

'Which means what? That he didn't want to risk his own people on a hit?'

'That's how I read it. We'll keep an eye on them and pull them in when we've got Carpenter.'

'Now what?' asked Roper.

'You and your family are on a flight to Florida. The DEA will put you under armed guard, with a watch at all airports for anyone who's even spoken to Gerald Carpenter.'

'Maybe they'll take us to Disneyland.'

'Maybe they will,' said Hargrove. 'But it won't be for long. We're entering the end phase now, Sandy. I promise.'

Roper nodded, but he wasn't convinced. Hargrove and Mackie had promised on a stack of Bibles that he and his family were safe in Milton Keynes, but the two men in night-vision goggles had just given the lie to that.

Carpenter waited until just before dawn before he assembled his phone. He listened at the door, and when he was satisfied that the landing was clear, he switched it on and called Fletcher's number.

'Yes, boss,' said Fletcher.

'We're gonna have to keep this short, Kim. Battery's on the way out. Get me another sent in, yeah?'

'Will do, boss.'

'How did it go?'

'Not good, boss.'

Carpenter cursed under his breath. 'Spit it out, Kim.'

'Roper's gone. The house was empty.'

'I thought you had the place under surveillance.'

'We did. He was there, no doubt about it. But we had to leave to brief Lewis and pay him. By the time he went in, Roper had gone.'

Carpenter ran a hand through his hair. It might just have been bad luck – the Church might be moving Roper around as a precaution. 'What does Yates say?'

'His mobile's off. I'll catch him tomorrow. But I've got the last set of tapes from him. I'll go through them now.'

'You think there might be more on them about Roper?'

'It's a possibility. Yates does his best but he can't remember everything.'

'Do it, Kim. I'll call you back tomorrow.'

'Boss, Lewis wants paying. The full whack.'

'That's okay.'

'But he didn't do the job. Bloody liberty, if you ask me.'

'Just pay him. It wasn't his fault. But keep your distance. If they moved Roper out, they might have had the place under surveillance.'

'There were no cops there, boss. Guaranteed.'

Carpenter swore. 'Just let me do the thinking, will you? They might be trying to link Lewis to me by letting him run. That's why we've got to pay him to keep him sweet. And get someone else to hand over the money. I've got to go. Don't forget that battery.' He cut the connection. He paced up and down with, the mobile in his hand. That had been the last thing he'd wanted to hear from Fletcher. Roper was the key to his freedom. With Roper out of the picture, the case against Carpenter would collapse. He could only hope that he'd be able to find out where Roper had been moved to. But at least he still had the inside track on everything the Church did. Or, more accurately, Carpenter knew everything that Roy Mackie, Head of Drugs Operations, did. And wherever Roper went, HODO wouldn't be far behind.

Shepherd spent the morning cleaning the ones with Charlie Weston. Amelia Heartfield was supposed to be overseeing them but she spent most of her time in the bubble with Tony Stafford. From time to time he heard her laughing. Shepherd wondered what she had to be so happy about. He never saw her in anything other than good spirits, yet she had a high-stress job with four children to take care of on the out.

There was no sign of Carpenter. At dinnertime Gilchrist came down from the threes and took a plate of food up to Carpenter's cell. In the afternoon Amelia was back on the ones. Shepherd asked her if it was okay to use the phone. 'You know you're supposed to wait until association,' she said.

'It's personal,' he said. 'During association every man and his dog listens in, you know that.'

Amelia looked concerned. 'Wife trouble?'

Shepherd shrugged. Lying was a way of life when working undercover and it came naturally to him, but he still felt bad about being dishonest with Amelia.

'Go on, then,' she said.

Shepherd went over to the phones and tapped in his pin code followed by the number for Uncle Richard. A man answered.

'Richard, it's Bob,' said Shepherd. 'I'm calling to see how everything went.'

'He had visitors but he wasn't in.'

'Anyone we know?'

'We're on the case.'

'But no one known?'

'No one obvious.'

'And our man's well?'

'Fine and dandy. And you?'

'As well as can be expected,' said Shepherd. 'Tell Sam that the Walkman's working fine, but I've nothing worth listening to yet.'

'I'll tell him,' said the man. 'Do you need anything else?'

Shepherd tapped the receiver against his head. What he needed was to be on the out with his son. But first he needed Carpenter on tape, incriminating himself. And that was all down to Shepherd. 'No,' he said. 'I've got everything I need.' He replaced the receiver and went back to cleaning the floor.

Carpenter waited until an hour after lock-up before he took the Nokia from its hiding place in his stereo and phoned Fletcher. His man had obviously been waiting for the call because he answered it on the first ring. 'You've got a major fucking problem, boss. There's a grass in there.'

'What the hell are you talking about, Kim?'

'Mackie talked about a guy in prison. He only refers to him in passing, but he says he's got balls of steel. "Twenty-four hours a day among some of the hardest bastards in the realm" is what Mackie said. His name's Shepherd.'

'Why didn't Yates tell you about this?'

'It was a throwaway line, boss. Easy to miss unless you know the context.'

'That's all you've got?'

'I ran it by Ryan. And he came up trumps.'

Malcolm Ryan cost Carpenter upwards of a hundred grand a year but he was one of his most useful police sources. He worked in the Metropolitan Police payroll and pensions office and had access to the Met's personnel records. Carpenter was grateful that Fletcher had used his initiative rather than waiting for the go-ahead to contact Ryan. 'What did he say?'

'Said there's a Daniel Shepherd who worked for the Met for a year but who was seconded to some Home Office undercover unit.'

'Have you a picture?' asked Carpenter.

'Got better than that, boss. Ryan sent me a copy of his file.'

'Get it to me, Kim. You paid off Lewis?'

'Got the money to him,' said Fletcher. 'Did it through a courier. No link back to us, guaranteed.'

'Good man. Don't go near him again, not even a phone call. *Persona* bloody *non grata*.'

Carpenter cut the connection and put the phone away. He smiled savagely. As soon as he found out who the grass was, he'd take care of him. Permanently.

The next day the newspapers and mail weren't delivered until after dinner. Carpenter was lying on his back listening to Mozart on his headphones when Healey appeared at his cell door with his papers and two letters, one from Bonnie, the other from his lawyers. Both had been slit open. All his mail, incoming and outgoing, went through the prison censors. 'Short-staffed again,' said Healey. 'Lot of lead-swinging at the moment.'

'Gym's still on?'

'Yeah. The problem's over at admin,' said Healey. He left and Carpenter pushed the door shut.

The manila envelope was inside the *Guardian*. Unlike the posted mail, it was sealed. Carpenter opened it. There were three sheets of

A4 paper, a printout of a computer file. There was a name at the top of the first sheet. Daniel Shepherd. There was a photograph in the top left-hand corner. As he recognised the man Carpenter swore. Bob Macdonald. Bob fucking Macdonald. Carpenter felt a surge of anger. He'd talked to the man, shared confidences with him. And everything Macdonald had said had been a lie. It had been a set-up, right from the start. Bob Macdonald was Daniel Shepherd, and Daniel Shepherd was a lying, cheating undercover cop.

Carpenter read through the file. School in Manchester. Studied economics at Manchester University. Left before taking his finals and joined the army, the Paras. After two years passed selection for the SAS. Left to join the police. Currently attached to a Home Office undercover unit but his salary was still paid by the Met. A list of a dozen commendations.

Carpenter flicked through the sheets. Married. One son. Carpenter smiled. He'd take care of Daniel bloody Shepherd. Inside and on the out. He'd show him what it meant to cross Gerald Carpenter.

Moira ruffled Liam's head. 'Gran, I'm concentrating!' moaned Liam, his thumbs flicking across the controlls, his eyes glued to the television set.

'Those video games are bad for your eyes,' said Moira.

'So's reading,' said Liam. On the television, a racing car was hurtling along a crowded city street.

'Oh? Who told you that?' said Moira.

'Everyone knows that if you read too much you need glasses. All my teachers have glasses.' Liam groaned as the car crashed into the side of a bus and burst into flames.

'Doesn't that have a parental-guidance warning?' asked Moira.

'It's a video game, Gran.'

'Why don't you go and help your granddad in the front garden?' she said. 'He's pruning the roses.' She looked through the sitting-room window. Tom was standing at the garden gate, talking to two men in dark coats. Moira frowned. They weren't expecting visitors. The men looked like policemen. The man talking to Tom was smiling a lot. He had very white teeth, Moira noticed, too white to be real.

As she watched, Tom and the two men walked towards the house. Moira's stomach lurched at the thought that something might have happened to Daniel. She clasped her hands together and took a deep breath. It had been two police officers who'd broken the news of Susan's death. She'd opened her front door and known from the look on their faces that something bad had happened, and as soon as they'd asked her to confirm her name she'd known it was Susan they had come to see her about. They'd wanted to step inside the house, but she made them tell her on the doorstep and collapsed in the hallway. Her heart raced, but then she saw that the man with the white teeth was smiling and Tom was chatting to him. It couldn't have been bad news.

'What's wrong, Gran?' asked Liam.

'Nothing,' said Moira. She went to the front door and opened it, just as Tom and the two men arrived on the doorstep.

'These are two policemen, love,' said Tom. 'They want to check our security.'

'Why do we need security?' asked Moira defensively. 'Has something happened?'

'Nothing's happened, Mrs Wintour,' said the man with white teeth. He had a slight lisp, Moira thought, giving credence to her impression that his teeth were false. 'Just better safe than sorry.'

'But why would we need security?' asked Moira.

'It's okay, love,' said Tom. 'They just want to look round. Check the locks, the windows, that sort of thing.'

Moira sighed. 'I suppose you'd better come in,' she said. Tom waved the men inside. They wiped their feet on the doormat before stepping into the hallway. 'Would you like a cup of tea?' asked Moira.

'Tea would be lovely,' said the man with white teeth. 'Where's Liam, then?'

'In the sitting room, playing video games.'

Tom shut the front door.

'Kids!' said the man with white teeth. He pulled a large revolver

286

from his coat and pointed it at Moira's face. 'Now, do as you're told, you stuck-up bitch, or I'll put a bullet in your face!'

Carpenter was sitting in his cell, reading a copy of *Investor's Chronicle*. Most of his investments were offshore, well away from the grasping hands of HM Customs and police assert-seizure teams, but he liked to keep an eye on the UK stock markets.

He looked up as Rathbone appeared at his doorway. The officer glanced back down the landing, then ducked into the cell. 'Special delivery,' he said, slipping a brown envelope from under his black pullover. 'Rush job, yeah?' He handed it to Carpenter, then bent down and slipped a mobile-phone battery out of his shoe.

Carpenter took the battery, and studied the envelope. 'Have you opened this, Craig?'

Rathbone smiled easily. 'Might have done,' he said.

'Have you forgotten what we agreed?'

Rathbone pointed at the envelope. 'That's Macdonald's boy in there, isn't it? Saw him visiting.'

'Why's that of any concern of yours?'

'Because you're up to something. If Macdonald gets hurt, I could too.'

'Have you opened my correspondence before?'

Rathbone shook his head. 'That one felt different,' he said. 'Lucky I did.'

'Luck doesn't come into it,' said Carpenter. He sighed. 'Look, there's nothing for you to worry about. You've brought in other stuff for me, and you've been well paid for it. I gave you ten big ones for the phone. You get a grand for every letter you take in and out.'

'Yeah, but that's not a letter, is it?' said Rathbone.

'So, you want more?'

'I want five big ones for that. And I want five for any other envelope that's got more than a sheet of paper in it. Agreed?'

'Agreed.'

Rathbone turned to go.

'One more thing, Craig. I don't want you opening any more of my mail. Five grand pays for confidentiality, right?'

'Don't worry, Gerry.'

Rathbone left. Carpenter glared after him. He wasn't worried in the least.

Shepherd was doing press-ups in the corner of the exercise yard when a pair of white Nike trainers appeared in front of him. He looked up, holding his weight on his fingertips. It was Gilly Gilchrist, the prisoner who fetched and carried for Carpenter.

'What's up, Gilly?' asked Shepherd.

'The boss wants a word.'

'Okay. Tell him I'll be up when exercise is over.'

'He says now.'

'Yeah, well, I only get an hour a day in the fresh air, Gilly, and I want to take advantage of it.' He continued his press-ups.

'He says now,' repeated Gilchrist.

Shepherd stopped again. 'You're starting to piss me off, Gilly.'

'He said it was important,' said Gilchrist. 'If I go back without you, he's going to be pissed off at me. So I'm not going back without you.' He stood where he was, his hands on his hips.

Shepherd got to his feet and wiped his hands on his jeans. He walked back into the spur, with Gilchrist following. Something was wrong. If it was just a friendly chat, Carpenter himself could have come out into the exercise yard. Or talked to him in the gym. Or on cleaning duty. There was no need to summon Shepherd to his cell. Unless there was a problem. He walked up the stairs with Gilchrist behind him. That was a worry, too. If it was just a chat, Gilchrist would have been friendlier. Shepherd fingered his Walkman. If Carpenter had become suspicious, it might be a good idea to leave it at his cell. But if it was a chat, it might be the sort that Shepherd should record. He ran through everything that had happened over the previous twenty-four hours but couldn't think of anything that might have raised a red flag. He forced himself to relax, then pressed the pause button. Whatever happened, it would be recorded.

He reached the threes and walked down the landing to Carpenter's cell. The door was ajar but Shepherd knocked. There was no answer so Shepherd pushed it open and stepped inside.

It was the first time Shepherd had seen inside Carpenter's cell. There were photographs of his wife and children on the wall – not snaps stuck on with tape, like in most of the other cells, but large prints in wooden frames. There was a carpet on the floor and a brand new Sony tape-deck and speakers on top of the wall cabinet. The room smelt of lemon, and Shepherd saw a small air-freshener under the sink.

Carpenter was sitting on the only chair and when he stood up Shepherd saw that there was a blue silk cushion on it. He had been reading a book and he put it down on his bunk. It was about opening moves in chess. Carpenter smiled, like a kindly uncle. 'Well, you've been a busy bee, haven't you? He said.

'What's up?' said Shepherd.

'What's up? You've got the fucking audacity to ask me what's up?' Carpenter pointed finger at him. 'I'll tell you what's fucking up, Mr Plod. Your fucking number!'

Carpenter clenched his teeth and breathed heavily. Shepherd heard a noise behind him and looked round, but it was only Gilchrist with his back to the cell door. Shepherd ran through his options: he could stand his ground and try to bluff his way out; he could rush out on to the landing, hit the alarm button and hope that the officers got to the threes before Carpenter or his men did him any real damage; he could attack Carpenter, disable him, and Gilchrist if necessary, do whatever it took to save his skin.

'What the hell are you talking about, Gerry?' he said, hands swinging loosely by his side in case Carpenter should get physical. He looked for weapons but Carpenter's hands were empty and there was nothing obvious within reach.

'It's a bit late to play the innocent, Shepherd. It's a bit bloody late for that.'

As soon as he heard his name, Shepherd knew there was no point in trying to bluff his way out. If Carpenter knew his name, he knew everything. But the fact that he hadn't simply had him knifed in the showers meant that he had other plans. And that could only be bad news.

'I thought you were my fucking friend,' said Carpenter. 'I trusted you.'

'What can I tell you?' said Shepherd. 'A man's got to do what a man's got to do, right?'

'A man doesn't sneak around lying and cheating. Crawling around on his belly in the shit. That's not what a man does.'

'What do you want, Gerry?'

Carpenter continued to glare at him, then he smiled slowly. 'I suppose you think you've been pretty clever, don't you?'

Shepherd said nothing. He was still wondering why Carpenter had summoned him to the cell. If the man knew he was an undercover cop then he knew, too, that his plan to kill Roper would come to nothing and that he was going to prison for life. The drugs charges plus conspiracy to murder a Customs officer meant he'd be behind bars for ever.

'Did you think I wouldn't spot you? Do you think I can't smell an undercover cop a mile off?'

It was over, Shepherd realised. First, Carpenter wouldn't say anything incriminating. Second, by tomorrow everyone on the block would know he was an undercover cop. Within two days everyone in the prison. He was blown. But he doubted he'd done anything to show out. Someone must have grassed him up, and Shepherd wanted to know who. That was the only reason he was still in the cell.

Carpenter handed Shepherd an envelope. It had already been opened. 'What's this? My P45?' he asked.

'Open it and find out,' said Carpenter. 'It should knock that self-satisfied grin off your face.'

Shepherd slid back the flap. His stomach lurched. There was a Polaroid photograph inside. Even before he took it out he knew what had happened and that his life was about to change for ever.

He stared at the picture in horror. Liam was sitting on a wooden chair, staring at the camera, tight-lipped, his hands on his knees. Moira and Tom were behind him, their faces fearful.

'They weren't hard to find, not once I knew who you were,' said

Carpenter. 'You marry a girl from Hereford, she kicks the bucket, it makes sense that your lad would go and stay with her parents.'

'You hurt him – you hurt any of them – and you're dead,' said Shepherd.

'Nothing's going to happen to them, not if you're a good little piggy.'

'What do you want?' asked Shepherd.

'I want you to get me out of here,' said Carpenter.

'What?'

'You heard me. You've fucked up my plans well and good, so now you're going to get me out of here. That, or your kid dies.'

'You're not making any sense,' Shepherd said, confused.

'I'm making perfect sense,' said Carpenter. 'You've just got to listen to what I'm telling you. I have your son. You've stitched me up on the outside, you've had the Church spirit Roper away, you've been trying to put together a case against me in here. The way I see it, it's up to you to get me out.'

'Do I look like I've got a set of keys?'

Carpenter rushed at Shepherd and grabbed the front of his shirt. The Polaroid slipped from his fingers and fell to the floor. 'Don't get smart, Shepherd. Smart is what got you into the shit you're in.'

'How am I supposed to get you out, Gerry?' asked Shepherd calmly. He made no move to defend himself. There was no point: Carpenter held all the cards.

'That's up to you,' said Carpenter. 'But I'm telling you, here and now, if you don't get me the hell out of here, your boy dies.'

Shepherd held his hands out to his side while Hamilton patted him down. Then he went into the exercise yard. He took deep breaths of fresh air, then swung his arms and jogged on the spot. He wanted to run until he was exhausted, until he couldn't run any more. He wanted to get a gun and put it to Carpenter's head and pull the trigger. He wanted to grab the man by the throat and squeeze the life out of him.

Shepherd bent down and touched his toes, then arched his back, feeling his spine click into place. He wanted to kill Carpenter, but that wasn't an option. He couldn't kill him and he couldn't tell anyone. The fact that Carpenter knew who Shepherd was meant he still had a mole on the outside, someone who was passing information to him. If Shepherd told Hargrove or anyone else in the police, Carpenter might find out. And if that happened, Liam would be dead.

The strength went from his legs at the thought that his son might die because of what he'd done. He went down on one knee and put his hands on the Tarmac. His heart pounded and he fought to stop himself passing out.

A hand touched his shoulder. 'Are you all right, mate?' It was Ed Harris. 'You look like shit.'

'Stomach ache.'

'You want me to tell Hamilton that you've got to go to the medical centre?'

'I'll be okay.'

'Sure?'

'Sure.'

Shepherd stood up and took more deep breaths. He needed to plan, to find a way out. What he didn't need was to panic. Harris flashed him a worried look, but walked away. Shepherd gazed up through the anti-helicopter cables. What Carpenter was asking was unreasonable. How could he be expected to get him out of a Cat A prison?

He saw Justin Davenport on the opposite side of the exercise yard. It was hard to miss him in his escape-risk uniform with the patchwork of blue and yellow squares. He was walking on his own, looking through the wire mesh to the perimeter wall in the distance. Shepherd went over to him. 'How's it going?' he asked.

Davenport was in his early twenties, stick-thin and with a rash of acne across his forehead.

'I'm Bob Macdonald,' said Shepherd.

'The guy that shot the cops. Yeah, heard about you.'

'One cop, and I didn't pull the trigger. You're the guy they caught on the Eurostar.'

Davenport chuckled. 'Nah, I went round to see my girlfriend and the cops were there waiting for me. You can't believe anything you hear inside.'

'Everyone's innocent for a start,' said Shepherd. 'There's not a guilty man in here.'

Davenport giggled like a schoolboy.

'They say you escaped from Brixton,' Shepherd went on.

'Maybe.'

'Did you?'

'That's what they say.'

'Think you could get out of here?'

Davenport giggled again. 'It's escape-proof, this place. Didn't they tell you that?'

'If it's escape-proof, why do they make you wear that gear?'

Davenport looked down at his colourful clothing. 'To punish me – make me look like a twat.'

'It'd make them look like twats, if you did get out.'

Davenport snorted, then wiped his nose with the back of his hand. His fingernails were bitten to the quick. 'Yeah, that'd show them, wouldn't it?'

'So?'

Davenport shrugged. 'Can't be done.'

'Because?'

Davenport looked at him as if he was stupid. 'Because it's escape-proof.'

'Yeah, well, they said the *Titanic* was unsinkable.'

'Great movie, wasn't it? That Kate whatsername, I'd give her one.' Davenport started to walk round the yard, his trouser hems scuffing the Tarmac.

Shepherd hurried after him. 'You got over the wall at Brixton, right?'

'They say.'

'Made a ladder in the workshops.'

Davenport giggled again. 'Made it in bits, I did. We made crutches and walkers. You know, those things old folks shuffle about on. I made two walkers that could be taken apart and reassembled with four crutches as a ladder. Went up on to the roof of the workshop, legged it to the wall, up, over and away.'

'What about CCTV?'

'They had it but nobody watched the screens during the day, not when we were working. No point, right? That was the weakness in the system. They thought that because they had cameras covering all the walls nobody would climb over in broad daylight. But the screws in the coms room spent most of their time reading the papers and nattering on about the footie. They had fifty-odd cameras but only six monitors so most of the time the section of the wall I was going over wasn't even on screen.'

'What about when you were on the other side?'

'I legged it.'

'That was it?'

They'd worked their way round the exercise yard and were back at the entrance. Davenport didn't speak until they were out of earshot of Hamilton. 'I wasn't wearing gear like this. I had regular denims on. Just walked to a phone box and called my brother. He drove to south London and picked me up.'

'Could you do it here? Get over the wall?'

'You can't get to the wall. End of story.'

'But if you did?'

'That's an anti-climbing device on the top,' said Davenport, pointing to the top of the wall. 'You can't get a grip on it.'

'Tunnelling out?'

Davenport laughed. 'You've been watching too many prisoner-of-war movies, you have. That wall's thirty feet high. But it goes down thirty feet below ground, too. You can't go over or under. But like I said, you can't even get to the wall, that's the beauty of the design.'

He pointed at a wire fence some six metres away from the wall, topped with razor wire. 'Before you get to the wall, you have to get through or over the wire fence. That's got motion sensors so sensitive that a strong wind can set them off. Between the wire fence and the wall is what they call the sterile area. Inside there are

294

microwave detectors and motion-sensitive cameras.' He grinned. 'You know it's the same design they used in Belmarsh, where they keep all the terrorists?'

'Yeah?'

'Yeah. Four blocks, all linked by a secure corridor. The only way in and out of each block is through the corridor. Every time a prisoner's in the secure corridor, there's an officer with him. And the corridor's covered by CCTV. The officers can open all the doors in the blocks, and all the doors in the secure corridor, but the door out of the corridor is monitored by the control room at the main entrance. If they don't press the button, the door won't open. And they won't press the button until they've checked the CCTV.'

That meant that there was no way of breaking out of the secure corridor, Shepherd thought. Which meant there was no way of getting to the wall. Even if a prison officer was being held hostage and his keys taken, the ones at the gate would simply refuse to open the door.

'That's the way it works in a Cat A,' said Davenport. 'In a Cat A you're escorted everywhere, in a Cat B you're watched everywhere, in a Cat C you have freedom within the walls, and by the time you get to a Cat D, you're practically on the out. You want to know the best way to get out? Keep your nose clean and play the system. Go from here to a Cat B and then a Cat C and by the time you're Cat D you'll be going home one day every fortnight.'

'I was hoping you'd be more creative, Justin.'

'This place was built to be escape-proof,' he said. 'You know I'm on the twos, right?'

Shepherd had seen him coming out of a cell on the other side of the landing from his own.

'All escape-risk prisoners are put in the twos in Shelton – so that we can't dig up or down. Now, how stupid is that? We're observed through the spyglass every hour, right? So how can anyone dig in here? And what would you dig with? We're searched everywhere we go, right? And even if I was to dig my way out, where would I be? I'd be in the secure corridor, which means I'm under CCTV surveillance. And, like I said, you can't go over the wall or under it.' He turned away and lowered his voice to a whisper. 'Hamilton's watching us. Careful, everyone I speak to gets written up.'

Davenport walked away. Shepherd touched his toes and sneaked a look between his legs at the entrance to the exercise yard. The officer watched Davenport for a few seconds, then began patting someone down.

Shepherd swung his arms round, then jogged on the spot. Bill Barnes walked over, grinning. 'You're full of beans,' he said, took out a packet of Silk Cut and lit a cigarette with a disposable lighter.

Shepherd stopped jogging. He wanted to be on his own. He wanted to think. He wanted to be able to let out all the anger that was building up inside him, but he couldn't. He had to stay in his role. He was Bob Macdonald, armed robber and hard man. He couldn't show any emotion, any weakness. 'You told me you sold stolen watches, but I heard you were a cat burglar,' he said.

'Never stole a pussy in my life,' said Barnes.

'But you climb through windows, yeah?'

'It's been known.'

'Could you climb out of here?'

Barnes looked at him. 'What the fuck are you talking about?'

'This is my first time inside. I'm just putting out a few feelers.'

Barnes thrust his head closer to Shepherd's. 'You're talking about getting out?'

'I'm just considering my options.'

Barnes grunted. 'You're wasting your time.' He gestured up at the four CCTV cameras covering the exercise yard. 'Big Brother's watching you everywhere you go,' he said. 'You're escorted every move you make. Don't bother looking for a way out. There isn't one.'

'Escape-proof?'

'This place and Belmarsh were built to hold the most dangerous criminals in the country.' Barnes grinned. 'That's you and me, Bob.'

'And no one has ever got out?'

'Not from here.' Barnes started walking round the perimeter of the yard and Shepherd followed him. 'Guy got out of Belmarsh once.'

'Yeah? How?'

'Swapped identities with a prisoner who was being released,' said Barnes. He took another drag on his cigarette. 'The guards don't know every inmate's face and most of the file photographs are out of date by the time a guy's let out. So if you can find someone who's going to be released and persuade him to change places with you, you might get out.' Barnes grinned. 'Thing is, he's going to get another ten years for helping you. You either pay him off or threaten his family. If he's under duress, maybe he won't get sent down for it.'

Shepherd cracked his knuckles. Finding someone to change places with Carpenter was out of the question. He didn't have time and, besides, he had to escape with Carpenter. If they didn't go out together he had no guarantee that Liam would be released.

'There's always transit,' said Barnes.

'Transit?'

'You've got to make regular court appearances so that they can keep you on remand. Let Securicor take you through the gate. Minimum wage in uniforms, they are. The vans are heavy-duty, but they're still only armoured cars driven by monkeys. You've got mates with shooters?' Barnes made a gun with his right hand and faked shooting Shepherd in the face.

Shepherd nodded thoughtfully. Yeah, he had mates with shooters.

Rathbone unclipped his spaniel's lead and let her run free, in ever-increasing circles, sniffing and growling, happy to be out in the open air. Rathbone's mother took care of the dog when he was working, but she had a bad hip and couldn't do more than let her out into the tiny back garden. She had been on an NHS waiting list for a new hip for the best part of four months, but there was no sign yet of her getting anywhere near a surgeon's knife. It wasn't fair, thought Rathbone. His father had paid a lifetime of tax and

National Insurance contributions and had died of a heart-attack two weeks after he retired. Now his mum had to wait in line for medical treatment while asylum-seekers stayed in hotels and got money in their pockets. It wasn't fair, and life wasn't fair. But at least he was doing something to redress the balance. Five grand for delivering the photograph to Carpenter. Ten grand for the phone. With any luck Carpenter would stay behind bars for years. And if Carpenter got out, the prison was full of wealthy guys who could afford the service Rathbone offered: access to the little comforts that could make life inside a bit more comfortable.

The dog ran off, barking. Rathbone twirled the lead and walked after her. He'd have liked nothing more than to whisk his mother into a private hospital and have her pain taken away, but if he did that he risked losing everything. The money had to stay untouched until he left the prison service. Until then he had to live at home, drive a three-year-old car and watch his mother hobble upstairs to bed each night.

A man was walking along the path towards him. He was in the centre so Rathbone stepped to the side but the man moved the same way. Rathbone smiled an apology.

'Nice dog,' said the man. He had unnaturally white teeth and they seemed slightly too big for his mouth.

'Yeah,' said Rathbone, disinterestedly. He had no wish to get into a conversation with a stranger. He didn't mind talking to other dog-owners, but the man had no lead in his hand and there was no dog nearby. Rathbone called his dog, but the spaniel was having too much fun to respond.

'Cocker spaniel, isn't he?' said the man.

'She,' said Rathbone. 'She's a bitch.'

The man smiled. 'Yeah. So's life.' He pulled a hunting knife from his coat pocket and thrust it into Rathbone's chest. Rathbone fell back and the knife came sucking out, still in the man's hand.

Rathbone turned and tried to run but another man was in the way. He, too, was holding a knife, and he slashed it across Rathbone's throat. Rathbone tried to scream but his windpipe was full of blood and all that came out was a soft gurgle. He fell to his knees, clutching his throat, feeling the warm blood pump through his fingers.

'You shouldn't have opened the envelope, Craig,' said the man with white teeth. He kicked Rathbone in the chest and he fell backwards into the grass.

'Big mistake,' added his companion.

'Huge,' said the first man. Rathbone's eyes glazed over and his mouth fell open, bloody froth on his lips. 'Get his wallet and watch. Let's at least try to make it look like a mugging.'

The spaniel watched them from behind a tree, her body low to the ground.

'Do you want to kill the dog?' Rathbone heard the second man say, his voice far off in the distance.

'No, Pat, I do not want to kill the fucking dog.'

That was the last thing Rathbone heard, and he found it strangely comforting. At least his dog would be okay.

Shepherd waited until no prisoners were waiting to use the phones, then walked over and dialled Jimmy Sharpe's number. It was a mobile and when the detective answered he could hear an approaching siren in the background.

'DC Sharpe, this is Bob Macdonald.' He spoke quickly so that Sharpe would know they had to stay in character.

'How's prison food?' asked Sharpe.

'I need a favour,' said Shepherd. 'I need you to check on my boy.'

'You think there's a problem?'

'If there is, I don't want you to do anything about it,' said Shepherd. 'You've still got that number I gave you?'

'Yes.'

'If there's anything untoward at the house, call my friend and tell him what's happened. But that's all. Don't start raising red flags.'

'Okay,' said Sharpe, hesitantly.

'Mum's the word on this,' said Shepherd. 'Any comeback, any shit heading towards the fan, and you know nothing.'

'Understood.'

'Thanks,' said Shepherd.

'Are you okay?'

'Not really, but there's nothing you can do to help. Just check on my boy, and make that call. Then forget we spoke.' Shepherd replaced the receiver and walked up the stairs to the threes. He went along the landing to Gilly Gilchrist. 'I need to talk to him,' said Shepherd.

Gilchrist went into the cell, and reappeared a few moments later. He waved Shepherd inside.

Carpenter was sitting on his chair, a pair of headphones in his hand. 'Mozart,' he said. 'Nothing better than a bit of Mozart in the afternoon.'

'I think I've got a plan,' said Shepherd.

'I'm very glad to hear it,' said Carpenter. 'And I'm sure Liam will be, too.' He smiled.

Shepherd wanted to grab him and slam his head against the concrete wall until the back was a bloody mess. 'When's your next court appearance?' he asked.

'Next week,' said Carpenter. 'Tuesday morning.'

'That gives me enough time,' said Shepherd.

'Time for what?'

'I can get you out while you're in transit. In the van on the way to court.'

Carpenter scowled. 'Do you have any idea how they take me to court?' he asked.

'In a Securicor van. Same sort they brought me in, right? It's not a problem.'

'The problem isn't the van, Supercop. The problem is the car full of armed police front and back, and the helicopter overhead.'

Shepherd showed no reaction. 'Like I said, it's not a problem.'

'I'm going to need more than that, Shepherd.'

'I know people.'

'Yeah, well, I know people too.'

'You know what I did before I was a cop?'

'Army.'

'Not just army. SAS.'

'I know,' said Carpenter.

Shepherd filed the information for future reference. There weren't many ways that Carpenter could have discovered he had been in the SAS. 'So a few armed police and a helicopter aren't going to worry the people I know,' said Shepherd.

'And they'll do it?'

Shepherd nodded slowly.

'How much are you paying them?'

'Nothing. They're friends.'

'So, Tuesday it is.'

Shepherd stared at Carpenter. 'If you hurt my son, I'll kill you.'

'Sticks and stones,' Carpenter said laconically.

Shepherd rushed forward and thrust the heel of his left hand against Carpenter's chin, pushing him against the cell wall. He drew his right fist back, ready to smash it into Carpenter's face. Carpenter stared at Shepherd, his hands hanging at his side. There was no fear in his eyes. Shepherd was breathing hard, his left hand clamped round Carpenter's throat. 'I'll kill you now!' he hissed.

Carpenter's face reddened but he made no sound. He just stared at Shepherd.

'I'll do it here and now.'

Shepherd heard a noise at the door. Carpenter's eyes flicked towards it, then back to Shepherd.

'Stay where you are or I'll drive his nose into his skull,' said Shepherd, without looking round.

Carpenter looked over Shepherd's shoulder and nodded at Gilchrist. Shepherd tightened his grip on Carpenter's throat. It would be so easy to kill him. One punch. The cartilage would spear the soft brain tissue, severing blood vessels, and bringing about almost instantaneous death. But what then? Would killing him get Liam back? Carpenter glared at him. There was anger in his eyes now, but still no sign of fear.

Shepherd released him. Gilchrist took a step towards Shepherd but Carpenter held up his hand. 'It's okay,' he croaked. 'Leave it.'

Gilchrist backed away. 'Watch the door,' said Carpenter. He unscrewed the top of a bottle of Highland Spring water and drank deeply, then wiped his mouth. Gilchrist went back out on to the landing. Carpenter took another drink. Shepherd stood at the foot of his bed.

Carpenter put down the bottle. 'I understand your anger, Dan. If I was in your place I'd be angry, too. I'd lash out. I'd do exactly what you're doing. But in my heart I'd know that getting angry wouldn't get my boy back.'

'You hurt him and you're dead.'

'The whole point of this is that Liam doesn't get hurt,' said Carpenter. 'You get me out of here and you get your boy back. Everyone gains. The only way Liam gets hurt is if I have to stay behind bars. If that happens we all lose. You lose your boy and I lose my freedom.'

'I'll do what I can, but if it goes wrong, if I fail, then you're not to hurt him.'

Carpenter said nothing.

'Did you hear me?'

'I heard you. But you've no bargaining power here, Dan. I hold all the cards. And just so there's no misunderstanding, my men on the outside will kill Liam if anything happens to me in here.' He pointed a finger at Shepherd's face. 'I'll put down what just happened to the stress you're under, but you touch me again and I'll have your boy slapped around.'

Shepherd said nothing.

'Did you hear me, Dan?'

'Yeah,' he said Shepherd. 'I understand.'

'Good man. Now, tell me exactly what you've got planned.'

There were three phones on Major Allan Gannon's desk. One was a general line that went through the switchboard at the Duke of York barracks in London, another was a direct line to SAS headquarters in Hereford, and the third connected him to the Special Boat Squadron base in Lympstone. Next to his desk, on a table of its own, was the briefcase containing the secure satellite phone they called the Almighty. It never left Gannon's side. It rarely rang, but when it did, all hell usually broke loose. The only people who had access to it were the Prime Minister, the Cabinet Office, and the chiefs of M15 and M16. And they didn't call Gannon for a chat about the weather.

It had been several weeks since the Almighty had rung, and Gannon felt like a caged lion. Three-quarters of the SAS personnel had gone to Iraq, and half had been in country before hostilities had officially commenced. But Gannon had been told in no uncertain terms that his services were required in the UK in case of a local terrorist incident. He and his team had waited for the expected terrorist backlash but none had been forthcoming and Gannon had spent the Iraqi war watching reporters in flak jackets describe the offensive on BBC World, Sky News and CNN.

He stood up, walked to the window and stared out through the bomb-proof blinds at the parade-ground, where a lone soldier on a discipline charge stood ramrod straight, his weapon at his side, sweating under the midday sun. He'd been standing at attention for three hours, ever since he'd been marched out by a grim-looking sergeant-major. Gannon had grinned when he'd seen the sergeant-major giving the squaddie a dressing-down. Standing still for three hours wasn't what Gannon would consider a punishment. A beating by six SAS troopers, now that was lesson the young man would never forget.

A phone rang. Not the Almighty. The Almighty's commanding call to arms could never be confused with a regular telephone's half-hearted warble. It was the cream-coloured phone. The switchboard line. He picked up, knowing that, more likely than not, it would be a wrong number.

'Gannon,' he said, into the receiver.

'Major Allan Gannon?' said a voice. Scottish. Not a voice Gannon recognised.

'Yes?'

'My name's Sharpe, Jimmy Sharpe. You don't know me but I'm calling on behalf of a mutual friend who needs your help. Spider Shepherd.'

Gannon reached for a pad attached to a metal clipboard. It was stamped 'Eyes Only – Top Secret. Not For Distribution'. Strictly speaking the pad was only for official work, but Gannon doubted that anyone would mind. 'What does he need?' asked Gannon.

Shepherd's name was on the gym list again, presumably because Lloyd-Davies had been pulling strings on his behalf. His main motivation for using the gym had been to get close to Carpenter, but that had been blown out of the water. He had stopped carrying the Walkman. There was no longer any point. He'd left a message with Uncle Richard, telling him that things were progressing slowly. He just hoped Hargrove didn't decide the investigation had stalled and pull him out.

He waited at the bubble. Amelia Heartfield was inside, talking to Tony Stafford. She was crying, brushing away tears with the back of her hand. Bill Barnes was standing at the stairs wearing his England football strip with a towel round his neck.

'What's wrong with her?' asked Shepherd, indicating Amelia.

'Rathbone's been killed,' said Barnes.

'How?'

'Mugged. Knifed.'

'What?'

'He was walking his dog. They found him stabbed. No wallet, no watch.'

'Bloody hell.'

'I tell ya, Bob, you're safer in here sometimes, the way the world is,' Barnes went on. 'He was okay, was Rathbone. Fair. Treated us like people, not numbers. That's rare in here.'

Carpenter came down from the threes with his bottle of Highland Spring. He ignored Shepherd and went to stand by the barred door.

'They know who did it?' asked Shepherd.

Barnes shook his head. 'It's in the *Evening Standard*. Stabbed in the chest and had his throat cut. Police are appealing for witnesses, blah, blah, blah.'

Shepherd frowned. Stabbed in the chest *and* a cut throat? It sounded like two assailants, but if it had been a mugging and there were two of them there'd have been no need for that degree of violence.

Amelia came out of the bubble and unlocked the door to the secure corridor. She checked the eight names of the men on the gym list, then escorted them down the secure corridor. Shepherd walked with Barnes, who wouldn't stop talking, but that was fine. Shepherd let the words wash over him. Carpenter brought up the rear of the group. Shepherd didn't turn to look at him but he could feel the man's eyes boring into his back.

As soon as they'd been checked in, Shepherd went over to a tread-mill and started running. Carpenter appeared at his side and stabbed the stop button. Shepherd slowed to a halt. Carpenter leaned close to him. 'You heard what happened to Rathbone, yeah?'

'That was you?'

'What the fuck do you think? Time's running out, Shepherd. You get me out of here or your kid gets the same.'

Shepherd glared at Carpenter. 'It's in hand.'

'It'd better be,' said Carpenter. He jabbed at the treadmill's start button and walked away as Shepherd started running again.

Moira banged on the door with the flat of her hand. 'Moira, please,' said her husband. He was sitting on the floor with his back to the wall. 'You'll just annoy them.' Liam was sitting next to him, his head against his grandfather's shoulder.

'Liam needs food,' said Moira, 'and water. And we need to be able to use a toilet.' She glanced at the red plastic bucket and toilet roll in the far corner of the basement. 'We're not using that.' She banged on the door again. 'You out there! Come here!'

'Moira, they've got guns.'

She ignored him and continued to bang on the door. She stopped when she heard footsteps on the other side of the door.

'Now what?' said a muffled voice.

'We need food,' Moira shouted. 'My grandson's hungry.'

'I'm all right, Gran,' said Liam.

'Stand away from the door,' said the voice. Moira did as she was told and they heard the sound of bolts being drawn back. The door opened. Despite his mask she knew it was the man with the gleaming white teeth. She didn't understand why they

305

were bothering to hide their faces because she'd seen them when they'd walked up the garden path with Tom. She didn't have the best memory for faces but she'd never forget those two men after what they'd done. They'd called her a bitch in her own house and waved a gun in her face, bundled them into the back of a van and made them pull hoods over their heads, terrorised young Liam and threatened to shoot them all if they didn't do as they were told.

'What do you want?' said the man.

'I want you to let us go, but I suppose that's out of the question, so I want food and something to drink, and I want to use the loo. A real loo, not that bucket.'

'We'll bring you food later.' He was holding his pistol and pointed it at the bucket. 'Use that or keep your fucking legs crossed.'

'How dare you speak to me like that?' said Moira.

The man pushed her in the chest. She gasped and staggered backwards.

'Don't you hit my gran!' shouted Liam. He rushed across the basement and kicked the man in the shins. The man lashed out with his foot and caught Liam in the groin. He screamed and fell to the concrete floor.

Tom pushed himself to his feet and walked over to the man, his hands bunching into fists. 'There's no need for that,' he said. 'Hitting women and children, you should be ashamed of yourself.'

The man raised the gun and slashed it across Tom's head. He grunted and dropped to his knees, then fell sideways next to the wall, blood trickling down his cheek.

Moira screamed and knelt down beside him. 'You've killed him!' Liam was crying, his knees drawn up to his chest.

'He's not dead!' yelled the man. 'But carry on the way you are and you fucking well will be. This isn't a fucking game. If I get a phone call telling me to put a bullet in your heads, then that's what I'll do. You are *this* close to being dead.'

Tom put a hand to his head and groaned. 'Thank God,' said Moira. She leaned over and held Liam's hand. 'It's okay, Liam. It's okay.'

The man bent down and poked her in the back with the gun. 'No, it's not okay. It's as far from okay as you can get. Now, shut up or I'll give you what I gave your fucking husband.' He jabbed her with the gun again, spat at her, then stamped out and bolted the door.

Tears ran down Moira's face as she comforted Liam. She stared at the door and, for the first time in her life, she wished another person dead.

Shepherd pulled on his yellow sash and joined the queue of prisoners waiting to go into the visiting room. The Welsh officer who'd originally escorted him from reception to the remand wing was patting down prisoners. Shepherd smelt garlic on the man's breath as he carried out the search. He figured that few prisoners would be trying to smuggle anything out of the prison, the contraband would all be coming in.

His visitor was already seated. He was a big man with a strong chin, wide shoulders and a nose that looked as if it had been broken at least once. He was wearing a baseball cap and sunglasses and kept his head down as Shepherd walked to the table. He waited until Shepherd had sat down before he said anything. Then he leaned across the table so that his mouth was only a few inches away from Shepherd's ear. 'Fuck me, Spider, I always knew you'd come to a bad end, but I never thought you'd end up behind bars.'

'Thanks for coming, Major,' Shepherd murmured.

'Do you want to fill me in on what the hell you're doing in here?' said Gannon.

Shepherd looked around the visitors' room. One prison officer was at the far end of the room but he seemed more interested in two married couples who were kissing as if their lives depended on it. The Welsh guard was still patting down arrivals at the door. Keeping his voice low, Shepherd told Gannon everything. The robbery. The new assignment. Gerald Carpenter. Sue's death. And Liam's kidnapping.

Gannon listened in silence, his face tightening as he learned of Sue's accident, eyes hardening as Shepherd told him what had happened to his son. When he had finished, Gannon gave a soft whistle. 'You've packed a lot into the last few weeks,' he said. 'I'm sorry about Sue. No one told the Regiment.'

'No one outside my team knows. There won't even be a funeral until after this is all over.'

'And who knows about Liam?'

'You, me and Carpenter.'

'What is it you want, Spider?' asked Gannon.

'I want to get out of here.'

The SAS major nodded slowly. 'Consider it done,' he said.

Gannon slotted the slide cartridge into the projector while Martin O'Brien poured coffee from a pewter pot into five dainty cups. O'Brien was in his late thirties, broad-shouldered, and he'd put on a few pounds since he'd last served with the major. He was now doing close-protection work with World Bank executives, and two years of lunches in expensive restaurants and overnighters in five-star hotels had taken a toll on his waistline.

O'Brien handed cups of coffee to Geordie Mitchell and Billy Armstrong. Mitchell and Armstrong had left the Regiment a decade ago, but were still trim and fit. Mitchell ran ten kilometres a day with a rucksack filled with housebricks, and Armstrong swam two miles in the sea every morning. Mitchell was doing something shady out in the Far East, and Armstrong ran survival courses down in Cornwall. Mitchell sipped his coffee. He grimaced as it hit a bad tooth. He had a mouthful of crowns, half of them gold. Armstrong ran a hand through his receding hair and stretched out his long legs.

Gannon looked at his Rolex Submariner. Only one member of the group was absent but he wasn't surprised: Jimbo Shortt was a notoriously bad timekeeper. He knew more about tele- and radio communications than anyone else Gannon had met so he would be invaluable for what he had planned. All four knew Shepherd well and had agreed to drop everything when Gannon had told them of his predicament. Shortt had the furthest to come: he was teaching close-quarter combat techniques to Ukrainian

308

SWAT teams but had promised to get on the next flight to the UK.

Armstrong drained his cup and stood up to help himself to more. Gannon knew the men would have preferred mugs, but room service in the hotel just off Piccadilly had supplied cups and saucers more suitable for a lady's knitting circle than a group of military men brought together for a tactical briefing.

'Two sugars in mine, Billy,' said Shortt, as he strode in. He was a stocky five feet nine with a sweeping Mexican moustache. He shook hands with Gannon. 'Sorry I'm late, boss. Traffic.'

Gannon smiled, but said nothing. Shortt always had an excuse, but considering that just twenty-four hours earlier he had been in the Ukraine, Gannon reckoned he had nothing to complain about.

Armstrong handed Shortt some coffee and the two men took their seats. Gannon dimmed the lights and switched on the projector. He hadn't bothered with a screen: the wall above the television set was pristine white. A satellite shot of four cross-shaped build-ings surrounded by a wall came into focus as he fiddled with the lens. 'Her Majesty's Prison Shelton,' he said. 'Same design as the better-known Belmarsh in south London. You all know why we're here, and you all know what we've got to do, so there's no need for a sit-rep. The fact that you're all here means you're up for it, so I'm going to run through the operation start to finish.'

'Who else is in on this?' asked Armstrong.

'Just you,' said Gannon. 'After this briefing I'll have no further involvement, not because I wouldn't give my eye-teeth to be with you but we can't afford to have any official connection to whatever happens. You guys are all—'

'Expendable?' said O'Brien, with a grin. He tore open a Mars bar and took a bite.

'No longer on the Regimental payroll, is what I was going to say, Martin. But, in your case, expendable will do.'

'I don't want to sound negative,' said Mitchell, 'but even I can count, and I make it four of us. That's one brick against a maximum security prison containing how many guards?'

'A full complement of a hundred and sixty during daytime hours. About fifty at night. But none are armed.'

Mitchell frowned apologetically. 'And again, without raining on anyone's parade, aren't these places designed to withstand pretty much anything?'

Gannon smiled. 'That's the whole point, Geordie. Prisons are designed to keep people in. And they make a bloody good job of it. But there's one thing they're not designed for, and that's what we're going to take advantage of.'

The four men exchanged confused looks, wondering what the major wanted them to do.

Gannon grinned. He pressed the switch in his hand and another slide flashed on to the wall: a photograph of the main entrance of the prison taken through a long lens. 'Now, if you ladies would allow me to continue with the briefing, I'll take questions later.'

The four men settled back in their chairs and listened as Gannon outlined what he wanted them to do.

Martin O'Brien and Geordie Mitchell arrived in Belfast on the afternoon ferry but they waited until it was dark before driving their green Range Rover out of the city and to the west on the M1. O'Brien drove slowly, then left the M1 at Lisburn, checked that he wasn't being followed and headed for Armagh.

The churchyard was exactly as he remembered it, bordered by a shoulder-high stone wall festooned with ivy, the grass well tended and the gravestones weathered by centuries of Irish wind and rain. There was a noticeboard at the entrance, detailing times of services and a phone number on which the priest could be reached, twenty-four hours a day. O'Brien smiled when he saw it was a mobile number: there was something amusing about a priest using new technology to keep in touch with his flock.

There was a half-moon overhead and a relatively clear sky: enough light to see by. O'Brien nodded at Mitchell and pushed open the wooden gate. It creaked like a rheumatic joint. The church was in darkness, the nearest house a hundred yards down the road. The two men had sat in the Range Rover for thirty minutes until they were satisfied that no one was in the vicinity, no late-night lovers or insomniac dog-walkers to stumble across them as they moved aside the two-hundred-year-old gravestone and dug into the hard earth with their spades.

They worked in silence and were both breathing heavily when they uncovered the first package. It was wrapped in polythene and O'Brien slowly peeled it back to reveal an oily cloth package. Inside he found a Chinese automatic pistol, with rust on the handgrips. He showed it to Mitchell, then put it aside and picked up a bigger package, almost three feet long, handed it to Mitchell and pulled out another. Both contained Hungarian 7.62mm AKM-63 automatic rifles, copies of the Soviet AK-47, with plastic socks and handgrips. 'These'll do,' said Mitchell. The weapons were serviceable but, more importantly, they looked the part.

O'Brien used his spade to lever more polythene-wrapped parcels out of the soil. One contained ammunition for the AKM-63s. Another contained half a dozen Second World War revolvers. He wouldn't want to risk live firing those.

The arms cache had been put together by the Real IRA in the late nineties. The organisation was poorly funded in comparison with the Provisionals and they had a tendency to buy whatever weaponry was offered to them. Most of the consignment buried in the graveyard had come from a Bosnian gangster, who had travelled from Sarajevo to Belfast to arrange the shipment. Special Branch had the man under surveillance from the moment he'd landed on British soil and MI6 had followed the shipment from a warehouse outside Sarajevo to a beach on the south coast of Ireland, from where it had been driven up to Belfast. Unbelievably, MI6 had lost the truck in Belfast and the consignment had vanished.

O'Brien had been working undercover in West Belfast and had penetrated a Real IRA cell that had been authorised to withdraw a number of weapons from the cache to use in a building-society robbery. He and three terrorists had removed several handguns. O'Brien hadn't passed on details of the cache to his handler. It had been a flagrant breach of procedure, but he had seen too many cock-ups to put his life on the line by revealing what he'd seen. If his bosses had decided to go in and neutralise the arms, it wouldn't have taken the Real IRA high command long to work out where the information had come from.

O'Brien was supposed to have driven the getaway car for the three robbers, but there'd been a change of plan at the last minute and he had been told that his services wouldn't be required. The raid had ended in disaster – not through action by the security services but a road accident. The replacement driver had gone through a red light on the way to the building society and a bus had side-swiped the car. The petrol tank had exploded and all four were killed. The following day the Real IRA executive who had organised the purchase of the arms had been assassinated by a Unionist death squad, and O'Brien realised that he was the only man left who knew the location of the arms. It was a secret he'd kept even after leaving the army. The only person he'd ever told was Gannon, and the major had recommended he kept the information to himself. Until now.

O'Brien unwrapped another package: a Polish Onyx short assault rifle with a folding stock and two curved thirty-round magazines. The gun was a copy of the Russian-made AKS-74U submachine gun, capable of firing 725 rounds a minute. An excellent bit of kit. 'I'll have this,' he said.

Mitchell picked up a small package and opened it: a Polish Radom, a heavy 9mm pistol. 'Why would they buy this crap?' he asked.

'Beggars can't be choosers,' said O'Brien. He pulled apart another small package, and whistled softly. It was a brand new SIG-Sauer P-228, a compact Swiss pistol with a thirteen-round magazine.

'I'll have that,' said Mitchell, reaching for it.

'My arse you will,' said O'Brien. 'Finders keepers. Anyway, you and Billy are using the AKMs.'

They worked through the cache. The prize was at the bottom: a wooden box the size of a small suitcase that had been wrapped in a dozen black rubbish bags. O'Brien grinned. 'Bullseye,' he said.

*　　*　　*

Jimbo Shortt paid off his black cab, then headed west along the King's Road, checking reflections in shop windows before crossing the street and heading back the way he'd come, checking for tails. When he was sure he wasn't being followed he crossed the road and headed for a black door between an antiques shop and a hairdresser's. To the right was a small brass plaque inscribed 'Alex Knight Security', a bell button and a speaker grille.

Shortt pressed the button and was buzzed in. He headed up a narrow flight of stairs. A striking brunette had the door at the top open for him. 'Jimbo, I didn't know you were in London,' she said, giving him a peck on the cheek.

'Flying visit, Sarah,' he said. 'Is he in?'

'Ready and waiting for you,' she said.

Alex Knight was sitting behind a pile of electronic equipment and a stack of manuals. The walls of his office were lined with metal shelving stacked with boxes and more manuals. There was a single chair on Shortt's side of the desk but it was piled high with unopened Federal Express packets.

'Can I interest you in a sat-phone scrambler, Jimbo?' asked Knight. 'State-of-the-art from Taiwan. I can do you a deal.'

'Not this time, Alex.'

Knight came round from behind his desk and several inches of bony wrist protruded from his dark blue blazer when he stuck out his hand out to shake Shortt's. He was tall and gangly, with square-framed black spectacles perched high on his nose.

'So, what can I do you for?' he asked.

'Scanner that'll key me in to police frequencies,' said Shortt.

'Ask me something difficult,' said Knight. 'You can buy them at Argos.'

Shortt chuckled. The sort of equipment Knight sold was most definitely not available on the high street. 'This'll do the trick,' he said, pulling a box off a shelf and examining the label. It was a model he hadn't seen before. 'And I need a mobile-phone jammer. A biggie.'

'Illegal in this country, of course,' said Knight.

'Of course,' said Shortt.

'How big?'

'How big have you got?'

'I've got hand-helds that can block all signals up to a hundred feet,' said Knight.

'Bigger,' said Shortt.

'There's a model just in from Hong Kong that can shut down all signals in a building, pretty much.'

'Bigger,' said Shortt, grinning.

'Jimbo, why don't you just tell me what it is you want shutting down?'

Shortt's grin widened. 'You don't want to know, Alex, but let's say it's the size of a football stadium.'

Knight went back behind his desk and tapped away on his computer. He frowned, and tapped again.

Shortt continued to walk along the shelves, picking up the occasional box and examining its contents. Some of the equipment Knight had was so cutting-edge that even Shortt wasn't sure what it was supposed to do.

'What frequencies?' Knight asked.

'UK only,' said Shortt.

'Sale or lease?'

'I was hoping you'd lend me one, Alex.' Knight raised an eyebrow, and Shortt laughed. 'I'll need it for a couple of days.'

'I can let you have one for a week at five grand, but I'm going to need a deposit. This is expensive kit. When do you need it by?'

'Yesterday,' said Shortt.

Shepherd was in the corner of the exercise yard doing vigorous press-ups when his name was called. It was Hamilton. He got to his feet and went over to him, brushing his hands on his jeans. 'Legal visit,' said Hamilton.

Shepherd followed him off the spur and along the secure corridor to the visitors' centre. Hamilton said nothing during the long walk and Shepherd didn't want to start a conversation. He hadn't requested a visit from Hargrove. If the superintendent had discovered what had happened to Liam, it was all over. Shepherd forced himself to relax as he was shown into the glass-sided room.

Hargrove shook his hand. 'How's it going, Spider?'

Shepherd sat down. 'Slowly.'

'Hadn't heard from you for a while so I thought I'd drop by and see how you were.' Hargrove took his seat. His briefcase was on the floor.

'Soon as there's something to report, I'll be on the phone.'

'Are you okay?'

'I'm fine.'

'You look a little tense, that's all.'

'I'm in prison, for fuck's sake,' Shepherd snapped. He saw the look of concern on Hargrove's face and held up his hands. 'Sorry,' he said. 'It's just that being Bob Macdonald twenty-four seven isn't easy.'

'Anything I can do?'

Shepherd shook his head.

'Anything taped we can use?'

'I'm only wearing the recorder when there are officers around. That way he can't start searching me if he gets suspicious. Problem is, with the officers around he's not going to say much. I want to get him talking in his cell but I'm not in there often.'

'We need something, Spider. You know how important this is.'

'I can't push it any more than I'm doing or he'll back off.'

'And he hasn't said anything we can use?'

'He's not stupid,' said Shepherd. 'He's in here because he was set up by pros, and he's keen not to make the mistake again.'

'You don't think he suspects anything?'

'I'm being careful.'

'Carpenter's got a remand hearing in a couple of days. Might give you something to talk about.'

'I'll give it a go. He's not going to get bail, is he?'

Hargrove grinned. 'Not a snowball's chance in hell. He might have torn holes in our case but the judge is aware of what's going on and he's a safe pair of hands.'

'I'm doing my best,' said Shepherd.

'I know you are, Spider. Do you want me to go and see your boy?'

315

'Best stay away until it's all over.'

'You sure?'

'I'm sure.'

Hargrove stood up and adjusted his cuffs, picked up his briefcase, then held out his hand. Shepherd stood up and shook it. He hated lying to Hargrove, but he had no choice. There was nothing the superintendent could do to get Liam back. It was all down to Major Gannon and his team.

Jimbo Shortt brought the van to a halt about a hundred yards from the prison wall. Armstrong and Mitchell were in the back. O'Brien twisted round in the front passenger seat. 'Okay, let's get to it,' he said. 'From the moment we go in, we'll have eight minutes, maximum. If we're unlucky and someone calls it in, that's how long it'll take SO19 to get here.'

'Assuming there isn't an armed-response car driving by,' said Mitchell.

'Let's look on the bright side, shall we?' said O'Brien. 'This time of night, that's not likely.'

Armstrong slotted a magazine into his AKM and adjusted his black ski mask. Armstrong, Mitchell and O'Brien were wearing black fireproof overalls, ski masks and sneakers. They had black leather belts on their waists with spare ammunition, a handgun each and a radio transmitter nestling in the small of their backs. There was no need for the ballistic jackets or helmets – there wasn't a single gun inside the prison. The only risk of firepower was from the Metropolitan Police's SO19 armed-response teams. Shortt was the only member of the team wearing civilian clothes. He had on a leather jacket over blue overalls and a New York Yankees baseball cap.

'And again, if we do come up against armed cops, defensive fire only,' said O'Brien. 'Understood?'

Armstrong and Mitchell nodded.

'Fire over their heads and get the hell out,' said O'Brien. 'The cops aren't used to taking automatic fire. Okay, let's get to it.' He pulled on his mask, climbed out of the van and jogged round to the rear, his Polish short assault rifle strapped to his back. Armstrong and Mitchell opened the doors and pushed the wooden box towards O'Brien, then helped him lower it to the ground.

Shortt hefted the briefcase-sized phone jammer on to the passenger seat. He had already disabled the local BT sub-station that handled the landlines from Shelton. The jammer would take care of any mobiles in the vicinity.

'Check comms,' said O'Brien. 'Alpha on air.'

The men had on microphone headsets under their masks, wired to the receivers on their belts.

'Beta on air,' said Mitchell.

O'Brien gave him a thumbs-up. His voice had come over loud and clear through the earpiece.

'Gamma on air,' said Armstrong. O'Brien nodded.

'Delta on air,' said Shortt.

O'Brien knelt down and opened the wooden box: a Russian-made 7V rocket-propelled grenade launcher nestled in a bed of polystyrene balls. Mitchell nodded approvingly. 'Nice bit of kit,' he said.

'Oh, yes,' said O'Brien. 'The Somalis used one of these to bring down that Blackhawk. Accurate up to three hundred metres with a moving target, five hundred if it's stationary.'

'Makes a change from friendly fire,' said Mitchell.

O'Brien took the metre-long launcher from the box and hefted it on to his shoulder. He walked a few paces towards the prison entrance.

'Sure you've got it the right way round?' asked Armstrong.

'Aye, fuck you too,' said O'Brien. He looked at his watch, then knelt down on one knee and sighted on the main gate, a hundred metres away. 'Are we all set?'

'Mobile signals are down,' Shortt said. 'All signals blocked. Rock and roll.'

O'Brien took a deep breath. His heart was pounding as adrenaline coursed through his system. He'd fired RPGs before, more than a dozen, but there was always the risk that something might go wrong and it blew up in his hands.

In the distance the occasional car drove down the motorway but all they could see were the headlights carving through the darkness. The prison had been shielded from the road by landscaped hills and trees so that the sensibilities of law-abiding citizens in north London wouldn't be offended by high walls and surveillance cameras. The hills would block any sign of the explosion, and the most that would be seen from the road was a flash of light.

The four men stared at the prison walls, which were thirty feet high, as was the metal gate, the only way for vehicles to enter the prison. No CCTV cameras covered the exterior – there was no way even for the officers inside to see outside. As Major Gannon had pointed out several times during his briefing, the prison had been purpose-built to keep six hundred unarmed men confined in specific areas. Every security measure was directed inwards. Four armed men who knew what they were doing should, in theory, be able to bring the place to its knees.

'Stand clear,' said O'Brien. Armstrong and Mitchell jogged to the far side of the van. O'Brien braced himself and pulled the trigger. The grenade whooshed from the launcher, leaving a plume of white smoke in its wake. It arced through the air and hit the door, dead centre. The explosion was a dull thud that O'Brien felt as much as heard, and then the massive metal door crashed to the side, twisting off its opening mechanism.

Shortt revved the engine. O'Brien tossed the launcher to the ground and ran to the passenger seat. Mitchell pulled the rear door shut. Shortt stamped on the accelerator and the van sped forward, towards the shattered gate.

Shepherd squinted at the luminous dial of his watch. It was three o'clock in the morning and he'd been awake all night. Lee had switched off the television just after midnight, and by half past one there had been silence on the landing. The spyglass had opened at two thirty and the next check wasn't due for another half-hour.

Lee was snoring softly, but he woke with a start as Shepherd climbed down from the top bunk.

'What's up?' he said sleepily.

'Did you hear something?'

'Like what?'

'I don't know. Outside, on the landing.'

Lee swung his feet to the floor. 'What time is it?'

'Three.'

'It'll be one of the guards doing his checks.'

'I heard an explosion.'

'Bollocks.'

'What if there was a fire somewhere in the block? Would they let us out?'

Lee sniffed. 'I can't smell anything.'

'I didn't say I smelt smoke, I said I heard a bang.'

Lee walked to the door. Shepherd moved to the side to let him pass, then grabbed him from behind. Lee could barely grunt before Shepherd had his neck in a tight lock. Shepherd squeezed as Lee tried to twist round. He held him tight, and for more than a minute they shuffled backwards and forwards. The head lock applied pressure to the carotid arteries, cutting off the blood supply to Lee's brain. All Shepherd had to do was hang on and keep applying pressure to the sides of Lee's neck.

When he felt him go limp, he dragged him over to his bunk and rolled him on to it. He pulled the laces from Lee's trainers and used them to bind his wrists and ankles. Then he ripped a strip of material off the sheet and used it as a makeshift gag. He checked that the laces were secure, then went to the door. He switched on the light and started stretching, loosening his muscles for what was to come next.

3.00 a.m.

The van screeched to a halt in front of the gatehouse. The back door flew open and Armstrong and Mitchell jumped down. They both fired short, controlled bursts. The 7.62mm bullets ripped through the door and shattered the lock. The two men stepped to the side and O'Brien jumped out of the van, ran at the door and kicked it, hard. It crashed to the side and he ran into the gatehouse, his submachine-gun in front of him.

There were two prison officers behind the glass panel, one in full uniform, the other in short sleeves. The one in uniform had a phone to his ear, his hand on the keypad. Both men were staring at the shattered door, their mouths open.

'Get down!' shouted O'Brien. They stood where they were, too shocked to move. O'Brien gestured with his Onyx short-assault rifle. 'Get down, now!' he yelled.

The officers dropped to the floor. O'Brien fired a short burst at the security glass. It wasn't designed to take the impact of an assault rifle at short range and it shattered into a million shards.

Armstrong vaulted over the counter, his gloved hand crunching on the broken glass. He put his foot on the back of one of the officers and shoved the barrel of his gun against the other's neck. 'Just stay calm and no one gets hurt,' he said. The man he was standing on had a long keychain on his belt and Armstrong ripped it off. He tossed the keys to O'Brien, who caught them.

Mitchell looked through the doorway and Shortt gave him a thumbs-up. He had turned the van so he could see through the doorway. Outside the prison, everything was in darkness.

'Come on, come on,' said O'Brien. 'Get the doors open.'

Armstrong bound the arms and legs of one officer with a plastic tie, then dragged him to his feet.

Access to the prison was through two security doors that could not be opened at the same time. The gap between them was effectively a quarantine area and the second door wasn't opened until the identity of those entering or leaving had been checked. O'Brien and Mitchell walked up to the first security door. Armstrong shoved the muzzle of his weapon under the man's chin. 'Open the outer door,' he hissed.

The officer, trembling, stabbed at a button. The gate slid open. O'Brien and Mitchell moved into the quarantine area.

'Now close it,' said Armstrong.

He stabbed at another button.

Once the outer door had clicked shut, Armstrong jabbed the gun into the man's chin. 'Open the inner door.' The officer was already reaching across the console to press the button.

O'Brien and Mitchell rushed through the gap and sprinted away. Armstrong tied the officer's wrists behind his back with another plastic binding. He watched on the monitors as O'Brien and Mitchell ran across the second courtyard to the door that led to the secure corridor.

'Which button opens the door?' asked Armstrong.

The officer nodded at the console. 'The red one.'

Armstrong pressed it. 'Gamma, door is unlocked.'

'Roger that,' said O'Brien, in his earpiece. 'Alpha and Beta going in.'

'Delta, outside is clear.'

'Roger that,' said O'Brien.

On one of the monitors, Armstrong watched O'Brien pull open the door and Mitchell run into the secure corridor. O'Brien followed him. Then Armstrong pushed the officer to the floor and tied his feet together. When he straightened up, he scanned the monitors: O'Brien and Mitchell were running down the secure corridor, automatic rifles clutched to their chests.

3.01 a.m.

Lloyd-Davies sipped her coffee and flicked through the observations book. It had been a quiet day – a couple of minor scuffles, a racist remark that had been reported to the governor, and a new arrival on the ones – he had been crying so much he'd been taken to the medical wing. Tonight her colleague in the bubble was Paul Morrison, a former landscape gardener who had only been in the prison service for three months. He was a few inches shorter than she, and although he was only in his early twenties he was losing his hair. He was keen, and had made a special effort to learn the first names of all the men on the spur. Lloyd-Davies hoped he'd maintain his enthusiasm, but she knew that, after a year on the job, most officers became hardened. The lies, the occasional flashes of violence, the boredom changed even the most altruistic soul. She closed the observations book and took another sip of coffee.

As she put down the cup she heard rapid footsteps and turned to look down the secure corridor. Her eyes widened as she saw two figures running full tilt towards her, holding automatic rifles close to their chests. She stared at them in disbelief, then gasped and grabbed her radio. The men rushed up to the barred door. One shoved the barrel of his gun through it. 'Put that down!' he hissed. 'Now!'

Morrison whirled around. He and Lloyd-Davies were transfixed.

'Down!' the man repeated. 'Put the radio down.'

Lloyd-Davies did as she was told.

Morrison got to his feet, trembling. He looked across at Lloyd-Davies. 'It's okay, Paul, stay calm,' she said.

'Shut the fuck up,' hissed one of the marked men. 'Lie down on the floor, face down.'

The second man had a key on a long steel chain and unlocked the barred door.

'What do you want?' asked Lloyd-Davies.

'Just get down on the floor. Now!'

Morrison dropped to his knees, then put his hands on the floor.

The man with the key pulled open the door, then aimed his gun at Lloyd-Davies. 'Down!' he said.

They looked like SAS troopers, thought Lloyd-Davies. Black ski masks, automatic rifles. Black uniforms with equipment hanging from black leather belts. But why would the SAS be storming a prison? It didn't make any sense.

The man with the key stepped forward and grabbed Lloyd-Davies by her ponytail. 'We're not fucking around here!' he hissed. 'Now, get down on the floor.'

Lloyd-Davies realised that she wasn't scared. She was angry, but she wasn't frightened. If the men had intended to shoot them, they would have surely done it straight away. Whatever they were up to, they weren't there to kill anyone. She went down on her knees, her eyes never leaving the man's face. She was trying to memorise as many details as she could. The colour of his eyes. Brown. His height. Just under six feet. One of his canine teeth was crooked. He was clean-shaven. Right-handed. Slightly overweight.

'On the floor!' repeated the man.

Lloyd-Davies did as she was told. The other man was fastening a plastic tie round Morrison's wrists.

The man with the key pushed her down and she lay still as he pulled her arms behind her back and tied her wrists together. She turned to look at him but he put his gun to her forehead. 'You keep staring at me and I'll give you something to remember,' he hissed. He had an accent, but it was hard to identify. Irish. Or Scottish, maybe.

He pressed the gun into the small of her back. 'Who else is on the spur?'

'Healey,' said Lloyd-Davies.

'Where is he?'

'Should be on the ones.'

'Anyone else?'

She shook her head.

'If you're lying, you'll be putting their lives on the line.'

'Just the night staff. Three of us.'

He took the gun away from her back. 'Stay on the ground, keep your eyes closed and this'll be over before you know it,' he said.

Lloyd-Davies shut her eyes. 'You'll never get out,' she said.

The man pushed the barrel of his gun against her neck. 'You'd better hope we do or I'll be putting a bullet in your head,' he muttered. 'Now, shut the fuck up.'

3.02 a.m.

O'Brien tossed Mitchell the key and told him to go and get the prison officer on the ground floor. Mitchell left the bubble and unlocked the barred door that led to the landings. He peered over the railing through the wire-mesh suicide net. A large West Indian was walking slowly towards the far end of the spur. Mitchell put the key into his pocket.

He crept along to the stairs, his gun at the ready, past a cell where rap music was playing. He kept his eyes on the officer below, ready to duck at the first sign that he was turning round. Rock music was coming from another cell. Mitchell imagined the prisoners lying on their bunks, listening to their stereos, with no idea of what was being played out beyond their doors.

He reached the top of the stairs and crouched, his attention fixed on the West Indian. The officer reached the end of the spur. He was swinging his keys on a chain as he stood reading a notice pinned to a board. Mitchell waited. The man was unarmed but he had a radio clipped to his belt, and Mitchell didn't want to give him the chance to call for help. He took a quick look at his watch. Almost two and a half minutes had passed since they'd driven in through the shattered gateway. If he waited for the West Indian to walk back down the spur that could take a full two minutes at the speed he moved.

Mitchell took a deep breath. He took the stairs two at a time, on his toes to minimise the noise. The West Indian continued to swing his keys and read the notice. Mitchell reached the floor and sprinted down the spur, keeping his breathing to a minimum.

The West Indian began to turn. Mitchell sprinted across the linoleum towards him, his assault rifle clutched to his chest.

Armstrong looked up at a clock on the wall above the CCTV monitors. It was several minutes slow and wasn't even showing three o'clock. He saw movement on one of the monitors. It was Mitchell, running hard and fast along the spur towards a fat West Indian officer. As Armstrong watched, the man turned and saw Mitchell running towards him. His mouth opened and his hands went up to defend himself, but before he could do anything Mitchell had slammed into him.

The West Indian must have been twice Mitchell's weight but Mitchell had the advantage of momentum. He hit the man with his left shoulder, and the officer spun then crashed into the wall, face first.

Mitchell lashed out with his foot, kicking him just above the knee. Then, as he slumped forward, he hit him across the back of the neck, open-handed, a stunning blow rather than a killing one.

Mitchell stood back as the guard fell to the ground. Then he rolled him over and dropped on to one knee to bind his wrists and ankles.

Jimbo Shortt looked at his watch. He gunned the engine, keeping up the revs. If anything went wrong they'd have to move quickly. If SO19 headed their way, running was their only option. It was one thing to break one of their own out of prison, quite another to shoot at cops. O'Brien was right: even the specialist armed police units weren't used to serious firepower, but Shortt wasn't convinced they'd duck for cover at the sound of automatic weapons. And what then? The van they were using was a workhorse and the police would have high-powered cars, motorbikes and helicopters. Shortt chuckled as he pictured himself, O'Brien, Mitchell and Armstrong standing in the dock at the Old Bailey. The Four bloody Musketeers. How would they explain themselves? They'd broken into a high-security prison because a friend needed their help. Would a judge understand that? Would a jury? Shortt understood it. He'd fought alongside Spider Shepherd, and seen him take a bullet in the shoulder. It had been Shortt who'd stemmed the bleeding and got Spider to a medic before he'd bled to death. He had saved Spider's life then, but he knew that Spider would have done exactly the same had their roles been reversed. The bonds formed in combat were like no other, but there was no way Shortt could explain that to someone who hadn't been through it themselves. He hadn't hesitated when Major Gannon had phoned him. Spider was in trouble, that was all he needed to hear.

Shortt looked over at the gatehouse. He couldn't see Armstrong, but he knew he was there. He couldn't see O'Brien and Mitchell either, but he knew exactly what they were doing. And in five minutes it would all be over, one way or another.

3.03 a.m.

Mitchell stood up. He yanked the officer's radio off his belt and tossed it down the spur. He was breathing heavily but he wasn't tired. So far it had been a walk in the park. 'Beta, ground floor is neutralised,' he said.

'Roger that, Beta,' said O'Brien in Mitchell's earpiece. 'Move back up to the first floor.'

'Beta, on my way,' replied Mitchell.

He ran back to the stairs, not caring now how much noise he made. The spur was secure, and even if any of the prisoners heard what was going on, they couldn't see out of their cells.

He raced up to the first floor, nodding at O'Brien as he passed the bubble. O'Brien was looking at his watch. He moved quickly along the landing, glancing at the pieces of card with the names and numbers of the prisoners fixed to the side of each door. Major Gannon had said that Shepherd's cell was the fourth on the left, but Mitchell checked all the doors as he passed them.

He reached the fourth. R. Macdonald, SN 6759. He pulled out the key and slotted it into the lock, turned it and pushed open the door.

Shepherd tensed as the door opened. It was only when he saw the figure in black standing there that he realised he'd been holding his breath. Even with the ski mask on, he recognised Geordie Mitchell. 'You're a sight for sore eyes,' he said.

'Your chariot awaits, m'lord,' laughed Mitchell. He took a pistol from the holster on his belt and handed it to Shepherd. 'Martin said you should have this.'

Shepherd reached for the gun but Mitchell tossed it on to the bunk. 'Said you should wear these first.' He took a pair of surgical gloves from his pocket and gave them to Shepherd, who pulled them on and flexed his fingers, then hefted the weapon in his hand. It was a Yugoslavian Model 70, a weapon he'd heard of but never fired. 'You can thank the boyos for that,' said Mitchell. 'Carpenter's on the top floor, yeah?'

Shepherd nodded.

'Let's get to it, then,' said Mitchell. 'Beta, moving to second floor,' he said into his microphone. He headed back to the stairs. Shepherd followed.

3.04 a.m.

O'Brien grinned as he saw Shepherd following Mitchell down the landing, holding the handgun they'd taken from the Real IRA arms cache in Belfast. Shepherd moved fluidly and easily, and was clearly as fit as the day he'd left the SAS. His years with the police clearly hadn't taken his edge. As Shepherd reached the stairs he saw O'Brien watching him and waved.

Mitchell stood to the side to let Shepherd run up the stairs first. He ran along the top landing and stopped outside Carpenter's cell. Mitchell put the key in the lock and turned it. Shepherd pushed open the door. Carpenter was asleep on his bunk with his back to the door.

'If it wasn't for your boy, I'd slot him now,' said Mitchell, pointing his assault rifle at Carpenter.

Shepherd put a hand on the weapon. 'Once we've got Liam back, we'll take care of him,' said Shepherd. He reached out and flicked on the light. Carpenter rolled over in his bunk, blinking and grunting.

'What is it?' he said, shading his eyes with the flat of his hand.

'Get up,' said Shepherd.

'Bob?'

'Get the fuck up,' spat Shepherd.

'What the hell's going on?'

'We're getting out of here.'

'What?'

'We haven't got time for this,' said Mitchell. 'Come on.'

'I'm not going anywhere,' said Carpenter, pulling his legs up to his chest.

'You wanted out,' said Shepherd. 'This is out.'

'You said the van was going to be ambushed,' said Carpenter. 'You said we'd break out on the way to court.'

Mitchell pushed Shepherd out of the way, grabbed Carpenter by the collar of his pyjamas and yanked him out of his bunk. He slammed him against the wall. 'You're coming with us.'

'Fuck you!' shouted Carpenter.

Mitchell smashed the stock of his Kalashnikov against Carpenter's temple. Carpenter pitched forward, his eyes rolling up in their sockets, but Shepherd caught him before he hit the ground.

'Carry him,' said Mitchell. 'We have three minutes and counting.'

Shepherd tossed Carpenter over his shoulder and followed Mitchell out on to the landing. Prisoners were banging on their cell doors and shouting obscenities. The houseblock echoed with screams and yells as the banging built to a crescendo.

3.05 a.m.

Armstrong watched on the CCTV monitors as Mitchell emerged from the cell and ran down the landing, followed by Shepherd, with Carpenter over one shoulder and a gun in his hand. They reached the stairs and headed down to the first floor.

One of the officers at his feet started to struggle so Armstrong kicked him in the ribs, not hard enough to break anything but hard enough to make him scream. He bent down and pushed the barrel of his AKM-63 into the man's neck: 'They're not paying you enough to take a beating. Now lie still.'

The man did as he was told, and Armstrong straightened. On another monitor, Mitchell had reached the bubble.

Mitchell banged on the glass wall with the flat of his gloved hand. Shepherd came up behind him, breathing heavily. O'Brien nodded at Carpenter. 'Tell me you didn't shoot him,' he said to Mitchell.

'He was being uncooperative,' said Mitchell. 'I just tapped him.'

'Let's get out of here,' said O'Brien. 'Alpha and Beta are leaving the block with objectives,' he said, into his microphone.

'Delta, roger that,' said Shortt, through their headsets. 'All clear outside.'

'Gamma, all monitors show zero activity,' said Armstrong.

O'Brien headed for the door.

'Bob, think about what you're doing,' said a voice.

Shepherd looked into the bubble. Lloyd-Davies was lying with her face towards him. 'I'm sorry,' he said.

'Come on,' said O'Brien. 'Two minutes and counting.'

'This won't solve anything,' said Lloyd-Davies. 'They'll get you eventually. Your fingerprints, your DNA, your picture, they're all on file. If you run, they'll lock you away for ever.'

Shepherd had a sudden urge to explain everything to her. That he wasn't Bob Macdonald, career bank robber, he was an undercover cop and he wasn't running away from a prison sentence; he was helping Carpenter to escape because if he didn't his only son would die. But Shepherd knew he couldn't tell her anything – and even if he did she wouldn't believe him.

'I've no choice,' he said. 'Trust me.'

'How can I trust you after this?'

Mitchell pointed his assault rifle at her. 'Shut up!' he hissed.

Shepherd reached out and pushed the barrel of Mitchell's gun to the side. 'It's okay,' he said.

'It's not okay,' said Lloyd-Davies.

'I told you, shut the fuck up and close your eyes!' shouted Mitchell.

O'Brien patted Mitchell's shoulder. 'Come on,' he said.

Mitchell nodded, and followed O'Brien out of the bubble and into the secure corridor.

Shepherd gave Lloyd-Davies one last look. 'I'm sorry,' he said.

'You're throwing your life away.'

Shepherd shifted Carpenter's weight. 'It's my life,' he said. He turned and left the bubble.

Armstrong scanned the CCTV monitors. There were more than a dozen each divided into four views, with three showing full screen images. From where he was he could see the wall, the secure corridor, the offices, the hospital wing and interior views of all the blocks.

He watched O'Brien, Mitchell and Shepherd leave the bubble and run into the secure corridor. He could also see the white van, with Shortt at the wheel.

On one of the spurs on Block C, a female officer was walking along the top level, checking the spyhole at all the cells.

On Block D, two officers were standing on the ground floor, laughing.

O'Brien and Mitchell reached a corner of the secure corridor and waited for Shepherd to catch up.

Armstrong grinned: Shepherd was panting under the weight of the man on his shoulders. Then he saw movement on one of the monitors.

'Gamma, hold your positions,' he said, into his microphone. 'We might have a problem.'

Lloyd-Davies rolled over so that she was facing Morrison. 'Paul, are you okay?'

Morrison's eyes were tightly shut, and his whole body was trembling. 'Have they gone?' he whispered.

'Yeah. It's over.'

Morrison opened his ears. Tears ran down his cheeks. 'Jo, I think I've wet myself.'

'It's okay, Paul. I was scared too. There'd be something wrong if you weren't.'

'What did they want?'

Lloyd-Davies realised he hadn't seen Shepherd and Carpenter leave with the men in ski masks, and that she didn't have time to explain now what had happened. They had to sound the alarm.

She rolled on to her back and sat up. Her radio was on the desk but she doubted that she could operate it with her hands tied behind her back.

'How did they get in?' asked Morrison.

It was a good question. Had they come in over the wall? Lloyd-Davies wondered. Dropped in by helicopter? Or come storming in through the front gate? Did anyone else in the prison know that armed men were on the loose? 'Help me get up,' said Lloyd-Davies. 'Sit back to back and push.'

Morrison rolled over and sat up, then shuffled around so that his back was against hers.

'On three,' she said. She counted aloud, then they pushed hard and raised themselves. Almost immediately Morrison lost his balance and fell back against a filing cabinet, cursing.

Lloyd-Davies looked at the monitors. There was no sign of the men, so they must have left the block. That meant the only prisoners they'd released had been Shepherd and Carpenter. An armed robber and a drug-dealer. Where was the logic in that? Armed men in ski masks meant terrorists, but most of the terrorists were in the Special Secure Unit on the far side of the prison. None of this made any sense.

3.06 a.m.

'Gamma, you have two prison guards heading your way.' Armstrong's voice crackled in O'Brien's earpiece.

'Shit,' said Mitchell.

Shepherd looked at the two men. 'What's wrong?' he asked. He leaned against the wall, allowing it to take some of Carpenter's weight.

O'Brien pressed a finger to his lips, then pointed down the corridor and held up two fingers.

'Alpha, how far away?' he asked.

'Gamma, one hundred metres from the corner ahead of you,' said Armstrong.

'Alpha, have they got radios?'

'Gamma, affirmative.'

O'Brien cursed under his breath. The two prison officers might be going to another block or the administration centre. Or they might be leaving, which meant they'd buzz the gatehouse to unlock the door from the secure corridor. If they went to the administration block, he and the team would be in the clear, but either of the other two options meant the officers would have to be confronted and overpowered. They wouldn't be able to summon help from outside the prison but they could use their radios to call colleagues from other blocks.

O'Brien glanced at his watch. Time was running out. 'Alpha, if they stop at the door, let me know.'

'Gamma, will do.'

O'Brien made a clenched fist, telling Mitchell and Shepherd to wait.

Lloyd-Davies groped for the radio. As her fingers closed round it she saw the alarm button on the wall and decided it was a better bet. She hopped over towards it. It was on the wall next to the monitors at shoulder height so she couldn't reach it with her bound hands. She tried to hit it with her shoulder but failed. She cursed, then pressed it with her forehead but that didn't work either. She tried again and fell forward, banging her nose against the wall. She felt blood spurt from her nostrils and blinked away tears. She pushed herself away from the wall, then hopped as close to the desk as she could get and allowed herself to fall forward. Her nose slammed into the bottom and she felt the cartilage crack. Tears streamed down her face and mixed with the blood, but she heard the alarms burst into life and smiled despite the pain.

O'Brien swore as the alarms went off. 'Where are they, Gamma?' Mitchell was looking back the way they'd come, cradling his rifle and shifting from foot to foot.

'Still heading your way,' said Armstrong. 'They're about fifty feet from the corner where you are.'

'We're going to have to take them,' said O'Brien. 'Are you ready, Beta?'

'Let's do it,' said Mitchell.

O'Brien put a hand on Shepherd's arm. 'Are you okay?' Shepherd nodded. 'We'll rush them but, whatever happens, you keep going, okay?'

Shepherd nodded again.

'Gamma, they're running your way.'

O'Brien jerked his head at Mitchell, then pointed down the corridor. Both men started to run. Shepherd hurried after them.

As they rounded the corner, they saw the two prison officers heading towards them. They were big men with the build of rugby players. They stopped dead when they saw O'Brien and Mitchell.

O'Brien pointed his gun at the men. 'Down on the floor!' he shouted.

The men didn't move, too shocked to react. Mitchell stepped forward, his finger on the trigger of his AKM-63. 'Do it – *now!*' he shouted.

The men got down on the floor and lay there, spreadeagled. Mitchell a bound the wrists of one. O'Brien told Shepherd to go on ahead and knelt down to tie up the second.

Overhead, the alarms were ringing, but O'Brien knew they were internal with no connection to the authorities outside the prison. It was an inconvenience but they were in the end phase now: a few unarmed prison officers wouldn't stop them.

Shepherd ran along the corridor. Carpenter was moaning, but he wasn't moving. Ahead he saw the door that led out of the secure corridor to the courtyard, then heard rapid footsteps behind him and turned. O'Brien and Mitchell were running towards him. The two officers were on the floor, face down, their hands tied behind their backs.

He wondered if the alarm had been sounded back in Block B or if the problem lay ahead, at the gatehouse. His heart was pounding and his back ached from Carpenter's weight. He stopped at the door.

O'Brien skidded to a halt and jabbed at the intercom button to the left of it. 'Alpha, ready for exit!' he shouted.

Mitchell ran up behind O'Brien. The lock clicked and O'Brien shouldered open the door. Then he put his hand to his ear. 'Alpha, say again.' He frowned.

'What's wrong?' asked Shepherd.

'More officers in the corridor, from Block A.' O'Brien glanced at Mitchell and pointed down the corridor, then held open the door for Shepherd. He carried Carpenter through and hurried across the courtyard, Carpenter's feet banging into his thighs.

Armstrong scanned the monitors. O'Brien was holding open the door from the secure corridor. Mitchell was racing towards Block

A. Shepherd was coming towards the gatehouse with Carpenter on his shoulders. And Shortt was gunning the van engine.

No cameras covered the outside of the prison so he had no idea what was going on beyond the walls. For all he knew armed police units were already stationed there. He said a silent prayer that Major Gannon was right and that even if they knew what was going on it would take SO19 at least eight minutes to get to the prison.

There was movement on another of the monitors – the secure corridor outside Block C: three prison officers, two male and one female, were running from the bubble.

'Gamma, three more guards in the corridor,' said Armstrong. 'Time to call it a day.'

'Alpha, roger that, said O'Brien, but he stayed where he was, keeping the corridor door open.

Mitchell stopped running. He could hear booted footsteps round the corner ahead of him. He stood with his left leg slightly forward, ready to absorb the kick of his AKM-63. He took no pleasure in shooting at unarmed men, but he had to show them he was capable of using his firepower.

The two men reached the corner first. One was short and dumpy, the other tall and lanky. The tall one yelped when he saw Mitchell, the other ducked and tripped over his own feet.

Mitchell was amused by their confusion. 'Get down on the floor!' he yelled.

A female prison officer came round the corner. She swerved to avoid falling over the officer on the floor and slammed into the wall.

Mitchell fired a short burst into the ceiling above their heads. A light shattered and ceiling tiles showered down on them. 'I won't tell you again!' he shouted.

The overweight guard and the woman dropped on to the floor next to the other.

'Link your fingers behind your neck!' ordered Mitchell.

They did as they were told.

'Anyone follows us, I won't be firing warning shots,' he shouted.

'Tell your friends – they come after us, they're dead.' He turned and ran back to O'Brien.

'Nice speech,' said O'Brien.

'What can I say?' said Mitchell. 'Winning friends and influencing people.'

O'Brien held the door as Mitchell ran into the courtyard, then chased after him. The door clicked shut. Hopefully, with the gatehouse disabled, no one would be able to follow them out of the secure corridor.

Shepherd was breathing heavily by the time he'd reached the gatehouse. Carpenter was still groaning, but his body was limp. The interior door was already open and he ran through it. To his left Armstrong was cradling his automatic rifle. He acknowledged Shepherd, then went back to studying the CCTV monitors.

The second door, leading to the outside, was shut. Shepherd stood in the holding area and waited.

O'Brien and Mitchell ran in from the courtyard, rushed through the interior door, then turned to check that no one had come after them. The courtyard was clear.

Armstrong hit the button to close the security door. Seconds ticked by as it shut. O'Brien and Mitchell turned to the second door. 'We haven't got time for this,' said Mitchell, levelled his gun at it and let loose a short burst. The glass shattered.

Armstrong vaulted over the counter and ran out into the courtyard. Shepherd raced after him, his trainers crunching over shards of broken glass. Armstrong jumped into the back of the van and held out his hands to heave Carpenter in. O'Brien and Mitchell were running towards them. They turned and faced the gatehouse, weapons at the ready as Shepherd clambered into the van. 'We're in!' he shouted.

O'Brien and Mitchell ran together, jumped in and Shepherd pulled the door shut.

'Go, go, go!' screamed O'Brien. Shortt stamped on the accelerator and the van shot towards the gate.

*   *   *

The van swerved and Shepherd's head smacked against the side. He put out a hand to steady himself. O'Brien and Mitchell sat with their backs towards the seats, cradling their weapons. Shortt was keeping just below the speed limit as he pulled a series of tight turns. It was important to put as much distance between themselves and the prison as they could, but there were speed cameras in the area and they couldn't risk being photographed.

Armstrong scratched his chin under the ski mask as he stared down at Carpenter, who was lying on his back, his eyes shut, breathing heavily. 'Doesn't look like much,' he said.

'Worth twenty-eight million,' said Shepherd.

'Yeah, well, his money's not going to get him out of this,' said O'Brien.

Mitchell held out a hand. 'Hang on, now, boys. Let's at least hear what he has to say. I mean, Spider's one of the lads, but twenty-eight mill is a shedload of money.'

O'Brien thumped Mitchell's shoulder. 'Why don't you just go out and write one of those kill-and-tell books? Make some money that way.'

'Can't string two words together, me,' said Mitchell. 'Why don't we just hold him to ransom? He's got money. Let him pay for what we just did.'

O'Brien pointed a warning finger at him.

'Joke,' said Mitchell.

The van swerved again and the tyres squealed. O'Brien was monitoring police radio frequencies but so far no one had called in the raid on the prison. 'We're in the clear, Jimbo,' he said.

Shortt eased off the accelerator.

Carpenter rolled on to his side, and Armstrong placed a foot casually on his neck.

They drove to an industrial estate on the outskirts of Watford, close to the M25. O'Brien climbed out and unlocked a metal shutter, pushed it open and Shortt edged the van inside the building. It was a small warehouse, a bare space with metal rafters overhead and a small plasterboard office in one corner. There were no windows.

Armstrong and Mitchell opened the rear doors of the van and dragged Carpenter out as O'Brien pulled down the shutters at the entrance. Shortt got out, holding a bottle of Evian water. He unscrewed the cap and poured it over Carpenter. Carpenter coughed, spluttered and sat up.

O'Brien, Shortt, Mitchell and Armstrong stood in a semi-circle facing him, their submachine-guns at the ready.

'Who the hell are you?' asked Carpenter, running his hands through his wet hair.

'We're the guys who pulled your nuts out of the fire,' said O'Brien, 'so a bit of respect is called for.'

Carpenter got to his feet. His lip was split and blood was dribbling down his chin. He grinned at Shepherd. 'I knew you'd be able to do it,' he said. 'You just needed an incentive.'

'I got you out,' said Shepherd. 'Now I want my boy back.'

'I think we should celebrate, don't you? It's not every day that you get to break out of a Category A prison, is it?' Carpenter laughed, but no one laughed with him. 'A friend of mine always made the same toast when he opened a bottle of bubbly,' said Carpenter. 'Champagne for our real friends, and real pain for our sham friends.' He moved quickly, stepping forward and grabbing the gun from Shepherd's belt. Then he flicked the safety-catch. 'That's what I want for you, Shepherd. Real fucking pain.' He pointed the gun at Shepherd and pulled the trigger.

In the confined space the explosion was deafening. Shepherd staggered back, clutching his belly. Carpenter grinned in triumph. He waved the gun at the men in ski masks, then frowned when he saw they were all laughing, guns at their sides.

Shepherd straightened. He held his hands up, palms out to Carpenter. No blood.

Carpenter stared at the gun in disbelief. He aimed at Shepherd's stomach and fired again. Shepherd stood where he was, his ears ringing.

'You stupid twat,' said O'Brien. 'You don't think we'd give Spider real bullets, do you?'

Carpenter tossed the gun away. 'Fuck the lot of you,' he said.

O'Brien aimed his gun at Carpenter's face. 'Why don't we just have done with it and slot him now?'

'Do that and he'll never see his boy again,' said Carpenter.

'Where is he?' asked Shepherd.

'I don't know.'

Shepherd's jaw dropped. 'You what?'

'I don't know and I don't want to know. My guys have taken them somewhere. Once you've let me go, they'll let your boy and his grandparents go. That's the deal.'

'We can't trust him,' said Mitchell. 'After what he just did, we can't believe a thing he says.'

'You've no choice,' said Carpenter. 'There's nothing you can do to me to make me tell you where his boy is, because I don't know. And if you kill me . . .' He left the sentence unfinished.

'It's your call, Spider,' said O'Brien, scratching at his ski mask.

Shepherd picked up the gun. He stared at Carpenter as he tapped the gun against his leg. If he let Carpenter go, there was no guarantee he'd release Liam, Moira and Tom. Mitchell was right, there was no way they could trust him.

'Yeah, Spider,' said Carpenter. 'It's your call.'

'Your guys have mobiles, yeah?' said Shepherd. 'Throwaways?'

'Sure.'

'Okay, here's what you do. You call your guys and tell them to release Moira and the boy. They're to give them a mobile and let them go. As soon as they're safe, they can call me. We release you, and then you call your men to let Tom go.'

'Nice,' said Carpenter. 'That way the most you'll lose is your father-in-law.'

'He's my boy's grandfather,' said Shepherd. 'His life means more to me than a thousand of you. You hurt him – you hurt any of them – and you're dead.'

'Sticks and stones,' said Carpenter.

Shepherd raised his gun to smash it across Carpenter's face, but held himself in check. There was nothing to be gained from hitting

Carpenter. All he wanted was to get Liam back safely. He lowered the weapon. Carpenter grinned.

'Give him a phone,' said Shepherd.

Fletcher was picking his teeth with a playing card when the mobile rang. He answered it immediately. Carpenter was the only person who had the number. 'Yes, boss.'

'I'm out, Kim. Free and clear.'

'Great news, boss.'

'How are they?'

'They're behaving. I had to give the old man a slap but they're as right as rain now.'

Neary looked over from the sofa where he was stretched out reading the latest Harry Potter. Fletcher flashed him a thumbs-up.

'Right, here's what we do. Let the grandmother and the boy go. Give them a mobile and get them to call this number as soon as they're away from the house. Keep the old man with you until I call you again. Then, assuming everything's still okay, leave him and come and get me.'

'No sweat,' said Fletcher. The phone went dead. Fletcher smiled at Neary and shrugged. 'We let them go,' he said.

Neary sighed. 'Good,' he said. 'I never like hurting women and kids. Doesn't seem right, you know?'

Fletcher nodded.

Carpenter handed the mobile back to Shortt. 'Next time that rings, it'll be to say that the boy and his grandmother are free,' he said.

Gannon took the phone. 'Why don't we just slot him?' asked O'Brien.

'Because if I don't call back in ten minutes to say I'm okay, the old man gets shot,' said Carpenter.

O'Brien shrugged. 'We slot you then we hit the redial button and tell your guys you're dead so they might as well knock it on the head.'

'They'll still take care of him, whatever you say.'

'Leave him alone, Martin,' said Shortt.

'Who are you guys, anyway?' asked Carpenter.

'They're friends of mine, that's all you need to know,' said Shepherd.

Carpenter ignored him and continued to talking to Shortt. 'I could use a crew like you.' He gestured at Shepherd. 'I don't know what he's paying you, but I can give you ten times as much.'

'He's not paying us a penny,' said O'Brien.

'Skills you've got, you could be rich men,' said Carpenter.

'This isn't about money,' said Shortt. 'Now, shut the fuck up.'

Carpenter settled back in the van. They waited in silence until the mobile rang. Shortt gave it to Shepherd. It was Moira, sobbing.

'Are you okay?' he asked.

Through her tears she told him that she and Liam were safe but that she didn't know where her husband was. Shepherd told her that Tom would soon be with her. 'What's happening, Daniel?' she asked.

'I'll explain later,' he said. 'First thing is to get you all home. Where are you?'

Moira sniffed. 'There's a road ahead of us. I saw a bus go by.'

'Go to the road and find out its name. Call me back and we'll come and get you.'

'I'll call the police,' said Moira.

'No,' said Shepherd quickly. 'Don't do that.'

'We've been kidnapped, Daniel. They had guns. They said they'd kill us.'

'Moira, please, listen to me. Whatever you do, don't call the police. I'll explain everything, I promise, but there's nothing the police can do right now. Trust me.'

'Daniel . . .'

'I mean it, Moira. Wait until Tom's back with you and I can talk it through with you. Just get to the road and call me.'

'All right . . .'

'Can I talk to Liam?' He heard the phone change hands.

'Dad?'

'Are you okay?'

'They hit Granddad. With a gun.'

'It's over now, Liam. You're safe.'

'Who are they, Dad?'

'Just bad guys. Don't worry, it's all over now. I'm coming to get you.'

'Are you out of prison?'

'Yes.'

'So you're coming home?'

'Definitely,' said Shepherd.

He cut the connection and held out the phone to Carpenter. 'Okay, now let my father-in-law go.'

Carpenter grinned. 'That's not how it works, Shepherd.' He held out his hand. 'I'll need some money for the call-box.'

O'Brien tossed him a handful of change.

'You screw me over and I'll hunt you down and kill you,' said Shepherd.

'Of course you will,' said Carpenter.

Armstrong and Mitchell opened the rear door of the van. They'd parked in a side-street a short walk from Brent Cross tube station. Carpenter climbed out. He turned to Shepherd. 'Be lucky,' he said, then jogged down the road towards the station.

Armstrong scratched his ski mask. 'Didn't even thank us,' he said.

'He's probably going to write,' said Mitchell.

'A card would be nice.' Armstrong pulled the door shut. 'Or flowers.'

Even though the road was clear behind the Rover, Stan Yates still switched on his indicator before pulling over to the side. Force of habit. Twenty-seven years as a professional driver and never an accident – not even a speeding fine – but what did he have to show for it? A clean driving licence and a one-bedroomed basement flat in east London, and somewhere up north an ex-wife and two kids who didn't know him. Didn't need to know him, either, not now his ex-wife had her fancy-man solicitor with his detached house and his yacht moored in Portsmouth.

Yates wanted a cigarette but the Rover was a smoke-free zone. His boss was a stickler for it and no amount of air-freshener would get rid of the smell. He made do with a stick of foul-tasting nicotine gum.

He ran his hands round the steering-wheel, enjoying the feel of the leather. As soft as a young woman's skin, he thought. Not that he'd touched many young women over the past few years, but all that would change soon. He'd quit his job, sell the flat, and move to the Philippines. He'd heard great things about the Philippines. How a man could live like a king, even on a government pension. How the women were soft, pretty, accommodating . . . and available. Yates's smile widened: he'd be arriving in the Philippines with more than his pension.

He stretched out his arms and arched his back. The Rover still smelt new. It was less than six months old and had done only three thousand miles. Ray Mackie didn't travel much – the car was more of a status symbol than anything else. A badge of office to show that he'd climbed the slippery pole and was now master of all he surveyed. Head of Drugs Operations. Mackie would be retiring with a real pension, thought Yates bitterly, and he earned real money. Not the pittance that HM Customs paid him.

Yates reached out and touched the gleaming wooden veneer around the car's instruments. Real craftsmanship, he thought.

A car pulled up behind the Rover. It was a BMW, a nice motor, the five series, thought Yates, but it didn't have the quality of the Rover. The BMW was a car to drive but the Rover was a car to be driven in. It was a crucial difference. Long before he'd become a professional driver, Yates had been a car salesman and had spent a year selling Rolls-Royces in a Mayfair showroom. He'd always been able to spot a serious buyer because they'd get into the back of the car, not the front.

Yates watched the BMW in his rear-view mirror. The headlights flashed. Yates frowned. Normally they came to him. He twisted in his seat. The men stayed in the BMW. He frowned. What the hell were they playing at? He switched off the engine and climbed out. The BMW's headlights flashed again.

Yates walked to the driver's side. The window wound down and Pat Neary grinned up at him. 'Stan the man,' he said.

'What's going on?' asked Yates. 'I'm not supposed to see you until next week.'

'Change of plan,' said Neary.

'There's no plan to change,' said Yates. 'I give you information on HODO's movements, you give me a brown envelope.'

'Our boss wants a word,' said Neary.

Kim Fletcher was in the passenger seat. He grinned. 'He'll make it worth your while, Stan.'

Yates looked up and down the road. There were headlights about a mile away but the car turned off to the left. 'What does he want to talk about?'

'He wants to pick your brains.'

'About what?'

'That's why he wants to see you, Stan. Says he doesn't want to work through me on this.'

Yates licked his lips. 'How much?'

'Didn't want to tell me, Stan, but he said he'd make it worth your while.' Fletcher sighed. 'Look, if you're not interested just tell me and I'll pass the message on.'

'I'm not saying I'm not interested,' said Yates hastily. 'It's just I've always worked with you.'

'And I work for him,' said Fletcher. 'It's his money you're salting away.'

Yates thought about it. 'Where?'

'He's waiting for you, not far away. Follow us in your motor, okay?'

Yates went back to his car, spat out his chewing gum, climbed in and started the engine.

The BMW flashed its headlights, then pulled out and drove on. Yates followed at a safe distance. His mouth was dry and he wanted a drink. Yates never drank while driving. In his twenty-seven years at the wheel he'd never so much as touched a glass of shandy while he was working. But as he followed the BMW through the darkness, he wanted a whisky, badly. And he wanted a cigarette.

The promise of extra money was tempting, but Yates wasn't sure if he really wanted to meet Fletcher's boss. Fletcher had approached

343

him two years earlier as Yates was sitting in a bar round the corner from his bedsit. Yates didn't like being at home: it felt too much like a prison cell. Six paces long, three paces wide, a single bed, a cheap chest of drawers and a wardrobe with a loose door, a microwave oven on a rickety table and a cramped shower room with a leaking toilet. Looking back, it had been a slow courtship. The occasional drink. A late-night curry. Fletcher listened to his complaints about his ex-wife, his job, his boss. Fletcher had always seemed interested in Mackie, who he was and whom he met. Then one night Fletcher slipped him an envelope containing five hundred pounds. It was a gift, Fletcher had said, just to help him out. Yates had taken it. That night Fletcher had asked some specific questions about Mackie. Where he lived. What car his wife drove. Yates had answered without hesitation. He'd had a few drinks, but it wasn't the alcohol that had loosened his tongue. It was the resentment. At the way his life had gone down the toilet. At his wife for stealing his children. At Mackie for lording it over him, treating him like shit.

The meetings with Fletcher had become less social: weekly debriefings, then a brown envelope full of cash. After six months Yates had asked for a rise and Fletcher gave him a thousand pounds a week. Pat Neary had started to attend the debriefing sessions. But Fletcher made demands, too. Specific questions about Mackie. Who he met. Where he went. Then, after another year, Fletcher had asked him to take the Rover to a garage in Shepherd's Bush in West London. It was a tiny place under a railway arch. A mechanic had fitted tiny microphones into the rear of the car and a micro tape deck in the glove compartment. The money went up to two thousand pounds a week and Yates had to hand over a bag of tapes at his weekly debriefings. There were no more late-night curries, no chatty drinking sessions, just a straightforward trade. Information on HODO for money. Lots of money. Yates felt no guilt, no shame. The way he looked at it, if his wife hadn't dumped him and run off with her fancy-man solicitor, if Mackie had treated him better, maybe he wouldn't have had to do what he'd done. But he'd made his bed and was quite happy to lie in it. Especially if that

344

bed was a king-size in the Philippines with two beautiful young girls. Maybe three.

The BMW indicated a right turn. Yates indicated, too, even though there was nothing behind him. Yates had never asked what Fletcher and Neary were doing with the tapes and the information he gave them. He hadn't cared. Fletcher and Neary hadn't seemed over-bright and Yates had always assumed they were working for someone else. He popped a fresh piece of nicotine gum into his mouth and grimaced at the taste. He'd been meaning to switch to patches but kept forgetting to visit the chemist.

The BMW turned down a rutted track. Yates cursed as the Rover hit a pothole and mud splashed over the door. Mackie insisted that the car was always in pristine condition so he'd have to be up early in the morning, washing and polishing. The Rover's headlights picked out a wooden sign with faded paintwork. It was a limestone quarry. Yates was annoyed at the cloak-and-dagger. The meeting could just as easily have taken place in a pub.

The track curved to the right and Yates lost sight of the BMW. He flicked his headlights to main beam and huge tunnels of light carved through the night sky. Ahead he saw huge metal sheds with corrugated-iron roofs and two silos with conveyor belts running up to the top. The road curved back to the left and Yates saw the BMW. It was parked in front of a metal-mesh fence. Yates frowned. The gate into the quarry was padlocked and there was no other vehicle to be seen.

He brought the Rover to a halt and sat there, chewing slowly. Fletcher climbed out of the BMW and walked towards him, his hands in his coat pockets. Yates wound down the window. 'Where is he, then?' he asked.

'Pat's calling him on the mobile,' said Fletcher.

'What's the story?'

'He's a bit wary of being seen, that's all. Come on, stretch your legs.'

Yates climbed out of the Rover. Fletcher took a pack of cigarettes from his pocket. Silk Cut. He offered it to Yates. Yates was going to decline, then changed his mind. He spat out his gum and took a cigarette. He shielded it from the wind with his cupped hands while Fletcher lit it for him.

Neary got out of the BMW and leaned against it, his hands in his pockets.

'How much is he going to give me, your boss?'

'Don't worry, he'll take care of you,' said Fletcher.

Yates shivered. 'I'm going to the Philippines,' he said. 'Fed up with this weather. Fed up with the whole country.' He took a long pull on his cigarette and blew a plume of smoke down at the ground.

'Don't blame you,' said Fletcher.

Neary waved for them to go over to the BMW.

'Now what does he want?' said Fletcher.

Yates started walking towards Neary. He took another pull on his cigarette and filled his lungs with smoke. It wasn't just the nicotine he missed, but the smoking. The feel of the cigarette in his hands, the inhaling, holding the smoke in his lungs, exhaling. Even the flicking of ash. They were all tactile sensations that were missing from the gum and the patches. He was going to start smoking again, he thought. So what if he got cancer down the line? He was just as likely to get hit by a bus while crossing the road. 'How long have you been smoking, Kim?' he asked.

Fletcher didn't answer. As Yates turned to see what Fletcher was doing, a .38-calibre bullet exploded into the back of his skull and blew away most of his face.

'Run it by me again, Spider. From the top.' Superintendent Hargrove leaned back in his chair as Shepherd told his story for the third time. Hargrove steepled his fingers under his chin and listened. They were in an interview room in Paddington Green police station at the junction of Harrow Road and Edgware Road. Shepherd didn't know why Hargrove had wanted to interview him at Paddington Green. It was the most secure police station in the country and the place where Special Branch interviewed suspected terrorists. Shepherd didn't know and didn't ask.

The story that Shepherd told the superintendent was close to the truth. The best lies always were. The interview room had a tape-recorder with two decks, but it wasn't switched on. It was an informal debriefing, Hargrove had said, but if it had been that, they could have chatted in a pub or a coffee shop. So Shepherd checked and cross-checked everything he told the superintendent. One slip and he knew the man would pounce.

The story he told was simple. Shepherd had been sitting in his cell. The door had been opened by a man in a ski mask. Then he'd been taken to Carpenter's cell. The man in the ski mask had knocked Carpenter out and forced Shepherd to carry him. That was pretty much the truth. Shepherd had no choice in that because it would all have been captured on CCTV.

They'd been taken to a van and driven out of the prison. Somewhere on the outskirts of London, Shepherd had been thrown out. Carpenter had gone off with the masked men. End of story. End of lie.

'Did they have accents?' asked Hargrove.

'Irish, maybe.'

'Maybe?'

'Everything was staccato. Rushed. It's hard to pin down an accent when all they say is "Run, run, run." But if I had to choose, I'd say Irish.'

'North or south?'

'I couldn't say. Hand on heart.'

'We found a discarded Russian RPG launcher. Fire and throw away.'

'That was how they got in?'

'Blew the gate off. It was part of a shipment from Bosnia that Six tracked during the late nineties. Disappeared when it got to Belfast. Red faces all round but no heads rolled.'

'IRA?'

'Real IRA. The nutters.' Hargrove leaned forward. 'So, why do you think the Real IRA would break into a Cat A prison to break out a drug-dealer and not rescue their own?'

Shepherd pulled a face. 'Money?'

'Carpenter paid them? Is that what you think? Terrorists for hire?'

'Overseas funding is down since September the eleventh. Carpenter's got millions stashed away.'

'So he pays politicals to break him out?'

Shepherd didn't say anything. Hargrove was being either deliberately vague or setting a trap for him.

'You ever have any dealings with the IRA in your former life?' asked the superintendent.

'Some,' said Shepherd. 'Provos mainly.' Hargrove knew exactly what Shepherd had done in the army, where he'd served and who with.

'What's your opinion of the Real IRA?'

'Like you said. Nutters.'

'Well trained?'

Shepherd exhaled deeply. 'Not really. They don't have the same discipline as the Provos or the training facilities.'

Hargrove nodded. 'That's my opinion – and, in fact, most people I've spoken to don't think the Real IRA would be physically capable of mounting an operation like the one at Shelton.'

Shepherd tried to look relaxed. Hargrove was an experienced interrogator so his body language wasn't necessarily an indication of what was going through his mind.

'At least we know who Carpenter's man in the Church was.'

'Who?'

'Stan Yates. He drove the Head of Drugs Operations. Carpenter knew about everyone Mackie met outside the office, every phone conversation he had from the car.'

'Yates is talking?'

'Yates is dead. At least, we assume he is. He went missing the day after the breakout. Car's gone too.'

'He might have done a runner.'

'His stuff's in his flat. Passport, money, personal stuff. Carpenter's had him killed, for sure.'

'Red faces at the Church, then.'

Hargrove chuckled. 'Mackie will probably be processing VAT refunds until he retires,' he said.

'And Rathbone was Carpenter's man inside Shelton?'

Hargrove nodded. 'We've arrested Stafford. Gosden has been suspended pending an inquiry. I doubt he'll ever run a prison again.'

Shepherd had no sympathy for the governor. If he'd done his job properly, Carpenter would never have been able to run his operation from behind bars.

'You didn't have any clue that Carpenter was planning to break out?' asked Hargrove.

Shepherd forced himself to relax. The interrogation was back on. 'None at all,' he said.

'And if you had?'

'Hypothetically?'

'Hypothetically,' said Hargrove.

'I'd have called the number you gave me. Or gone through the governor.'

'You wouldn't call anyone else?'

Shepherd frowned. 'Such as?'

'We ran a check on all phone calls made prior to the breakout. There was just one from you. To DC Jimmy Sharpe.'

Shepherd looked at the superintendent, keeping his eyes steady and his breathing regular. No looking away. No fiddling with his hands. No biting his nails. 'I wanted him to check on Liam.'

'I can understand that. You were worried about your boy. It's only natural. Did he go to see him?'

'I'm not sure. He said he'd write to me.'

'And he never wrote?'

Shepherd shook his head. 'It's water under the bridge now, isn't it?'

'It might be,' said Hargrove.

'Did you talk to Jimmy?'

'Oh, sure. He said he was about to call on your in-laws when the shit hit the fan. He never got the chance to see if Liam was okay.'

Shepherd nodded slowly. 'That sounds about right.'

349

'He was a bit vague about the other thing you asked him to do.'

'What was that?' asked Shepherd.

Hargrove smiled tightly. 'Your memory really is giving you problems, isn't it?' he said. 'I hope it's not early Alzheimer's.'

'I've been under a lot of pressure.'

'You said if there were any problems, he was to call a number you'd given him.'

'Don't remember saying that.'

'So you don't remember who Sharpe was to call?'

'Sorry. No.'

'Must be contagious,' said Hargrove. 'Sharpe said he couldn't remember the number either. Said he didn't call because there wasn't a problem.'

'There you are, then,' said Shepherd.

Hargrove studied Shepherd with unblinking brown eyes. Shepherd looked back at him. Now he knew what was coming. He forced himself to relax.

'You had a visitor. On the fifteenth.'

'I guess.' He smiled. 'You lose track of the days in prison.'

Hargrove was still staring at him. 'You applied for a visiting order. Joe Humphreys. You put him down as a cousin.'

'Bob Macdonald's cousin.'

'Who is he, Spider?'

'Just a friend.'

'Must have been important if you were prepared to compromise the operation to see him.'

'I needed to see a friendly face, banged up in there.'

Hargrove chuckled. 'Interesting choice of words,' he said. 'I had a look at the CCTV footage for the visiting room, the day Joe Humphreys visited.'

'And why would you do that?'

For a brief moment Hargrove's eyes hardened. 'Just to put my mind at rest. It wasn't the best picture quality in the world, but there wasn't much of his face to see anyway, not with the baseball cap and sunglasses.'

'It was a sunny day, when he visited.'

'Yeah, that's what I thought,' said Hargrove. 'How long have you known him?'

'A few years, I guess.'

'An elusive character, this Humphreys.'

'In what way?'

'He had photo ID to get in, but the address on the visiting order is a newsagent's in Battersea.'

'He moves around a lot.'

Hargrove settled back in his chair. 'Going back to the phone conversation you had with Detective Constable Sharpe. Can you remember what you said?'

Shepherd had been expecting the change in subject so he wasn't fazed by it.

'Not word for word.' A deliberate lie. Shepherd's memory was faultless when it came to conversations.

'Because I've listened to the conversation. Word for word.'

Shepherd kept on looking at the superintendent, kept a smile on his face, kept breathing regularly, kept his hands in his lap.

'I think your exact words to Sharpe were that if there was anything untoward, he was to call the number you'd given him and tell him what had happened. "But that's all. Don't start raising red flags." That's what you said. What did you suspect might have happened?'

'I just wanted reassurance that my boy was okay, that's all.'

'This man you wanted Sharpe to contact, he wasn't the mysterious Mr Humphreys, was he?'

'No.'

'You're sure of that? You being confused and stressed and everything.'

'I'm sure.'

'I'd like to talk to Mr Humphreys.'

Shepherd looked pained. 'Like I said, he moves around a lot.'

'You've always been one of my best men, Spider,' said Hargrove. 'I know you're not bent, so I've got to ask you, unofficially and off the record without the machine running, is there anything you want to tell me?'

Shepherd stayed silent.

'Anything at all?'

Shepherd shook his head.

There were two dozen DEA agents working out of the American embassy in Grosvenor Square, but Matt Willis was the one Major Gannon regarded most highly, not least because Willis had spent seven years as a Navy Seal and had seen action in the Gulf and Afghanistan.

The American's Special Forces background gave the two plenty to argue about whenever they met up, and often led to early-morning drinking sessions in the Special Forces Club, behind Harrods in Knightsbridge.

Gannon arranged to meet Willis there at lunchtime, so they would not be tempted to embark on a drinking binge. The club was in an anonymous red-brick mansion block. The brass plaque identifying it had been taken down after 11 September and now passers-by had no idea that were some of the most specialised soldiers in the world were inside the building, or that drunken SAS and SBS officers often hurtled down the stairs on metal trays – a makeshift toboggan run.

Gannon signed in and went up to the first-floor bar, all dark wood and leather armchairs. Willis was already sitting in a corner, his back to the wall, nursing a tumbler of whisky and ice. He stood up, shook hands with Gannon, then slapped him on the back and ordered him a whisky as the major dropped into an armchair. 'Busy?' asked Gannon, placing his case on the floor next to the chair.

'As ever,' said Willis. 'You?'

Gannon pulled a face. 'Sitting on my arse in the barracks,' he said.

'Really?' said Willis, grinning.

'The Provos are finished, what's left of the Republican movement are nutters, pretty much, and Al Qaeda aren't up to much here. All quiet on the western front.'

'Pity you missed out on Iraq.'

'Tell me about it. Three-quarters of the Regiment were there but all I did was babysit the bloody sat-phone.' He gestured at the case by his side. Wherever he went, Gannon had to take the Almighty with him.

The two men clinked their glasses and drank. 'Have you got time for lunch?' asked Gannon. The club's dining room offered the sort of food that soldiers enjoyed – good solid meals with no-fuss service. Willis shook his head. 'We've got a satellite conference with Langley this afternoon.'

'It was a lot easier before the spooks got involved in drugs,' said Gannon.

'It was the end of the Cold War did it,' said Willis. 'Had to find themselves a new role and drugs was the war of choice. Half the undercover operations we run come up against CIA agents. They treat us like we're the enemy.'

'Same with the cops and our spooks. Hate the sight of each other, and we end up in the middle.'

Gannon waved at the elderly barman for more drinks.

'So?' said Willis.

'What?'

'You didn't ask me here to complain about the security services, did you?'

Gannon grinned. Willis knew him too well. 'There's a drug-dealer we'd like to sort out. Gerald Carpenter.'

'I know the name.'

Gannon smiled. Of course the American knew the name. Carpenter was one of the biggest players in the country, and his escape from Shelton prison had been plastered across the newspapers for the best part of a week.

'Why didn't you sort him out when you had him?' asked Willis.

Gannon's eyes narrowed. 'What are you getting at, Matt?'

'Don't try to kid a kidder,' said Willis, evidently enjoying Gannon's discomfort. 'The papers might fall for that crap about the Real IRA breaking into Shelton to get their men out, but I'm a bit too old to believe in fairy stories.'

'So what do you think happened?'

'I haven't a clue. But I know one thing for sure. The Real IRA don't have the expertise to break into a shoebox, never mind a high-security prison.'

'And?'

'Hell, I don't know, Allan. Why don't you tell me? Four men in black use an RPG to blow their way into a high-security prison. They cut all communications, overpower a couple of dozen trained officers and disappear into the night with two prisoners from the remand wing. Sounds like special forces to me, buddy.'

'You might be right.'

'Then there was the other prisoner that got out with Carpenter. What was his name?'

Gannon shrugged.

'Macdonald,' said Willis thoughtfully. 'Armed robber. Seems strange company, doesn't it? A big-time drug-dealer and a small-time thief. I mean, if the Real IRA had gone to all that trouble, don't you think they'd have gone the extra mile and broken into the Special Secure Unit and got a few of the boyos out?'

Again, Gannon shrugged.

Willis leaned back in his chair and sipped his whisky, watching Gannon over the top of his glass. 'So, where were you when it all went bang?' he asked.

'I was playing squash with my staff sergeant.'

'You win?'

'I did,' said Gannon.

'Interesting,' said Willis.

The barman brought over their drinks and they waited until he'd gone back to the bar before continuing their conversation. 'We'd like to undo the damage,' said Gannon.

'All the king's horses?'

'And all the king's men. Snag is, we don't know where Humpty Dumpty is.'

'But you're looking?'

'The Regiment doesn't have that expertise. And the security services don't usually react favourably to requests from us for help. We work for them, not vice versa.'

'And you're looking for the two of them? Carpenter and Macdonald?'

'Just Carpenter.'

Willis looked up at the ceiling. 'Why am I not surprised?' he mused.

'Just the big fish,' said Gannon.

'And you're assuming he's left the UK?'

'He'd be mad to stay,' said Gannon.

'And am I to assume that's the end of it, so far as MI5 and MI6 are concerned?'

'I wouldn't be coming to you if they were on the case,' said Gannon. 'Interpol are on the lookout for him, but Carpenter won't be travelling on his own passport.'

'What about his family?'

'They left the country the day after he was taken out of prison. Got on the Eurostar to Paris and vanished.'

Willis ran a finger round the lip of his glass. 'You want me to get our guys active on the case?'

'He killed one of yours.'

'I know he did, but there's no proof. If there was, we'd have had him back in the States.'

'Couldn't have been extradited, not with the death penalty a possibility.'

Willis grinned. 'There are ways around that. We'd have had him. But, like I said, there's the little matter of proof.'

'The cops and the Church had proof, but Carpenter came close to getting off.'

'Inside help, I hear,' said Willis.

'What big ears you have.'

Willis swirled his whisky in the glass. 'So, going back to your request, you want the DEA to find Carpenter, and then what?'

'Put in a request for the Increment to go and get him.'

'That'll depend on where he is.'

'He won't be in the States, that's for sure.'

'And then what?'

'We take him back to prison.'

Willis took a long pull on his whisky, his eyes never leaving Gannon's face. He put down his glass. 'Are you sure about that, Allan?'

Gannon looked at Willis levelly. 'Absolutely.'

'Cross your heart?'

Gannon grinned. 'And hope to die.'

The organist started to play a hymn that Shepherd could only dimly recall. Weddings and funerals were pretty much the only times that he walked on hallowed ground. The vicar closed his Bible and smiled reassuringly at the congregation. A small hand slipped into Shepherd's. 'Don't be sad, Daddy.'

Shepherd smiled down at his son. They were sitting in the front pew at the small stone church down the road from the house where Moira and Tom lived. They'd wanted their daughter buried close to them and Shepherd had agreed. His in-laws were sitting in the same pew on Liam's other side. Liam was in his school uniform, his shoes polished, his tie neat. Shepherd was wearing a suit.

'I'm not sad,' he said, and put an arm round his son to pull him close. That was a lie. He was sadder than he'd ever been in his life. He hadn't had time to grieve for Sue while he'd been in prison, but as soon as it was all over the enormity of what he'd lost had washed over him.

'What happens now?' asked Liam.

'We live our lives,' said Shepherd. 'We remember her all the time and we think about her and we miss her, but we have our lives to live.'

'And then we see her again in Heaven?'

'That's right,' said Shepherd.

'Are you still going to be a policeman?' asked Liam, squeezing his hand.

'I'm not sure,' said Shepherd, and that was true.

'I want to be a policeman when I grow up.'

'Really? Why?'

'Because they help people.'

Liam was right, Shepherd thought. Sometimes policemen did

help people. And sometimes they killed them. And sometimes they brought misery to those around them.

He looked over his shoulder. At the back of the church he could see Major Gannon, in a dark suit, flanked by O'Brien, Shortt, Armstrong and Mitchell. Gannon nodded at Shepherd, who smiled thinly. It was reassuring to know that they were there, watching his back literally and figuratively. Shepherd didn't believe in angels with wings and harps, but guardian angels were a different matter and the five men at the back of the church were just that.

Shepherd walked out with his son and into the churchyard with Moira and Tom. Tom was wearing a tweed hat that hid the plaster covering his head wound. He had his arm round Moira's shoulders.

Outside, Shepherd stopped and stared up at the cloudless sky. It was a perfect summer's day. Birds were singing in the trees that bordered the churchyard. Butterflies flitted around yellow-flowered bushes on either side of the path that led from the church to the road. It was a perfect day for a wedding, thought Shepherd, but a lousy one for a funeral. Funerals should be held on rainy days, with cold winds blowing from the north and leaden skies overhead.

Gannon came up behind him and put a hand on his shoulder. 'I'm sorry about your loss, Spider,' he said. He was carrying the sat-phone briefcase in his left hand.

'Thanks, Major.'

'Do you know what you're going to do?'

'It's all up in the air.' He gestured at Sam Hargrove, who was walking to his car. 'He wants me back in harness.'

'You do good work,' said Gannon.

'Thanks.'

Gannon knelt down so that his head was level with Liam's. 'You should be very proud of your father.'

'I am,' said Liam.

Gannon ruffled the boy's hair. 'Is that your gran over there?'

Liam glanced at Moira and nodded. 'Why don't you go over and see if she's all right?' said Gannon. 'I want a word with your dad.'

'Okay,' said Liam, and ran over to his grandmother.

Gannon straightened up. 'We've found him,' said Gannon.

'Where?'

'On a Colombian ship in the Atlantic. Used the ship's sat-phone to talk to his wife and kids and the NSA tracked it.'

'And?'

'We're going out to get him.'

'Officially?'

'Oh, yes. The DEA has formally requested that the Increment do the dirty.' The Increment was Gannon's unit, an ad-hoc pulling together of SAS and SBS troopers capable of carrying out tasks deemed too dangerous for the Security Services. On the far side of the graveyard, Moira held one of Liam's hands and Tom took the other. 'Do you want to come?' asked Gannon.

Shepherd watched Tom and Moira walk away with Liam. He knew that his place was with his son, being a father. But the adrenaline kicked in and his heart beat faster. He wanted to be a father, but he wanted to see Carpenter pay for what he'd done. Carpenter had kidnapped Liam and threatened to kill him. He'd forced Shepherd to help him escape. And he'd ordered the killing of Jonathon Elliott. Carpenter had to pay for his crimes, because if he was allowed to get away with them then everything Shepherd had done would count for nothing.

'Yes,' said Shepherd. 'Yes, I do.'

It was a vision from Hell, Shepherd thought. Black figures with protruding snouts, huge eyes, and massive humps on their backs, crouching by the walls, bathed in red light. Their chests rose and fell as they pulled air into their lungs through tubes that ran up to the roof. The troopers were all bent forward, not wanting their parachutes to rub against the fuselage of the Nimrod. They were cradling their Heckler & Koch submachine-guns, barrels pointing down. They were all kitted out with full high-altitude parachute life-support system equipment. All the men wore black balaclavas and helmets, oxygen masks, bottles and carriers, boots and insulated over-boots. They wore felt gloves close to the skin for insulation and leather ones for protection, goggles to protect the eyes from the icy wind. Strapped to their chests were the LCDs of their computerised navigation systems. Their black thermal suits had felt liners to protect them against the high-altitude sub-zero temperatures. A thermometer on the fuselage of the Nimrod gave the temperature as minus 48 degrees Fahrenheit, and once they jumped, the wind-chill factor would kick in. Without the protective clothing they'd be blocks of ice by the time they reached the target.

On their backs were parachute canopies, two-thirds larger than a standard sports parachute, attached to a standard army harness, with a smaller reserve chute at the front of the rig. They had handguns in holsters and knives strapped to their legs. The submachine-guns were on webbing harnesses. All the troopers had the Heckler & Koch MP5SD4, a silenced model with a three-round burst facility in addition to single and full automatic fire. It had no butt stock so it was less likely to get tangled in the parachute rigging, and the silencer meant they'd have the element of surprise. They had extra ammunition in pouches on their webbing belts. Everything, in fact, that the trooper about town needed to drop in from thirty thousand feet and kill people.

They'd all been weighed at the Royal Navy Air Station in Culdrose and equipment had been distributed to equalise the men's weights. The time taken for a high-altitude high-opening jump was dependent on weight. The heavier the man and his equipment, the quicker he'd descend, and for what Gannon had in mind it was vital they landed together.

Gannon was at the front of the plane, closest to the crew exit door. There was a loader there, a man in olive green overalls and a quilted jacket linked to the fuselage with thick webbing straps. The Nimrod was designed for high-altitude surveillance not for dropping two four-man SAS bricks out at six miles high, so the loader was far from happy about what he was being asked to do. He was more at home in a Hercules C-130 transporter. Like the SAS troopers, he was breathing from an oxygen mask connected to the plane's central system. The Nimrod had been depressurised ten minutes earlier, when they had come close to the dropping-off point. Two of the four jet engines had been switched off so that it could be slowed to below a hundred knots.

'Okay, communications check,' said Gannon, into his radio microphone. One by one the troopers went through their call signs. Shepherd was Alpha Two.

Then Gannon told them to set the altimeters they were wearing on their right wrists. Thirty-two thousand feet above sea level. It would take them almost an hour to reach the target and during that time they would travel forty miles. A needle in a haystack didn't come close to hitting a converted oil tanker sitting in the Atlantic Ocean, but the GPS-linked navigation system brought the odds down to an acceptable level. But there was no margin for error: they were doing the drop at night and if anyone missed the ship it was one hell of a long swim home.

The eight troopers split into twos and checked each other's equipment – the oxygen supply, the webbing straps, the Irvine height-finder and the device that would ensure all the chutes opened at precisely twenty-six thousand feet.

Shepherd checked Gannon's rig, then gave him the OK sign, a circle formed from the thumb and first finger of his right hand. Gannon checked Shepherd's then clapped him on the shoulder. He put his masked face close to Shepherd's ear. 'You okay?' he yelled, over the noise of the engines. 'Stay close, yeah?' He was shouting because if he used comms the rest of the troopers would hear what he was saying.

'I'll be fine,' Shepherd shouted back. He'd done high-altitude high-opening drops before, admittedly never on to a ship in the middle of the ocean with little in the way of a moon, but the principle was the same: exit the plane; hope the parachute opens; guide the canopy down to the target; don't break anything on landing. Simple.

The ship was a medium-sized oil tanker. There was a superstructure at the rear containing the bridge and crew accommodation, but all over the quarter-mile long deck there were hatches and pipes that could easily snap a leg or a hip. It would have been a difficult jump at the best of times. A HAHO drop would give them plenty of time to make the right approach, though, and the chutes were so big that they'd move in slowly. The alternative, HALO – high altitude, low opening – wouldn't give them time to make a safe approach and Gannon had been discounted it, even though it would have reduced the risk of them being spotted in the air.

There was a third option – high altitude, no opening – but the SAS tried to avoid that manoeuvre as far as possible. A twelve-stone trooper with fifty pounds of kit travelling at a hundred and twenty miles an hour made a hell of a mess on impact. Shepherd flashed back to his first HALO jump high over Salisbury Plain in the West Country. He had been one of six on the course, under the wing of a grizzled sergeant who'd been with the Regiment for going on fifteen years. As the sergeant was lining up Shepherd and the others, he'd stuffed a large piece of parachute silk into Shepherd's pack. When it was Shepherd's turn to exit the plane, the sergeant had tapped his shoulder. Shepherd had turned, seen what looked like a ripped chute, and the sergeant had pushed him out. It was the longest two minutes of Shepherd's life, hurtling towards the ground at terminal velocity in full kit, not knowing if he had a faulty chute on his back. It had been a week before he'd seen the funny side.

The red light on the bulkhead flicked off and the amber one went on. The troopers took off the oxygen masks linked to the plane's supply and replaced them with their own, then shuffled towards the front of the plane. The loader nodded at Gannon and opened the crew exit door. Shepherd stood next to Gannon, breathing slowly but deeply, the adrenaline coursing through his veins, heart pounding, stomach churning as his body geared up for what was to come. Part of him was terrified at the thought of jumping out of a plane six miles above the ocean, but another part relished the fear. He was doing what he'd been trained to do.

The engine noise died down as the pilot pulled back on the throttles of the remaining two engines to idle and the nose of the plane went up. Shepherd almost lost his balance and Gannon reached over to steady him. The Nimrod shuddered as the pilot fought to keep it steady at the close-to-stalling airspeed. Shepherd looked through the open door at the black night sky, peppered

361

with a million stars. Far below was a layer of thick cloud, from fifteen thousand feet to six thousand, which meant gliding through nine thousand feet of close-to-freezing water vapour. That and the landing would be the most dangerous phases of the operation. It was easy to get disoriented in cloud and there was a risk of collision – dealing with tangled chutes in cloud at night was an interesting proposition that Shepherd was keen to avoid.

The amber light winked off and the green light went on. Gannon grinned at Shepherd, behind his mask, then jumped out of the exit door, thrusting out his arms and legs in a starfish pose. Shepherd took a deep breath and followed him. He gasped as the wind tore at him, pulling, twisting, pummelling. He fought to keep his arms and legs out as he fell through the slipstream. As soon as his descent stablished he pulled in his arms and legs slightly, adopting the stable position, his back arched so that his centre of gravity shifted towards his stomach.

Gannon was to his right so Shepherd crabbed towards him, feeling the air pressure shift under his body. More of the troopers joined them and Gannon turned slowly, checking numbers until he was satisfied that everyone was in free fall.

They reached twenty-six thousand feet above sea level and the automatic opening devices kicked in. Shepherd felt a tug at his shoulders as his canopy deployed, then his arms snapped in and his legs went down as the chute filled with air and slowed his descent. He reached up for the toggles that controlled his direction and pulled the left one, heading after Gannon, then checked his jet-black canopy. It was fine, totally rectangular, no tangled lines. In the distance, the engines of the Nimrod were a dull roar.

Shepherd tilted his head down and looked at the chest-mounted liquid crystal display screen of his GPS system. It showed his position and, some forty miles to the south, a red dot that represented the tanker.

He looked over his shoulder. Behind him, he could see the rest of the troopers, their canopies unfurled. He did a quick count. So far so good.

The harness was biting into his groin and Shepherd kicked out with his legs, moving the webbing. He took a deep breath of oxygen and let it out slowly.

'You okay, Alpha Two?' Gannon's voice crackled in Shepherd's earpiece.

'No problems,' said Shepherd.

'Just sit back and enjoy the ride,' said Gannon.

Carpenter hated ships. He hated the cramped rooms, the constant motion, the never-ending distant throb of massive engines. Bonnie had been nagging him for years to take her on a luxury cruise, but he'd steadfastly refused. There was a certain irony in the fact that the safest place for him had turned out to be a tanker prowling around the Atlantic.

His place there had been arranged by Carlos Rodriguez, a Colombian with whom Carpenter had dealt for more than a decade. The Rodriguez cartel had links to the Colombian government and was one of the country's biggest and most successful cocaine and heroin dealers. The tanker had been Rodriguez's idea, a floating warehouse that went into port twice a year for maintenance, and only when it was empty. It was a quarter of a mile long with facilities for two dozen men. Drugs were flown out from South America and dropped into the sea where they were picked up by small speedboats sent out from the tanker, then taken aboard and kept in compartments at the bottom of the hold. In the event of a raid, the compartments could be emptied, sending the drugs to the bottom of the ocean, far out of reach.

The tanker had once been owned by a Greek shipping magnate but now sailed under a Panamanian flag. Buyers, only people known to Rodriguez, paid offshore and collected from the tanker in their own boats. Rodriguez shipped drugs worth more than a quarter of a billion dollars a year through it. It was a perfect system. Usually there were only two dozen men on the vessel, a crew of ten and fourteen armed guards, and Rodriguez had vetted them all personally. It was equipped with state-of-the-art radar and sonar so that a surprise attack by the DEA or Customs was virtually impossible. But Rodriguez had more than enough law-enforcement

363

officials on his payroll to ensure that no one took him by surprise. He was untouchable, and as long as Carpenter remained on the tanker, so was he. He was arranging for a new passport to be sent out from the UK, based on a whole new identity. The paperwork would be faultless, reflecting the premium price he was paying. Once he had it he would go to Brazil for extensive facial surgery. When his new identity was in place, he'd set about removing the old one from the Police National Computer in the UK. It would cost an arm and a leg, but it would be money well spent. Without his prints on file, he'd be able to disappear for ever.

He'd have to stay in South America – Europe would never be safe for him and the United States would be out of bounds. But there were plenty of countries in South America where a man with money could live in privacy. Bonnie and the children could join him eventually. He would buy them new identities, and Bonnie had been suggesting she had a facelift anyway. It wasn't a perfect solution, but it was far better than twenty years behind bars.

Carpenter appreciated the irony that his present living space was similar to his cell at HM Prison Shelton. His cabin wasn't much bigger and he had no choice in his companions. There wasn't little natural light unless he went up on deck, and the bulkhead doors were like the cell door that had clanged shut on him at night. The food was better – Rodriguez had hired a top Argentinian chef – and he could use the well-equipped gym whenever he wanted. There were more TV channels than he had had in Shelton, too: the tanker had a state-of-the-art satellite system and a library containing thousands of DVDs. There was plenty of alcohol, too. But it was still a ship, and Carpenter hated ships.

He was sitting in the mess, a large room with a pool table, a big-screen television and several large sofas. Five Colombians were playing poker at a card table, laughing loudly and drinking a bottle of Chivas Regal. They were playing with stacks of hundred-dollar bills and their Kalashnikovs were close at hand. The Colombians were for protection; the crew were Ukrainian.

One of the crew came in and barked at the Colombians in fluent Spanish. He was in his fifties, his face flecked with broken blood vessels, his nose almost blue from years of hard drinking. He spoke passable English but had said barely ten words to Carpenter since he'd arrived on board. Like the rest of the crew, he seemed to resent Carpenter's presence. The only man who'd been friendly had been the captain, a guy in his thirties who wore a pristine white uniform and a peaked cap. He saw Carpenter as a chance to practise his English, but Carpenter had soon got bored with the man's interminable conversations about twentieth-century novelists and avoided him when he could.

The Colombians got up, grabbing their weapons as they headed up to the bridge.

Carpenter went up to the bridge. He asked the captain if he could join him. The bridge was the captain's domain and only the crew or invited guests were allowed in. The captain nodded. He was looking aft through a large pair of binoculars. Two other crew members were with him, monitoring the radar and sonar systems, and the five Colombians stood at the windows, their Kalashnikovs slung over their shoulders, talking to each other in Spanish.

'What's the excitement?' asked Carpenter.

'Plane, coming from the north,' said the captain. 'It was up at thirty thousand feet but it started descending and now it's heading back this way under the cloud cover.'

'What sort of plane?'

'We don't know, but it's moving fast so it's not a small plane. Maybe a jet.'

'Is it a problem?'

'It's too big to be a seaplane and even the Americans wouldn't blow us out of the water, but it might be a spotter plane. Surveillance.'

'DEA?'

'Or Customs. Who knows?'

'What will you do?'

'Watch it. We'll only dump the gear if we see a boat approaching.'

'How much is on board?'

The captain grinned. 'A lot.'

Carpenter stood up. 'If you even get a whiff of a ship heading this way, I want off this tub,' he said.

'Don't worry. No one has ever tried boarding us at sea,' said the captain. 'We are in international waters so we are free to defend ourselves,' he chuckled, 'and we are well equipped to do that.'

Carpenter knew he wasn't joking. The Colombians were all crack shots. He'd seen them throw oil drums into the sea and fire at them for target practice. And he'd been told that there was a major arms cache below decks with enough firepower to fend off anything short of a full military attack, including Stinger surface-to-air missiles. 'Can you see it?'

'Not yet.' The captain turned and spoke in rapid Ukrainian to one of his crew, who answered him.

'It's down to four thousand feet and descending,' said the captain.

'Engine trouble?' asked Carpenter.

'They're not broadcasting on the emergency frequency, and it looks as if they're under power,' said the captain. 'Don't worry, Mr Carpenter. One plane isn't going to do us any harm. And if it looks as though it is, we'll shoot it down.'

The cloud was disorienting. Shepherd couldn't see more than ten feet in front of him. The parts of his face that were exposed were ice cold and the surface of the black thermal suit was soaked. His body was dry, though, and surprisingly warm.

There was no sense of movement. He felt as if he was suspended in fog. And other than the occasional static through his earpiece, it was eerily silent. He looked up but could barely make out the black canopy above his head. It was a GQ-360 nine-cell flat ramair canopy that was designed to be virtually silent as it moved through the air. He checked his watch: forty-four minutes since he'd jumped out of the Nimrod. He checked his altimeter: eight thousand feet. They should reach the ship in sixteen minutes. Give or take one minute, and they'd miss it by a quarter of a mile.

He wiggled his toes inside his boots, then worked his fingers in his gloves, keeping the circulation going. The last thing he needed was cramp as he came in for landing.

'Comms check,' said Gannon, in his earpiece. 'Alpha One.'

'Alpha Two,' said Shepherd.

One by one the remaining eight troopers sounded off.

Shepherd looked down past his feet. He saw wisps of cloud, and then suddenly he was through it, hanging in the darkness. Above him, there was cloud, and far below, the blackness that was the sea. In the distance he could see Gannon's canopy, a dark shape in the night sky. He checked his LCD display. Their forward speed had slowed while they'd been in the cloud, but that had all been calculated for. Hopefully. According to the computerised display, the target was eleven miles away.

The captain swept his binoculars right, then stopped. 'I see it,' he said. 'It is a jet. Four engines. It's big, too.'

'Any markings?' asked Carpenter.

'Can't see any. And I can't make out the number.'

'Not Army or Customs?'

'It looks like a Nimrod, but it's flying close to stall speed,' said the captain.

'I thought Nimrods were for high-altitude surveillance,' said Carpenter.

'They are. Six miles and above.'

One of the Colombians said something in Spanish and the other four laughed. Another took out a cigar, but before he could light it the captain spoke to him. The Colombian glowered and put away the cigar.

'So what the hell's it playing at?' asked Carpenter.

'Could be lost,' said the captain. 'Navigation system might have failed and they've dropped down below the cloud to get their bearings.' He muttered to one of the crewmen, who reached for a radio microphone. 'We'll try to make radio contact with them,' said the captain.

Carpenter stared into the darkness. He was getting a bad feeling about the plane.

★   ★   ★

'Alpha One, I have visual on the target.' Gannon's voice crackled in Shepherd's earpiece.

Shepherd peered into the darkness. He could see Gannon's black canopy in the distance, swooping down like a giant bat. But he couldn't see the tanker. He looked down at his LCD display. The red dot was less than a mile away. He checked his altimeter. Two thousand feet. That should be more than enough height to reach the target. He looked back to Gannon, then beyond. Lights. Red, green and white. As he stared at them he could make out the shape of the tanker. It was sailing towards them at an angle. The superstructure was at the rear.

'Alpha Two, I have visual,' said Shepherd, into his mike.

Then Shepherd saw movement in the air, several miles beyond the tanker. It was the Nimrod, flying low. If Gannon's plan worked, everyone on the ship would now be staring aft and the troopers should be able to land without being seen.

'Alpha Three has visual.'

Gannon's chute swung to the right, lining up with the tanker. Shepherd waited ten seconds, then did the same. He concentrated on keeping his breathing slow and even. It was easy to hyperventilate under stress.

'Alpha Four has visual.'

Shepherd flexed his fingers on the toggles that controlled the direction of the chute. The key to landing without getting hurt was all down to the toggles. Getting the direction just right, slowing the descent, emptying air from the chute so that it deflated. Done right, it should be as easy as stepping off a chair. Done wrong, he'd slam into the deck or, worse, miss it.

'Alpha Five has visual.'

The troopers were stacking up behind Gannon, drifting down towards the tanker. Shepherd wondered how many had done a similar jump before. The SAS regularly trained at HALO and HAHO, but during his days in the Regiment they'd never jumped on to a ship.

'Alpha Six has visual.'

By the time the last trooper had the tanker in his sights, Gannon was only two hundred metres from the prow. Shepherd used small tugs on the toggles to keep his descent even. Suddenly he was no longer flying over waves but over metal plates, glistening wet, pipes and manholes, welds and rivets. Ahead he saw Gannon's chute flare, then heard a thump as Gannon hit the deck and rolled, the chute flapping like a huge, dying bird. Gannon had hit midway down the length of the tanker, more than a hundred metres from the superstructure.

Shepherd pulled hard on both toggles and let his knees give as his boots hit the deck. He let go of the toggle in his right hand and hauled on the one in the left, deflating the canopy. He heard a dull thud behind him. Alpha Three. He grabbed armfuls of black silk, rolled it up tight and unclipped his harness. Gannon ran over, bent low. They shoved their chutes under a pipe and unclipped their oxygen masks. 'Nice job, Spider,' said Gannon, clapping him on the back.

Shepherd took off his mask and unclipped the oxygen cylinder. 'Hell of a ride,' he said.

'You should knock the cop job on the head and come back to the Regiment.' Gannon's face hardened and Shepherd realised the major had remembered why Shepherd had left the SAS in the first place. Sue.

Shepherd waved away any apology that the major was about to make. 'Let's get to it,' he said.

Another bump. Alpha Four. Shepherd looked up. The six remaining troopers were lined up in formation, coming in to land.

Shepherd unhooked his MP5 from the webbing. Gannon had made it clear at the briefing that no one was to be hurt unless absolutely necessary. The mission was to apprehend Carpenter and take control of the vessel. The tanker was then to be sailed into US waters. The Americans would take it and the drugs, the British would apply for Carpenter to be extradited to London. Everybody would win. Except Carpenter and Carlos Rodriguez.

Gannon waited until all of the troopers had landed, stowed their chutes and oxygen tanks, and checked their weapons. Then he motioned for them to head towards the superstructure. He and Shepherd led the way. Four of the troopers moved across to the port side, and the second brick took starboard. They moved slowly, keeping low.

It took them several minutes to reach the base of the three-storey superstructure. Three hatches led from the deck into it, one each on the port and starboard sides, and one in the centre, facing towards the bow. Four men headed for the port, four went starboard, and Gannon and Shepherd took the centre. They opened the hatches and slipped inside, Heckler & Kochs at the ready.

The captain took his binoculars away from his eyes and spoke to the communications officer in Ukrainian. He replied tersely.

'No communication,' the captain translated for Carpenter's benefit, but the officer's shaking head had already told him that much.

In the distance, the plane was climbing again, showing that it wasn't having engine problems.

'Whatever the problem was, they seem to have sorted it,' said the captain.

'And there's no ship heading our way?'

'Nothing within fifty miles,' said the captain.

'And they weren't talking to anyone?'

'No radio communications,' said the captain. 'The direction they were heading, they might not even have seen us.'

Carpenter nodded thoughtfully. He still had a bad feeling about the plane. He left the bridge and headed down to the mess. It was deserted, but through the open doorway he could see half a dozen Colombian heavies sitting at a table. Roast meat was piled high on a platter and they were helping themselves to rice. Three more Colombians came up from the cabins. They had handguns in shoulder holsters and were all wearing skin-tight T-shirts with designer jeans. They headed into the canteen. They, too, regarded him as a nuisance.

As Carpenter turned for the stairs to the cabins, he heard footsteps. Several people, moving quickly. He frowned. There

370

were five guards on the bridge, nine in the canteen. That was the full complement. The crew who weren't on the bridge were in the engine room.

Carpenter dropped behind a sofa, his heart pounding. He knew instinctively that the men running up the stairs were connected with the mysterious plane. And that they meant trouble.

Major Gannon had obtained structural plans of the tanker from its original builders, a huge industrial conglomerate in South Korea. They'd rehearsed the storming of the superstructure a dozen times in the Stirling Lines barracks in Hereford with troopers from the counter-revolutionary warfare wing playing the part of the Colombian foot-soldiers. Gannon had never managed to seize the objective without taking fewer than two casualties. But the counter-revolutionary warfare wing troopers were the best-trained soldiers in the world bar none, and the Colombians on the tanker were just thugs with big guns.

Shepherd had been at the briefing and at the rehearsals. Twice he'd taken a fictional bullet in the chest. Not that it worried him: that was the purpose of rehearsals, to iron out all the kinks so that no one got hurt during the real thing. Now he followed Gannon up the narrow stairway that led from the deck to the crew's quarters. Troopers were already moving through the cabins. All were empty. Four troopers headed down towards the engine room.

The rest moved up the stairs to the mess and canteen level, with Gannon and Shepherd.

They rushed through the mess area, sweeping their weapons from side to side, and heard laughter from the canteen. The lead trooper burst through the open doorway, telling the men to get down on the floor. One of the Colombians got to his feet, grabbing for his Kalashnikov. Two more troopers piled into the canteen. One let off a three-round silenced burst and the Colombian slammed into the wall. The rest raised their hands as their colleague slid to the floor in a pool of blood. The troopers pushed them to the ground and started to bind their hands and legs with plastic ties.

Shepherd did a quick head count. One dead, eight captured. No home team casualties. So far so good.

Gannon waited until all the Colombians had been bound and gagged, then motioned for three of the troopers to move up the stairs to the bridge. The fourth stood guard over the Colombians. There were two stairways, at either end of the mess room. The three troopers went up the right-hand side, Gannon and Shepherd the left.

As Shepherd reached the bridge he heard the muffled explosions of a three-shot burst and saw a Colombian slump to the floor over his Kalashnikov. The captain was standing with his hands held high. Another Colombian had his weapon up and was about to fire. Gannon let loose a burst and the Colombian spun round, blood spurting from his neck.

There was more gunfire from Shepherd's left and a third Colombian slammed against the window and fell to the floor, blood pouring from his chest. The last two dropped their weapons and raised their hands.

Shepherd looked round the bridge. There was no sign of Carpenter.

Gannon went over to the captain and jabbed him with the barrel of his MP5. 'The Brit, where is he?'

'Downstairs.'

'Where downstairs?'

'I don't know,' said the captain. 'He left just before you got here. Who are you?'

Gannon turned to Shepherd and nodded for him to go downstairs.

'Who are you?' asked the captain. 'Americans?'

Gannon grinned at him. 'If we were Yanks half our men would have been hit by friendly fire.'

'You are SAS?'

'Just do as you're told, Captain, and you'll be fine.'

'I am just a seaman, doing my job.'

'You can argue that with the DEA when we get to port,' said Gannon, 'but if you make a move to dump any of your cargo I'll personally tie you to an anchor and throw you in after it.'

Shepherd headed for the stairs. The mess was still empty so he went to the canteen. The eight tied Colombians were struggling in vain to get loose.

Their Kalashnikovs had been piled on the table. Shepherd frowned. An SAS trooper was supposed to have been standing guard over them. He pushed the door open. The trooper was lying on the floor, face down.

Shepherd cursed. He stepped out of the canteen and felt the cold barrel of a gun press against his neck. 'You couldn't leave well alone,' said Carpenter.

'It's over, Gerry.'

'Drop your weapon.'

'I can't. It's on a sling.'

'Let go of it.'

Shepherd let the MP5 slide through his fingers. It swung loose on its webbing.

'You're my ticket out of here, Shepherd. Again.'

'They won't wear that, Gerry. This is officially sanctioned. The government wants you back. The Americans want the boat.'

Shepherd raised his hands and turned slowly. Carpenter stepped away from him. He was holding a blood-smeared Kalashnikov. 'You're not taking me in,' said Carpenter.

'We'll see about that,' said Gannon. He was standing in the middle of the mess room, his MP5 aimed at Carpenter's chest.

'I'm not going back to prison,' said Carpenter.

'That's your call,' said Gannon.

As Carpenter looked across at Gannon, Shepherd took hold of his MP5 and slid his finger on to the trigger.

'I want off this boat,' said Carpenter.

'That's what we're here for,' said Shepherd.

Carpenter looked back at Shepherd. 'You're not taking me back. You were there. You've seen what it's like. I can't take twenty years.'

'If you can't do the time . . .'

'Fuck that!' said Carpenter.

'No one forced you to do what you did,' said Shepherd. 'You made choices every step of the way. You dealt drugs, you had Jonathon Elliott killed, you had Rathbone and Yates killed, you tried to kill Sandy Roper, you kidnapped my son. Did I forget anything?' He frowned. 'Oh, yeah, you tried to shoot me.'

'I should have done it when I had the chance,' said Carpenter.

'One of life's missed opportunities,' said Shepherd. 'It's over, Gerry. They've got Fletcher and he's singing like a canary. Can't shut him up.'

'Bullshit.'

'Pat Neary, too. The guys they paid to break into Roper's house got caught in a black-on-black shooting in Harlesden and they gave up Fletcher to cut themselves a deal. And Digger's become very co-operative. Selling you down the river and Tony Stafford, too.'

The colour drained from Carpenter's face. 'So it's over,' he said quietly. 'Bar the shooting.'

'Pretty much.'

'I could shoot you now,' said Carpenter. 'Easy as pie.'

'It's an option.'

'You'd get off one shot, so you'd better make it count,' said Gannon coldly, 'because if you fire that weapon, I will take you out.'

'That's all it would take, one shot,' said Carpenter.

'You'd be firing at an unarmed man,' said Gannon.

'What?' said Shepherd.

Gannon continued to stare at Carpenter. 'You didn't think we'd give him live rounds, do you? Spider here's out of practice, he'd be a liability firing real bullets.'

Carpenter frowned. 'Bullshit.'

'Not that shooting unarmed men is a problem with you, is it?' said Shepherd. 'Jonathon Elliott didn't have a gun. Neither did Sandy Roper.'

'If you're going to shoot anyone, I'd be the one to aim at,' said Gannon.

'I don't care about you,' said Carpenter.

'Making it personal is a big mistake,' said Gannon.

'Shut up!' shouted Carpenter. 'Let me think!' He kept the Kalashnikov levelled at Shepherd's stomach.

Shepherd stared back at him. Gannon's revelation that his MP5 was loaded with blanks was worrying, but Shepherd figured it was a bluff. But he had one secret that he was keeping from Carpenter: underneath the black thermal suit he was wearing a Kevlar vest. The Kalashnikov was a powerful weapon and Carpenter was up close and personal, but with luck the vest would hold. It would hurt like hell but the bullets shouldn't penetrate.

'There's nothing to think about, Gerry,' said Shepherd. 'It's over. Put the gun down.'

'If I go back to prison, I'll never get out,' said Carpenter. 'You know that. The drugs charge. Kidnapping. Conspiracy to murder. Perverting the course of justice. They'll throw away the key.' His finger was tightening on the trigger.

'You've no choice,' said Shepherd.

'There's always a choice,' said Carpenter. 'You've just got to have the balls to make it.'

'Don't do this,' said Shepherd.

Carpenter had the Kalashnikov at waist height and tilted it so that the barrel was pointing at Shepherd's head.

'Lower your weapon or I will fire,' said Gannon. There was no doubt that he meant what he said.

'You understand, don't you?' asked Carpenter, his eyes still on Shepherd. He was ignoring Gannon.

'Yeah,' said Shepherd. 'I understand.'

'Fuck it,' said Carpenter.

'Yeah.'

Carpenter swung the gun towards Gannon. Gannon pulled the trigger of his MP5. Three bullets rat-tat-tatted into Carpenter's chest, dead centre. He fell back, three red flowers blossoming on his shirt. The Kalashnikov clattered to the floor. Carpenter's legs buckled and he fell to his knees, then slumped on to his back. His chest juddered, bloody foam frothed between his lips, and then he was still.

'It was his choice,' said Gannon. 'He wanted it that way.'

'I know,' said Shepherd flatly.

'He could have surrendered. He could have come with us.'

'I know,' said Shepherd. But he also knew how Carpenter had felt. There was no way he could have spent twenty years in prison. That went for Shepherd as much as Carpenter. Life was for living. It was about being with family and friends. Watching your children grow. Being with people you loved. And if you couldn't do that, then maybe a bullet was better.

He turned and walked back to the bridge.

'We gave you real bullets,' Gannon shouted after him.

'I know,' said Shepherd.